BLOOD METAL BONE

Lindsay Cummings is a #1 *New York Times* bestselling author of eight novels and co-founder of the Scribbler Box for writers. She lives in Texas and writes part-time, when she's not chasing around a toddler or running media for her church. You can find out more at www.lindsaycummingsbooks.com and follow Lindsay @authorlindsayc on Twitter or @authorlindsaycummings on Instagram.

Also by Lindsay Cummings

THE BALANCE KEEPERS SERIES
The Fires of Calderon
The Pillars of Ponderay
The Traitor of Belltroll

THE MURDER COMPLEX SERIES
The Murder Complex
The Death Code

THE ANDROMA SAGA
(with Sasha Alsberg)
Zenith
Nexus

BLOOD METAL BONE

LINDSAY CUMMINGS

ONE PLACE. MANY STORIES

This novel is entirely a work of fiction. The names, characters and incidents portrayed in it are the work of the author's imagination. Any resemblance to actual persons, living or dead, events or localities is entirely coincidental.

HQ
An imprint of HarperCollins*Publishers* Ltd
1 London Bridge Street
London SE1 9GF

www.harpercollins.co.uk

HarperCollins*Publishers*
1st Floor, Watermarque Building, Ringsend Road
Dublin 4, Ireland

This edition 2021

4

First published in Great Britain by
HQ, an imprint of HarperCollins*Publishers* Ltd 2021

A catalogue record for this book is available from the British Library.

ISBN: 978-0-00-829279-9

This book is produced from independently certified FSC™ paper to ensure responsible forest management.

For more information visit: www.harpercollins.co.uk/green

This book is set in 11.5/16 pt. Adobe Garamond by Type-it AS, Norway

Printed and bound in Great Britain by
CPI Group (UK) Ltd, Croydon, CR0 4YY

For Dan the Man, the horse that started it all.
And as always, to my dad, Don Cummings.

CAST OF CHARACTERS

The Kingdom of the Deadlands

Azariah of Stonegrave, a mysterious stranger*
Jaxon of Wildeweb, Sonara's closest friend*
Markam of Wildeweb, his mischievous brother*
King Jira, ruler of the Deadlands
Razor, the wyvern

The Kingdom of Soreia

Queen Iridis, ruler of Soreia
Sonara, the Devil of the Deadlands*
Duran, Sonara's steed
Crown Prince Soahm, heir to the throne

The Kingdom of the White Wastes

Queen Marisk, ruler of the White Wastes
Thali the Cleric, companion to Azariah of Stonegrave

The Crew of the *Starfall*

Captain Cade Kingston, captain of the *Starfall*
Karr Kingston, his younger brother

Communications Manager Jameson, Karr's closest friend on the *Starfall*
Rohtt, the medhead

Beta Earth

Friedrich Geisinger, a famed inventor and businessman
Jeb Montforth, a scavenger and space pirate

* indicates Shadowbloods

TEN YEARS AGO
The Kingdom of Soreia

Tears trickled down Sonara's cheeks as she crouched in the shadowy corners of the Soreian royal stables.

She'd awoken early that morning to find the word scraped in the sand between the aisles of stalls. Exactly where they knew she'd find it.

BASTARD

It had been gouged deep, as if drawn with the sharp edge of a warrior's sword.

Many times, Sonara of Soreia wished the goddesses had never granted her life in her mother's womb. For what was living, when you spent your days tucked away in the shadows, disowned and unwanted?

Sonara had scraped the awful word away with a mucking fork, then spent the rest of the morning cleaning out stalls, telling herself she wasn't going to cry.

The damned tears came anyway, pesky drops that fell hard and fast the moment her brother entered the stables.

Soahm came as he always did: unannounced and disguised in a cerulean hooded cloak that did little to conceal his true identity.

Everyone knew the Crown Prince of Soreia.

He stood a few paces away, a pale mare nuzzling at his pocket, trying to uncover the hidden wintermints he'd purchased on his latest journey to the neighboring kingdom of the Deadlands. Soahm's azure hair and eyes, deep as the sea, were the mark of Soreian purity; a trait that had passed down from generation to generation, marking the worthy from the not.

"If I were you," Soahm said as he stroked the mare's nose with a bejeweled hand, "I'd consider it a blessing that mother doesn't look upon you at all. Some days I swear the goddesses are punishing me beneath her wretched stare."

Mother.

Sonara flinched at the word.

"Careful," she said softly. She glanced over her shoulder, where a quiet stablehand hauled hay around the corner. A chorus of nickers followed after it, steeds poking their heads out of stall windows in hope of sneaking a bite. "You're speaking words of treason, Prince."

But the stablehands and grooms were sworn to secrecy. Their very lives, their *children's* lives, depended upon it. The last one who'd uttered a word of Sonara's lineage was still displayed as an ornament upon the palace gates.

"Perhaps," Soahm said. He shrugged out of his cloak and placed it on a bridle hook just outside the nearest stall. The mare huffed at it, then stuck her head over the polished gate and promptly removed it with her teeth. The cloak tumbled to the sand in a heap, the fine silk worth more than an entire year's worths of wages for Sonara. Soahm sighed as he lifted it from the sand, a golden chain dangling from his throat as he shook out the dust. "But these aren't the words of the crown prince. They're the words of an older brother, who is doing his utmost to comfort his little sister."

"That could be treason, too," Sonara said. "Calling me such a thing."

The crown prince held his arms wide. "Then let the queen send me over the cliffs to my death. I don't fear the Leaping. And besides, when Rhya takes the crown in my stead and spends half the kingdom's wages on flagons of liquor and ladies in waiting, mother will be begging the goddesses to pull me back from the depths." He flashed that summertime smile of his. "You're my *sister*, Sonara. You always will be, regardless of how much shared blood runs in our veins."

He'd meant the words as a comfort. But Sonara sniffed, and more tears slipped from her eyes. They were darker than Soahm's crystalline blue; a brown so deep they were almost black, her pupils scarcely visible in the dim light of morning.

She holds the darkness of night in her eyes, her mother's voice whispered into her memories. *The darkness of a demon.*

"Don't waste your tears," Soahm said. He gently patted her shoulder, then tucked her long braid behind her ear. The strands caught in a ray of sunlight peeking through the gabled stall window, revealing the natural smudges of muddy brown mixed with pure Soreian blue. "Not on a single one of them."

As he spoke, Sonara saw the royal family in her mind, the outline of the Queen, a shimmering crown perched atop her blue braids. And the three other half-siblings, all manicured menaces whose hearts had never known softness, never longed to show compassion. Not like Soahm.

"Easier said than done," Sonara answered.

Soahm was older by several years. He'd traveled all across the continent, visiting the neighboring kingdom of the Deadlands, even traveling so far as the White Wastes up north. He'd seen other castles and cultures, dined with kings and queens and learned to wield a sword as any Soreian warrior should. He bore the weight of their kingdom's future upon his shoulders, for someday, their mother's crown would become his.

Soahm knew a great many things. But he would never truly understand what it was like to bear the burden of *bastard.*

It was whispered behind Sonara like a devil's hiss in the city streets.

It sung wickedly to her each night in her dreams, when the wind sighed and the stars came out to shed their light on the kingdom below.

Sonara was a child without a known father to claim her, with a royal mother who'd never wanted to bear her at all.

"Well," Sonara said, as her tears dried up. "I've work to do, and seeing as you're here…"

"Fine," Soahm said. "But I'm not going anywhere near Duran."

Sonara raised a brow. "Scared, princeling?"

Almost as if in response, a great *boom* exploded against the stall door at the edge of the aisle.

Sonara clicked her teeth and went to soothe the source of the noise.

Duran, a beautiful beast with a coat the color of desert sand, mane and tail deep as blackest night, stood at the stall door, pounding his wide hoof against the gate. The entire stable seemed to shake with each kick. Some of the other steeds whinnied or snorted in response, their ears twitching this way and that. Dust kicked up outside Duran's stall, the lock doubled to ensure he wouldn't escape.

"That's enough now," Sonara said, as she stopped just out of his reach.

The beast looked at her with eyes that glowed as red as the bleeding suns.

He was in the last few months of being a young steedling. His dark heavily feathered legs had grown stronger, his back broader, his thick neck arched and noble. Soon, he'd be fitted for armor with the rest of the young steeds. They were a tougher, broader breed than the royal procession, bred for war instead of elegance. For death instead of life.

Sonara reached into her pocket and plucked out one of Soahm's wintermints.

"Don't bite me, beast," she warned him. "Or I'll bite you right back."

Duran's ears flattened against his head. But he promptly lipped the mint off of her palm, crunching it down before releasing a wintry *huff* in her direction.

"I can't believe you touch that thing," Soahm said, eyes wide.

"*Steed,*" Sonara corrected him. "He's harmless."

"Tell that to the rider whose back he broke last week."

Sonara's stomach sank at the thought of Duran's future. As soon as he could be tamed, he'd join the steed army, paired with a warrior who'd ride with a heavy hand, a blue sword at his or her side.

She'd likely never see him again, and it was that thought that hurt, strangely, worse than any words of cowardice the royal siblings could scribble in the sand.

"I have half a mind to take Duran and ride far away from here," Sonara said as she undid both locks and entered the stall, pushing Duran back a few steps. He tossed his head but relented as she clicked her teeth and stared him down. The beast stilled as she ran a brush across his back in steady strokes, even going so far as to lower his head to her. Sonara sighed and gave him another mint. "Imagine, the life he and I would have in the Deadlands. Freedom, Soahm. As wild as the winds."

Soahm chuckled from the stall across the aisle. "You, in the Deadlands? If you don't die of starvation or thirst or getting lost in the endless sands, you'll definitely die of an attack by outlaws. The desert has eyes, Sonara. And they're always watching, waiting for their moment to strike." He shivered as if his memories of traveling to the neighboring kingdom were more than enough to set him on edge. "And their king, I might add, is one who thirsts for blood. He sits upon a throne of bones."

"Laugh all you wish, Prince." Sonara tossed him a glare worthy of any war mare. "But I'm plenty capable of surviving anywhere. Outlaws be damned."

"Are you?" Soahm crossed his tan arms over the stall door,

gemstone rings glinting in the stray tendrils of sunlight. "Prove it."

Sonara weighed the onyx brush in her hand. Before he could react, she hurled it at him. It spun, bristles over back, until it landed with a dull thud against Soahm's chest.

It left nothing more than a smudge of dirt against his tunic before it fell to his polished boots.

"Terrifying." He arched a blue brow.

"I warned you."

"You'll need a name, if you're to be a dangerous outlaw."

"Sonara the Shadowrider," she mused, catching the brush as Soahm tossed it back to her. Duran huffed and shifted his weight as if he were tired of their game.

"Too obvious," Soahm said. "Something more sinister. Sonara the Stabber? You'd carry a warrior's sword, of course."

She snorted back a laugh as she brushed Duran. "That's ridiculous. I'm no weaponsmaiden."

They paused as a commotion rose outside the carved stable windows. Murmured voices of distant onlookers mixed with the soft sigh of seashells dancing among braided wind chimes. Cheers rose up as hoofbeats pounded against the sand, and a conch blew in three long blasts. Sonara paused to glance outside Duran's stall window as the royal procession snaked past.

Warriors rode on the backs of glamorous steeds as they escorted the Queen of Soreia towards her towering fortress at the ocean's edge.

Sonara glared from the shadows as Queen Iridis rode past. Her long hair was loose, a brilliant natural blue that hung in long coils down her back. "She makes the steeds' sides bleed from whipping them," Sonara said.

Sonara groomed and fed all the young steeds. She helped train them when allowed, and though Duran was especially stubborn, and though he didn't like to listen, he'd stolen her heart all the same, far more than any of the other steeds ever had.

"Do you know how many of them she's turned sour?" Sonara sighed and felt Duran's hot breath on her neck as he drew her attention away from the window.

It was as if he could sense her mood dropping, sense the light within her fading the more she stood in her mother's presence.

Sonara dug her hands into Duran's mane. "If the devil of a woman *ever* touches you, Duran..."

"That's it!" Soahm cried out. He clapped his hands together just outside the stall door, so loudly that Duran skittered sideways at the sudden sound.

"Some War Steed you'll make," Sonara murmured with a smile. Duran's ears flattened as if he very much disagreed.

"The Devil," Soahm said, crossing his arms atop Duran's stall door. "Someday, Sonara, you're going to become the She-Devil, riding on Duran's back, spreading hell across Dohrsar. And don't forget the sword."

He reached to his hip, where his blade was held.

Lazaris; the blade of their ancestors. A sword Soahm had trained with since he was only a boy, beautiful in its simplicity. The blade was solid black, with a strip of Soreian blue steel running down the middle, cool as a river.

The sword was once their mother's, wielded as she slew her way to the crown. But Soahm had been gifted Lazaris upon birth, a sword he'd finally grown into with age. Sometimes, Sonara watched from the stables as Soahm trained with the royal weaponsmaidens, who forged blue Soreian steel into weapons capable of withstanding a lifetime of warriors' hits.

When Soahm held Lazaris in the bright light of day, practicing on the elevated castle grounds in full view of the citizens, Sonara hid in the shadows of the stable, and mirrored his motions with a mucking fork.

At night, he trained with *her* on the Devil's Dunes, the twin moons their only watching eyes. She was not skilled, by any means.

But holding Lazaris gave her a reason to believe in herself.

For what was a sword, without a warrior to wield it? Perhaps someday, she'd be strong enough, skilled enough, to earn her own weapon.

"Lost in your thoughts, She-Devil?" Soahm asked, drawing Sonara's attention away from Lazaris. The Queen's procession faded away and the sound of chewing steeds took its place. A red bloodfly buzzed past Sonara's ear.

"Not quite," she said, and swatted the bloodfly away. "No, I don't think that's the right name. The She-Devil? It doesn't have much of a ring to it. But it was a worthy try."

Soahm sighed. "I'll figure it out eventually." He turned over a water bucket and sat down on it to keep her company while she worked, his chin propped upon his ringed hands.

"Tired already?" Sonara asked, tossing the brush at him again. "You're becoming lazy, princeling."

"She-Devil," Soahm said with a wink as he stood to help her. "*Definitely* a She-Devil."

***

Sonara leaned against the rough edge of a round pen, watching the royal trainers with longing in her eyes.

Duran had already thrown three riders from his back, his tail fountaining behind him in silkiest black as he pranced, feathered legs dancing with each pound of his hooves against the sand.

The day was uncomfortably warm. The scent of steed sweat mixed in with the nearby smell of the sea. Across it, a pasture of golden seagrasses waved in the wind, the sky above darkening. A storm would soon arrive from far across the sea. It would crash onto the shore like a maelstrom, and everyone in Soreia would head inside.

"Easy, Yima!" the head trainer shouted. "Don't give him too much control of his head, or you'll be thrown, too! We should head in. Call it for the day."

Yima was one of the finest riders, from a noble family of steed breeders in eastern Soreia. Sonara watched from outside the pen, clicking her tongue as Yima, heavy in her blue scaled armor, climbed atop Duran's back.

And dug her heels in deep.

"Not so easy," Sonara murmured beneath her breath.

She saw the telltale shift as Duran's ears flattened against his head, nostrils flaring.

Yima yanked on the bit as she clicked her own teeth at him. The steed's sides were already bleeding from countless riders and spurs, his breath heaving as he fought against their control.

Sand kicked up against Sonara's legs as Soahm appeared at her side, blue robes flapping in the wind.

He often left the castle during morning hours, but she hadn't seen him in days. Their mother kept him in the castle for hours on end. Taking requests, calling on visitors, learning the ins and outs of what it meant to lead a kingdom, a whole room full of ancient councilmen and women droning on and on about goddesses only knew what.

It was a life Sonara had never wanted. Deserved? Half of her blood said *yes.*

But wanted? That was a very different sort of thing. She would rather stand here now, hair unbound and face freckled from the sun, the kiss of the sea upon her tanned skin. And the sound of hoofbeats pounding in time with her heart as Yima tried to gain control of Duran.

"I stopped by the betting house this morning," Soahm said softly as he watched the steed crow-hop past. "I placed ten gold coins on Duran."

"People are betting on whether or not he'll be tamed?" Sonara sighed. The steed's reputation had spread across the capital, then. "Well, for what it's worth, I'd bet on him, too. He's going to throw her. Any moment now."

Soahm shrugged and leaned over the railing. "Looks like she's got it under control to me. But, ah… isn't watching Yima's impending doom a fine way to spend your birthday?"

"My birthday," she said with a frown.

She'd nearly forgotten.

Soahm laughed. Then he frowned, too. "I forgot to bring you a gift."

"No gifts," Sonara said.

Soahm looked at her as if he disagreed.

"*No* gifts, Soahm," she said again.

"Of course," he said with a wry smile, and pointed back at the round pen. "The height of the show."

Duran snorted and huffed, tossing his deep black mane. Sweat foamed upon his neck and chest as he fought against Yima's commands.

"I call it in three," Sonara said. She winked at Soahm and held up three fingers.

Across from them, Yima dug in her heavy-booted heels and pulled the reins sharply to the right. Duran's head turned with her, his body following chase… but Sonara could see him fighting, chomping at the bit.

"Two." She dropped a finger.

"You'd better be right," Soahm said.

Sonara smiled as Yima made the gravest mistake of all. She looked away from Duran's head, for only a moment, as a flock of fowl soared past, searching for refuge from the oncoming storm.

Sonara pointed her remaining finger inside the round pen. "One."

Yima's body took to the sky as Duran launched her off his back.

She hit the sand with a heavy thump, armor clinking as the beast pranced to the corner of the round pen. He snorted and stomped his front hoof into the sand, proud as only a young steed could be.

"No one will tame this demon," the head trainer said with a growl, while the others standing around, who'd been so hopeful before, groaned and booed as Yima brushed her armor off.

"I could," Sonara said softly.

Soahm turned around, leaning his back against the round pen as he looked at her. "Truly?"

"The trainer is a fool. He's not meant to be *tamed*," she said. "His spirit is as wild as the wind."

Some days she swore she could feel it, almost *sense* it in the gentle huff of his breath, when they sat alone in the stall, hidden from the judgemental eyes of the world.

Duran was like her.

Different to the others.

Misunderstood, because he didn't fit into their perfect Soreian mold.

"So what would you do differently, then, little sister?" Soahm asked.

Sonara smiled, tilting her chin towards the oncoming storm. The clouds were darkening now, rolling above the angry waves in the distance, where sky met sand and sea.

"For starters, I'd ride him without that heavy armor. Right when the rain hits."

Soahm laughed, for when it came to riding unarmored on a beast as fierce as Duran, that most certainly sounded like a death wish. Couple the storm with it, and any steed's attitude would change.

But Sonara had sensed Duran's fighting soul from day one. He was born too early, a squalling and scrambling thing, scrawny legs and thin neck and a mare that did not have enough milk to sustain his endless hunger.

"He won't survive the week," the royal horsemaiden had said, considering the beast a burden.

But Sonara had refused to give up on him.

She did not sleep for days, so focused was she on filling him with donor's milk. Bottle after bottle, she'd sustained him.

Duran grew quickly. He cheated death, and in the months after, Sonara spent countless hours grooming him, whispering her hurts and her pains into his fuzzy ears. Kissing him on his velvety snout. Sometimes, soaking her tears into his neck in the dark of night, when her problems surfaced and her demons tried to reel her in. Her soul always felt lighter in his presence. Like he was taking some of the burden off her back and placing it upon his own.

Sometimes, she swore he looked into her eyes and saw through to her soul.

He didn't know what she was, a bastard without a true call to a crown.

He just knew that she was *his.* He'd claimed her heart from the moment she laid eyes on him.

And he was hers.

"Then I'd open these blasted gates," Sonara said louder now, watching Duran's dark-tipped ears flick towards the sound of her voice. "He was not meant to be confined to a pen." His head turned to her and his blazing red eyes fell upon her face in recognition. He tossed his mane and pranced across the sand, snorting as he stopped before her. Sonara held out a hand, feeling his warm breath dissolve against her skin. *Home*, her heart whispered. "Then I'd turn him towards the crags, where the seagrass catches the breeze. I'd give him his freedom, allow him to think with his own head instead of a bit. We'd run until the storm broke. I wouldn't slow him. And when he grew tired…" she smiled, thinking of the freedom, "we'd stand on the edge of the crags, watching the horizon where the sky meets the sea."

Silence.

Then laughter, as Yima stalked over, catching Sonara's gaze.

"The groom thinks she can do better than a cadre full of riders."

"I don't *think*," Sonara shot back. The wind blasted her hair back from her face. "I know I can."

The other trainers standing around laughed. But Soahm…

"A gift, Sonara," he said softly.

He winked at her, just before he stepped forward and lowered his hood from his head. The crowd gasped, the riders dropping to their knees as they realized the Crown Prince of Soreia was in their presence. His blue curls lifted as a gust caught the strands. The storm wind pulled at the fabric of his cloak, tugged at the heavy chain around his neck and the black stone dangling from it, sealed carefully in a ring of forged gold.

For centuries, the amulet had been in the royal family, passed down from generation to generation, from one heir to the next, marking the successor to the Soreian throne. There was no story behind the stone. Only that it was ancient, that it once belonged to the very first Soreian queen, who'd always seemed to know how to find favor with her people. Beloved. Admired.

She wore the stone upon her neck until the fading sands of time called her home.

"You'll let Sonara inside the pen," Soahm commanded, that very same stone hanging from his neck. He placed his palm over Lazaris' pommel. "Give her a chance."

The gate opened with a creak as the storm rumbled overhead.

Sonara stared at Soahm blankly.

Go on, he seemed to say, with a nod of his head.

She swallowed, heart racing as she stepped slowly inside. Gently, she removed Duran's bridle and looped it over the railing.

She ran her hands against Duran's side, as if she were running a brush across him. Easy, *so* easy, she stepped closer.

"You and me," she whispered.

Murmured laughter sounded behind her, but she paid the riders no heed. She was used to drowning out the sounds of the world, the whispers. The lies.

Soahm gave her a leg up, and as she gently settled atop Duran's back, armorless and light as the air around them… something in her soul felt like it was home. Soahm commanded the gates be opened. They creaked with a warning groan, as if even the gates knew she should stop.

But Sonara leaned forward and dug her fingers into Duran's thick mane, heart hammering in time with his.

"You're sure about this?" Soahm said.

"I'm sure," Sonara said. She nodded, and stared between the tips of Duran's ears, right into Yima's judging eyes. Something inside of her seemed to shift. "I am not afraid."

Duran's ears flicked backwards, as if he'd heard her words.

Then the gates swung wide, and Sonara's stomach shot into her throat as Duran leapt into a lope, practically becoming one with the wind.

Hold on, Sonara told herself. *Don't you dare let go.*

They soared past Soahm, and Sonara heard his cheers mixing with the others. The prince leapt and clapped as he yelled, throwing all formality to the sky as he screamed, "Ride, Sonara, ride!" His amulet bounced on his chest, thunder cracking as the storm finally released its wrath on the world.

Rain fell in sheets across her eyes, but Sonara no longer

cared. For she and Duran were now one with the storm, furious. Untethered, as they left the castle grounds.

Together, they ran…

And they did not look back.

A gift, Soahm had said.

The greatest one he could ever give.

FIVE MONTHS LATER

Sonara found him at the ocean's edge.

The suns were just setting, a double green flash as they sank out of view beyond the furthest stretch of sea.

Seated on the sand, toes not far from the lapping waves, was Soahm.

A mere speck in the distance, she hadn't seen him in weeks, not since the battle. Not since he'd returned home, wounded from a skirmish in the neighboring Deadlands, his leg torn open and bloodied as he lay in the back of a soldier's cart.

"Slow, beast," Sonara murmured to Duran now, leaning back a bit.

The steed dropped to a calm walk, responding to the motion of her body. She'd trained him to respond only to the pressure of her legs, to the click of her tongue, to the shifting of her weight or a gentle murmur of a practiced command.

The trainers had called her a fool, at the beginning. But now the bastard girl of Soreia had become the beast's master. And perhaps one of the finest riders the kingdom had to offer.

"Go on," Sonara murmured as she stopped Duran and slid down from his back. "Eat your fill."

His nostrils flared as he trotted off towards the dunes, fresh pale seagrass waving atop it. Soahm's mare was already there, happy as could be. The wind blew, carrying her scent down the hillside, and Sonara swore she could feel a bit of peace wash over her.

Her footsteps were drowned out by the crashing sea as she approached her brother. The prince was busy sketching, the back of his left hand turned dark from smudges of charcoal. She rarely saw him without those telltale smudges. The moon was out in full tonight, a beautiful blue that cast a cool glow across the beach.

"What are you doing all the way out here, Soahm?" Sonara asked.

They were nearly an hour's ride from the castle, on the fringes of the freelands where herds of wild steeds still roamed. He often came out here, to think. To enjoy the silence, without their mother barking commands, or filling his list with countless princely duties.

Sonara wouldn't know a life like that. And in that, at least, she was grateful for her separation from the ones she could have called family.

"Sonara." Soahm sighed her name in greeting.

She could sense the sadness in him, as deep as the ocean floor. He tossed a lilac shell into the sea. "I can't lead this kingdom the way she wants me to." He glared at his injured leg, splayed before him in a splint. Beside him, a discarded crutch that had become his constant companion. "I'm broken, Sonara."

"Broken?" Her dark eyes widened. "You're injured, Soahm. That's a far cry from broken. You'll heal."

"There's a chance I won't." Soahm looked at her fully, and his blue eyes, so unlike hers, were rimmed with red. "The healers say it's possible that I'll never fully recover. The people want a *warrior*, Sonara. Like our mother. They want to know that their future king will rule with sword and shield, will not balk or falter in the face of his enemies. I cannot give them that."

"Perhaps you never could," Sonara said with a shrug.

Those blue eyes widened ever more.

She held up a hand and offered him a gentle smile. "You're not like that, Soahm. Before the injury, after it… it's never been *you.* If they want a king like that, they can move north to the Deadlands, and bow at Jira's feet. Or worse, to the White Wastes, and praise the ice queen."

Soahm frowned, his brow furrowing. "You think me weak?"

"The opposite," Sonara said. "I think you're strong. But in a different way. Perhaps a better way…" She considered for a moment, as a distant pod of sea wyverns splashed their tails above the waves. "Yima rides with heavy heels. The steeds respond, but they don't respect her." Sonara reached out, and scooped up a handful of sand, letting it fall through her fingertips. The grains danced away on the wind. "The people want someone they can respect, and it isn't always earned with a warrior's sword. Give them a reason to follow you. Give them a leader they can be proud of. Bend a knee to their level, and show them you understand their struggles, their worries and fears, that you care about filling their bellies and giving their children a safe place to learn and play and sleep."

"But how can I do that?" Soahm asked. "How can I do that like *this*? The Great War ended when Jira rose to power, but skirmishes still rise. There is still unrest on the borderlands."

Sonara grabbed her brother's hand and squeezed it, forcing him to pay attention. To look at her *clearly*, with her muddied blue hair, her dark eyes, her differences that marked her as a bastard. The lowest of the low. "*See them*, Soahm. *All* of them, not just the wealthy and the nobles. See them *all*, the way you have always seen me."

He squeezed her hand back, then let it go. They sat together for a time, watching the stars wink down from the sky. Behind them, Duran had crossed to the hills, his face buried in the seagrass as he filled his ever-hungering belly.

"Let's walk," Soahm said. His voice was a bit lighter, the heaviness replaced by what Sonara felt was, perhaps, hope.

She reached out a hand to help him stand. He took it gratefully, a prince that was never too proud, and together they walked, their cloaks dancing behind them in the wind. In the distant sky, a star was falling, a trail of glitter in its wake.

"I've spent more time sketching," Soahm said. "Mother doesn't know, of course. She'd slay me herself if she thought I was wasting my time sketching when I could be studying." He reached into his cloak pocket and pulled out his leather-bound journal. On the front, a stamped insignia of a rearing steed. He flipped through the pages until he landed on a sketch of a warrioress, seated atop Duran.

"It's me," Sonara said.

She smiled.

"The She-Devil," Soahm said with a wink. "Keep it." He passed her the journal. "I have plenty. Try your hand at a sketch, Little Sister. It's kept me busy during my recovery."

Sonara laughed, for she'd never been able to sit still enough to sketch, but she tucked the journal into her cloak anyway, to humor him. She was about to suggest they turn back, her body growing tired, when the star in the distance caught her eye again.

Stars didn't fall quite like that, cutting through the night like a beacon.

"Do you…" Sonara pointed. "Do you see it?"

Soahm followed her gaze through the sky, the light reflecting upon the black sea. It drew ever closer, the brightness intensifying until she saw that it was not a star.

Rather, it was a *shape*, a blazing trail of fire beyond it. A shape that looked like the head of an arrow, slicing through the sky; metallic. Not of this world.

The wind kicked up, gusting towards her as a rumble sounded from the object, shooting across the sky like a war drum.

Sonara's blood felt cold, her heartbeat rising to her throat. *Danger.* She felt it, a sickness spreading through her gut. Behind her, Duran and the mare cried out, then galloped over the hills, out of sight.

"Run," Sonara whispered. She gripped Soahm's hand, her nails digging into his skin as fear overcame her. "Soahm, *run*!"

She turned, tugging him along with her. The beach was a wide expanse of sand spreading into the dunes beyond. Nowhere to hide, nowhere to bury themselves in the shadows, except…

The cave on the edge of the Devil's Dunes.

A burial ground for the dead, a sacred space that was not to be disturbed, and yet Sonara found herself tugging Soahm towards the yawning black mouth of it, the safety of darkness calling them home.

"Slow down!" Soahm yelled. He stumbled, but Sonara tugged his hand harder, her fear a living thing inside of her now.

Run, it beckoned. *Run, and do not slow down.*

She had always been smaller than most, lithe and used to working long hours in the stables. She pushed herself, legs burning as she trudged through the deep sand.

Behind her, the object closed in, screaming from the sky as the winds kicked up. She looked overhead as light flared. She saw only metal, like a great beast in the sky, a crimson bird painted upon its belly.

At some point her sweaty hand slipped from Soahm's. She reached the mouth of the cave, darkness swallowing her up, safety wrapping its arms around her as she disturbed the domain of the dead.

She turned in time to see Soahm hit the sand. For a moment, her panic cleared at the sight of him, his crutch discarded, his hand reaching for her.

But fear snapped its angry jaws, freezing Sonara in place as her entire body shook. Soahm sruggled to his feet, then cried out in pain again.

He was crawling now, his leg splayed at an awkward angle behind her.

"Sonara!"

She saw his lips move, forming her name. But she could not hear him over the screeching of the metal beast in the sky.

She took a step forward, her whole body so seized in fear that her legs felt leaden.

Another step. *She could do this. She could save Soahm.* She reached out her hand, leaving the shadows just as a beam of blue light erupted from the belly of the beast. It surrounded Soahm, lifting him from the sand. He screamed and thrashed, trying to escape, but he was powerless to the beam's hold, as if it were some dark, powerful magic. His arms stretched, his amulet dangling from his tunic, shining in the beam as the beast's great metal belly yawned wide, pulling him inside before slamming back shut.

Soahm was gone.

***

The floor beneath the Queen's dais was bathed in blood.

It was a cool night, steam still rising from the rivers of crimson that had pooled between the pearlescent green tiles. They came to a stop at the edge of the throne room, where rows of soldiers stood guard, swords and spears in hand. Behind them, a thick crowd stood watching the public trial.

All had been called to file in, to boo and jeer and stomp their feet as Queen Iridis charged the Bastard Girl of Soreia with the murder of the crown prince.

"You will never shed your filth on this kingdom again," Iridis said. She lifted a hand in command. Another lash of the whip followed. The sharpened prongs tore Sonara's skin away in bleeding chunks, dragging through muscle down to bone. "You will spend the rest of your days wandering the planet alone like the bastard you were born as."

"I didn't kill the prince!" Sonara screamed. She hardly recognized her own voice, as if her vocal cords had been ripped to shreds with each scream following the lash of the whip.

The crowd began to boo, spitting as they stared at Sonara with disgust in their eyes. The skin on her back was torn to ribbons;

the blood that was half-Soahm's pooling around her body. *Gone.* Soahm was *gone.*

Some, watching from the sides, held hands to their faces, horrified as the Queen's guard slung the whip again. Blood and bits of flesh rained upon the floor.

But they hadn't uttered a word in her defense. Nothing to lay claim to the fact that they might have seen the great metal beast falling from the sky, lighting up the night like a beacon before it took Soahm.

Sonara hadn't known *true* pain, hadn't known agony, until this moment. She became only the rush of hot blood running down her back, knew only the wicked kiss of the whip as it feasted on her skin.

How many times would her mother order her flayed? How many strokes of that whip would she endure, before death stole her away?

It was a mercy she would have begged for, had she the strength to utter the words.

She'd come to the castle last night to *save* him. She'd ridden from that hellish beach as fast as Duran could carry them both. She'd burst through the gates, his hooves pounding across the cobbles like a war drum, not caring about the citizens diving out of the way, or the soldiers standing guard, the weapons they'd pointed as they'd commanded her to halt.

Nothing else mattered, for the crown prince was *gone.*

Up, and away, into the silent skies, as if he'd never existed at all.

Beneath the moon, Sonara had pleaded with the guards to wake her mother, and by the grace of the goddesses, the queen had come, wrapped in robes, her face gaunt as she listened to Sonara sob the truth of Soahm's taking.

Iridis hadn't believed her.

She'd placed the blame of Soahm's disappearance upon *Sonara,* refusing to believe her tall tale of a great metal beast soaring down from the night skies.

Now, Sonara lay dying,

"He was my firstborn. The heir to the Soreian throne," the queen said. She stood atop the dais, her voice ringing out across the throne room, sickeningly calm. "You killed him. For that, you will die."

The whip came down again.

"Bastard!" the crowd shouted. *"The Bastard Girl of Soreia!"*

Another lash.

"You have no name," the queen said.

Skin, torn away from Sonara's muscles.

"You have no kingdom."

Muscles, torn away from her bones.

And then the sentence came.

"Tonight," the queen said, as silence swept across the throne room, "you will die."

In her mind, Sonara escaped to thoughts of the girl Soahm had once spoken of: the She-Devil, the dream she should have grabbed ahold of when they'd thought it up together in the stables. She should have run far, far away.

Her other half-siblings, the princes and princesses of Soreia, stood with their arms crossed on the dais, the fringes of their robes flecked with her blood. They watched, unwavering as their mother beat Sonara to the end of breathing.

They left just enough life in her to perform the Leaping.

At dusk, Sonara was placed on an open wagon and carted to

the edge of the kingdom in full view, so that the watching crowd could gaze upon the fate of a kingdom's traitor.

They gathered and grew and followed to the edge of Cradle's Cliff. It towered so high the clouds kissed it, moistened the earth like it had been covered in a blanket of winter's breath. The ocean raged against the rocks below, sea-spray erupting in the air where it was picked up by the wind.

The salt air stung as it landed on Sonara's open back. Her vision flitted from dark to light as the cart wheels groaned to a stop, and strong hands lifted her ruined body.

She could scarcely hold open her eyes as the crowd chanted.

But one sound broke above it all.

A cry. A mighty, beastly screech that forced her eyes open.

Duran.

Her heart sank. There he was, the beast that had become *hers*, fighting for freedom at the edge of the cliff. Two trainers held a rope, their feet scrambling for purchase against the moist earth as Duran reared and threw his mighty head about, trying in vain to escape.

They made her watch as they bound him, man by man, ropes on his legs, ropes slung around his strong neck. His red eyes were ablaze, sides heaving as he stood there, a captive.

He was *hers.*

And that made him as good as dead.

Fight, Sonara wanted to tell him, as she was lifted from the cart by strong soldier hands. She hung between two men as they dragged her towards Duran, feet scraping the earth. *Oh, goddesses, just keep fighting.*

But in her presence, at her touch, the mighty steed calmed.

He allowed Sonara to be placed upon him, those very ropes used to bind them both together as the guards slung her on his back.

She knew this death: the Leaping.

A death reserved for a traitor. A coward. A deserter, tied to the back of their own steed, forced to ride over the edge of the abyss.

The crowd cheered, as Sonara slumped forward on Duran. They made a path, two sides that closed in, the nearer they got to the edge.

"Over the edge," the queen said. "To a death that has no peace. No silence. *No end.*"

The trainers released the ropes, cracking the whip over Duran's back as they commanded him forward.

His nostrils flared. But he steeled himself and did not move.

"Again," the queen commanded. The tips of her blue braids danced in the wind, mirroring her cold blue eyes. Soahm's eyes.

The whip cracked again, doubly as hard. Duran screamed as his skin split open. But still, he held his ground.

Tears streamed down Sonara's cheeks. She had only enough strength to utter a plea. *"Just me."*

But the queen only lifted her hand again, and the guards brought down the whip once more.

Duran finally took a step forward.

"Fight against them," Sonara thought to him. With everything in her, she wished he could hear her words, could take comfort in her presence. *"Don't let it end like this."*

Another step. This one a lurch as Duran sidestepped, another lash open on his side. The motion sent pain rocketing into Sonara's body, the wind howling, the cold salt spray like a knife reopening her wounds.

PART ONE

BLOOD

CHAPTER 1

TEN YEARS LATER
On board the *Starfall*
Outskirts of the Milky Way Galaxy

Karr

It took less than twenty-four hours for outer space to claim Karr Kingston as its own. Seventeen hours and forty-three minutes, to be exact.

The problem wasn't the warp speed at which the *Starfall*, the fastest ship in Jeb Montforth's black-market legion of Graters and Streakers, traveled through light-years of space and stars.

It wasn't even the two MREs Karr had downed right after he woke up on the ship, which could be more or less explained as eating freeze-dried cat, and may *not* have been one of his prouder moments.

It was the metal walls.

It was the feeling—the *reality*—of being so damn trapped.

Again.

"Not for long," Karr said, as he fumbled with a stubborn screw on a ruined escape pod in the belly of the *Starfall*. The pod was an ugly thing, battered and bruised and long since forgotten for flight.

Instead, it had been used all these years as one of hundreds of hiding places on board the massive ship.

The seats inside the pod had been torn open, the stuffing removed and replaced with sealed packages of smuggled drugs. They'd been sewn back together with an unsteady hand, as if a drunken surgeon had been given the job.

Karr sighed as he stared at the mess that would be his escape.

The cosmetics of the pod didn't bother him. And besides, he wouldn't have time to worry about the stitching on the seats when he was trying not to crash-land. All Karr cared about was the mechanics, those vital, running bits of the pod's insides that would hold his life in balance when he strapped himself in and ejected himself from the belly of the *Starfall*.

Tomorrow, Karr thought. *Tomorrow, I'll get the hell away from here.*

That is, if he could keep himself hidden until then. He'd shared plenty of false stories with the crew about his whereabouts, knowing that with their loose lips and watching eyes, he wouldn't be able to hold the truth off for long. He'd even rigged the locks on the storage bay's door so that when he was found, they'd have a hell of a time getting through.

The newly formed lump on his forehead throbbed as he thought of the Captain's wrath. If he was discovered… he'd never make it back to Beta Earth.

Heaven, Karr thought.

Or, at the very least, it had felt like it for the short time he and the rest of the crew had been docked there. Karr had traveled all his life, bounding around from one end of the Milky Way to the other, never staying on any one of its 8.8 billion planets for more than a few weeks at a time.

But Beta Earth?

They had stayed for five blessed months, while his captain was investigated by the Interstellar Trade Corporation for allegedly smuggling and selling illegal goods to black-market collectors across the shadier parts of the galaxy. They had no idea who turned them in for the crime.

Their Interplanetary Exploration license was put on hold, the *Starfall* was docked indefinitely, and even though it *was* true, and they were guilty as hell… the Captain had described the entire extended investigation as complete and total spacetrash.

Karr, on the other hand, had been given a gift by association.

"Five months," he said aloud as he worked with the stubborn screw.

The extended stay on Beta Earth had been enough time for Karr to discover just how much he'd been missing by spending a lifetime in the skies.

It wasn't entirely his fault. Earth was dying, and had been since 2052. The atmosphere had been torn to shreds, wild seas raged and continents drowned. Food sources had depleted, and people lived on bioengineered crops and pills meant to supplement their systems into survival. Something had gone wrong in the development of the crops along the way.

It had resulted in a disease called RP-53, more commonly dubbed the Reaper's Disease, for once it came calling, none survived.

Karr's parents had fled Earth, years ago, to escape the Reaper.

Like countless other travelers, they spent their lives working for the ITC, searching other planets in hope of finding some sort of substance that would turn into the miracle cure. Karr was born in the skies, in the *Starfall*, during that endless search. He'd never had a chance to get to know a home planet.

But Beta Earth had given him that chance. It was new. Alive.

A terraformed wonder that was fresh on the market, only a few years open to residents, and the place where Karr wanted to spend the rest of his days.

The streets of the docking sector on the northern continent were packed with hundreds of thousands, both native and alien, every race and religion and language in the galaxy mixing together like a glorious nebula. The buildings towered on all sides of him as he walked, or took a taxi ship, soaring through rows of blinking traffic lights looming over the city like dying stars, the smoke-filled, drink-laden clubs…

Beta Earth was a place made of adventure.

A destination planet where people came and saw and *lived.* Where those who hailed from old Earth had a chance to start anew.

It was on Beta that Karr had also discovered freedom.

For once, he could get away from the Captain of the *Starfall* and decide for his own damned self *what* he wanted to do, *when* he wanted to do it.

The Captain ran his crew like a pocketful of straight-backed soldiers, and Karr was always first to feel the burn.

Stand taller, Karr.

Polish your boots, Karr.

Go back and do it right, before you spend the rest of your time in the brig.

His personal favorite?

Shut your rutting mouth, before I eject you out the crapper tube, Karr.

Perhaps it was his age. Perhaps it was his attitude.

But when the sudden announcement was made that the *Starfall* was miraculously cleared, not a single bit of the drugs that lined the interior walls of the ship discovered, their pilot's license renewed to head back out into the depths of outer space… Karr did what every crew member wished they could do when they were sick of the rules and the grueling schedule.

He'd thrown a complete and total fit.

He *might* have burst into Jeb's holo bar, a recent purchase in the shadiest borough of the north continent, where black-market smugglers, pirates and privateers drank until the day's end. Karr had stumbled inside with whiskey on his breath and a hell of a hangover already on its way.

He'd gone right up to Jeb before anyone could stop him, shoved the drinks on the table aside, and planned to give him a piece of his mind.

I'm not going back on that damned ship, he'd started, though the words came out slurred and uneven.

The last thing he saw was Jeb's wicked half-smile, before someone cracked him over the head with the butt of his own Hammer rifle.

He'd awoken in his own cabin on the *Starfall*, the doors jammed from the outside. A trick he'd learned how to bypass, though it had taken quite some time with the hangover muddling his thoughts. He'd snuck his way through the ship, down to the storage bay, where he now sat.

And the damned lump on his head wouldn't stop throbbing.

All his life, Karr had done things without thinking of the consequences. It was what made good explorers, but even better thieves. Only this time, he wished he'd stopped for one second.

He wished he'd actually presented the Captain with something concrete before trying to make a stand against Jeb. Like, for instance, a completed application for the art school that he'd discovered during his stay, mere blocks away from the very bar where everything had gone to hell in a puke puddle.

Karr slammed his fist on the outer door of the escape pod. His father's old ring, hammered gold with a small ruby, clanged against the metal with a sound like a tolling bell.

"Come off, you Son-of-a-Saturn's…" And just like that, the screw finally popped loose. He yanked it from its hole and frowned at its condition. "Stripped."

Karr tossed it aside.

There was a single porthole next to the pod, just large enough to shed streaks of starlight on him as he worked. He leaned his head against the door, relishing the feel of something solid and cool on his skin.

And here he sat, staring out at the planet that was next on their manifest.

Dohrsar.

A glowing orb in the sky, surrounded by five colorful rings that reminded him of a curved rainbow. There was a single main continent on the dwarf planet, split into three distinct shades that set each place apart: the north, a frozen milky and mountainous white, tinged with bits of blue. The middle, the largest portion of the continent, was pale brown and red, a massive expanse of desert lined with a jagged range of purple and red mountainous land down its center. Beneath it, the only strip of green, leading into what could only be a tropical climate that spilled into the sea.

Pretty, from the outside. Beautiful, even.

But it was no surprise to Karr that the planet had yet to be colonized by outsiders.

It would require an armored S2—a spacesuit capable of blocking out Dohrsar's poisonous atmosphere. Many planets they'd visited required the S2s, but the Atmos ratings on Dohrsar were off the charts.

No suit, no survival.

Karr didn't plan on donning an S2. Not again.

While the crew was busy going over the manifest, he'd take this pod and soar away. If he programmed it right, it would get him back to a habitable planet in the next system. From there, he'd smuggle himself onto a transport freighter and head to Beta Earth.

Karr set back to work, looking for any weak points in the pressure seal, when a bang sounded from the doorway.

"KARR!" Another bang. "OPEN THIS DOOR, YOU LITTLE—"

Karr hissed and dropped his screwdriver. Greasy strands of hair fell into his eyes as he heard the telltale screech of metal, then another bang.

Karr had just enough time to squeeze himself in the shadowed space between the pod and the ship's curved metal wall before the door screeched open. A grunt sounded out, followed by footsteps.

Shock swept over him. How in the *hell* had they gotten through the bypass?

"You're smart, Karr," a voice said. A pair of boots glided into the storage bay. Polished to perfection, the laces tied evenly.

The Captain.

Karr sank deeper into the shadows.

"Smart." The Captain took a few lazy steps forward, past storage crates and massive Rover vehicles and rows of blood-red S2s. "But not smart enough. I'm the one who taught you that little trick with the airlocks."

It didn't matter how many turns he took, how many side trails he left for the Captain to find. The man was like a bloodhound, and Karr was always captured prey.

"Do you really want to play this game?" the Captain stopped before the pod, boots gleaming in the starlight. "Stop hiding in the shadows like a bug."

A second passed.

Karr held his breath.

Then a hand slipped into the shadows, gripping the collar of his oil-stained suit. Karr yelped as the Captain yanked him out into the open.

"That escape pod is *ancient.* You're signing yourself up for a death sentence!"

Blood boiling, Karr forced himself to stand tall as he glared up at his older brother's face.

***

"What the hell do you want, Cade?" Karr asked.

They could have been twins, the Kingston brothers, if Cade weren't thirteen years his elder. They shared the same hazel eyes. The same curly hair, strong jaw and lean build.

But where Cade was tall and strong, the picture of a captain, Karr was short and scrappy. The smallest on their crew, by far.

And the two could not have been more different on the inside.

Cade was all plot and plan, control and command.

Karr lived moment to moment, like space trash, tumbling head over heels, unsure of where he was going or if he'd ever make it there.

"I want to protect you," Cade said, his tone every bit like a disappointed father. "I can't do that if you're intent on throwing yourself into a pod that hasn't worked for over thirty years."

"Thirty years is generous," Karr said. "I can fix it."

But even as he spoke the words, he began to doubt them.

"You could," Cade said, inclining his head at the pod behind Karr, "if you had a year's worth of time, and thousands of creds' worth of parts that we don't have on this ship." He placed a hand on Karr's shoulder. "This is ridiculous. You can't just run away."

Karr barked out a laugh. "Isn't that what we're best at?"

That damned *throb-throb-throb* returned, which quickly reminded him that his dear brother before him was the one who'd ordered Karr knocked out, bound up, and placed in a locked room aboard the *Starfall.* Conveniently, just in time to leave Beta Earth and Karr's dreams of freedom behind. "Let me go back."

Cade stooped to pick up the old, rusty wrench. One of the few belongings left from their father besides Karr's ring. "We aren't free to choose our destinations. You know that." He turned the wrench around, grease marring his evenly trimmed fingernails. "You *also* know we have a mech drone you can use. It would make it easier to fix this junker up."

Karr took the wrench from Cade's hand. "I prefer to use my

hands. Just as I prefer *not* being kidnapped by my own flesh and blood."

"It was that or allow Jeb to handle you." Cade rapped the side of the pod with his knuckles. A bit of metal flaked away. "You were reckless. I did what I had to do."

"And you enjoyed it," Karr spat.

Cade worked his jaw back and forth in the very same way Karr did when he was trying to hold back a curse. But Cade had self-control. Karr had a mouth like a bottle rocket.

"Blood is stronger than fear," Cade said softly. A classic captain's line. "You've taken that to heart, and you've always had my back, even when you'd rather stab a knife in it."

"Screwdriver," Karr said. Cade raised a brow. "I'd choose a screwdriver instead of a knife."

Cade ignored that sentiment. "We have an opportunity before us, Karr. One that will award us the prize of our lives. Play our cards right, and we can go back to Beta. But not in a pod. We'll take the *Starfall.* Hell, we can buy Jeb as our personal pet, and make *him* do the smuggling for a change."

"You," Karr said as he looked into Cade's eyes, "have gone mad. We're never going to get away from this life. I've known it since the day Jeb plucked us out of the system. And if we'd been truly convicted by the ITC?" He dropped the wrench on the ground, wincing at the clatter. "We'd both be spending the rest of our lives behind bars. And he'd *still* be free."

The truth hung between them.

Bare naked and ugly.

Cade sighed. "We've had a change in employment."

Karr's neck cricked from whirling it so fast.

The brothers were prisoners to the black market; prisoners to Jeb and the illegal empire he'd built, selling drugs and smuggling goods to wealthy collectors galaxy-wide. They'd never be free of this life until they simply took a stand. But even then, Jeb would find a way to get back at them.

Cade removed something from his jacket pocket and held it out. At first glance, it was simply a dull hunk of jagged black rock. "*This* is our freedom. And it's not going to Jeb."

"You're going to double-cross him," Karr realized. "You want *us* to double-cross him. "With *who*?"

"Friedrich Geisinger."

Karr burst out laughing.

Friedrich Geisinger was the king of a pharmaceutical empire. A reclusive man who'd created so many medical advances, society practically bowed at his feet. It was his great-great grandfather that discovered the atlas orb, the cleanest and strongest source of power known to man. It was his great-grandfather that had cured the common cold, and his uncle that had cured cancer.

It was Geisinger's *father* that had created the supplemental vaccine that was supposed to save lives from the environmental changes. It was widely taken by all on Earth before it turned into the Reaper's Disease. It had wiped out *half* of humanity there; a fate that Friedrich Geisinger had spent his entire life trying to unwind. To clear his family name.

Though only in his forties, Friedrich had a pill on the market for every ailment. A patch for every problem. Small solutions... but he'd never cracked the code on the Reaper.

"There is no way in *hell*," Karr said through his laughter,

"Friedrich Geisinger would hire us for a job. He's busy trying to unravel the knots his father made."

But Cade wasn't laughing.

He crossed his arms and leaned back against the pod, face as stoic as a statue.

"Cade," Karr said. "Come on."

Cade only shrugged.

"Seriously?" Karr's laughter fizzled to nothing. "You're serious."

"A captain never lies. He recently purchased the dwarf planet at auction. A low-level acquisition, being that the planet is practically uninhabitable by outsiders. I think many were shocked to find one of Geisinger's emissaries wasting their time at the auction. But he's sending us out on a short-term mission to dig up some of the planet's resources. He's a powerful man, despite his father's history. He says he's on the verge of something *big.* And that little planet is the last key to helping him unlock it. One more job, and we'll have our freedom." He set the rock in the open doorway of the pod and backed away.

Karr chuckled beneath his breath. "It's a pipe dream. Jeb will kill us all."

"We have the protection promise of Friedrich Geisinger. Jeb can't compete with that."

True, Karr thought. For he knew that despite all of Jeb's contacts and threats, he could never hold a candle to a man as wealthy as Geisinger. "What does it do? The rock."

"Antheon," Cade said, staring out the porthole at the little poisonous planet that hung in the sky. It looked like a glistening marble, its center a trio of strangely split colors. "It's nothing in this form. But Geisinger swears it's revolutionary. *Another pivotal change in science,"* he added, in a voice that sounded oddly like the man's, clipped accent and all. "The job won't be easy, per se. We'll have to take a shipload, and… well, there are some minor wrinkles I still need to smooth out. But the crew's in, and I need you to be, too." He reached out and grabbed hold of the chain around Karr's neck. The necklace itself, a flattened bit of glass that looked like the sea, preserved for eternity. "They were scientists. Not thieves. We'll do it for them. In their memory."

Cade had given his time, his life, his freedom, to always stay by Karr's side. When he looked back on his memories, he saw his older brother taking swing after swing from the other boys in the orphanage when those hits were meant for Karr.

He saw every extra morsel of meat passed across the table, saved for him. So he could grow strong, and defend himself from the others when they deemed him an easy target because of his size.

He saw the extra blankets, stolen, so Karr could stay warm. The boots Cade nabbed from a shop, an act he was nearly hanged for. He saw a lifetime without his real mother and father, but with a brother who'd done his best to take their place.

It didn't matter what Cade was planning, because as much as he hated the phrase, blood *was* stronger than fear. He'd always take Cade's side.

"You and me, Cade. I'm with you. And I'm sure as hell with Geisinger."

Cade looked like he wanted to hug him, but he settled for a curt captain's nod instead. "Get some rest." He grimaced at the storage bay, in all of its controlled chaos. Artifacts from planets strapped down to shelves, ancient weapons and strange foods, foreign animal pelts and all manner of alien things. "I don't know how you can stand it down here."

"It's like art," Karr said. "A beautiful mess."

"Crew meeting in thirty. Details, specs… don't be late. And for God's sake, Karr, clean yourself up. You smell like a brewery."

With that, Cade spun on his heel like a soldier and left Karr in the belly of the *Starfall*, alone with his thoughts.

CHAPTER 2

The Planet Dohrsar
The Kingdom of the Deadlands

Sonara

There was a Devil in the Deadlands, with blood as black as her sins.

She stood disguised in the center of a sweltering golden throne room, her palms pressed close to the blades hidden within the lining of her skirt.

Death, the blades whispered.

Death in the shape of tiny bird bones.

Sonara would not use them yet. Not until the moment demanded, and in a sea of noblewomen hoping to become the king's next bride, death was not in high demand.

The throne room itself—thick with bodies, heavy with the heat of a Deadlands afternoon, the walls painted a starless black, polished golden floor tiles and carved black stone pillars stretching towards a domed ceiling made entirely of shimmering diamond—made Sonara feel small enough.

But it was King Jira himself, as his dark eyes scanned the crowd, that sent a shiver of cold fear creeping across Sonara's tanned skin.

There he sat, atop a golden dais high above her on a throne made of his enemy's bones, staring at the sea of potential brides. Jira was a beast of a man, shoulders wide, his muscles bared and honed from years of ravaging the Deadlands to become king. His large hands curled over the armrests of his throne, easily dwarfing the inset skulls that stared down at the crowd, eye sockets filled with glittering diamonds.

Those hands caught Sonara's eye, along with the gold and diamond rings on each of his fingers, each worth an entire small village outside the capital. They'd bring in enough coin to last for moons upon moons. Perhaps more, if Sonara could drive a decent enough deal at market.

"The Lady Anyta, of House Romar of the Blood Bucket!"

The trumpeteer's voice rang out as a woman at the front of the crowd ascended the towering dais, her blood-red hair braided back from her face to reveal her harsh beauty.

Jira lowered his gaze as she knelt before him, her guard placing a heavy stone box at his feet. Inside, another of many countless gifts the king had no need for.

The women around the room stood with bated breath, hoping that they would be chosen, not for a marriage to the monstrous king, but for the promised future it would afford their own territories and kingdoms.

Sweat trickled down Sonara's back. She fanned herself and held back a yawn.

The whole display was rather boring. She supposed the real Lady Morgana of House Kwell would spend her time smiling up at the king as he welcomed his potential brides. Perhaps she would even toss him a flirtatious glance as she angled her body just so.

But that was *not* Sonara. And the only thing she wanted to draw today was Jira's blood.

Preferably in a solid line across his throat.

"To hell with all of this," she whispered, hating the part she was playing. Hating everything Jira stood for.

Her lips curled into a snarl.

A fingertip gently prodded her side. "Smile, *Morgana*. Snarls aren't very becoming on a Lady."

Sonara tucked a strand of mixed blue-and-brown hair behind her ear and glanced to the right, where her partner Jaxon stood, tall and muscular in his stolen guard's uniform, a cap pulled low over his eyes to conceal the jagged scar that ran across half his face. He looked handsome in Soreian blue. Too handsome, perhaps. He was drawing too many eyes. She could practically taste the desire each time a woman cast a glance Jaxon's way.

Like spun sugar, sickly sweet upon her tongue.

A useless curse, her power to taste the emotions of others. She'd come back from death with it years ago, a tricky little side effect of re-entering the land of the living. Now, Sonara swallowed the insufferable tang of desire away, then pushed with mental fingers until her curse was locked back in its internal cage where it belonged.

If only she had a power like Jaxon's.

A power that could control the bones of the dead creatures among them; like the ones currently hidden in the fabric beneath her fists. The guards had all been cleared of weapons. None would think to check a Lady's outer skirts for a thin layer of bones.

"Perhaps snarls are not fit for a Lady," Sonara whispered back, resisting the urge to squirm in her skirts. Sweat was already trickling down her back, the skirt's inner slip sticking to her skin. Honestly, how could anyone *breathe* in these things, let alone move enough to put up a decent fight when the time came? "But they're delightful on a Devil."

The line of potential brides moved slowly, the Deadlands heat creeping across the throne room like a fog. It was a sea of colors, gowns in every shade and style rolling gently as women fanned themselves in the heat, or tossed their hair over their shoulders, or batted their lashes at the king.

Twenty paces, and Sonara would stand before him atop the dais.

Twenty more, and she'd finally steal a prize worthy of her outlawing name.

The woman before her, a baroness from the northern kingdom of the Wastes, was called forward. She ascended the dais, her hair a silken train of white behind her as she went to offer a gift to the king.

Sonara had no gift.

At least, not one that would last.

That was the trouble with items like the one Jaxon held in his pocket. An illusion made by their comrade Markam, much to Sonara's dismay… and one that would fade by day's end.

Sonara's toes reached the edge of the dais, her slippers damp from sweat.

"Lady Morgana," the trumpeteer began, his voice ringing out across the throne room, bounding off the diamond-domed ceiling far overhead. Fractals of light reflected off the golden tiles, making Sonara dizzy as she took Jaxon's arm. With a predator's grace, she ascended the golden steps to the throne.

The king's eyes were jaded as he stared at his polished fingernails, as if he hadn't a care in the world about the hundreds of brides come to grovel at his feet. She supposed the ceremony had lost its luster, as he took a new bride each year.

Sonara reached the top, Jira's throne drawing her attention. It was a morbid thing, even for her eyes, and somehow more menacing up close.

They weren't beast bones.

They were Dohrsaran bones, people that Jira himself had slain. Some of the bones, like the femurs that made up the backrest and the jagged spines lacing around the arched back, were cracked. As if Jira had split them in two with the sheer force of his will.

But Sonara knew the true cause of those split bones. It was the golden sword that hung at his side, unsheathed.

Gutrender.

Hell, the sword was a beauty. Her eyes fell upon the pommel in the shape of the Hadru, the mighty monster that was the sigil of the Deadlands. The pommel was shaped like the Hadru's barbed tail, ready to strike, the blade itself sticking out of the beast's open maw. Jira kept one of the beasts—the largest ever beheld in the kingdom—in a pit at the northernmost point of the Deadlands, waiting for victims to swallow whole.

Ancient symbols swirled across Gutrender's blade, markings that Sonara could not decipher but had seen carved across the Deadlands for centuries. Markings that whispered of times long ago, when the goddesses birthed Dohrsar from the abyss and swaddled it in a blanket of stars.

"Beautiful," Sonara whispered, as she looked at Gutrender.

Her curse whispered, too.

Blood, it said, begging to come out of its cage. *Hot blood and ripped metal and shredded bones.*

She allowed her curse to creep out, focusing with her breath as she pushed it slowly past the sword's aura until it landed upon the king.

His taste was powerful.

Prideful.

And utterly foul.

Jira looked her up and down as she stopped before him, her blue-and-brown braid hanging like a rope over one shoulder, seashells interwoven through the strands. Her body, covered in makeup to disguise all the scars.

"You have an appetite for dangerous things?" Jira asked. "That is… uncommon, for a Lady."

His voice was deep and booming and all too close.

It made her want to vomit onto her slippers.

This man… he sought out the hidden people like Sonara, with blood the color of shadows.

Demons, some called them.

Ghosts, claimed others.

Devils, Sonara thought, for she was the Devil incarnate, standing before him. Whatever the case, those rare few like her were sentenced to another death; the kind they couldn't come back from again.

"I beg your pardon, my king," Sonara said, bowing her head. *What would the delicate Lady Morgana say to gain his favor, to get him to reach out and touch her hand?* She swallowed and gave a pathetic attempt at a flirtatious laugh. "My mother was a skilled weaponsmaiden from Soreia. And the sword…" She released a gentle breath. "Well, there are a great many tales about what it can do, when wielded by a man with *true* power."

"Power," Jira echoed. His eyes flicked up and down her body, testing her curves. "And a bride who appreciates it."

Don't snarl, Sonara told herself.

"A gift, my king," she said. "From my providence in the southern kingdom. May I?"

Jira nodded.

She glanced backwards at Jaxon, who produced a crimson silk pouch from his coat pocket. Inside, the ring that Markam had crafted for the job. She'd been reluctant to team up with the Trickster, as he always had an extra surprise up his sleeve… but this time he'd sworn to be honest. And the ring he'd fashioned *was* lovely, with a plump diamond the color of blackest night, its band made of thick gold to match Gutrender.

"From the finest craftsmen and women Soreia has to offer." Sonara extended the ring, fighting back a tremor of excitement.

Her blood pulsed, hot with the promise of a true prize. The king's dark eyes narrowed. But he uncurled his fingers from the skull armrest and held out his hand. "Very well."

It dwarfed hers. Callouses from sword-fighting littered his palms. How many across Dohrsar had Jira killed? Not only enemies, but innocents? How many had been children? How many had held up their own hands in surrender while he brought down his blade?

Sonara smiled.

A real smile, for the girl she'd once been long ago would have shaken as she stood before him. But now, she was not afraid.

"You must be delicate when you make the switch. Swift as a fowl in

flight." The memory of Markam's voice whispered into her mind, instructions from the countless hours they'd spent practicing this particular sleight of hand.

Sonara had mastered it plenty of times before. It was how they'd bagged enough coin to survive the coldest nights on the run.

"I'd like to see you conquer more kingdoms," Sonara said, tilting her body so that she could draw the king's eyes back to hers. Mixed, muddied brown, with the slightest ring of outer blue. She fluttered her lashes. "If you would have me, my king."

Sonara made the swap, placing the false ring on his finger while she deftly slid another ring off. It was almost like magic, so smoothly the swap went.

Almost.

For just as she was about to release the king's hand, his grip tightened.

Pain lanced across her bones as he squeezed. "Perhaps I'm mistaken, my Lady. But I believe you've just taken something of mine."

Sonara's curse thrashed inside of her.

That was the taste of *fury* that rolled onto her tongue, like she'd swallowed a burning ember. She'd practiced that trick a hundred times, a *thousand* times, so how in the blasted gates of hell…

"Who are you?" the king demanded. So soft, so utterly calm, even as his eyes hardened, and she thought her hand might break beneath his crushing grasp.

He leaned forward, his face now so close to hers that she could sense every sinful aura soaring from him.

He tasted like blood.

He tasted like *death.*

Sonara tried to speak, but the mixture of his aura was too strong. Her tongue felt like it was burning to ashes. She took a step back, but Jira yanked her forward again, her useless slippers sliding on the dais.

Murmurs spread throughout the crowd, but Sonara could hear nothing but the sound of her own heartbeat, and her black blood roaring in her ears.

Before she could stop him, Jira dipped his hand into the hidden pocket on her skirts to produce his diamond ring. She stiffened, her mind wiped clean of any believable excuse.

"You'll have a visit to Deadwood for this, my *Lady.*"

Deadwood.

The prison camp in the north, where blood froze alongside aching bones.

Jira rose, his grip like an iron manacle. He produced a small blade from his gold robes and pressed it to her throat.

"Guards!" he growled. "Seize this traitor to the crown." His eyes flitted past Sonara, to where Jaxon stood, a guard who'd been forced to leave his weapons at the door. "And her guard, too. Take them both to the north."

"*No,*" Sonara said. She winced as the tip of his blade nicked her skin.

Any normal girl would've cried out in pain. But Sonara had become one with pain in all her years of outlawing, relished it, even. It was *fear* that she must conquer now, the true traitor, as her blood was drawn.

As not liquid, but living *shadow* slid from beneath her skin.

It soared out of the wound like a ribbon of black smoke. It

danced over their heads, twirling and twisting as it rose higher, fully alight in the rays of sunlight shining down from the diamond ceiling.

Jira's grip went slack. His eyes widened as he whispered, *"Shadowblood."*

A story thought to be untrue.

A curse deserving of death.

The word echoed outwards, circling around the throne room as everyone below registered the sight. It was one that had not been seen for centuries. It was whispered about around roaring campfires and echoed on long, desert rides, a story dealt as a warning to tricky children before they were tucked away into their beds at night.

Careful, or you'll be haunted by a Shadowblood.

"Seize them both!" Jira growled. "*Alive.*"

Sonara felt the seams of her outer skirt split.

A flicker of white shot past her gaze, so fast it was merely a blur. She heard the sickening *squelch* as Jaxon's magic sent the sharpened bird bone soaring home.

Right into Jira's eye.

***

Sonara didn't waste a breath. Screams rang out across the throne room as she moved, lunging for the only weapon in sight as Jaxon's curse continued to call upon the bones in her skirts, and Jira's guards poured up the dais.

Blood, Sonara's own curse sang.

The metallic aura in the air came from Jira's eye as he roared and tried to pry the bird bone out. But it was also coming from the massive golden sword at his hip.

Sonara had failed once already in losing her prize. And at this rate, death was imminent. Jaxon only had so many bird bones to go around. They'd left their real weapons beyond the city gates with Markam and their mounts.

But Gutrender… it was now, or it was never, for there were no prizes on the other side of death.

She would not become a prisoner today.

It felt like a dream as Sonara reached for the sword. Somehow, the king saw her coming, but a bird bone drove itself into the back of his hand, shooting a clean hole out the other side. Jira roared as Jaxon's power commanded another bone to fire, and suddenly Sonara's hand was around Gutrender's cold pommel.

She gripped with all her might and *pulled.*

It sang sweetly as it tore from the king's iron belt.

"Sonara, *now*!" Jaxon yelled.

She turned, the heavy weight of Gutrender so unlike her own weapon as she tested the balance, distorting her view of the ladies sprinting to safety or tripping over their own skirts as they cleared out of the throne room, abandoning their gifts to the king.

The sounds of chaos took over; a chorus of screams, shouts of guards commanding a calm that would not come; the stomping of boots and clinking of heavy golden armor as Jira's guards thundered up the steps of the towering dais.

The first guard reached the top.

Sonara felt the satisfying *snick* as the blade cut through the unprotected flesh between helmet and chestplate. She felt it flay bone, sever head from neck as blood sprayed. *Regular* blood, the kind that wasn't deemed unwanted or unworthy.

Sonara spat it from her lips, but the aura of it got to her all the same.

Bitter, like the hot venom of a desert snake.

All of Jira's guards had the same vile taste, that same soul-deep aura that Sonara's curse latched onto, even when she willed it not to be so.

The crack of the guard's head hitting the stones resounded around the throne room, the screams of the ladies gone now as the room cleared, replaced by the shouts of guards.

Sonara's curse tugged at her senses.

Left!

Fury, surging forth like a rogue wave.

She ducked as a spear thrust out from beside her. Before she came back to standing, she drove Gutrender upwards, out, and *through*. Innards spilled across the dais.

She swung again, taking out the next guard. Down, she marched, Jaxon at her side as they cut through their enemies.

Four guards dropped to two in a single swipe from Gutrender.

Two guards dropped to none as Jaxon's bird bones landed home in eyes or hearts or sliced across jugulars, draining their lifeblood.

"I'm almost out!" Jaxon yelled. "We need to go."

He was paces away, his hands raised as he called on his Shadowblood curse, the weight of Sonara's skirts lightening as bone by bone was removed.

Sonara let her own curse guide her, ducking when it beckoned, dodging when it tasted the sharp anticipation of a swing.

Her bare feet reached the bottom of the dais, slippers discarded in the bloodshed. She cut through a guard's spear, wood splintering with a sound like lightning. Another spear dove towards her gut. Sonara feinted backwards, but a bird bone spiraled past her ear to land in the man's chest. Two more followed, little white missiles, and he dropped, lifeless on the stones.

"I'm out," Jaxon said. He was breathless, hunched over as the exhaustion from using his curse weighed him down. "We have to leave."

The king was nowhere to be seen. The dais was empty, save for the corpses strewn about.

"He ran," Sonara said, wiping blood from her face. "Like a child."

Silence, followed by the *plink* of fresh blood dripping onto the gold tiles.

"No ring," Jaxon said.

"No ring," Sonara echoed, and lifted Gutrender. "But this will do."

Jaxon stared at the blood and the blade. "You frighten me, Lady Morgana."

"Lady Morgana is dead. And you will be too, if you don't drop the charade. You realize this changes things, don't you?" She lifted the sword. "They'll send more. Jira won't rest until we're placed among the other bodies in Deadwood."

The prison camp was far worse than any fate she could imagine.

Jaxon only shrugged. "We've made it out of worse situations."

A bold lie. But they turned towards the exit together anyway, ready to fight off their fate. The heavy doors groaned, ancient and tired as they heaved them open to let the Deadlands air rush in.

Jira's castle sat perched atop a single flattened mesa that

dropped hundreds of feet straight down to desert sands. At the front entrance, only a single stone road led down to the capital city of Stonegrave.

Sonara stared down that road now, the dry wind shifting from sweltering daytime heat to the sudden chill of a desert night.

Far below, she could see the red and brown rooftops of tightly crammed together homes, the sharp, knife-like Scholar's Keep cutting above the tallest buildings. Not far from it, the rounded bell tower of Stonegrave stood proudly, flocks of colorful fowl dipping and twisting in the sky as they soared past.

Beyond it all—the endless expanse of desert that made up most of the Deadlands, as far as the eye could see.

It was eerily quiet; no carriages waiting, no steeds lined up at the gates. The ladies and their guards had abandoned the castle, likely hidden deep within the city streets by now, far away from the two Shadowbloods that had poisoned the throne room with their presence.

"Strange," Jaxon said.

Sonara felt the hair on the back of her neck stand on end. "There should be more guards," she said. "There are *always* more."

Just as she said it, the bell tower began to ring.

A solid resounding clang, it echoed across the city. A warning to all.

Danger has come to Stonegrave.

Sonara saw, then, the snaking line of guards pouring up the single road. She heard the thunderous symphony of hoofbeats hitting stone, as guards came atop their steeds, weapons glinting in the dying sunlight.

One road out of the castle; straight towards the guards.

“Jax,” Sonara said softly. “There’s a hundred of them, and two of us.”

“Not great odds,” he admitted. “We should have let Markam come.”

“No,” Sonara hissed. “We’d be twice damned if he was with us.”

“Sonara, I can’t use my curse anymore,” Jaxon groaned. There was a darkness beneath his eyes; the heavy exhaustion of having used his power to free them from the guards in the throne room.

Sonara looked at him, the weary smile on his handsome scarred face. He’d fight as long as she did, and in the end they would *both* end up in chains, sent to Deadwood to die.

She checked the horizon. Trickster or not… Markam was hiding beyond the city walls, waiting for them with their mounts. He would hear the bells and come—of *course* he would come, when he assumed they’d gotten their hands on the prize. But the sky was still empty. How long until Markam noticed the commotion and soared for them on his mount? How quickly could his wyvern fly?

Not fast enough, Sonara’s conscience whispered.

In her mind, she saw a pair of cool, sea-blue eyes paired with a prince’s smile.

Soahm.

She’d lost him, then.

She wouldn’t lose another brother now, even if Jaxon wasn’t her blood.

“Five days,” Sonara said as she lifted Gutrender and admired the perfect blade.

Jaxon raised a brow. *Confusion* flickered from his aura on

a gust of wind. Sonara's head pulsed with pain at the sudden use of her curse. "What?"

She swallowed and faced him head on. "When they take me, Jax… I'll have only five days before the prison wagon reaches the north. Don't trust Markam too much. And… don't make me wait that long."

Before he could protest, she rammed the pommel of Gutrender atop his head.

He dropped like a stone.

Sonara dragged him, grunting from his unconscious weight, to the thick thorny bushes surrounding the castle and shoved him behind them. She placed Gutrender on his chest; a prize she could not afford to lose. Then she dragged two dead guards atop him, so if found, Jaxon would only be mistaken as carrion for the birds.

Sonara stepped back and admired her quick work. Darkness would fall soon, and he'd be well hidden until he woke. By then, Markam would have come and plucked him from harm.

Sure enough, she could see the ghostly outline of a black speck in the distance, taking to the skies. For once, he was reliable.

Sonara faced the guards, taking up one of the fallen blades.

The sound of hoofbeats heightened as the guards in the front of the cavalry thundered into the courtyard, surprise on their faces as they beheld her, alone.

A blue-haired beauty practically dripping blood-red.

The first guard was easy to take out. He fell from his steed in a burst of blood, and in a blink, she swung upwards into the saddle and yanked the reins to the right, swiftly kicking the beast into a lope and riding right back towards the rest of the guards.

They'd take her alive, soon enough.

Until then… Sonara gripped her sword, and prayed to the goddesses that her plan, however futile, would work.

CHAPTER 3

THREE DAYS LATER
The Northern Road

Sonara

Three days had passed since Sonara was captured, knocked out and bound, and had awoken here, a prisoner among twelve others, her back cramped against the rough wood of a prison wagon as it rocked its way across the northern road.

Three of the twelve were already corpses gone cold. Their eyes were open, staring past the iron bars on the windows as if they'd wanted to catch a glimpse of freedom as their spirits were called home.

It felt like a dream, waking here in the stink of sweat and piss and broken dreams.

Three days, and Jaxon was nowhere to be seen.

The crack of the whip sounded out.

Sonara bumped heads with the man next to her as the steeds hauling the caravan hastened their pace. Outside the barred window, she caught a distant glimpse of the armed guards that had been hired to escort the prisoners from Stonegrave to Deadwood.

The wagons snaked along a curve in the makeshift desert road. The escorts, ten on each side of the caravan, rode beautiful beasts from Soreia, backs broad and necks strong, hooves kicking up sand that was picked up by the wind.

Endless miles of it.

Sand, and sand and sand, spreading into the ghostly forms of the Bloodhorn Mountains, far beyond.

From here, the desert almost looked like the sea.

When Sonara closed her eyes, she could imagine it; the memory of the waves tugging at her bare toes. The sound of the gulls cawing overhead, the kiss of the salt air upon her lips.

The feeling of waking up from her own death on a distant shore, long ago, with a hazy memory of only spending a short time in the afterlife. She had her new curse as her companion.

And *Duran.*

Blessed, beautiful Duran.

They'd died together on the rocks, their bodies crushed during the Leaping. But somehow, the steed had come back to life alongside Sonara, unharmed and unmarred. It was like a sweet dream, that moment of waking, of blinking back the sun and seeing Duran step towards her on the shore. As if the goddesses—or whoever was in charge of the realm that held the living—couldn't bear to see his soul leave the world so soon.

She had no idea why they'd both been brought back.

How they'd been brought back.

Only that they were here, now, and for the past ten years they'd stayed together, wild and free.

Sonara's memory was broken by the sound of a scream. The mournful kind that ripped apart the soul.

"Goddesses be with them as they go," a woman across from Sonara whispered.

The scream heightened, turning to muted sobs from the wagon in front of theirs.

Another prisoner had succumbed to death.

"The goddesses can't hear your prayers," Sonara said. "And even if they could, I doubt they'd be listening."

The woman's whispered prayers fell silent.

Two days more, and they'd reach Deadwood, the prison camp at the edge of the Deadlands, where the rocky Bloodhorn Mountains turned to solid ice. The frozen land dropped straight off into what seemed an endless abyss. There, the prisoners would live the rest of their days carving out a frozen bridge that would span across the miles-long gap that separated the Deadlands and the northern kingdom of the White Wastes.

Sonara would rather die.

She was not fond of the cold.

The whip cracked again. The wagon lurched over a bump in the sand, and a man to Sonara's left leaned over and spilled his guts onto the wooden floorboards.

The smell of waste, of *fear*, hung heavy in the air.

Her manacles clinked as she shifted, her wrists red and raw. Each one of the links, shimmering beautifully, was made of diamond, and worth one hell of a prize.

It was also unbreakable.

Unless you had a wyvern that breathed emerald fire hot enough to melt the diamond.

Unfortunate, Sonara thought. For she *did* have access to such a beast, but Razor's shadow had yet to darken the skies beyond the wagon.

She looked back at the manacles around her wrists and sighed. "I don't suppose anyone has a key?"

"*Enough*," said the man across from her. His eyes were sunken, his lips cracked and dry.

"It's a pity, you know," Sonara said, "if I ever get out of this blasted wagon, I'll never be able to look at diamonds again."

When, Sonara told herself. *When Jaxon comes to free you.*

Her blood brother, her comrade, would never leave her to rot. Markam, perhaps, for he was a different story. But *three days*? Her troupe had never taken so long before. Perhaps her plan, her last shred of hope as she took a stand on that mesa, had failed her.

Sweat trickled down her skin, pooling at the small of her back. Each breath felt heavier, more labored than the next. But come nightfall, her teeth would set to chattering. Her very bones would quiver inside of her skin.

She sighed and looked back to the prisoner across from her. "Tell us, friend. What did you do to get a one-way ticket to the north?"

As she spoke, a tendril of deep blue-and-brown hair slipped from her braid and tickled her nose.

The man looked her over as if he were searching for a secret.

He would find nothing but scars, for Sonara shared no secrets, and gave no tells. That was how one survived in the Deadlands. And you couldn't simply *see* a Shadowblood. There was a reason they were told only as tall tales around campfires.

Sonara had tried to find others.

She'd never discovered any but the ones in her troupe.

"I killed a girl for asking too many questions," the man said. His smile was dark and toothless. "She was small like you."

Sonara raised a brow. "I have nothing to fear from a man in chains."

He barked out a dry, humorless laugh. "I like you, Blue."

A veiled threat, and one she'd have to watch out for, should the wagon make it to Deadwood with her aboard. Many of the people here were criminals. Killers. The worst the Deadlands had to offer. They didn't feel fear, for they themselves bred it and carried it like a torch.

Deep inside, Sonara's curse wriggled, begging to come out. *Only a tiny taste,* it whispered.

Every emotion and feeling had one, something that Sonara could breathe in and savor as plainly as if it were placed right on her tongue. She hated to use her curse; her *sense,* this strange trait that marked her second life. She hated the way it overcame her, caused her pain each time she used it, as if it were a tiny beastie that burrowed deeper into her body the more she lengthened its leash. Long ago, she'd learned how to control her curse, to press it deep inside a mental cage.

But that didn't stop it from reaching its little shadow-claws through the bars to swipe at her when it hungered most. It eased out towards the man, wanting to savor his aura.

A sharp, iron tang, like blood, as if his soul was soaked with it.

A murderer's aura.

"I work alone," Sonara said, holding his gaze without backing down.

"We'll see about that, Blue." He smiled a cold, unfeeling smile. "Go on, then. Share your tale. What brings a little lady like you to the north?"

He was goading her now. Perhaps she would let him have the truth.

"I stole Jira's golden sword," Sonara said with a yawn.

The man chuckled, light reaching his eyes. "You tell an interesting tale, Blue."

Sonara felt the eyes of the others sliding to her. As if they were coming back to life for the first time in days.

She'd last seen Gutrender on Jaxon's side, before she'd been taken.

She hoped, hell, even *she* was almost ready to pray, that nothing had gone wrong. And if something had happened to her steed along the way, she'd turn Jaxon and Markam inside out.

Soon.

They would come soon.

"She lies," the woman on the far side of the wagon scoffed. "The Devil wouldn't be caught alive, and forced into a prison wagon."

"The Devil?" another asked.

The woman nodded. "Heard tell of it just before they picked me up in Rothollow. The Devil stole the king's sword!" A few nods of approval followed. The woman coughed and glanced at Sonara with hollow eyes. "But this girl is just a stray sea urchin from the south. Nothing more."

Sonara barked out a laugh at the insult. If she wasn't chained, she would show the woman exactly what a *sea urchin's* sting felt like. But she was weaponless. She may as well have been naked without her sword.

The Devil of the Deadlands, Sonara thought. *Doomed to die.*

If her troupe really had forgotten her, she'd haunt them from the afterlife.

She wasn't truly afraid. And yet, she couldn't help the image that slid into her mind at the thought of a final death. A quest unfinished.

A face that materialized, long removed from her life, but *never* forgotten.

The face looked like hers, but it was older. Male, and handsome, with a square jaw and perfect Soreian blue eyes and hair to match.

If she died in the north, she'd lose all chance of finding her brother again. Though sometimes, she wondered if Soahm was already dead.

"What if she's not lying?" the other prisoner asked. Sonara blinked, and Soahm's face faded from existence, replaced by the man before her that continued smiling in the shadows. "You say you are the Devil?"

Sonara nodded. "I very well could be."

"Alright then, Blue. Prove it."

She opened her mouth to speak, but words failed her.

For outside the wagon, something had changed.

Sonara cocked her head to listen. Beyond the wind, beyond the breathing of her companions… the powerful beat of widespread wings cutting through the sky. A sharp screech echoed from afar.

The steeds hauling the caravan whinnied, and everything shifted. Indeed, beyond the barred window, the escorts turned in their saddles, then began to shout as they saw something in the sky.

The word echoed across the caravan, from one escort's mouth to another's, until it reached the front driver.

"Wyvern!"

The whip sounded. The wagons began to speed up. Sonara's head smacked against the person next to her, so hard she sucked in a painful breath. And as she did, her curse snapped loose.

Come back, she begged, but she already knew it would refuse.

Out the wagon window it went, spiraling into the desert as it preyed on everything in sight. She sensed the steeds hauling the whole caravan, their fear *sticky and dark as tar on the tongue* as the screech in the sky grew louder.

She sensed the corpses in the other wagons, bloated and decaying in the heat.

She sensed the salty tears on someone's face. The sweat on tightly pressed together bodies, on ruined wrists beneath thick diamond manacles.

Her head throbbed like someone had taken a hammer to it. Her throat burned like she'd contracted a sudden illness.

Still, the steeds tore across the sand, desperately trying to outrun the source of the wingbeats. Dust rose from the wheels, clouding the barred windows, the view of the escorts and their mounts.

"What's out there?" a prisoner asked. "Why are we speeding up?"

"You want me to prove I'm the Devil?" Sonara asked the others. "First, I suggest you all duck your heads."

They only had time to scream as a massive set of razor-sharp claws pierced through the roof of the wagon, just over their heads. A mighty roar followed, and the roof of the wagon was ripped away.

***

Fear.

It was all around her, so thick Sonara couldn't force the aura back.

But her troupe had *come.* They'd come for her, just as she'd hoped they would.

The twin suns were like daggers in her eyes, the sudden absence of shadows utterly jarring. Sonara blinked, a triumphant cry building in her.

For there overhead, soaring across the endless desert sky, was Razor, Markam's mighty wyvern as black as the night. The roof of the wagon still clutched in her jagged talons. She released it, sent it tumbling down from the skies.

The escorts, galloping across the sand, had drawn their swords and shields. But they would be useless against Razor.

Sonara had never been so happy to see the hideous beast. For there on her back was Jaxon and Markam, alive and well. Together, the brothers and the beast were a force of fire and flight, working in synchronized glory as they fought to free the prisoners below.

Sonara could sense the wyvern's fire before she released it: *a spark, building to a flame, the thickness of smoke spilling from mighty lungs* before Razor opened her massive jaws and sent a pillar of green flame down towards the wagon at the front of the caravan.

The wagon exploded. The steeds' harness melted at its touch, and they tore off across the desert, free at last, the very ground shaking under their feet.

Sonara cheered, her heart racing in her chest, blood roaring in her ears as the rest of the caravan finally came to a rolling stop.

The chains around her wrists bit at her skin as she tried in vain to free herself. She wanted out. She wanted to *fight.*

Razor banked again, screeching so loud Sonara felt it in her bones. The wyvern stretched out her talons, tucked her wings in tight, and dove straight for the escorts, who hefted their swords and readied for a fight they could not win.

One lifted a crossbow and shot.

The arrow spiraled towards Razor, who dipped sideways with ease, then continued her chase.

The steeds below skittered sideways, bleating in fear. Two of the guards were thrown overboard, their steeds abandoning them to tear off into the desert.

Razor roared again, jaws wide and smoke pluming from her nostrils. She landed effortlessly upon the sand and spread her wings high above her, barbed tail spraying the grains like droplets of a crashing wave.

There atop her sat Jaxon, with his wide-brimmed leather hat pulled low over his eyes. Markam was just behind him, a shade taller, both wearing brown leather dusters that settled behind them like capes. They dismounted, boots softly scraping up the sand as they approached the guards.

Razor growled, but Markam held up a gloved hand. She fell silent, smoke pluming from her nostrils. If she released too much of her fire too soon, she'd burn out like a candle, and be useless when they needed her most.

The guards dismounted and formed a circle around the brothers as they stopped fifty paces away.

Back to back, they stood. Two sentries ready to strike fear in the hearts of those who dared cross them.

"Stand down!"

The largest guard, a man with a red braid hanging down his back, hefted a sword that was made of black Deadlands iron. Supple material, though not as strong as Soreian steel.

It was so quiet, Sonara had forgotten she sat in a wagon full of other prisoners, who watched with breaths held; a wagon full of murderers and thieves and madmen, too fearful to utter a single noise as they watched.

"Stand down?" Jaxon's chuckle danced across the desert sand, carried towards Sonara on a gust of dry wind. She breathed in his aura, the *fearlessness, strong as a freshly brewed cup of hauva in the morning.* "You have something of ours. And we never leave without getting what we want."

"These prisoners are the property of the King of the Deadlands," the guard growled.

Markam smiled, a cruel thing that had Sonara's insides twisting. "Brainless beasts, the king's guards," he said in his casual drawl. "This fight is dull, Jaxon. Show him the way the bones call to your blood."

Jaxon lifted his hands, then. And all around him, the desert began to quake.

The sands shifted softly as his curse called upon the bones of the dead, begging them to uncover themselves; to shake off the dust, and answer the silent cry.

The bones of an ancient, long-dead fowl appeared, hobbling towards him as it emerged from the sand, wings bent and broken. A desert rat crawled forth from its unmarked grave. The body of a snake, no longer held together by muscle or skin, shaped together and slithered towards him, alive beneath the power coursing in Jaxon's blood.

"By… by the order of King Jira of the Deadlands," the head guard stuttered, fear lancing his words now. "*Stand… down.*"

Jaxon tilted his head sideways. The bones stopped at his feet in shapeless piles. "Free the Devil of the Deadlands, and you'll walk away from this fight unharmed."

His eyes flitted past the guards, towards the caravan, where Sonara herself sat waiting, still held by her insufferable diamond chains. The other prisoners watched her with widened eyes, as if they could scarcely believe what they were seeing was true.

"Sonara?" Jaxon cried out. "Now would be a good time to let me know you're alive in there!"

A smile spread across Sonara's dry lips. "Alive!" she called back. "And growing impatient!"

With a smile, Jaxon removed his hat and placed it beside him on the sand. It was that act alone, more than the risen bones, that confirmed no one would leave this place alive today.

Jaxon didn't like to get blood on the old leather. And blood was most certainly about to be spilled.

"Free the Devil," Jaxon said softly, his scarred face clearly visible now.

The guards did not lower their swords. "Stand down," the leader said. "In the name of His Majesty King Jira."

"You had a chance," Markam told them, with a shrug.

The guard growled and lunged, swinging his blade.

A ripple of the air… and Markam disappeared.

One moment there, gone the next. The guards gasped, the one lunging towards him stumbling as his blade hit only air where Markam had just been.

"*Shadowblood*," he growled as he turned his attention on Jaxon instead. "Kill them both!"

Jaxon only lifted his hands.

Like little white missiles, the bones shot forward across the sky, propelled by his power. They sank into the guard's body like a hundred tiny swords; small femurs and knuckle bones and kneecaps that turned on their sides, the better to slice.

The guard staggered sideways, eyes wide, jaw hanging open in shock as he registered what Jaxon had just done.

Then he fell: a lifeless lump, face first in the sand, useless sword still clutched in his fist.

"Well done, brother!"

Markam reappeared on the edge of the crowd, behind the guards.

They spun, stumbling backwards in fear as his cloak settled around his ankles, like he was a ghost stepping out of an invisible realm.

"KILL THE DEMONS!" a guard shouted.

Sand sprayed as they dove into the fight, half towards Markam, the other half towards Jaxon.

Sonara watched as Jaxon dropped to one knee and spun in a circle, hands held before him as he called upon the bones of the dead. They shot from the sand, arced and twisted through the sky as he himself spun, sending them in a full whirlwind of death.

They sliced through arms and jammed into kneecaps and weakened muscles as the guards fell, practically bleating with fear.

Behind him, Markam fought on; standing in the sand, his arms crossed as he hefted his trademark red dagger and spun it in his hand, jamming it into the thigh of a guard before disappearing in a blink.

Two heartbeats later, he zapped back into existence behind another guard, sliding that crimson dagger across the man's throat. Blood sprayed, and Markam was gone again. Only the mark of his footsteps shifting the sand revealed his presence as he sprinted across the desert, unseen, to fully form again at Jaxon's side.

One by one, the brothers of Wildeweb took the guards down until there were only four left.

Two for each brother; the desert around them, littered with bodies that were once proud to be called King's Men.

But Jaxon was beginning to stagger. Too long, too much of his power used, and he would lose his strength. Sonara saw it in the way his steps began to lose fluidity. The way the sweat was clearly beading on his scarred brow.

He earned a slice to his collarbone.

Sonara cried out as she saw his black blood soar to the sky.

"*Come on, Jax!*" she growled. "*Focus.*"

Markam was too busy, preoccupied with taking out the other two, who hefted their broadswords against Markam's single dagger. He was quick, but he wasn't as large as them, wasn't as strong.

"Come on!" Sonara shouted, wishing she could tear herself from her diamond chains, wishing she could run from the wagon and lift her sword and…

She screamed as a guard struck Jaxon in the back.

He stumbled, his face warped in pain even as he sent a bird's beak flying home into the man's jugular.

Jaxon fell to a knee, gasping, face twisted in agony. He was burning out. The other guard took the moment to close in on him, had nearly leveled his sword over Jaxon's neck as the bones around him began to fall from the sky. Markam shouted and tried in vain to get to him, but…

A *blast.*

A crackle that shook the very sky.

The hair at the end of Sonara's braid stood on end as a massive burst of blue light, of sparkling electricity, soared across the sand and blasted a hole in the ground. The guards before the brothers soared backwards like falling stars, smoking and charred and utterly, utterly dead.

Sonara gasped as silence spread across the desert.

She turned, slowly, to look towards the left.

As the smoke cleared, two steeds emerged, like specters stepping into the sunlight.

The first was a pale steed, ridden by a woman who looked to be wearing a mask made of a wolf's skull.

The second was Duran, Sonara's loyal steed, who'd died with her and came back to life again, ten years ago. On his back sat a woman adorned in a deep red cloak, black hair hanging to her waist, her palms held open before her.

Sonara had to blink a few times to confirm what she was seeing was true.

For the woman's skin was smoking and charred. Tendrils of still-glowing blue lightning snaked up her wrists—as if she held the power of a storm within her veins.

***

It didn't take long for the desert to clear of prisoners.

One by one, Jaxon, wounded but well, went to the wagons

and freed them, Razor's fire melting the massive lock that bound each wagon's set of chains.

Sonara waited, eyes closed as she leaned her head back and ignored the watching eyes of her fellow prisoners. Finally, *finally,* there was the clink of chains, a muted curse, and her wagon door fell to the ground.

Sonara coughed as the dust settled, and the prisoner across from her screamed.

Razor's massive, dripping maw was just inches away. The wyvern released a heavy breath, the smell of death enough to make plants wilt.

But Sonara only smiled. "You do know how to make an entrance, Razor." The knots in her chest fell free for the first time in three days as the wyvern growled. "It's good to see you, too, vile beast." The caravan driver's dismembered head was held between Razor's teeth. Sonara grimaced. "Enjoying a treat?"

Razor chomped down on the skull.

There was plenty of merit to choosing Razor. But Sonara preferred the swift gentle soul of her steed.

She felt for that little burning flame inside of her. It was always there, sometimes hotter than others. The most frightening of times, the *loneliest* of times, it was merely an ember close to cold. It had been so for these three days.

That little flame was Duran's soul, and it was tangled up with hers. A bond that could not be broken.

Sonara's blood was replaced with living shadows, the side effects being her curse and a soul connection with Duran. She wished only the latter had remained.

That soul-ember flared bright, signifying his closeness and safety.

"Alright, Sonara?" Jaxon appeared beside Razor as she spewed a breath of green fire. The diamond melted like liquid starlight, pooling and hissing into the sand.

So fast, the prisoners rushed to freedom, shaking off their chains, not caring that their manacles still held. No one uttered a thanks. They were gone before Jaxon could offer to set them free of those, too.

Typical, even for prisoners heading to Deadwood. Nobody wanted to be near a Shadowblood. Not even one that had just saved them from certain death.

The wound on his back wasn't as bad as she'd originally suspected. It was open, and bleeding, but he'd endured worse before. It was the use of his power that drained him far more.

"Next time, Jax," Sonara said, relief flooding through her as he smiled and crawled into the wagon, "try not to get yourself killed when you're saving me. You scared the hell out of me."

"I don't fear a second death," he said with a wink. "I have a pretty close relationship with the Devil herself."

Sonara cursed under her breath as he worked at her manacles, whistling softly to send tiny bones soaring into the locks of her cuffs. A twist, a sigh from Jaxon as he let the last dregs of his power loose, and the manacles fell free. He smiled up at her, exhaustion darkening his eyes. "If I remember correctly, you're the one who knocked me out and left me buried in a pile of corpses outside Jira's castle, leaving my fate to Markam, of all people."

Sonara winced. That *was* true. "What did it take, to get him to fly you here to save me?"

Jaxon closed his eyes. "I agreed to another job."

"Of *course,*" Sonara said with a groan. Markam never did any good deeds, even for family, without demanding a prize of his own. "No rest for the weary. Did you ask him for details of this job, before you signed the deal in blood?"

Jaxon's sudden silence, and the way his posture went rigid, was all the answer she needed.

He was helplessly, *hopelessly* loyal. "Blast, Jax. What have you done?"

"I've saved you, for starters," Jaxon said. "He wouldn't tell me the details until you were present and accounted for. But whatever it is, Markam has promised a fine prize. The Lady is wealthy beyond measure."

He glanced behind his shoulder, where the two strange new arrivals sat. The lady in crimson, who still had her hood pulled low over her eyes, stood in the sand beside Duran, staring down at the corpses.

Only the wind pulling at her cloak revealed that she was not made of stone.

Perhaps she'd never killed before. It changed a person; placed a coldness inside of their hearts that no other deed on the continent ever could.

"Come on," Jaxon said. "One can see that smoke for miles and miles. Jira's guards will be swift on their way."

He looked exhausted, as if he hadn't slept in days. And perhaps he hadn't… but Sonara knew a large part of that exhaustion came from using his curse.

Jaxon's only worked with the bones of the dead. Beasts were far more common, for the bones of dead Dohrsarans were often buried far, far beneath the earth. To summon the bones of a person would be to call upon every *ounce* of power inside Jaxon, pushing him too close to a second death.

Every curse had its own twists, its own walls that couldn't be broken. Sonara's curse was the same. She could only sense emotions—never manipulate them. She'd only ended up with a massive headache when she'd tried.

The rest of the time, there was pain, a constant ache that just wouldn't quit. The longer she held her curse within its cage, the more it plagued her. But once she released it, the world was hers to breathe in… until the after-effects kicked in, a dull throb that reminded her she was not entirely *normal* in this second life.

There was a cost to every curse.

"Well. You've a story to tell," Sonara said. *Blast,* it would take days to rid herself of the soreness. Jaxon helped haul her to her feet, despite his own exhaustion. His heavy breaths were warm on her cheeks. His aura, comforting as always. *A hard, heavy drink after a long day's ride.*

"I need to know *everything,*" Sonara said. "Starting with her." She glanced outside the wagon, where the woman wearing a bone mask had pulled the lady in crimson aside, speaking to her in hushed tones. "Shadowbloods don't come out of hiding. And here out of nowhere, one of the strongest we've ever seen just rides into the sunlight to save the day?"

"That would be a side effect of knowing my brother," he said, eyeing Markam, who was busy digging through the suits of the uncharred King's Men, likely for any extra coin or bits of gold. Heartless as ever, Markam broke rules that Sonara never would.

She always let the dead lie still.

She still wondered what the afterlife would have been like, if whatever sent her barreling back to live a second life would have just left her *alone.*

"The sword?" she asked suddenly, still swaying a little on her feet.

Jaxon swallowed. "It's safe. Stashed in the cache at Sandbank. But I do have this, to tide you over." Jaxon lifted his duster, revealing a glimpse of a sword tucked carefully into a black scabbard.

Sonara's heart practically sang at the sight of it. "Hello, gorgeous."

Lazaris, the menacing black blade with a single stripe of blue running down its center.

Forget diamonds. Blades were a girl's true best friend.

Sonara strapped Lazaris to her waist, the aura of the sword—that had once belonged to her brother—like a healing balm to her soul.

Blood and metal and bone.

Sonara smiled, and whistled twice, high and loud.

Duran's ears pricked up, and in an instant, he was trotting towards her, head held high.

Dirt and grime, the after-scent of hard work and summer heat and wheat sprouts, crushed beneath layers of solid teeth.

Beside his aura, Sonara could *feel* the ember of Duran's soul heating in her chest, *feel* his excitement as he tore across the sand. His coat was a blur of red-brown like cavern rocks, his body all muscle on large feathered legs and hooves. In his first life, his eyes were red as hot coals. But now they were dark as a starless night.

The steed was her family, the *only* family she needed other than Jaxon.

Duran reached her, dark eyes boring into hers, nostrils blowing hot air into her face. Their connection brightened, a certain feeling of *rightness* sliding into place as she patted him on the small white star in the center of his forehead. Sonara dug her fingers into his dark mane and flung herself onto his back. He snorted as if to say hello, and she was home again in an instant.

"To Sandbank, then?" Sonara said. "Where we'll receive the terms of this little deal you've made with Markam and his strange new companions."

Jaxon bit his lip. "I did it to save you. I hope you remember that, when we discover whatever it is that I've signed us up to do."

"Markam saved us both," Sonara said, as she watched Markam climb atop Razor's back. He whistled, waving for Jaxon to join him so they could fly south. "I'm grateful… however damned we might be, in his debt again."

Markam was a Trickster. A liar. A true Shadowblood, who cared not for the lives of anyone other than himself. He hadn't saved them out of the goodness of his heart. No, there was always a second layer to his actions; a driving force that made his heart beat so cold.

"Onwards, then," Jaxon said.

"Do me a favor?" Sonara asked, as Jaxon walked away, heaviness treading with him across the sand. "When you're up there, high above the clouds… push your brother off. Then we'll have no debts to pay."

Jaxon only chuckled, and went to join Markam and Razor. He climbed slowly atop her, just barely settling himself before Razor leapt into the skies. With each mighty beat of her wings, the wyvern rose until she was a mere speck in the distance.

Sonara watched the brothers go, chewing on her lip. Frustration threatened to build within her, but she forced it down. She trusted Jaxon. He was her counterpart, nearly as much as Duran. He'd earned that trust through fire and blood, over the course of ten years traveling together. Never once had he betrayed her. Markam, on the other hand…

Sonara sighed, her attention turning to the pale steed as both ladies galloped away. "Whatever you've gotten us into with them Jax, whoever they are… it had better be worth the fight."

She looked back at the wrecked caravan, the roofless wagons with smoke still snaking into the sky, the bodies of the fallen guards scattered around it.

Then she clicked her teeth and urged Duran forward.

She rode, on and on into the blazing suns, with the distant shadow of Razor's wings above them, the sharp kiss of her sword at her side, and the taste of sweet freedom on her tongue.

CHAPTER 4

Sonara

The Deadlands were hell.

Sonara had always hated them, from the first day she and Duran crossed over the kingdom's southern border. She'd been thirteen then, and now, ten years later, she hated Jira's domain even more.

It was like a fragment of home; sand, sky, and sweat, but there was something missing.

The sea. Deep blue and beautiful, like a little piece of heaven.

And even though it was the sea that had killed her, some part of it still called her home.

The Deadlands had only a few small bodies of water: the largest was the Briyne, a salt river that spanned from Soreia all the way to the Wastes. It snaked right through the gates of Jira's fortress, giving him the keys to the main trading route between all three kingdoms.

Duran thundered up a hillside, and Sonara paused him for a breath.

In the distance, she could see the distant shine of the Briyne, like an unraveled spool of emerald thread in the middle of endless pale sand.

She squinted in the bright suns, just able see the colorful specks on the Briyne that marked the sailboats that traveled north and south along the body of water. They were often targets for outlaws and bandits to pick off, hauling away their wares.

Sonara, Jaxon and Markam had spent years perfecting those attacks. Work was hard to come by in the Deadlands, especially for those who couldn't stay in one place too long, for fear of revealing their Shadowblood powers.

They'd become outlaws instead, for with their curses the prizes were quickly earned, and they paid bountiful amounts of gold, even split thrice. For years, the troupe worked the Briyne, but in recent months had grown tired of the jobs on the salt river. They'd turned their eyes to Jira instead; the ultimate prize. His ring had evaded them, but Gutrender… well, that was a prize far mightier, and one Sonara hadn't ever dreamt of getting her hands on.

A cry resounded overhead, and Razor banked in the sky, turning backwards as if Jaxon had wanted to check on Sonara. He removed his hat and waved, pointing as if trying to draw her attention to something.

Sonara lifted a hand, signaling back that she'd understood.

For she saw it then: the flash in the distance. The strange, otherworldly *thing* that bobbed across the sky at the base of the hill.

Metallic, fast, and heading further away by the second.

"Gazer," Sonara said. She clicked her teeth. "It's a *Gazer,* Duran!"

A kick of her heels had the steed tearing down the hillside to give chase.

Sonara leaned close to him, her fingertips digging into his mane as he thundered across the desert.

The Gazers had been around for years now. Strange, metal orbs in the sky, something from another planet, another *world.*

They did not show up often, but when they did…

"Faster!" Sonara shouted, squeezing her legs as she urged Duran onwards.

The world became a blur, her focus only on the metal orb that bobbed away, buzzing slightly as if some strange power was held within it, moving it along.

Most were the same, battered old floating orbs that catalogued information and sent them back to wherever they'd come from, in another world across the sky, beyond the domain of the goddesses.

But Jaxon was right to have signaled her. For as Duran's hooves caught up with the Gazer…

Sonara glanced sideways, the wind stinging her eyes as she tried to focus on the Gazer.

"Steady," she said, and her loyal beast held pace with it.

This Gazer was new, without markings or crude scribbles of anatomy from those who'd caught them and let them go. New Gazers hadn't arrived in years.

Sonara leaned, focusing as best she could until she could read clearly the two words inscribed on the side: GEISINGER CORP.

Something new, indeed.

Sonara couldn't quite be sure what it meant.

She'd been obsessed with the strange metal orbs for years,

dragging Jaxon all over the Deadlands in hope of gaining information on them.

The sight of it would have given any Dohrsaran pause; perhaps even filled them with terror, thinking of the strange Wanderers that had arrived, years ago, to announce their presence and demand a treaty of peace with the Dohrsarans.

The Gazers remained, a sign that Dohrsar was being watched, being measured up by them, at all times.

Civilians did not know exactly when the Wanderers would show, but those who saw them had a hard time ever forgetting.

Like their ships that ventured down from the skies, the Wanderers themselves were encased in metal. Gleaming armor molded to their bodies as if forged in fire. It had no breaks, no folds, no weak spots in which to drive a spear or sword. Some of the Wanderer armor was as black as Sonara's blood. Other sets were ice-white, or ember gold. But one thing was always the same: none had ever seen the faces of the creatures hidden within.

The ones who'd removed their helmets had burned to piles of oozing, steaming waste within minutes. As if the very air on Dohrsar was poisonous to them.

As the Gazer bobbed closer now, a flash of a memory suddenly slammed into Sonara.

A beam of blue light split the darkness, chasing her down as she sprinted across the sand, her hair yanked loose from its braid. She dove into the shadows just as Soahm's ragged scream split the night.

"Sonara!"

She turned to face him.

But he was already gone.

A flash of anger rippled through Sonara, threatened to pull

her under to a place she kept hidden, dark and deep. It was there, always, beside that ember of Duran's soul, beside the cage she kept her curse locked in.

Settle, Sonara told herself. For if she fell into that place, if she tumbled headlong into the abyss, she feared she'd never be able to climb back out again.

Duran's ears suddenly pricked up as he sensed the shift in her soul.

He slid to a stop, nearly throwing Sonara from his back.

"No!" she shouted. She dug her heels in deep. "It's getting away!"

But the beast would not move, so focused on relieving the tension he surely felt surging between the two of them, at the presence of the Gazer.

Perhaps he remembered, too, that night in Soreia.

Perhaps he still felt the fear of the events afterwards, when they'd been forced to perform the Leaping.

When their bodies had been broken on the rocks, and the current called them home.

Sonara sighed deeply as the Gazer bobbed away.

"It's alright, beast," she said, as Duran glanced backwards, peering at her with one big, dark side-eye. "*I'm* alright." He nickered as she ran her hand across his neck, that ever-gentle sound softening her anger.

It helped her to think clearer, to push aside the emotions so she could focus on the facts.

All her second life, she'd dug for information about the Wanderers, always seeking them out in hope of finding answers to what happened to Soahm. But she'd never discovered who had taken her brother, or *why.*

Sonara sat there, following the Gazer with her eyes until it was a speck in the distance. She stared until her eyes watered from the effort not to blink. Until the desert horizon swallowed it whole, and whisked it away as easily as Soahm had been that fateful night.

"I will find you," Sonara whispered to the horizon. She dug her fingers deep into Duran's mane. "Until it kills me, Soahm, *I will find you,* and bring you home."

***

Duran's hooves thundered across the sand as the day bore on, and Sonara held fast to his braided mane as she tried to catch back up with the others.

She was all body, no mind, just the beat of hooves and the flap of Razor's wings in the distance as she circled every so often, allowing Duran to follow her trail. Even as they came into view, Sonara kept her distance from the female riders on the pale steed, unwilling to get too close. Unwilling to trust them yet.

They shouldn't have paired with Markam in the first place, to steal the king's ring. It had been months since they'd seen him last, and only desperation had brought them to accept a job with the Trickster.

Now, whatever Jaxon had agreed to had extended that partnership with Markam.

Again.

That thought plagued Sonara all day, until the suns grew tired and tucked themselves away behind the Bloodhorns, in a natural valley that spanned a mile wide before stretching directly upward into mountains again. Despite the unknown, a weary smile widened Sonara's lips as she saw the telltale form of Sandbank in the distance, the trading post at the bottom of a sandy hill that stood like a lone sentry in the desert.

The trading post was old and dusty but, bless the blasted place, it had a saloon. The days were hot, but the drinks inside the saloon were cool. And the rumors that spread about guts and glory were plenty.

Sonara leaned back, and Duran slowed to a stop, his hooves squeaking in the windswept sand. Sweat dripped from his neck and belly, his sides heaving with heavy breaths. Foam had gathered on his chest, the mark of a steed who'd done his best to carry her, hardly stopping all day.

"You wonderful, beautiful beast," Sonara said, patting his neck and wrapping her arms around him, despite the fact that he smelled more like a wet steed than he ever had. He huffed, his heavy heartbeat pounding beneath her ear as his soul-ember heated with pride. A steed was never one to balk at a compliment. Especially not one as proud as Duran. She glanced at Sandbank in the distance as she pulled away. "You always know the way home."

Home.

There was a traitorous pang in her heart, the moment she thought the word.

Home was in Soreia, the southern kingdom. She thought of the red Sand Caves, and the scalding Demon's Dunes, guarded by spiraling rock monuments that stretched into the sky, carved with sigils of queens long ago cast to the stars. She ached for the bustling trade days by the water's edge, the crash of waves collapsing on shore, the distant cries of feral sea beasts as they gathered on the rocks and screeched at the twin moons. She ached for the summer season, with Soahm laughing beside her as they practiced with sticks for swords, then raced into the waves to cool off.

She'd never go home again. But Sandbank was as close as it got to something familiar; something safe.

"Alright, Sonara?" Jaxon called down as Razor landed upon the sand. The great wyvern blew out a hot breath, rustling Duran's mane and tail.

He whinnied a greeting to the other pale steed, who continued down the hillside with the ladies upon its back. The strange Shadowblood had yet to remove her hood, concealing her true identity. Sonara watched as they slid down from the beast, tying it up outside the saloon with the rest of the steeds.

Sonara sighed as she looked at the line of others stamping their hooves, many with saddles still on. Sonara rode bareback only, and she didn't like to keep Duran tied up outside, waiting on her beck and call. He was prisoner to no rope, no saddle, no Dohrsaran rider's command.

"Go on, then," she whispered to him. "Enjoy some freedom." He trotted away, off to find a watering hole and some much needed saltgrass on its banks.

"Evening, Sunny."

Sonara's whole body seized at the sound of that voice.

Markam's deep timbre was painstakingly similar to Jaxon's, but it held an air of superiority beneath it that Jaxon's never did. His pride was as strong as his scent as he dismounted and marched across the sand towards her.

Sour and sweet all at once, like the coolness of spring colliding with the heat of summer.

Sonara rolled back her shoulders and forced herself to greet him. "Hello, Markam," she said.

Then she spun around and, with all the strength left in her, slammed her fist into his face.

CHAPTER 5

Sonara

Sonara hated having history with people. History meant roots, and roots were things that could be tugged and pulled on, like heartstrings.

Roots meant weaknesses, and Markam was more than a root. He was a weed.

Markam was the biggest high-roller in all of the Deadlands. He knew every secret that passed from every set of lips, every little detail of who would be where and when. Bankers' carriages, boats on the Briyne, noblemen and women journeying from one fortress to another. None of their routes were secret or safe. Markam held the keys to his own sort of kingdom, and it was why Sonara had first been drawn to him, in hope of discovering something about Soahm and the ship that whisked him away ten years ago.

It was also why Sonara had later grown to mistrust Markam's every word.

He was a Trickster, after all, the only other Shadowblood she and Jaxon knew. Markam's curse manifested in illusions. They were some of the best Sonara had ever seen. He made bets with Fool's Coin of his own making and was a skilled liar, to boot.

Blast you, Sonara. Why did you ever fall for him? she thought, as she shook out her throbbing fist, satisfied at how hard she'd punched him.

"You always did like to play rough, Sunny," Markam said as he rubbed his nose. He laughed, and *blast,* it was molasses-sweet. She hated the way her curse shivered at the sound of that laugh, how it longed to dive deep into his soul and have a taste of what was once hers.

Don't look at him. Don't look at him.

Sonara lifted her chin anyway.

Damn him, Markam was a sight for desert-sore eyes. He was only a year older than Jaxon, and made of muscle, but not the king's Guard type. Markam was lean and mean, with cropped night-black hair. His eyes were dark to match, his blood roiling with the very same shadows as hers.

Handsome on the outside. But Markam was downright rotten to his bones.

"We agreed to one job," Sonara said as she spun away from Markam. "Get the ring in Stonegrave, *get out* once we split the profit three ways. And of course you've roped us into more. That's what you always do."

"Circumstances change, Sunny." Markam stepped forward, his duster waving past his ankles. He wore the finest clothes, gold buttons on the leather, diamond links on his cuffs. "And *you* did not get the king's ring. One third of payment for the ring: that's what I was owed. Therefore, our agreement is *not* done. Thanks to me, I've extended an invitation for you to join me on one of my own escapades. And it pays far more handsomely than any you've ever faced before. When we complete it, you can give me one third of your prize."

"I'm going to rip out your insides, Markam, and fashion you a pretty little necklace from them," Sonara growled.

Jaxon jumped in between the two, just in time. "What's done is done. The job in Stonegrave went south, but we got out alive, and now we've got to honor our deal with Markam."

"We don't owe him anything," Sonara said. "The ring he made wasn't even real."

"And yet," Markam said, lifting his right hand with a flourish. Out of thin air, a black-banded ring materialized onto his thumb, the fat diamond near-identical to the one he'd fashioned to give to Jira for the swap. "The ring I made was worth a barrel full of coin at market."

He shook his hand and with a *poof,* the ring was gone again.

Sonara glared down the hill towards the saloon. It was steep and sweeping. If she could only get her foot behind Markam's ankle, perhaps she could send him rolling. Perhaps there'd be a happy accident, and he'd break his neck on the way down.

Sonara crossed her arms. "You lost out on nothing but time."

"But the pain it caused me to create it," Markam said with a dramatic sigh, "along with the loss of what would have been true profit once we sold the king's actual ring, was real enough. Now... the ladies are eager to get started, and you wouldn't want to keep a client waiting, would you?"

Sonara and Jaxon used to work for Markam, for years. He'd been their trusted informant, a laughable thought, because he'd damned them far too many times for Sonara to count on both hands, and there was hardly a shred of trust left between them. They'd had a falling out, when Sonara and Markam's relationship crashed and burned… and kept burning. They'd only contacted him again for the job in Stonegrave because they'd been desperate for coin, practically starving with a lack of jobs to be found.

With his curse, Markam had a way of sneaking into the most secret of places, of gathering information from the most private of conversations. He caught wind of the greatest catches in town, wagons hauling coin that were an easy snag, a shipment of steeds from the southern kingdom that could be captured and sold off. A group of rich merchants whose caravans could be blocked, cleared out, and sent on their way.

With his intel, Sonara and Jaxon stepped in and got the job done. They got coin and more wanted posters placed across the Deadlands, and Markam kept his name clean. No matter the job, no matter how interested Markam seemed in helping, the moment he smelled danger, he'd push down anyone in his path in order to save his own skin.

Even family.

At the base of the hill, the saloon doors swung open, and music filtered out. The sad twang mixed with the setting suns as daylight grew tired and weary. Sonara's own weariness tugged at her. She wanted to fall onto a bar stool and drink until her daylights went out. But first, she'd have to learn whatever hellish deal Jaxon had roped them into.

Sonara simply raised her chin a bit higher as she turned to Markam. "What if we refuse? What if I break the deal?"

Markam picked at a loose thread on his duster. "I'll turn you in for your crimes against the king. Now… shall we? Drinks are on me, as a token of my good will."

With a wink, he started down the hillside, leaving Sonara and Jaxon alone with the wind.

CHAPTER 6

Sonara

The swinging doors of the saloon slammed against Sonara's back as she and Jaxon entered.

The place was near empty as usual, the road-weary patrons already several drinks in. Everyone's aura was bright and scrambled together, too many emotions dancing across the room for her curse to devour. She settled it with a wince, her head already spinning. She'd given it too much freedom lately. Too long of a leash.

The town sherriff was there, a man with his buttons threatening to explode from his worn brown uniform. Across from him, a young blonde woman sharpened her dagger and glared at anyone who passed by. In the corner of the room, beneath the stuffed head of a desert pig mounted to the wall, a wrinkled storyteller sat, telling her tales. Laughter erupted from the patrons listening in.

Music played from a small stage to their right. Suzie Quick and the Lightning Girls, who were never on key enough to make it in the king's Traveling Troubadours, were still the main act.

Sonara hated music. It made her feel things, made her think of memories she'd rather keep long forgotten.

A hand reaching out.

A scream that split the sky in two.

She couldn't block the memories of Soahm, but she could try to drown them. So she headed towards the only sanctuary in Sandbank.

The bar.

It was a place where secrets were spilled as often as drinks. And there just beside it, seated furthest from the rest of the patrons, was Markam, along with the two ladies who'd joined their troupe. They sat at a table near-covered in shadows, moth-bitten curtains drawn to conceal the window behind them. Holes littered the surface of the fabric, enough to shed sunlight in strange patterns across the room.

"Ah," Markam said, standing like the gentleman he pretended to be. He already had a bottle of oil in his hand, the dark liquid sloshing out as he bowed. "Ladies, may I present, better late than never… the Devil of the Deadlands."

The woman in deep red robes was seated in her chair with such impeccable posture that she may as well have been sitting on a throne. Of noble class, certainly. Her dark hair hung from the shadows of that large hood, which still concealed her face. Her hands, covered in smooth silk gloves, were folded before her on the table.

Those hands held the power of the storms. Sonara's curse hissed as she watched the woman, as if it knew it was in the presence of a power unprecedented. Reluctantly, she eased it out of its cage, the tether lengthening as she breathed in the woman's aura. *Dark, robust. The promise of life and death all at once.*

Again, Sonara's rules for the world were changing. Shaping themselves anew, for where once there were only three Shadowbloods on Dohrsar that she knew including herself, now there were four.

The second woman was perhaps more puzzling than the first.

She was small, a head shorter than Sonara, her shoulders thin beneath her dark robes. Her hair, a palest white as the northern snows, was bound into two long ropy braids that hung to her waist, woven through with ice-blue beads and bits of white that looked like bone. Her face was entirely covered by a skull fashioned into a mask, tied tight.

The Canis, Sonara noted now, a beast dreaded in the White Wastes for how its midnight howls resembled a lost child screaming out in distress. When one ventured too far into the snowy woods to save the child, the Canis attacked, and devoured only their flesh, leaving the rest of the body behind.

The girl's mouth was barely visible behind the Canis' jawbones, the jagged teeth still intact at the end of a long snout.

"My lady does not like to be kept waiting," she said. Her voice was as sweet as a fairy's. She folded her hands upon the table, tapping her fingertips on the worn wood. They, too, were covered in bone; carved gauntlets that peeked out from her long sleeves, the knuckles intricately designed to move with her own.

Sonara pushed her curse towards the girl.

She nearly choked on her aura.

Death and decay. Bones left in the sun to dry.

She swallowed it away, shoving her curse back into its cage. Her head throbbed painfully in defiance as she turned the key.

"Apologies," Markam said as he held out a hand for Sonara and

Jaxon to join them. Jaxon pulled out his chair and slunk into it. "The Devil does not take clients often. We had to iron out a small issue, but I assure you, she's ready and willing to help you in your cause. Just as I promised you she would be."

"Interesting," the hooded woman said. "That's the first time I've known you to hold true to your word, Markam."

He shifted in his seat, but held his tongue.

"The Devil of the Deadlands," the hooded Lady turned to Sonara. "A difficult woman to find an audience with. I apologize for the delay in rescuing you."

"And who, exactly," Sonara asked, though not unkindly, "are you?"

"This is Thali," the Lady explained, inclining her head towards the girl in the Canis mask. "A cleric from the White Wastes, and my loyal advisor."

That explained the mask, then. Clerics worshipped a great many things, depending on their beliefs. It often manifested in misunderstood ways.

"And you?" Sonara asked. "Who lies beneath the hood?"

It was then that the Lady finally reached up with those gloved hands and removed her hood.

She was beautiful, with hair the color of black desert roses. She had eyes that were so dark they were almost entirely black, with no pupils: the mark of a true Deadlander. But where her face was pristine, her lips red and full… her neck was marred by a deep scar.

It was the kind that was unmistakable, immediately drawing Sonara's eyes; for Sonara herself had seen countless others like it on the necks of prisoners across Dohrsar, anchored to chains on walls.

It was the mark of a prisoner's collar.

The mark of someone never meant to walk free.

"My name is Azariah of Stonegrave," the Lady said. She lifted her chin, as if she wanted Sonara to see her deep scar in the rays of pale sunlight. As if she wanted Sonara to very clearly hear her next words. "More formally known as the Crown Princess of the Deadlands."

CHAPTER 7

Karr

Karr Kingston, only a boy, trembled as he crouched in the shadows beneath the *Starfall*'s dash.

If he stared at his mother and father long enough, he could almost pretend they were deep within the safety of their dreams. Their eyes were closed, hands outstretched towards his hiding place.

They'll wake up soon, he told himself. *They'll wake up, and we'll walk out of here together.*

It was the fresh blood, bright as rubies as it dripped from the intruder's knife, that told Karr how wrong he was.

***

He woke up screaming again, sure that the knife was buried in his own chest. Certain that the criminal who'd murdered his parents years ago had come for him, too.

You're safe, Karr told himself as he touched the old wound on his chest, his heartbeat steady beneath his fingertips. It still ached on occasion, mostly when he slept wrong. He sighed and sank deeper into his pillow, the ceiling of his bunk drawing his attention.

A smattering of charcoal sketches was plastered there.

Some were landscapes, sprawling metropoles and broad sweeping plains with herds of alien creatures dotting the horizon. Others were closer work, portraits from those he'd met in all his travels. He loved the angles of their faces, the way that everyone across the galaxy was uniquely original to him, but commonplace, perhaps, to the ones on their own planets. There were action drawings, old acquaintances leaping Growlers from jumps on distant planets. Sketches of sunsets that looked eerily similar to sunrises, or the cool glow of a waning moon.

One aspect of his drawings was always the same, a recurring presence.

He drew everything in blue.

Blue as deep as the sea.

Karr had always loved the sea, the calming scramble of waves as they lapped upon the shore and tumbled backwards, exhausted, to perform the dance all over again. He craved the smell of salt water, the feeling of warm sand beneath his bare feet.

His heartbeat calmed, slowing in time with his breaths as he stared at the smattering of sketches. A sea of cool, calm. Karr relaxed deeper into his mattress, then shivered and reached for the blanket.

Something rough scraped his fingertips.

"Open viewport," Karr murmured, a yawn muffling the words. The small rectangular window by his bedside slid open, revealing the star-pocked sky and Dohrsar beyond, its rings glowing as if made of multi-faceted fire.

In the dim light, Karr recognized the black rock from Cade tangled up beside him in the sheets. He must have fallen asleep holding it last night, waiting for it to do something special. Anything to convince him why Cade was so certain of its ability to save them.

But if a man like Friedrich Geisinger was behind the job… hell, Karr supposed a person could make anything happen, if they had enough riches to support their cause.

With another yawn, he swung himself out of bed and went barefoot out the door of his cabin.

Karr could navigate the *Starfall* with his eyes closed. Many times, as a boy, he and Cade had raced through the corridors. A challenge, on weeks-long journeys, to keep themselves from going stir-crazy. And where Cade was always taller than Karr, with longer strides, Karr was small enough to fit into the hard-to-spot places.

The shortcuts.

The *Starfall* was shaped like a diamond, sharp around the edges, and comprised of the typical sectors on interstellar starships.

A left turn led him past a few open cabins where the crews' snores rumbled like sleeping dragons. He tiptoed past the sick bay, where Karr himself had puked up an entire bottle's worth of whiskey only a few nights ago.

At the end of the hall, he took the freight elevator up, tapping his toe to the music.

A few more paces, a twist down the next empty hall, and he found himself standing at the captain's quarters, the black rock clutched in his hand.

It was more revolving door to Karr than *do not disturb unless you want to be incinerated* as it was to the rest of the crew… But when Karr lifted his hand to knock, muffled voices made him pause.

He knew he shouldn't listen in. But how many times had that stopped him before?

Instead of knocking, he looked to the com beside Cade's door.

It was a simple trick to reverse the audio, something he'd learned ages ago from the old mech that Cade ended up firing for screwing around on the job.

Karr popped open the com box, glancing over his shoulder to make sure he was still alone. Not even their obnoxious sweeper droid in sight. Karr made quick work of swapping the wires, then slipped the face of the box back in place. A simple override code, a long press of the com button, and…

A voice came through the static.

"This conversation is over."

Karr smiled. *Bullseye.* That was Cade's voice, commanding and clipped as always.

A short bark of a laugh sounded back.

Rohtt, Karr realized, the new Crossman who seemed to stare straight *through* every face he'd ever looked at. He hadn't been on the crew long, just enough time to scrape the surface of acquaintance, but Karr didn't like him.

He'd never met a Crossman who didn't drink, for starters. The Crossmen and women were some of the best medics in space travel, the kind that had pieced soldiers back together on the front lines of brutal, bloody wars. They'd been lucky enough to come across a few Crossmen in their days, the medics usually deserters on the run from their pasts. They all drank—some of Karr's most vivid memories were of himself and the crew, scattered across the lounge in the sector above, listening to a drunk Crossman tell his tales. To a Crossman or woman, drinking was like a badge of honor: the more they could hold down, the more they deserved your respect.

But Rohtt wouldn't touch a drop.

He'd joined the crew just before they left Beta Earth. Since then, he'd been a near-constant shadow to Cade, always watching.

"You listen to me, Kingston…" Rohtt's voice hissed through the combox.

"No." *Cade's voice again.* "This is my ship. I give the orders here. Patch me through to him."

"He is otherwise detained at the moment."

Bodies shifted inside. There was the telltale squeak of Cade's swivel chair, followed by footsteps. "I can't eat. I can't sleep."

"All normal side effects of anxiety, Kingston," Rohtt said. "Take a mood suppressor."

"You're mocking me."

"I wouldn't dare."

Silence. Then muffled sounds, a heavy sigh and the whine of Cade's chair again as he likely sat back down.

"You know what lies inside of…" Rohtt's voice trailed off as the connection fizzled. Karr cursed beneath his breath and scrambled to adjust the wires. "…the consequences if we fail."

Cade was silent for a moment. "I'm well aware. At least… give me a sleeping draught. I want my mind clear when we land."

There was the squeak of boots, as someone shifted towards the door.

Karr's thoughts were running so fast that he hardly had time to move when the door slid open. He backed into the shadows beside Cade's doorway, in a small alcove with a window that looked out at the stars. During sleeping hours, the corridors were lit only by the emergency exit lights. He pressed himself flat against the window as the two men marched past, blocking out the light of Dohrsar.

First came Rohtt, with a red medbox tucked under his arm. Cade followed after in his nightclothes. Behind them, Cade's door began to slide shut.

Before he could stop himself, Karr slipped through the opening and into his brother's quarters. The lights were dim, only the bunk lamp on.

Where Karr's room was plastered with his belongings, photographs and sketches and stolen knickknacks—all signs that he'd made a life aboard the *Starfall*—Cade's room was entirely absent of a personal touch. It was nothing more than a bunk, a built-in silver desk that protruded from the wall, and the old swivel chair that was once their father's, soldered to the floor.

He'd thrown his dark captain's coat over the built-in desk, leaving it rumpled, as if he'd taken it off in a hurry. A rare thing, for Cade not to leave his coat hung in the small closet beside the rest of his clothes, pressed and clean.

"What are you doing in here, Karr?" he asked himself.

Cade said the plan had wrinkles. He wanted to know what they were, and how best to iron them out.

Now that Karr was considering the job at hand, a question popped into his brain. It was one that had been lingering there since Cade had mentioned Friedrich Geisinger, but he hadn't quite been able to put the question into words until now.

A man with his power, with his standing, should be able to soar onto any planet in any nearby galaxy and simply pay for what he wished. So what was so special about this Antheon that would make him hire a shipload of black-market criminals to acquire it for him?

Karr sat down in Cade's chair, the question hot in his mind. Perhaps he'd sit here until Cade came back. He sighed, then reached down to remove the black rock from his pocket and ponder over it some more. But as he lifted it, his arm accidentally ruffled the edge of Cade's coat.

The screen beneath it lit up.

Karr cursed at the sudden brightness and reached down to slide the screen back into sleep mode.

But something caught his eye.

A blueprint, glowing brightly on the screen.

Karr glanced over his shoulder at the door. Still shut, no sound of footsteps bounding down the metal corridor. He turned back to the screen, sweeping Cade's coat aside to get the full view of it.

The blueprint looked like an alien beetle. It was the closest way to compare the headless mechanical creature with four hinged legs, sharp sword-like tips at the end of each. There were all sorts of numbers and equations, mathematical symbols and measurements written in the margins of the page, scribbled in a strange, tiny hand at each hinge. And Cade's handwriting, scribbled on the far side of the screen, as if he'd pulled up the blueprint and began to write notes of his own.

Heat-resistant. Water-resistant. Exterior shell? Impenetrable.

"What the hell is this about?" Karr whispered.

He leaned in closer, tapping the screen to enlarge the image. More notes, and something written in a language he did not understand. But he assumed it was one of the ancients, from old Earth. Karr zoomed again, eyes widening as he found a signature at the bottom right-hand corner.

As if the blueprint itself were a sketch. A work of art.

Friedrich Geisinger

His brows knitted together as he stared at the man's blueprint. Their new employer, no less. Was this the *wrinkle* Cade had mentioned?

Karr looked up as the sound of footsteps arrived from down the hall, still distant... but drawing closer. He quickly tapped the screen back to dark, then swiveled Cade's chair around and stood just as the door slid open.

Cade stood in the doorway, eyes narrowed. "Karr?"

"You really should keep your door locked," Karr said nonchalantly. "There's no telling who could stumble in here under cover of night."

"You should be sleeping." Cade crossed his arms as he looked around the room, eyes narrowing further still, as if he were searching for a ghost.

"I could say the same to you," Karr answered. "I saw you walk off with the medhead."

"I'm not entirely fond of him either," Cade said, wincing at the slang term for Rohtt. "But he's here on Geisinger's command. An emissary, if you will, to ensure we complete the job."

Cade wore a thick robe each night, to ward off the chilly recycled air on the *Starfall.* His old fighting scars peeked out from the opening.

They reminded Karr of the times he'd stood in the midst of a raucous crowd, surrounded by sweat and skin and fists full of money on the line. If he closed his eyes, he could still feel the struggle not to cry out as he watched Cade in the fighting ring, covered in blood.

It took him months to win his first fight. And months after that, to actually make money for them to pocket after giving their cut to Jeb.

But the blood and the bruises, the pain and the small payments didn't matter. Cade had always done the best he could to keep the *Starfall* afloat. To keep the crew happy. Most of all, to keep Karr alive.

"What's going on?" Cade asked now, drawing Karr back to the present. He sat down on the edge of his bunk, looking more exhausted than Karr had seen him look in ages. "Something you wanted to discuss?"

A thousand lies he could have made up.

Instead, Karr went for the truth.

"Why *us*?" he asked. "Geisinger, I mean. Why would a man like him hire a bunch of black-market criminals to dig up this rock? If he's as rich as the galaxy thinks him to be… if he owns the planet, why not just take a ship himself, hire his own crew, and dig it up?"

Cade shrugged. "We don't ask questions. We get in, get what we're asked to recover, and get out. You know that."

"But it's strange," Karr said.

"Aren't all our jobs?"

He tossed the small chunk of Antheon to Cade, who held it towards the dim bunk light. "There's a place near the center of the continent, on Dohrsar… old mines, on the outskirts of a Dohrsaran temple. Geisinger has been keeping an eye on things, upping his research. He's been in communication with one of their leaders. He previously picked up on a hot spot for this Antheon. It's worth trillions, in the right hands, in the right form."

Karr shifted his position. The chair squeaked beneath him, a sound that brought forth a memory. His father, seated in this very room, this very chair, arms held out as he grinned and said, *Come on, K. Come and help me decide where we'll fly next.*

"But why hide it?" Karr asked. "He owns the damned thing now."

He'd never questioned a job before. But since Cade had mentioned their new employer's name… something in Karr's stomach hadn't felt quite right. Like an obnoxious little gnat that wouldn't quit, it picked at his conscience. Begged him to dig a little deeper.

Cade glanced over his shoulder, then lowered his voice, as if he feared the entire crew was standing behind the door, listening. "We're scrubs, Karr. People who fly below the radar. The outcasts of the galaxy."

To hear him say it aloud… Cade had never acknowledged what Karr had always thought.

He was always seated on a mountaintop, no matter their situation. But tonight, he looked like a man defeated, the circles deep beneath his eyes. "But not after this. I've spoken to Geisinger myself. I've heard the terms. I'm keeping you out of it, so that if we're caught…" He shrugged. "I'm protecting you."

"What exactly from?"

"There are laws. Planets are purchased, but they're still managed by the ITC. Emissaries from all across the galaxy check in. And their recorders are always watching."

The recorders were orb-like camera drones that were sent across the stars, to all planets under the arm of the ITC, taking snapshots and video intel.

"They check for ethics when there can't be boots on the ground," Cade said. "Things must be done correctly, you know."

"So Geisinger's going to do something illegal and let *us* be his fall guys."

Cade shifted. "Geisinger has… taken the liberty of disabling the ITC recorders for the time being. He'll be watching on his own that he's previously sent planetside. That footage will seamlessly interrupt the ITC feed. It will hold *no* record of us having been to Dohrsar. The crew's identity will be kept safe. I've signed that in a contract."

Karr stared at him. This plan had been in the works for quite some time and Cade hadn't told him a lick of it.

"And what makes you think he'll honor any contract, if he's found some way to screw with the ITC's recording system?" Karr spread his hands before him.

Cade frowned. "You have to trust that I'm doing what's best for us. Stop asking questions. I've thought of the details, Karr, gone through all the steps you're going through right now. I've ironed them all out. And besides. They…" He swallowed, and his voice took on a different tone. A *longing* tone, a weapon he used rarely, but accurately when he chose to. "They made me promise to take care of you. I'm doing that by doing *this.*"

"Don't." Karr shook his head. "Don't turn this into something about them. It's not fair."

The memory of his parents' deaths, that hideous dream he'd awoken from earlier, drove into him like a knife. No matter how hard he tried to push it away, the sharp blade only sank deeper.

Their parents had traveled to nearly a hundred planets in their lifetime, faced dangers the likes of which no Traveler would ever see. Everything they did was for the good of the galaxy. Everything they discovered was handed right back to science, in hope of discovering something to cure the Reaper's Disease.

All it took was one raider to sneak aboard their ship while it was docked and slit their throats.

And then they were nothing.

Names on a gravestone. Ashes on the wind.

Karr wasn't supposed to be in the ship that night. He wasn't supposed to see their chests stop moving, their mouths agape, deep crimson pooling onto the metal floor. He wasn't supposed to feel the warmth of their blood as it slid towards his bare toes.

His chest ached. He rubbed at the old scar on it, just one of the many he'd received when he was a scrawny young boy in the system, picking fights with boys far larger than he was to fuel his anger.

Cade's expression turned worrisome. "Are you alright?"

Karr folded his hands into his lap. "I'm *fine*."

"But you're—"

"I'm *fine,* Cade. And it's not fair, how you've turned the tables. We don't speak about them."

"I do." Cade crossed his arms over his chest. "I always will. And this Antheon… this is something they would have gone after, Karr, something they would have been *proud* of." He leaned in, blue eyes wide, as he held up the black rock. "In this form, Antheon is nothing more than a rock. It's likely why the Dohrsarans don't have any idea what they're sitting on. But Geisinger has resources, and reach. Once we deliver it to him," he said, tossing the rock back to Karr, "he'll use it to make medical miracles. He could eradicate the Reaper for good."

"We don't have the manpower to mine at the level you're speaking of," Karr said. "To get the amount this guy likely needs. We have twenty men. A single drill. It will take years."

"I have it all taken care of," Cade said. "There are workers waiting for us on Dohrsar. And he's supplied us with tools to get the job done."

Karr hadn't seen those tools on board, but he supposed the storage bay, with its messy rows upon rows of gear, was likely hiding plenty Cade hadn't shown him.

"Look." Cade reached out and gripped Karr's shoulders, his fingertips cold in the recycled *Starfall* air. "I promise you, with everything that I am. This is the last job. We do this… we'll be free. We'll make a difference. Not just for us, but for *so many* in the galaxy."

It had always been the two of them against the world.

He tapped the exit panel beside his door. It slid open, revealing the red-lit corridor beyond. "No more questions. Just follow my lead and believe in our future."

Karr stood, the chair squeaking again beneath him. "Tomorrow, then?"

"Tomorrow." Cade nodded. "Get some rest. You're going to need it."

As Karr walked away, he glanced over his shoulder, and found Cade frowning down at his desk, where his captain's coat was ruffled, not in the space he'd last seen it.

As if someone had moved it aside to stare at the drawing on the screen.

CHAPTER 8

Sonara

Lazaris was in Sonara's hand in an instant, held before her as Jaxon leapt to his feet and took his place at her side.

The Crown Princess of the Deadlands?

At any moment, guards would be pouring into the saloon. Markam, *damn him,* what had he gotten them into?

But Markam didn't move an inch. He sighed and plucked a bit of lint from his duster sleeve, as if he hadn't a care in the world. "Save us the dramatic exit, Sunny. Azariah means you no harm. Perhaps myself, depending on how she sees the past, but…"

"The past is of no worth to me any longer," the princess said. Careful words, calmly spoken, but she glared at him with a sudden intensity that had Sonara seeing, for the first time, the darkness in her eyes that matched King Jira's. "But the future of my kingdom *is* of great value to me. It is why I came calling."

The Princess of the Deadlands.

Sonara would have pulled on her curse, tested the air for a taste of *truth,* sweet and succulent, or *lie,* bitter as crushed greens.

But she was so shocked by the revelation, that the cage inside of her fell dark and silent.

"There's no Princess of the Deadlands," Jaxon said, as if he were thinking the same exact thought. "Jira doesn't keep the females."

The words were not meant to be unkind. For they were all anyone in the Deadlands had ever known. But Sonara saw the way Azariah's shoulders stiffened. The way her fingers curled into fists. "Everything you've ever heard about him and his children… it all stands to be *true*."

The rumor was that when Jira took a bride each year, he sired an unwanted female. Furious, he'd dump the child into the Hadru's pit. There were countless stories out there of brides he'd taken, who disappeared into his palace only to reappear nine months later, mere shells of themselves. As if he'd stolen something from them that could never be replaced.

Some of his brides never reappeared at all. But every year, at the Choosing, he took another new one. And every year, he was given a daughter instead of a son.

"My father wants a male heir," Azariah said. "And yet the goddesses have never blessed him with one."

Now Thali turned her Canis gaze onto Sonara and Jaxon. "Months ago, I journeyed far to find the Lady, when I heard talk of her existence. The clerics have many eyes and ears across the continent. We speak of the hushed things. Whisper of the stories yet untold, beyond our hiding places of worship. I didn't know if I believed it myself, when I heard tell of the princess that survived. But just because you have never seen something with your own eyes does not make it untrue."

"So it's true, then," Jaxon said softly. "The king feeds his children to the Hadru."

At this, Azariah chuckled softly. "Not quite," she said. "The real truth is far darker. My father only sires females. And when he does, he takes us, not to the Hadru, as many whisper in the streets of Stonegrave. He takes us beneath his castle, to the depths of the kingdom itself. And there, he takes a blade and slits our throats."

The world seemed to have fallen silent.

Even Suzie Quick and her girls were in between songs, their silence nearly unbearable.

"Many have died," Azariah said. "Countless before me, and countless after. But for some reason, I survived. I came *back*."

"Even if it were true…" Sonara started, swallowing hard as the story suddenly began to mix with her own past, in her mind. A girl from one kingdom, slain by her father. And a girl from another, forced over the edge of a cliff by her mother. "Why would he keep you hidden all these years?"

Azariah looked to Thali, her gaze shifting from something like sadness to wonder.

"Because the princess goes against everything the Three Kingdoms have ever stood for," Thali whispered. "She is a Child of Shadow. She was brought back to live another life, and such is the reason the king slew her and her siblings in the first place. In hope that one would come back again, with powers that belong in the stories of old."

The King came from centuries' worth of Shadowblood hunters and huntresses. They'd wiped them from the surface of Dohrsar, signed a long-ago decree that ensured none would ever rise to power again, after the ancient Shadowbloods rose up. And once the Shadowbloods disappeared, their tale was told as a warning. A way to scare children into hiding. A way to ensure that if a Shadowblood was ever to appear, years later, their bloodline somehow missed in the destruction… people would fear them.

They would hand them over or hunt them down. There were paintings and depictions of slain Shadowbloods all across Dohrsar. In the Soreian palace, they were hung up like portraits in the Hall of Dead. Sonara had seen it, only once, when Soahm snuck her inside. In the White Wastes, there was a Night of Reckoning, where families threw black coals into their hearths, the dark smoke rising into the sky to ward off the evil, to keep the curse of the Shadowbloods from ever entering their lands.

Jira's family had led it *all.* The backbone of the Shadowblood extinction.

It wasn't possible that he'd try to *create* one. Let alone, keep one alive, especially his own daughter.

"He longs for power such as this," Azariah explained. She held out her gloved hands, and Sonara remembered the lightning swimming across her palms. She found herself glancing suddenly upwards, at the girl's scar. The mark of a collar upon her throat. Only a lifetime of bearing such a burden would cause a scar like that.

She suddenly felt sick.

"He despises Shadowbloods. But not because he fears us. He *longs* for what we have, deep down. He has everything any man could ever want. Servants and riches and power and brides, countless lovers beyond that… but he does not have *this.*" Azariah held up her gloved hands, her dark eyes wide. She looked at Sonara next. "I saw you in that throne room. I was there when you stole the sword, in a secret chamber beneath his dais, when you so fearsomely slew a room full of my father's men. It was my job, held in chains, to always be on lookout. To protect my father with my dark power, should there ever be a threat that his men would not be able to handle. But I stood idly by in the shadows when you attacked. I let you live. And in that moment… I wanted to be *with* you, walking out those doors. So that night I escaped the palace with Thali's help, and sought out an old companion of mine."

Markam raised his glass, already empty of its contents.

Azariah nodded at Sonara. "I then joined with Markam and Jaxon to come find you."

"But why?" Sonara asked. "Why *me*?"

"My dear Devil." Azariah's dark eyes narrowed as she took a sip of her own drink and patted her lips with a silk handkerchief, the picture of a princess. "I am here to ask for your help. To hire you for a job that will work against my father's might, for he is about to write the pages of a story that will damn Dohrsar, and all of its kingdoms, for eternity." She paused, eyeing the rest of the room as she leaned closer. "But before I give the details, I must have your oath of silence. I have journeyed far to pass along this message, for I believe you three may be some of the only few in the Deadlands up for the job. And I can pay you handsomely. Thali?"

Her guardian lifted a second silk pouch, carefully spilling its contents onto the wooden table.

Diamonds tumbled out like delicate raindrops. They caught the sunlight from the holes in the curtains, sent it sparkling in fractals as if the diamonds themselves were miniature stars. They were perfect, each one of their facets. And *massive*, some of the largest Sonara had ever seen. They rivaled the very ones that sat upon Jira's ringed fingers. With them, she'd be rich.

Not just rich.

Wealthy.

Among them, a fat golden ring that Sonara would recognize anywhere, for that very ring, days ago, had been pressed tight against her skin as the king gripped her wrist like a vice, and demanded she be sent to Deadwood to die.

It was his seal.

"I stole it myself," Azariah said. "As proof of my lineage, should you question me."

Sonara's eyes narrowed as she leaned forward to investigate further.

"Some of the finest craftsmanship I have ever seen," Markam said, turning to glance at Sonara and Jaxon. "If you won't trust my word, at least believe that the ring is real. And she is who she says she is."

"I can offer this as an advance payment," Azariah said, holding out a hand to the diamonds, "if you agree to take the job. And I can offer ten times this amount once the job is completed. Diamonds enough to fill an entire barrel."

Sonara's face remained impassive, but her blood hummed at the thought of so many diamonds. But working for the king's daughter, for *anyone* with his blood made her feel sick. As if the oil she'd drunk was getting to her, too fast, too soon.

Azariah's smile fell. She chewed on her bottom lip, the first sign of nerves since she'd begun speaking.

"Markam?" Sonara asked. She quickly nodded at Jaxon to stay put. "A word?"

Markam yelped as she grabbed his shirt collar and hauled him with her out the double doors of the saloon. She stormed outside, where she promptly shoved him up against the wall. Dust rained down from the ceiling above.

The steeds tied up at the railing barely lifted their heads, as if they were used to drunken patrons stumbling out of the saloon at a moment's notice.

"What the hell are you up to?" Sonara growled softly. She pressed him harder against the wall. "Why would you ever want to ally yourself with the Princess of the Deadlands?"

His breath tickled her lips as he leaned forward. "Need you even ask? She's the wealthiest mark we'll ever find."

"You're lying."

His aura reeked of it.

She recoiled, yanking him with her before shoving him against the wall again. He only chuckled.

"Come on, Sunny. It's a game."

"It's always been a game with you." She narrowed her eyes. "You want me to pay off the debt? We'll sell the damned sword. Split our profit three ways, just as you wanted, and then Jax and I can go free. Never see or speak to you again."

"The sword hardly counts as payment," Markam said.

"And why is that?" Sonara asked.

"Ask him." Markam glanced sideways, where Jaxon stood just outside the saloon doors. His eyes narrowed, when he saw Sonara pressed against Markam on the porch.

Sonara stepped away. "It's not what it looks like."

Markam chuckled and smoothed out his shirt. "Isn't it, though?"

"No," Sonara said. "It most definitely is not. Jaxon, fetch the sword from where you've stashed it. We're to sell it immediately and give Markam his cut. Pay off our debt and walk free of this mess. I want no part in this deal with the princess."

Markam clicked his teeth as if scolding a child. "Oh, Sunny. How precious little your comrade has shared with you after all."

Jaxon's body went rigid. He took off his hat and ran a hand through his dark hair. "I… I was going to tell you, Sonara, but…"

She turned to him, slowly, as the truth began to dawn on her. "You said the sword was safe. Stashed here in Sandbank."

Jaxon held up his hands in pre-apology. "It's… safe… yes. That much is true. But I don't precisely know *where*."

"And why, exactly," Sonara asked softly, "is that?"

"Because…" Jaxon took a step back, his shoulders scraping against the saloon doors. "I gave it to Markam as an up-front payment for helping me free you."

Goddesses be damned.

Sonara placed her hand on the pommel of Lazaris, suddenly wondering what it would feel like to skewer both brothers at once. Why, after all the years she'd known them both, was she *always* getting caught up between the two? It was like being passed between two dance partners who couldn't tell their left foot from their right.

"I was desperate, Sonara," Jaxon explained.

She could sense that desperation on his aura now, as her curse peeked its head out of the cage. *Like spun sugar on a stick.* His voice even tremored as he turned to face her, eye to eye.

Her anger tried to win over. But Jaxon was so damn *loveable* with his honesty. She saw him, for a moment, as she once had, ten years ago, standing before her with all the care in the world as he lifted her head from the sand and pressed a waterskin to her cracked lips.

I've got you, Jaxon had said then. *It's alright.*

Once he chose to let a person into his life, he let them in for good. Even if they were as rotten to the core as Markam. He sighed now, as if trying to explain his actions once and for all. "You were almost to Deadwood by the time I got to you. If I'd ridden Duran, I wouldn't have made it on time. And Markam wouldn't agree to help without payment. You know I had to, right?"

Sonara glanced to Markam, who was clearly flexing his arms while checking out the curve of his muscles beneath his jacket.

"What's she paying you?" Sonara asked. "Why are you so intent on getting us to join you and her? She's our enemy, by birthright and by blood."

"Because," he said, his voice missing that mocking tone for the first time, "someday, as long as she survives, she's to take her father's place. She's to become *queen.* And in a Deadlands ruled by her, Sonara, we'll be *free.* Better than free, we'll be on her court for doing this. We only need to help her do one little thing…"

Sonara laughed in his face. "You want us to become some sort of pieced together, ragtag *court*? Help her waltz into Stonegrave and steal her father's throne out from under him? By the looks of her she's been his prisoner for years. She can't become queen."

"She can," Markam said. "It's her birthright. Shadowblood or not, prisoner to him or not, she's entitled to his crown. This is our chance to align with her. And we'll be richer than rich, if we do this job. I know her, Sonara. Perhaps better than anyone does." His eyes took on the sheen of a man thinking of the past. "We can trust her."

"Why?" Sonara asked. "Tell me why you think you can trust her."

He glanced away, his jaw rigid. "Because we were lovers."

"Oh, Markam," Sonara said. "Don't tell me… *her?*"

Because suddenly she pieced it all together. *This* was the other woman. The one who'd stolen Markam's heart… and broke it. A few years ago, he'd disappeared for six months, fully out of touch, only to return one night, tears in his eyes as he came to Sonara.

I don't want to talk, he'd said. *I just want the pain to go away.*

Sonara had taken his hand and led him into the dark. There, they'd traded their pain: kisses to cover up the lies they were telling themselves, tangled breaths to take the place of heartless words. What followed was a whirlwind romance, one that would never last, for they were too broken to love each other truly.

The double doors next to them opened suddenly, brightness and laughter spilling out as two drunken patrons stumbled into the sands.

"This is the job of a lifetime," Markam said. "She needs us to do one thing, Sonara. One little job, and we'll be cleared. Names wiped from the scrolls, life ready to go on in blissful oblivion, and someday, when she takes his place… Don't you want to be a princess, Sonara? She could make you one."

She recoiled at the word.

"Give me a bigger, better job out there," Markam said. "I dare you to come up with a prize that large."

"The sword—" Sonara started, but she knew he was right.

"We work for her," Markam said, "we do whatever it is she asks, especially if it's against her father's wishes… It's a win-win, Sonara."

He was right.

She hated him even more for being so… but he was. She gave Markam her very best Duran-worthy look. "Fine."

"Alright!" Jaxon clapped his hands. "That's settled, then."

Sonara thought of Soahm, with his nice clothes and his lavish castle and the mystery surrounding him; a mystery she may never be able to uncover. Unless, perhaps, she had the riches to help. There was no mystery money couldn't buy the answer to. Or at least get her far closer to the truth.

She just hoped she didn't get killed in the process.

***

"The King has been in contact with the Wanderers," Azariah said, back in the saloon. A fresh bottle of oil sat opened on the table before her, along with a tray of roasted meats that were surprisingly delightful, unlike most backwater saloon food tended to be. "As you know, the treaty signed long ago is about to expire, and the Three Kingdoms have decided to renew it, as per their initial contract. The Wanderer leader will soon arrive on Dohrsar to complete it. The signing will take place at the Garden of the Goddess. Specifically, at the upcoming Gathering. It is there, after the treaty has been signed, that the Wanderers will begin their mission. The Gathering, as you know, is a very blessed experience. A coming together of the Three Kingdoms. A celebration of our similarities, despite our differences."

The treaty between the Three Kingdoms of Dohrsar was still in place, but it was a shaky thing, in near-constant imbalance.

Years ago, when Dohrsar's main continent only comprised Soreia and the White Wastes, Jira's father had discovered Gutrender, created an army, and razed his way through the entire middle of the continent. He created the borders around the Deadlands, declared himself king, and summoned both queens to his fortress walls.

The three rulers spent five days discussing the treaty that would keep peace in place, that outlined the new borders. It still held to this day, but the hatred between the three leaders was palpable. It was a skirmish between the Deadlands and Soreia that had called Soahm away to the front lines, that had resulted in his injury. There were other skirmishes like it, but someday, Sonara guessed that her mother and the Queen of the White Wastes would likely join forces to dissolve the Deadlands and take back what was once their ancestors' lands, splitting the desert between the two.

"I've been to a Gathering before," Sonara said. "Any good outlaw ensures they're in attendance."

Gatherings meant traders from all over Dohrsar would come, bringing their wares, ripe for the taking with the thick, bustling crowds. And the Garden of the Goddess, specifically, was one of the most fascinating places on Dohrsar. Plenty of places to hide, as it marked the entrance to the twisted network of mines that dove deep beneath the surface of the planet. It was there that many dug for gold, which was used to fashion into coin: the ever-driving force of man.

"But this is no common Gathering, Devil," Azariah said. "For the Wanderer leader comes not only to extend a treaty of peace.

He intends to take something from the planet." She paused for a moment, just as Suzie Quick's tune changed, growing louder and more raucous with the night crowd. "My father doesn't know where it lies, this object… Long has he sought it, but to no avail. He will wait for them to uncover it. And then he will steal it out from under them."

"An interesting turn of events, to have the Wanderers in attendance," Jaxon said. He glanced sideways at Sonara, as if he knew that the very word plagued her.

She was already leaning forward, itching for answers, the image of the Wanderers on her mind. Their skeletal armor, their strange, otherworldly weapons and starships. Their faces, *if they even had faces*, hidden behind dark helmets. They could have been goddesses, as some liked to believe.

Sonara thought they were the true devils.

But if the Wanderers were to be in attendance, she would be closer to answers about Soahm. Closer to a chance of recovering her brother, once and for all.

Wait, Sonara!

Wait!

She pushed the ghostly memory of Soahm's voice from her mind and focused on the group before her. "What is it they come to steal?"

Azariah paused. She looked to Thali and nodded.

"Antheon," Thali said. "A powerful orb that lies hidden beneath the planet's surface."

"An orb," Jaxon echoed. "Hidden inside the planet. It sounds like a tall tale."

Thali nodded. "And so does the tale about the Children of

Shadow. Yet here you all sit, with darkness coursing through your veins."

"What does it do?" Sonara asked instead. "The Antheon."

Silence, from both women.

"My father does not uncover all of his secrets, Devil. Just as you do not uncover all of yours."

Jira was as wicked as they came, a man who lusted for power, would do anything to secure more of it.

"Your job is to lie in waiting until they uncover it. The Wanderers have blessings from their world, blessings that will allow them a far better chance than we could ever have at finding the Antheon."

"So your father is double-crossing them," Sonara said. "The King is allowing the Wanderers to do the heavy lifting for him. Then he intends to take the Antheon. And you… will triple-cross him?"

Azariah nodded. "He is unaware that I overheard his conversations and plans. And unaware that I intend to stop him."

"Why stop him?" Jaxon asked.

"Because he is a monster," Azariah said. "And I fear what amount of power my father might rise to, should he get his hands on it."

The collar scar on her throat confirmed the former part of her words. Still… Sonara couldn't help but think back on Markam's words. *She is to be queen.*

What if Azariah was just as wicked as her father?

Blood doesn't always copy blood, she told herself, thinking of her mother, and the fate she'd endured at the Queen of Soreia's hands. She wasn't like her mother. She never would be.

Perhaps the same would be true for Azariah.

"How many Wanderers?" Sonara asked.

"A single starship," Azariah said. "With our abilities combined, we shouldn't have trouble securing the Antheon. We simply have to be clever, and not get caught by either party."

She made it sound simple enough. And yet Sonara knew no job was ever as it seemed, once the tide got moving. She looked at Jaxon and Markam, then stood. "When do we leave?"

"Sunrise," Azariah said. She reached into her jacket, and revealed an overflowing coin pouch, which she gently slid across the table. "Take the night to enjoy yourselves, to rest and replenish your supplies. We leave at first light."

Sonara snatched up the coin pouch before Markam could.

"Shall we, gentlemen?" Sonara crossed the room, the men trailing behind her. But she paused, glancing back over her shoulder to smile at Azariah. "If I find out you're lying, and you're working *for* your father… I'll cut your scar wide open."

CHAPTER 9

Karr

Curiosity was a traitor.

For no matter his hesitation about a job, landing day would always tug at Karr's mind. Today was no different.

He'd sat there in the bridge, in his normal seat towards the back, buckles snapped and straps taut, as they'd broken through the atmosphere into Dohrsar.

It was a dwarf planet, with only a single large continent, surrounded by sea. The continent itself struck him as strangely beautiful, enough that he found himself pulling at his straps to see better as the *Starfall* passed through the clouds.

He could draw this planet, as he'd drawn countless others. But to dip it all in blue would steal its glory.

The continent was split into three distinct shades: the top, an expanse of white and ice blue, a tundra that dipped into a frozen sea at the north, pocked by icebergs so large they could have been continents themselves.

Beneath it, spanning miles and miles wide, was a red-brown desert. It looked like a sea of its own, rippling sands with red and purple mountains zigzagging across its northern half like freshly sewn stitches.

Beneath the desert, in the south, the sands were separated by a jungle of lush green that bled into pale sand. Almost white, but not as stark as the north. It was white in a softer sense. The kind Karr wanted to sink into, as the ocean sand dipped into the southern sea.

The closer they drew towards the Dohrsaran ground, the more the continent began to take shape. The north and the south faded as they zeroed in on the center. Small townships were interspersed throughout the desert, multiplying towards a large circular central fortress surrounded by golden walls. Red-topped buildings and a few towering structures paled in comparison to the golden castle. It stood proudly atop a towering hill in the middle of the city, the castle itself topped with a domed ceiling that sparkled like it was made of diamonds.

They soared above it, still so small from such heights, as they barreled towards the center of the desert. Towards a sight that Karr knew he *would* draw, this time without his signature blue.

"Landing zone, boys." Cade tapped the viewport, the glass rippling as it zoomed in on a specific area of the desert. "The Garden of the Goddess."

The flight crew set the gears for landing, and the *Starfall* soared over one of the most alien sights Karr had seen in ages.

Jagged red rocks jutted into the sky like fingertips, all formed in a wide circle that was too perfectly placed to be an accident.

The mountain range that had moments ago looked so small, now looked monstrous, swirls of red and purple rock just barely missing the underbelly of the *Starfall* as the pilots sent her down for landing.

Too quickly, it was over. Too quickly, they hovered above the sand. The viewport slid shut, and they were cast back into their metallic world, lit by the steady glow of the ship's lights.

Karr swallowed a lump in his throat, realizing, suddenly, that this was the last exploratory landing he'd ever make with Cade.

It was not sadness. It was *relief.* As long as they finished the damned job and got Geisinger his Antheon. And put enough hope in the man to see that he'd deal with Jeb for good.

"Rock and roll, kid!" Jameson, the ship's communications manager, shouted from Karr's left. She was lean, mean muscle paired with a tiger's smile. She patted Karr on the shoulder as he unbuckled himself and stood, his legs uneasy as ever on landing day. No one else could call him *kid* and get away with it. But Jameson was like an older sister to Karr, one of the few aboard the crew who'd joined at the start and never left. Some of his sketches even hung in her quarters. On holidays, she always gifted him flagons of foreign alcohol, and they drank together until the edges of the world blurred.

"Sky legs?" Jameson asked now, raising a triple-pierced brow as Karr paused to look at Cade. The Captain was normally the first to rise, but he hadn't moved from his seat. He simply sat there, staring ahead at the closed viewport.

"You've got them, too," Karr said with a grin, gently pushing Jameson sideways. She teetered a little, but he had a feeling she'd done it just to entertain him. She could destroy him in games of muscles *and* wit, and they both knew it. His smile softened. "But no, I'm good. Go ahead, Jameson. I'll catch up."

She shrugged, then followed the rest of the piloting crew out of the bridge, where they headed down to the loading dock to don their S2s. They'd need them, before they set foot on the poisonous planet.

Karr waited until the bridge emptied, then slid into the pilot's seat next to Cade.

"Hey," he said, nudging him. "You alright?"

Cade blinked, nodding as he seemed to come back down to earth. He was always stoic upon landing day, in the way that Karr imagined a surgeon might prepare themselves for surgery. Or a soldier might sit in silence before a battle that would surely bring death.

"We've spent a lifetime in this ship," Cade said softly. "Our father—you may not remember the way he used to prepare for an expedition."

"I remember," Karr said.

He could picture it; their father, seated in the very same seat Cade was in now. Scrolling through a manifest with worn leather piloting gloves on. If he closed his eyes, Karr could still remember the smell of the leather. The squeak of it as his father flexed his fingertips and murmured softly to himself, going over notes, preparing to embark on another journey across alien soil. Their mother, with her ever-kind eyes, would stand behind him, humming as she stared out the viewport and admired the beauty of another place waiting to be explored.

"They respected every planet, saw them for the beauties that they were. They did their best to preserve them. To wander, but leave no trail. We've never honored that legacy, Karr. We steal things. We tear away a piece of every planet we ever visit. And today?"

Karr dared not speak. He placed his hand on the dash, where two sets of initials were carved.

MK. CK.

Myria and Charles Kingston.

"Today will be the last time we ever betray the Kingston name."

With a sigh, Cade unbuckled himself and stood. His dark captain's coat was ruffled from the buckles, and he smoothed it out across his chest, repeatedly, as if there were a wrinkle that just wouldn't quit. When he was satisfied, he held out a hand for Karr to go ahead of him.

But Karr didn't move.

"Cade." He cocked his head. "You're… bleeding."

Cade frowned.

He looked down at his hand, where a smear of fresh blood stained his fingertips.

"Strange," he said. He wiped the blood on his lapel.

"Did you cut yourself in the landing?"

It hadn't been rocky. If anything, it hadn't even felt like a landing at all, for how smoothly it went. Karr stepped forward, all formalities aside, to check his older brother for the source of the blood.

But Cade suddenly stepped away, waving him off. The strange sense of stoicity was gone, his captain's smirk back on his face. "The future is out there, Karr. Let's not keep it waiting."

With that, he turned and marched out of the bridge without another glance back.

CHAPTER 10

Sonara

Two days, they'd traveled, and only now was Sonara able to see the faintest glimpse of the Garden of the Goddess dotting the horizon. It was a mile-wide valley halfway up the mountains, where a circle of blood red rocks protruded from the ground like giant fingertips stretching for the sky.

The Garden of the Goddess was a celestial graveyard.

Each time the moons went dark, it was in remembrance of the time the goddesses slayed one of their own: the youngest, who rose up against the others in her greed for *more*. With great force, the goddesses slew her, and placed her body in a bed of stars.

As she lay dying, the goddesses began to mold Dohrsar around her, shaping the planet bit by bit until it became her tomb. Her last breaths were met with a curse: for eternity, she would find no rest.

The dying goddess stretched out her hand as the last pieces of the planet formed around it. Only her fingertips remained, poking through the earth as if she'd used every last bit of her strength to reach them.

"They're not as morbid as I thought they would be."

Sonara glanced backwards.

Azariah rode several strides away, with Thali perched behind her on their pale steed.

"The fingers of the goddess," Azariah said as she stared at the shadowy outline on the horizon. They were still a day's ride away from the Bloodhorns, and half a day's ride from heading up into the mountain valley. "People tell tales of them, all across the Deadlands. The details change, depending on who delivers it. The way the tale goes in Stonegrave, I always imagined you'd feel sad, looking at them. A goddess, cast out. Left to rot for eternity. But looking at them…" She tucked a tendril of dark hair behind her ear, and smiled sadly. "There's a strange sense of beauty to it."

"There are a great many tales about a great many things," Thali answered. "It is up to us, my Lady, which tales we choose to believe."

The two women were so starkly unalike it made Sonara smile.

Thali, on the back of the mare with her lazy, relaxed posture, her Canis mask protruding from her face, bone gauntlets wrapped around Azariah's middle. The picture of a Deadlander, though missing a much-needed weapon. And Azariah, riding sidesaddle, as rigid as a princess could be. It wouldn't surprise Sonara if she had a pole for a spine.

"Do you believe the tales you've heard about me?" Jaxon asked.

He'd purchased a mare in Sandbank before they left. And with how quickly he'd ridden out of town, Sonara guessed it had been with illusioned coin provided by Markam. The mare was a pretty thing, a white-and-black overo. Her multicolored mane was braided up to show off the intricate swirling patterns on her neck.

Each time she drew closer, Duran held his head a little higher, his steps more of a dance than a stride.

Some war beast you are, Sonara thought to him. *Prancing like a show steed.*

He swatted his tail in response.

"The only tales told about you, Jax, are how you accompany the Devil and do her bidding."

"Careful," he said with a smirk. "I'll send a bone soaring towards that ego of yours."

Sonara spat towards him. Jaxon laughed, and Azariah looked like she might be sick.

"Must you be so… vile?" she asked.

Sonara shrugged. "So tell us, Princess. What do you know of Markam of Wildeweb?"

"Ah." Azariah looked skyward, where Markam sat atop Razor's back. She waved a lace fan in front of her face, her silk gloves darkened from sweat. She wouldn't last one day in the Deadlands without a guide like Thali. "I only know one tale, about the businessman whose ego weighs nearly as much as his coin purse. The businessman who runs away in the dark of night, without a word of goodbye." Azariah's smile was laced with acid. "But that is not a tale worth telling."

Sonara's eyes narrowed.

For she'd experienced a very different version, when Markam came to her that night with tears in his eyes. Love was a tricky thing. Broken hearts, even more so, and they never did seem to break even.

"How much further?" Azariah asked, clearly changing the subject.

"A day's ride." Sonara stared between the tips of Duran's ears at the horizon. "We'll be there by nightfall. Camp on the outskirts, then ride up the pass into the Garden in the morning. The Gathering begins at the setting suns. We'll wait on your Wanderers to arrive. Watch them, until they make a move towards uncovering this Antheon you speak of. And once we recover it for you?"

Azariah fanned herself again. "You'll have your payment, on my honor."

"Will he be there?" Sonara asked. "The… king?"

Azariah glanced to the right, where another group of riders joined the road. "Yes," she said. Sonara could have sworn the girl shivered despite the heat. "You would be wise to hide yourself from him, when he arrives."

She tucked her fan into her cloak, and for a moment, the fabric slipped aside to reveal that awful scar around her throat.

Her eyes flicked upwards, catching Sonara's gaze.

All throughout the day, caravans had passed by, heading towards the Garden. It was not a rare thing for the desert trails to be packed with travelers. If not to get a look at the strange, armored Wanderers, then to reunite with friends from Soreia or the White Wastes, or make proposals to provinces from other kingdoms.

The royalty was always in attendance.

The other group on desert cats drew closer, their striped bodies nearly as large as Duran.

He tossed his head, his aura reeking of fear, his soul-ember blazing.

"Easy," Sonara said to him. "You'll embarrass yourself in front of the mare."

He simply snorted in response, tossing his mane as if his fear outweighed his need to prance and act pretty.

"I've never met a steed like him," Azariah said. "It's as if he listens. Responds."

Sonara chuckled. "All beasts do that. You just have to know how to listen." She ran her hand across Duran's hot neck. "Though, yes, he is different. He died with me. Came back to life at the same time."

"Shadows," Azariah said. "Shadows and… a gift."

"Curse," Sonara corrected her. "I've never known it to be a gift."

Thali answered this time. "The stories of old would disagree. It is magic we hold. Magic that once had the power to strike fear in the hearts of every living being on Dohrsar."

Magic.

She'd never heard the word before, and it was strange on her lips as Sonara echoed it. "Magic?"

"Magic," Thali said again, resolutely.

Jaxon, humming softly to himself on his mare, had fallen silent. He lifted the brim of his hat and spat a mouthful of chew into the sand. "What does it mean?"

"It is ancient," Thali said. "A word that means power, of the most unearthly kind. A beautiful thing to behold. Though the word itself has lost meaning in recent years as magic has crept far into the shadows, afraid to come back out."

"Which is exactly why Jira's forefathers slayed every last Shadowblood on Dohrsar," Jaxon said. "Their descendants, and their descendants, too. Because they were cursed, and undeserving of a second life. Tainted bloodline to bloodline."

And that was how Sonara had always felt, since coming back to life. *Tainted. Undeserving. Cursed.*

She'd lived two lives already, but she was still trying to figure out why in the hell she was deserving of even *one.*

Her own mother hadn't thought she was, and her father… well, Sonara supposed she'd never learn of the man that had sired her. She worried that if she ever did, she'd kill him.

Pay him back for the pain he'd caused her all those years in her first life, not knowing who she was. Not knowing *why* she'd even been born, if she was to remain unwanted.

The wind howled, kicking up the sand. It was days like this, out in the wild, where she considered opening the cage inside of her. If she did, the physical pain of it, the pressure of holding back her curse, would fade for a time. If she could have a few moments of freedom… it was as intoxicating as the urge to spill guts and gain glory. To track down the truth about Soahm.

Even if letting the pressure out meant it would only come back stronger later.

A tiny taste, her curse whispered. *Just for a moment, let me out to play.*

She glanced at her companions, silent, despite Jaxon's off-key humming, which Azariah was kind enough not to object to.

Perhaps Sonara could enjoy the ride, too.

She was the Devil of the Deadlands, after all.

She was alive, and she was free.

Sonara unlocked the mental cage and let her curse soar.

The tether lengthened as it soared down the foot-trodden path across the sand, landing upon a brown mare as her rider stopped for rest. She sank her muzzle into a trough of water. Her aura revealed *simple joy, cool as a rushing river.*

Sonara pushed the tether outwards with a heavy breath, testing her control.

Her curse soared only as far as she was able to see to command its direction. It went past two children as they giggled and chased a bony black feline around a wagon. She sensed *rage as rough as a grinding stone,* as the feline howled and tried in vain to escape.

The further the tether lengthened, the more her head lightened. She knew she should reel it back in, but she allowed it a bit more.

It bounded off the leather skirting of a wagon, sensing the *exhaustion,* the *anticipation,* from all who rode within. It danced past a flock of fowl swooping low in hope of plucking bugs from the sand, was *almost* back to her as Sonara mentally reeled the tether in, when the wind suddenly picked up.

"Do you feel that?" Azariah asked.

Sonara paused. She thought she'd imagined the rumble in her bones. But there it was, as she looked skyward. The glowing fireball of a ship breaking through the atmosphere.

"Next ship's landing," Jaxon said. "Just as you said it would."

"I've never seen a landing before, so close," Azariah answered, with equal parts fear and awe.

Come on back, Sonara told her curse. *It's time now.*

But the moment she'd thought the command… her curse soared away. A mistake she'd only made once before, giving it far too much time to play.

It flew into the distance, chasing the horizon.

The sky, sweet as hard candies.

And beyond that, as the ship lowered and began to slow enough that she could see its outline…

Black of night, bitter as crushed bones.

Sonara gasped. That was *death* she sensed, as clear as any day.

She could hear Razor let loose a trembling screech, and then Markam was landing beside them, covering his ears as the ship soared from the sky.

Sonara could sense the grains of sand beneath his feet, the tired leather of his boots, the sweat on Razor's belly…

Too much. Far, far too much.

She gasped, clutching her throat.

Azariah and Thali did not notice, but Jaxon dismounted and strode over, hands wrapping around Duran's mane as he stared up at Sonara from beneath his hat.

"Out of control," she hissed, panic rising in her chest.

"Breathe. Just breathe," Jaxon said.

The tether stretched. The pain was so deep she heard a whimper slide from her lips. She felt the wind of the Wanderer ship as it soared past, and her curse followed in its wake.

Dark, dark, dark. Fire and fury and the promise of spilled blood.

Sonara whimpered again. From the pain, but also from the memory. For she *knew* this sense, as if her body remembered it, even though she hadn't been a Shadowblood when she'd first encountered it years ago on her last night with Soahm.

"Sonara!" She heard his voice in her mind, saw the ghostly memory of his hands stretching towards her, the panic in his eyes, his leg splayed beside him at an awkward angle. *"Sonara!"*

The tether on her curse stretched so hard it might snap.

"You must control it," Jaxon said. "You must bring it back."

At his words, her curse turned. As sudden as it had soared upwards, it spun back to the ground and exploded against the sand.

The aura it found there was a new one. *An ancient and furious presence, gnashing its teeth, like the last warm trickle of sunlight before an endless black winter.*

Sonara clamped her eyes shut.

Come back, she begged her curse. *Come back, come back, goddesses damn you, come back.*

Jaxon's hand pressed against hers as she dug her fingertips into Duran's mane. She was on fire. She was going to burn until she became nothing but ashes, scattered away on a rogue wind.

"Sonara," Jaxon said again. He shook her gently. The very same way he had, years ago, when she'd lost control of her curse for the first time. When Markam had backed away, fear in his eyes, but Jaxon had entwined her fingers through his and together, they'd waited the pain away. "Sonara. You're not alone."

She wasn't.

She had Duran with her, the soul-ember in her chest warm and welcoming as she focused on it. And she felt Jaxon's hand tighten over her own. They held onto Duran together, breath by breath.

She wasn't alone.

She could bring it back. She was stronger than this.

Something seemed to *pop* in her senses. The tether recoiled. Her curse slammed into its cage, and the lock turned tight.

The heat was swept away, as if the wind had changed course and carted it to someplace distant. Sonara took a nervous breath and found it mercifully empty.

"Blast," she said, pointing up with a shaky finger. "The… the ship, Jax."

The sky was on fire. The Wanderer ship rocketed across it, metal and blazing as always. But this one had a red emblem painted on its underbelly. A bird with flaming, outspread wings as sharp as knives.

"Soahm," Sonara said, and in her mind, she saw the ship as she once had.

A shadow blotting out the stars, the red bird bathed in moonlight as the ship banked and rose higher. She'd never forget that bird. Not in a million years.

"That's the one," Sonara said. "I'm sure of it."

The shadows in her veins roiled, as the very ship that had stolen Soahm, years ago, finally returned to Dohrsar.

CHAPTER 11

Sonara

A half-day later, their mounts breathing heavily, they crested the final stretch of road up the mountain pass.

The Garden of the Goddess.

It was nestled in between the two smallest peaks of the Bloodhorns. Where the rest of the Bloodhorns were jagged terrain, rocky purple and crimson crags and treacherous mountain faces of shale that crumbled beneath the feet of even the most agile mountain beasts… the Garden itself was flowing with life.

An oasis like none other on Dohrsar.

Sonara's eyes watered from the mere brightness of it all.

Grass, so lush it looked like an emerald sea, swayed gently in the wind, a carpet rolled across the entire valley. Among the grass stood tents in every shade of beast skins and stitched fabrics from across Dohrsar; natural sun-dried leathers and vibrant, dyed blue and purple and red skins. Through the valley, cutting through the grass like a silver tongue, a pure mountain spring that boasted the freshest, coolest waters. Some healers across Dohrsar traveled days just to fill their jugs from it.

Sonara followed the gently flowing river upwards, towards the center of the Garden of the Goddess: where the legend itself was born.

The jagged crimson fingers of the fallen goddess stood like ancient sentries.

They stretched upwards right out of the ground, towering crimson rocks that were so massive Sonara had to crane her neck back to follow them with her gaze. They rose far above the valley, surpassing even the surrounding mountain peaks until they disappeared into the clouds beyond. None could tell how far the fingertips of the fallen goddess stretched.

Thick blue vines stretched and twisted up the towering crimson rocks, glowing even in the daylight. Sun blossoms, with their jagged petals, hung from them in silken auburn and golden clusters. At night, the petals would fall. Moon blossoms would sprout to take their place; softly glowing flora that could be crushed and spread to make a paint that looked dipped in moonlight.

A waterfall trickled from one of the goddess' fingers, thick blankets of moss hanging from it like an emerald curtain, sunlight glinting off it.

Large hunting fowl chirped and flitted from rock to rock, clinging to the vines with their talons before they leapt, wings tucked tight to their bodies as they pursued angelflies for a mid-morning snack.

The entire Garden filled with their song.

And with it… the sound of *life.*

Sonara didn't have a hope in the world of holding her curse back. The cage door practically blasted open, her curse soaring out as she breathed in the aura.

Fresh flower petals and sun-warmed dew and bread rising over a smoldering fire.

It was the aura of laughter, of love, of distant souls greeting each other after months spent apart. It was happiness and joy and lovers reuniting, family members embracing, old acquantainces becoming friends once more.

"The Garden of the Goddess," Jaxon said from his mount.

Sonara echoed his smile as she breathed it all in.

The sounds echoed back, music and laughter and conversation, the whinny of steeds and the roar of desert cats greeting their companions. The sound of blades clashing, as old comrades sparred together once more.

All around the Garden, interspersed around the rocks, were tents and makeshift booths. Citizens from across Dohrsar had come: Soreians, Deadlanders and those who'd made the journey from the northern White Wastes by wyvern.

Their sky wagons were docked to the far left of the goddess' fingertips, sails made of stitched hide pulled down taut so as not to catch the wind. The great metal harnesses for the wyverns had been removed and set aside, and the wyverns themselves stood clustered in a makeshift pen.

Overhead, Markam and Razor circled, coming to land by Sonara.

Razor cried out at the sight of her own kind, watching the northern wyverns in the pen. A pile of raw mountain goat legs was stacked in the middle: a free-for-all.

"We don't get too close to royals, my love," Markam said to the beast, as he landed and slid from the saddle. Delicate whorls of emerald smoke plumed from Razor's nostrils, but she lowered her head as he unstrapped her saddle. "They are not kind to desert rats like us."

He glanced at Azariah with coldness in his gaze.

She simply lifted her chin and glanced past him, her near-black eyes wide as she took it all in. She reached up and lowered her hood, a genuine smile on her lips. "It is a marvel," she said in a breath. "I never imagined it to be this way."

"The Gathering?" Sonara asked.

"No." The Princess only smiled and wrapped her arms around herself. "*Freedom.*"

She looked like a child receiving a gift. A warrior, being granted their very first sword at sunrise, toes dipped in the raging sea.

"When will they arrive?" Sonara asked.

Thali, all emotion hidden beyond her Canis mask, only looked skyward. "Dusk. The Wanderers will wait for the feast."

"And then?" Sonara asked.

The jagged teeth of the Canis flashed bright white beneath the sun as Thali beheld the Gathering. "Then we will begin."

***

The Wanderers had not yet arrived. But the Gathering was in full swing. And, stars above, *the silk*.

It was so soft against her cheek, Sonara wanted to bury herself in it.

She wasn't even past the outer ring of tents and booths when she'd found it. Her curse went wild, so close to something like this.

Cool, smooth water, like diving into an oasis after a long day's ride.

Damn it all to hell.

Outlaw or not, a girl needed fineries like these.

"Seven coins for a swatch, my blue-haired beauty," the booth-keeper chided, pulling Sonara from her thoughts. She flicked her long, bony fingers across the booth, and gave Sonara a saber-toothed grin. Around her neck, the red sigil of the Blood Bucket out west, a now-barren place where Jira's grandfather had first slain a man with Gutrender in the name of his conquering cause. Those who hailed from the Blood Bucket were fiercely proud of their city's history with Jira's forefathers.

"I'm all out of coin," Sonara said to the woman, and released the silk, her lips forming into a full pout.

Liar, her curse whispered.

The shopkeeper turned her predatory gaze on another young woman who approached the booth, and Sonara deftly slipped a piece of deep crimson silk into her duster. She silently blessed Jaxon for insisting she wear one to keep up her outlawing image, for it was perfect in times like this.

Thieving times.

After last night, and what she would face today… Sonara needed a distraction.

"Blood red is your color," Jaxon said, stepping up beside Sonara.

She laced her arm through his, and sighed. "Better than Soreian blue."

He chuckled. "Sonara, I…"

"I don't want to talk about serious things, Jax," she interrupted him as they walked. "I can sense the anxiety all over you."

"I just want to make sure your mind is clear, before we begin."

"It's clear, Jax."

"Is it?" He removed his hat and squeezed the brim, the leather darkened from years of his fingertips worrying at it absentmindedly. "Truly?"

Sonara's stomach twisted. He wanted to talk about *feelings.* Those pesky little beasts that plagued the living, day and night. Didn't she experience enough of feelings? Her curse lusted after them, a near-constant fight against releasing it so it could devour the auras of everyone who crossed its path.

It was exhausting, sensing the sadness of others. The euphoria, the anger, the bitter green of jealousy, the delicate rosy sigh of first love.

But the past ten years had also been taxing in their own right, searching for Soahm. For *something* to tell her where he'd been taken in that ship. And now…

"What does it taste like?" Jaxon asked. He waved his hand as a bloodfly buzzed past, likely chasing the scent of so many beasts in the distance. "What do you sense?"

He nodded out at the beautiful chaos all around them. The Wanderer ship with the red bird was nowhere in sight, concealed by the ring of mountains surrounding them. But Sonara swore she could feel its presence, like an almost-imperceptible pulse. Was Soahm inside the ship, returned to Dohrsar once more? Or had they taken him away from this world and left him somewhere else, never to return again?

It was here. Finally *here again,* and soon, she would have the truth.

"It tastes like hope," Sonara answered Jaxon's question. He raised a brow, and with a sigh, she added, "It tastes a little like hatred, too."

She'd once been lost under the power of that word, in the days after losing her brother. It no longer controlled her like it used to, this hatred for a strange, armored entity that came down from the sky and had its way with him. But it was still there. An old friend, ready to be called upon when she needed it to fuel her.

"Ah." Jaxon snapped his fingers at her truth. "*There* you are. That's the Sonara I know, never afraid to speak her mind."

Those first three words were the very same ones he'd spoken the first time they met. When Sonara had awoken on the sand to find Jaxon kneeling over her, the sunlight like a halo around the fringes of his hat. *"There you are,"* he'd said with a smile as she came back to consciousness. *"Thought you were dead."*

In her first days as a Shadowblood, unable to return to Soreia for fear of a second death, Sonara had had no choice but to roam endlessly through the Deadlands, as uninhibited as the wind.

Those days were still muddled. Full of pain and fear and the desire to simply give up. She'd gone nearly three days without water when he'd found her. They'd stayed together for a time, first only as comrades who agreed to help each other in a job.

But Sonara found that the more time she spent with Jaxon… the more he began to remind her of Soahm. Not in every way, but in the ones that mattered; in the ways that eased her conscience when she thought of her brother and remembered him screaming her name in the dark.

Jaxon was someone else to share knowledge with, to tease and laugh with and relent when she forced him to give over his blanket on the coldest Deadlands nights. He was someone to feel the hot blaze of competition with, on days when they both needed the extra push to keep going.

He'd saved her second life, literally, by simply offering to share his water skin. First it was the fear of being alone, of having *no one* besides their beasts, that first brought Sonara and Jaxon together. But it was their friendship, forged in the fires of life as outlaws and outcasts, that had made them an inseparable pair.

They'd become blood-bonded, with the slash of a blade, their palms pressed together. A pact, a promise sworn with the shadowy tendrils of their blood, to always look out for one another. Comrades in arms *and* in life.

She wouldn't make the same mistake with Jaxon that she'd made with Soahm.

She wouldn't lose him, too.

"I'm going to get my answers tonight," Sonara said now. Not far away, a troupe of musicians began playing a joyful tune. The people around them began to shift and move. In the distance, the single entrance to the Garden still flowed with caravans arriving. "I'll do the job. I'll be present, I swear. But when I get my chance…"

"You're going to take it," Jaxon said. "What are you going to do?"

"Find my answers. Even if they're on board the ship."

Surprise filled Jaxon's tone. "You're going to sneak onto a Wanderer ship?"

She smiled. "It's not as if they're going to invite me aboard. Though I can be convincing enough, should the need arise."

He frowned. "They're dangerous, Sonara. Creatures from another world. There's so little we know about them."

"They could say the same about us," Sonara said. She patted Lazaris on her hip. Its pommel was cold and solid. The sharpened blade, ready to strike.

He nodded. "Yes, but… there are too many variables. And are you prepared for what's to come, if there aren't any answers to find? It's been ten years. *Years.* He's not going to be sitting on the ship, waiting for you to rescue him with open arms, and—"

His voice trailed off.

His aura instantly flared with *regret.*

"I'm not a fool, Jax," Sonara said. She narrowed her eyes as she caught a child eavesdropping at the edge of a tent. "I know the odds. But I also know the odds of that ship having returned. I don't believe in fate. But perhaps I should. My entire second life has been leading to this moment. To finding my brother and bringing him home. You won't talk me out of it. You won't stop me."

"No, I won't," Jaxon said with a sigh. "But at least I can try. And I can be there with you, when the timing is right."

Duran whinnied suddenly, high and loud, as he caught a view of Sonara through the crowd. She smiled, for his call echoed across the Garden, audible even over the music.

"It's my mission to find Soahm," Sonara said to Jaxon. "My burden to bear. Not yours, Jax. Focus on the job. The riches and the freedom we'll gain once we have the Antheon. I'll handle my brother."

Jaxon nodded, his kind eyes watching Duran stare out across the crowd towards Sonara. "Perhaps it's not my burden to bear. But that's the thing with family, Sonara. When you love someone… you do whatever it takes to stay by their side."

***

"Collecting yourself a nice purse already?" Markam emerged from the crowd, a drink in his hand.

The moment between Sonara and Jaxon broke.

She whirled around and lifted a brow. He hadn't been there only a second ago, though she sensed the *smoky burn* of his curse sighing away on the mountain breeze. "It's not wise to sneak up on a devil."

He laughed and put his muscular arm around her shoulders, guiding her away from Jaxon, through the booths and back towards their group.

Jaxon followed, keeping his distance.

"The sword," Sonara said. "I don't suppose you're going to tell me where it is, now that we've made the journey here?"

"Dear Sunny, you always did have such a good sense of humor." Markam laughed. "It's safe. That's all you need to know, until we finish the princess' job."

She shook her head and sidestepped a man offering samples of fried mountain beast.

"So," Sonara asked, switching the subject as Markam plucked a sample off the tray and popped it into his mouth. Green juice oozed from it as he crunched down and promptly gave a look of instant regret. He spat it out as they kept moving. "What happened between the two of you? You never did tell me."

Markam glanced ahead of them, where Azariah was holding up a large black-pearl necklace from Soreia, her smile wide and genuine, sparkling up to her eyes. Thali stood beside her, arms crossed and looking worthy of every strange glance she received as people walked past, keeping their distance.

"She *is* beautiful," Sonara admitted. More beautiful than she'd ever dream of being. A princess, worthy of her title, despite the mark of the chain around her throat.

Sonara bristled, thinking of her own once-half-title, if she could even call it that.

"If you must know, Sonara…" Markam sighed as Sonara glanced to him. "She was the target of a high-profile job. I was there, impersonating a palace escort, in hope of gaining her trust and securing access to the royal catacombs, where the king guards the entrance to the diamond mines. I stayed too long, got too close to her, and she discovered the truth about my identity." He sighed and waved a gloved hand. "The rest, as they say, is history."

"History that resulted in a broken man," Sonara said. "It took you months to return to yourself after her."

"Perhaps it was not because of her," Markam said. His tone softened, and his eyes took on a sheen of sorrow. He leaned a little closer, lowering his voice. "Perhaps… perhaps it was because I was bedding a Devil."

Sonara gasped, then punched him in the arm, earning a satisfying yelp.

"You are as beastly as you've ever been, Markam of Wildeweb. And you don't deserve her. You never will."

But Sonara found herself smiling at him anyway, for she and Markam had always brought out the very worst in each other. The darker sides, that did not mind trading personal jabs even when they stung.

"When Azariah discovered the truth about me, she nearly had me killed. I had to flee in the night, chased by fifty of Jira's Diamond Guard. She told me if she ever saw me again, she'd request my head, served to her father's beasts on a platter. But

I fooled her, for too long. Which is why I'm not surprised she came to find me for this job to double cross her father. I am the best in the business."

Sonara shrugged. "I've known better."

"Doubtful." Markam flicked a coin to a woman selling a leg of mountain lamb, then took the leg and bit into it, groaning softly. "We'll be done here in no time. Easiest job you've ever been handed. That's a promise."

Her stomach rumbled, and she reached out to rip a piece of the meat away.

"Ah-ah-ah," Markam said, waggling a finger. "Patience, Sunny. It's something you've never quite learned."

"Beast," Sonara growled. But she smiled as Jaxon slipped up behind him in the crowd, just in time, and plucked the meat from his brother's hand.

Jaxon tore into it, then tossed the rest to Sonara.

She ripped into it, not caring that she probably resembled Razor feeding on a fresh kill. The meat was so good she groaned. She couldn't remember the last time she'd actually eaten a full meal that wasn't rations, let alone taken the time to enjoy one.

"Shall we, boys?" Sonara asked, as she downed the meat and tossed the bone against Markam's chest. His lip curled up halfway, his aura surging with hot annoyance.

Jaxon held out an arm. "We shall."

Sonara laced her arm through his, and they set off into the mess of tents and makeshift stalls, like two fine travelers ready to spend their heavy sacks of coin on whatever their hearts desired.

For a time, they lost themselves in the joy of it.

The simple motion of making their way across a valley of goods ripe for the taking. Sonara was able to forget the job ahead; and the *task* ahead, as they awaited the arrival of the Wanderers.

She and Jaxon had just settled down in the scattering of tents, drinking from full water skins, when the horn sounded.

Someone was blowing into a giant conch, the sound like a beast bellowing at the edge of its offspring's grave. She wouldn't be able to get that sound out of her ears even if she tried. And yet, on instinct, her head tilted towards the sound. Her heartbeat hastened its pace.

In her mind, she saw Soahm smile. *Race you to the sea,* he said, and she swore she could feel the ghost of long-gone wind on her face, the splash of distant saltwater against her ankles, hear the bubble of faded laughter as she and Soahm sprinted towards the crashing waves.

Soon, Sonara, she told herself. *Soon, the Wanderers will arrive. And you will get your answers.*

Her blood sang at that fact. Her curse hummed from within.

She stood and turned towards the entrance to the valley, where through the booths she could just catch a glimpse of the road into the Garden as the Queen of Soreia arrived.

Salt of the sea; the sprawling Black Waters.

The aura of a kingdom that was no longer home.

The flagbearer of Soreia arrived first. She sat astride a glorious black steed, the beast's tail like a river of shimmering silk. The flagbearer herself was adorned in Soreian armor, made of metallic blue interlocking scales. They were impenetrable to most weapons, almost undulating in the sunlight as they shifted between blue and green.

The Concher walked beside her, wearing flowing robes in sea green as he announced Soreia's arrival.

"Showy as ever," Jaxon grumbled, and Sonara felt his hand graze her wrist. A gentle touch, enough to show her that she was not alone. "You were never meant for them, Sonara. You're too wild. Too free."

"Too rabid," Markam added.

Sonara spat onto his boots.

Next came the cavalry. Trainers rode alongside, faces that Sonara recognized from her past. Ones that had not tried to stand up for her the day she died.

She'd deserved it.

A part of her knew she always had.

Banishment, a hundred lashings, a full day locked in the stocks that accepted the tides, that turned from dry ground to a neck-deep crashing sea… she could have endured them all.

Her mother had demanded the Leaping instead.

Duran lifted his head from a bucket and whinnied a greeting as his kin passed, their hoofbeats like the steady roll of thunder.

"Traitor," Sonara murmured to him.

The steeds were loyal and strong and sturdy, so beautiful it made Sonara's heart ache. In her mind, she was cast back to Soreia again, polishing their armor in the royal barn, lulled by the smell of sweet grain and fresh hay and fowl chirping in the rafters.

The steeds were wrapped with custom-fitted armor, sharp twin horns spiraling from their masked foreheads. The warriors on their backs were just as fierce, men and women wearing matching breastplates of blue, their helmets painted with the Soreian sigil.

Again, Duran whinnied, and Sonara didn't have the heart to silence him.

She knew he longed for home, had only left it because his heart was intertwined with hers.

The conch blew again, three short blasts.

People began to bow, dropping to a knee as the procession closed in towards Sonara. Others began to toss desert roses into the line of steeds.

Sonara's lip curled. From her place at the back of the crowd, she did not bow.

She would never bow again.

A mare she'd known well came into view. It had once been Soahm's favorite. With lethal grace, the pale beast carried Queen Iridis to the front of the pack. Cheers sounded out, more roses tossed at her feet.

Queen Iridis' hair was such a deep, beautiful cerulean it rivaled the sea, flowing down her back like ocean waves. She wore fitted blue armor, and atop it, a colorful braided sash, each colored strand signifying how many she had slain in her efforts to become queen as a much younger, fiercer candidate for the crown. It was perched atop her curls, gold with bits of opal on each of its glittering spires.

Let me go, Sonara's curse begged her. *Let me sense the soul of the wicked queen.*

It hammered against the cage.

It bashed and caused Sonara to grit her teeth with the effort to hold it in. But as the queen rode past, her curse won, shoving the cage door wide.

Pride, sweet but rotten. Fallen petals crushed by a storm.

Beneath it, the oily metallic tang of someone who had spilled blood.

"Easy, Sonara," Jaxon murmured gently, as if he could sense the hatred coming off her in waves. "Remember who you are. What power she no longer holds over you."

Sweat began to bead on Sonara's brow. She rooted herself to the spot, gripping Lazaris like a vice as Queen Iridis turned her gaze to the left.

She looked right at Sonara with a glare that could stop a heart.

Looked right *through* her, the bastard child she'd once sentenced to death.

"Sonara?"

Jaxon's voice drew her back to the present, where she stood with Lazaris still gripped in her fist as the sound seemed to snap back into place. Cheers and laughter and light all around her, but inside…

The Devil of the Deadlands snarled.

Soahm's name for her future had stuck. It had fueled her and given her a reason to become stubborn and deadly and *strong.* Her heart beat faster, whispering the promise it had held for years as she glared at her mother's retreating form, remembering the day she and Duran died and came back to life.

Today was a new day.

The ship that stole Soahm had returned to Dohrsar. Its riders would soon arrive at the Garden of the Goddess, and Sonara felt, deep in her shadowed blood, that her answers would also come.

When she found Soahm, she'd ride south with him. Then she'd fight her way through Soreia until Lazaris pierced their mother's heart. She'd carry on, leaving nothing behind but blood and metal and bone, until Soahm was seated on his rightful throne.

***

The life of the Gathering grew with each traveler that arrived. Music whistled across the Garden of the Goddess, laughter and song and stories, and it was that, coupled with time, that allowed Sonara to find the strength to rein herself back in.

A pull on the threads that made her *her,* tiny tug after tug, until she wove herself a steady mask to hide behind. Until she could breathe again.

The merchants from the Carcass Coast arrived, a desolate territory in the northwest Deadlands. After them came the sailors from Crooked Cove, shipmakers whose intricate sailboats floated along the Briyne. Countless others arrived, from every small and large territory in the Deadlands.

Still, Jira did not appear.

Queen Marisk of the White Wastes arrived next, soaring in on her pale wyvern. She, and the riders that flanked her, wore bone-white armor, made from the tusks of great northern sea beasts. It was lightweight but strong, a piece of loot Sonara had always wanted, but never had the chance to take for herself.

People cheered, throwing flowers into the sky as the Queen's wyvern landed with the others from the north.

Jira came last, an army of Diamond Guard at his back.

They rode on identical sand-colored steeds. Everything, from the tips of their ears down to their heavy hooves, was covered in hammered gold armor. The soldiers, carrying spears and swords adorned in diamonds on their pommels.

And Jira himself…

"Oh, goddesses be damned," Sonara said with a huff.

He stood on the back of a golden chariot, pulled by six steeds. The chariot was intricately designed, patterned with hadrus and sand beetles made of rubies and emeralds and more diamonds. His crown, atop his large head, was so bright it cast fractals all across the Gathering as the crowd erupted into murmurs. Others stood in equal parts of terror and awe as the King of the Deadlands rolled through the valley, his monstrous frame practically glowing like a beacon in the sunlight.

All the while, Azariah stood motionless in the thick of the crowd, her hood pulled low, her body pressed close to Thali's.

There was *fear* that filtered from her. But there was also hatred, as the crowd began to drop to a knee; a deep burn that had Sonara stepping away from the princess as her very insides felt set aflame.

"They bow when they should boo," Azariah murmured. "They kneel when they should point their swords at him instead. When we are done here, when we make our mark and we steal from him what the Wanderers uncover…" Her eyes followed her father's retreating chariot as he went to join the queens. "None will ever bow again."

On and on, the territories arrived from all across the continent. From the east, workers from Miner's Hope, on smaller, wingless cousins to the wyvern, scaled skin as red as blood. From the south, weaponmakers from Gutshot Bluff, who were known for their skill in blacksmithing. Years ago, Sonara, Jaxon and Markam had paid a visit there to get her sword fixed after a run-in with looters traveling from Soreia to trade in the north. They weren't as good as the weaponsmaidens from Soreia, but they had done well enough.

With every territory that came, Sonara's curse itched for escape.

She could scarcely focus on anything *but* the effort to hold it in. A place like this, with so many come together… her curse would soar out of control. She may never be able to get it back once it did.

It was Jaxon and Markam's turn to stiffen when a small group of travelers arrived from Wildeweb, their sigil of a tree revealing them. Those who lived in Wildeweb made their homes among the treetops, cautious of the beasts that hunted on the ground. It was the only territory in the Deadlands that had towering plants, a tangled jungle of overgrowth that many of the medicines in the Deadlands were derived from.

Their leader rode on the back of a wagon, hauled by a young wyvern, not yet having grown its full wings. Its jaw was sealed shut with chains.

The steady stream of travelers coming up the mountain pass slowed to a trickle. The valley was filled with hundreds when Sonara first heard the sound:

A buzzing, far away.

Nearing them with every passing second.

"What is that?" Azariah turned and tilted her head. Sonara got a whiff of pure curiosity, *sweet as edible stalks of wheatgrass.*

The taste traveled outwards from her, to everyone now slowly turning towards the western edge of the Bloodhorns, at the other entrance into the pass.

A pillar of dust rose from between the mountains.

"Sonara! Sonara, wait!"

Fear surged through her, and with it, curiosity like a soaring wraith. She turned and ran, Jaxon shouting her name. She wove through the tents, leapt across smoldering coals.

"Sonara!" Jaxon's voice followed close behind. "What's wrong?"

But she faded into the mess of booths, passing by until she came to the closest finger of the fallen goddess. With trembling hands, she gripped the vines, hauling herself up with the others who climbed in hope of getting a better look.

Her palms stung as the prickly blossoms scratched at her skin. But she climbed, ever higher. Up and up, until she saw them coming along the mountain pass.

Adorned in red armor, riding on black two-wheeled machines that roared as if they held the souls of wyverns within…

The Wanderers had arrived.

CHAPTER 12

SIX MONTHS AGO
Beta Earth

Cade

It wasn't hard to play a part.

After thirty-one years, Cade Kingston found it easy to slip into the act of being someone else. He kept those *someones* filed away in his mind. He memorized their mannerisms, the way some of them smiled with half their mouths. Some stuttered in the face of fear, or acted a drunken fool, unable to utter out a single clear word.

Part by part, person by person, he kept them filed neatly away, ready to change himself out at a moment's notice.

It was how he'd managed to claw his way up the ladder of this broken universe. How he'd managed to bite his tongue, grit his teeth, and keep quiet when Jeb was on one of his power surges. Jeb was a man of many threats, and Cade was a man of survival.

For himself.

For his crew.

Above all, for his younger brother Karr.

It was playing parts that allowed them to live their life with the illusion of freedom, because some was better than none. A starship could go anywhere, see anything, and yet it was the art of surviving that kept Cade crawling back to Jeb's doorstep, dropping off the next lot of illegal goods every time.

It was several months ago, sitting in a holo bar on the northern continent of Beta Earth, that Cade finally played the part he'd been dreaming of playing for years.

***

Jeb Montforth lived and breathed smoke, and he'd blown a faceful across the table at Cade, the stinking cloud twirling right through the holo between them.

It was one of a dancing girl, half-naked and whole perfect, though nothing about her was real.

But Jeb liked perfection.

And he was less than thrilled about the *Starfall* getting caught by the ITC.

So *less than thrilled*, in fact, that he'd made the threat that brought out the hidden monster in Cade Kingston.

"We've had plenty of eyes on us in the past," Jeb had said. "You screwed up, Cade. And now thanks to you, we have more eyes than ever before. I have half a mind to march down to the skyrise I've put you up in and tear your precious brother's skin from his face. That would teach you, hmm?"

Oh, that smug smile.

Cade's blood boiled while his mind said: *Play the part. Protect Karr.* And so he'd simply become the smooth criminal the man across the table had made him to be, Cade laughing along with Jeb as if he'd just made a stellar joke.

"You know my little brother does whatever I say, Jeb," Cade answered, "and that means he does whatever *you* wish. Let's not be rash. Punishing him isn't the wise way to punish me. We both know who holds the power here."

Jeb lifted his glass of swirling, glittering purple, and raised a scarred brow. "You're like a son to me, Cade. But family isn't everything. Mistakes have a way of breaking apart even the strongest of bonds."

Cade nodded. "It won't happen again, Jeb. I'll find whoever tipped off the ITC, and deal with them."

Here he was, groveling like a dog, even though his crew hadn't done a thing to give themselves away. Nobody on his crew would have crawled to the ITC for a measly tip-off sum. It was Jeb's fault they'd gotten caught. *Jeb's* fault that they were docked indefinitely. The man had feds eyeing his every move. *Of course* his hired hands were bound to get caught, now and then.

But the bastard couldn't see beyond himself.

Cade focused on the diamond ring glittering on Jeb's finger. It was the size of a river stone. He and Karr and the crew had stolen that ring for Jeb, thinking he'd hock it off on the trade planet Xanthar. Jeb had kept it for himself. Glittering perfection, even though a man like him could have purchased ten of those rings on his own.

Cade thought everything was clear. He'd been given an earful, accepted a threat for his brother's safety… and now?

"Another drink, Jeb?"

Cade raised a hand to signal the barkeep.

But Jeb suddenly lashed out to grab Cade's arm. He pulled him forward with the force of gravity, until they were forehead to forehead. Sweat to smoky breath. The lights that made up the holo girl flashed beneath their chins, so bright Cade's eyes burned. He could smell the alcohol on Jeb's breath, almost taste the fury pulsing out of him.

Jeb Montforth was not a man to be crossed.

"You screw up again, Cade Kingston," Jeb said, squeezing so hard that the corner of his diamond ring broke through Cade's skin, "and it will be the last you ever see of your brother, your ship, and your entire crew. You can't run from me. I own some of the deepest, darkest corners of this galaxy, every*one* and every*thing* in them. I will make you a ghost of yourself."

"Nothing you do can hurt me," Cade said through gritted teeth.

It was those words that had made Jeb smile his crooked demon's smile.

"My dear, foolish boy." Jeb leaned back and pressed a kerchief to his skin. He smiled at Cade, the very same way he once had, when he'd waltzed into the orphanage on a distant, forgotten moon and purchased the Kingston brothers for a mere hundred tokens. He took another sip of his drink and set the glass down. "I'm not going to lay a finger on you, Cade. I'm going to cut your little brother apart, piece by pathetic piece. And I'm going to make you sit there and watch me do it."

His stare held.

And Cade was reminded, with a sudden finality, of the true darkness that brewed within Jeb's heart.

"Pick up the tab, would you?" Jeb patted Cade on the cheek. And then he'd simply gone, whistling as he walked away.

Cade couldn't stop shaking.

He hadn't felt fear like this in ages, not since the day he'd walked into the *Starfall* to find Karr alive beside their dead parents.

And so Cade drank, and he kept on drinking those fears into a deep pit, hopeful that with each sip, they'd stay away longer in the days to come. At some point in the night, he'd been cast out by the bar's owner.

He stumbled down the street, tripping over his own feet, where he ran into a group of looters, and soon after, fell into darkness, covered in his own blood.

***

When he woke, it wasn't in his motel room in the West Sector that he shared with Karr, but instead, a pristine private hospital room. Crisp and clear and bright white, a chandelier over his head and a pretty, red-lipped nurse at his side. One of her eyes was replaced by a digital implant, a red light blinking in the center where a pupil should be.

"Where am I?" Cade asked with a groan. Certainly not anywhere near his apartment. He ran his hands across the silken sheets, blinking back the brightness from the small chandelier.

"Just a moment." The nurse smiled and left the room, sweeping past a silver curtain to where Cade heard a door open and then close.

Footsteps.

The door opened again and the curtain was swept aside as a salt-and-pepper-haired man walked in, wearing a slick silver three-piece suit, a pressed red kerchief in his lapel pocket.

"You drink like a fish," he said. "It's a wonder you survived the night."

"You…" Cade opened and closed his mouth in shock, unable to find the right words. "You're…"

"Friedrich Geisinger," the man said, smiling as best he could through a tight, wrinkle-free face. He held out a large hand. Cade didn't move to shake it. "You have me to thank for saving your life."

"My brother," Cade said instead. He blinked a few times, as if he could force himself to fully wake. "I have to go."

"Not so fast, Mr. Kingston." Geisinger settled into a high-backed chair beside the glass window-wall that overlooked the entire city below. Overhead, the crystal-and-gold chandelier tinkled as the air powered on, cooling the room. "I'd like to have a word with you first. It won't take long."

Cade almost laughed, stricken with confusion and shock and… where in the hell *was* he?

It wasn't the West Sector, with its looters and call girls and slick criminals running the streets like Jeb. Cade looked out the glass wall. The view was golden, and glimmering, buildings towering into the sky around him, and in the distance, a shimmering river with boats rocking on its windy surface.

The City of Stars, just across the new arched bridge that resembled one from Old Earth, centuries past. He could almost make out *his* apartment building, far across the bridge, amid the stacked slums.

"What's going on?" Cade asked. He ripped a needle from his arm, hissing through his teeth at the pain. "What do you want from me? I'll… go to the authorities, if you don't explain."

Geisinger smiled a wolf's smile. "You're a criminal, Mr. Kingston. I wouldn't suggest you do that."

Pure silence, thick and uncomfortable, as the man simply sat and watched Cade fumble for reality.

"If you hurt my brother..."

"Your brother is the least of my concerns," Geisinger said. "I understand he is the greatest of yours, though. I also understand that you are not in the position, judging by the joyful little conversation you shared with Jeb Montforth last night in the West Sector, to truly protect your brother right now. Your ship is locked away in an ITC storage bay, and there is no hope of it ever getting out." He looked at a golden watch on his wrist. A strange, ancient thing. "Right about now, there's a team of men about to uncover a thousand kilos of Stardust in the walls of your ship. You'll be locked away for life, and your brother... well, he's only eighteen, and with twenty being the new age of adulthood on Beta Earth, it means he'll be sent back into the system. And with his record, I can assure you, it won't bode well for him. He'll probably spend a lifetime melting trash on Old Earth. A few days there, and it's likely he'll contract the Reaper's Disease." He sighed. "I believe these are all problems you must solve, Mr. Kingston. And I can help you solve them."

Cade's pulse raced, beeping as some hidden scanner in the room kept track of his vitals.

What in the hell was going on? He crossed his arms, wincing as he saw all the bruises, and glared at the polished monster across from him. "What do you want from me?"

Friedrich leaned further back in his chair, as if he were prepared to take a nap in the sunlight that was now streaming through the wall of glass. A warm chuckle came from him, so out of place in this strange, stark moment. "Confusion is a funny thing, Cade. Shall I call you Cade?"

Cade nodded.

"Very good." He leaned forward, his eyes narrowing as much as his tightened skin would allow. "I'm not one to waste time, because it requires much of me. I'll get straight to the point. You and I have a common enemy, Cade. The Reaper's Disease has plagued Old Earth for centuries. It's since stretched past the borders, carried to other planets across the stars. A silent killer. Your parents, I believe, spent their entire adult lives searching for the cure?"

Cade nodded.

"I've spent a lifetime searching for the cure, as they once did. And I believe, Cade, that I may have finally found it."

Cade's mouth fell open. "You…" He almost laughed… but then he stopped himself. Because here, for the very first time, he saw an opportunity. A glimmer of hope.

"I've recently acquired a dwarf planet on the edge of the galaxy. It's not one commonly known—a newly discovered one, I might add. To most, it's useless. A poisonous atmosphere, and too small to bother wasting precious resources to send colonizers too. But it belongs to me now. And it holds a secret, Cade. A secret I intend to be the first to uncover."

Cade's head spun.

Geisinger Corp was a pharmaceutical kingdom that spread its wings across the stars, and the man before him, who'd put Cade up in this shimmering room and saved his life, despite the fact that Cade still *felt* he was in danger… Friedrich Geisinger was the leader of it all.

"What does any of this have to do with me?" Cade asked.

Geisinger leaned forward. "Geisinger Corp is a burgeoning business. And as soon as your ship is cleared, I plan to send you on a job to retrieve, quite possibly, the greatest substance in the history of medical advancement. The Reaper's Disease will be eradicated. And Old Earth… perhaps she may yet stand a chance of recovery."

The door suddenly opened beyond the silver curtain, and the red-lipped nurse shuffled in.

"Sir? There's someone here to see you." Her tone was perfectly even, her smile and her lush curls so motionless it was like they were sculpted out of clay. The red light in her eye flashed twice.

Geisinger nodded. "I'll be right with you." He turned back to Cade as the nurse scurried away. "If you accept my offer, and agree to my terms in silence, I will reshape your very existence. You and your brother will become men worthy of your last name. You will be as rich as kings."

Kings.

Cade churned the word around in his mind, and with it, Jeb's face appeared, that snarl and sneer, that jagged scar and his words last night, *not* forgotten even with all the alcohol.

To accept this job would be to double-cross Jeb. It would be to put Karr's life in certain danger.

But this was Friedrich Geisinger, seated before him, a man so powerful he made Jeb look like a slug.

Cade leaned his head on his fist and looked casually at Friedrich Geisinger, as if he were only mildly interested. "What exactly do you want me to recover?"

"That's the only stipulation I have, Cade," Friedrich said. He removed a small disc from his pocket, set it on the bedside, and tapped it once.

Light beamed from it, casting a hologram in the air just above.

There was nothing but a single solid line that snaked to life, a black X criss-crossing just beside it.

A contract disc. Cade raised a brow.

"You must agree to the job, and all that it entails, before I show you the manifest." He then called out for the nurse. She scurried back in, seconds later, her eyes wide and waiting. "Call Mav, over at the ITC. Tell her I'm ready to phone in that favor. The *Starfall* will be cleared of all charges, and please, get someone to dispose of those drugs. Dreadful side effects, truly. Dispose of them in Jeb Montforth's skyrise. Make it look convincing." He looked back to Cade. "And see to it that Karr Kingston and the rest of the *Starfall*'s crew are given whatever amount they need, to fill their ship with materials, rations… and alcohol, yes?"

Cade sat frozen in shock and awe.

This man oozed power, lived it and breathed it, and Jeb?

Jeb was a slug. His mind was racing so fast, muddled thoughts shooting through him, that he hadn't noticed the silence. He looked up and saw that both Geisinger and his nurse were watching him.

It was time to make a choice.

"The job," Cade said, finding his wits again. "Will not harm me, my crew, or my brother? And you'll handle Jeb Montforth for me?"

"As long as the job is completed, no harm will befall any of you." Geisinger nodded. "I consider you an investment, Cade. If this goes over well, I'd like to keep you on for quite some time.

We'll dine together on the rooftops of towers. We'll drink the finest wines from the finest planets, and when your brother comes of age, he'll drink with us, too." He smiled, genuine and bright. "Or, with the money you'll make from delivering the substance to me, he can pay someone to age him up. Age him down. He can become whoever and whatever he wishes. He won't have to lift a finger if he doesn't want to. His future will be very, very bright, and you will have been the one to give it to him. You'll be a hero. The privateer who set out to the ends of the Earth, to recover the cure to send the Reaper away for eternity."

It was too good to be true.

Cade had been in Jeb's shadow all his life, and Karr's by default. Would it be so bad, to accept this deal? It didn't matter what the job was, as long as no harm came to his brother or his crew.

This job?

It would be their last.

The choice was bright and clear. "You'll cover all expenses for the mission? And I need a few new crew members, to replace the ones that disappeared after we were docked."

Jeb had likely already tracked them down, killed them as he'd threatened to kill Cade.

Geisinger considered, for a moment. "You're a smart man, Cade. Sign the disc, and what you wish will be yours."

"You can truly cure it?" he asked.

Billions had died because of it. Old Earth was a biohazard now, a quarantined wasteland.

"I can," Geisinger said. "And I will, with your help."

Cade had hated Beta Earth since they'd landed here, wishing, with every minute of every day, that he could be back on his ship, out among the stars. But Karr…

Karr was *happy.* Thriving.

He deserved a future on solid ground. A future without Jeb.

"I'll do it," he said.

He traced his finger across the holo, sealing the deal.

"I'll be back later, with details." Geisinger said, and shook his hand. "In the meantime… rest. You're going to need it. I'll send over my man, later. Rohtt is… a talented Crossman, to say the least. Creative."

Cade smiled, and lay back on the pillows. He realized, before he closed his eyes, that he hadn't had to play a part to secure this deal. He'd been himself, plain and simple.

And he was about to become very, very rich.

***

Now, Cade Kingston shifted in his seat at the table in the center of the Garden of the Goddess. Dohrsar was beautiful, and the Garden around him…

So much more wondrous than Geisinger had prepared him for. This valley, these people, the music and laughter. It was *alive.*

But he'd signed on that dotted line. He'd taken the necessary steps to be ready for this task.

He told himself he was prepared. That fear wasn't already tightening in his chest, beside a pain that had only worsened since the day he'd walked out of Geisinger's hospital. Cade shifted his position again, ever so slightly, but with the S2 suit on, the pressure on his chest heightened.

The suit no longer fit the way it was supposed to.

And so he glanced quickly backwards to distract himself, to where his younger brother stood. Karr's face was practically lit up from inside, his smile so broad that it was clear as day beyond the tinted S2 visor as he watched the Gathering unfold.

Cade couldn't tell him the truth.

He didn't have the heart to.

I'll give you the world, Karr. No matter the cost.

Soon, the attack would begin.

CHAPTER 13

Karr

Karr Kingston did not mind this planet, one bit.

Most jobs, the crew of the *Starfall* had simply come and gone in a flash, leaving enough chaos behind to last a lifetime. The guilt of that past, those planets, weighed heavily on him.

A few of the planets were advanced, with glimmering cities made of glass, and technology the likes of which most non-travelers would never see. On Appona, the *Starfall*'s crew had had to dance with a cave full of naked, shapeless beings as Karr and Cade snuck away and stole from their private gem stores.

On Zeprin, Karr and Cade made the mistake of thinking interplanetary relations were peaceful, as per the last time they'd set foot on the planet, only to arrive years later and be chased away by ironclad warriors shooting red bullets that could obliterate an enemy in one shot.

But here, on Dohrsar?

It was the first planet where they were treated like equals, even sitting alongside the two Dohrsaran queens. They welcomed them with warriors, then directed them through the crowd.

The people parted like a river, split down the center. And together, the crew followed the queens and the monstrous king to the center of the valley; in between the towering rocks wrapped with vines, the flowers shifting before his gaze from dark as black silk to a softly glowing moon blue.

A small table had been placed at the base of the pillars. Warriors in leathers dyed white and blue draped fabric over it, bowing as they backed away.

And on its center, a dark stone tablet. Etchings were carved into the stone, alien markings Karr could not decipher with his own eyes. But his S2 visor translated the inscriptions.

It was a treaty of sorts; the kind meant to bind three kingdoms together. And at the bottom, they'd left room for a fourth.

Karr watched as the two queens spoke with Cade, seated on small stools.

The King, a man who could have picked up Karr and snapped his body in half with his bare hands, stuffed himself with food and drink, only speaking when he commanded one of his soldiers to bring him more. Always, *more.*

"Earth," Cade was saying, his helmet com relaying the message in the lyrical Dohrsaran language. "Our homeland is… a dying place. But we've secured relations with many across the stars. We've found other places to survive until we can fix what's been broken."

The blue-haired queen, beautiful and fierce, inclined her head. "What is death, but a passing from one place to another?" She smiled at him, but the light did not reach her eyes. "On Dohrsar we believe nothing ever truly stays *dead.*"

The other queen was a willowy woman, with skin and hair so

pale she could have been made of snow and ice. She did not smile as she said, "We are pleased to re-sign the treaty, to secure once more our peace with the Wanderers. You are… most welcome here."

She was not aware that her planet, her kingdom, belonged to a man stars away; that her freedom and her rule were all an illusion in the end.

The Dohrsaran king only grunted as he took another bite of animal leg, ripping through skin and vein in a way that made Karr's stomach twist.

He remained standing behind Cade as he was instructed, but his mind strayed, bored by the conversation. He yawned, breathing in the recycled oxygen pumping through his S2.

Cade's smile had been a ghost of itself behind his visor all day. Even now, his gloved hands clenched and unclenched into fists, and though Cade kept a casual, diplomatic conversation with the royals, he was not himself.

Karr wanted to move. To *do* something.

He'd been trained, as he always had done on jobs, to be extra eyes and ears for Cade. But today they had Rohtt for that, who stood a few paces away like a loyal dog, a few of the other gunners beside him.

The other crew members were lounging not far off, on the other side of the rocks.

Nobody was paying attention to him. And Cade said the job wouldn't begin until dusk, after the treaty had been re-signed.

So Karr simply took a step backwards, away from the Dohrsaran royals. Then another step, sliding out of Rohtt's peripherals, until no one could see him. A few more steps had him standing behind the next closest pillar. He followed it upwards with his gaze, where it disappeared beyond the billowing clouds.

Karr sat with his back against the pillar, pressing close to the thick, flowering vines.

He couldn't smell them behind the S2 visor, but he imagined it was luxurious. Beautiful.

And from here, he could truly watch the Dohrsarans without distraction. It was his favorite part of coming to any planet… sitting back, silent and unseen, to watch life unfold in an entirely different way.

The Dohrsarans were all humanoid beings, walking on two legs. Their creatures resembled many that Karr had seen on other planets, enormous war horses in armor, sleek muscular cats double the size of Beta Earth tigers, and fearsome wyverns that screeched and tore apart animal legs from their pen. The clawed tips of their wings shone in the sunlight, sparkling like blades.

The Dohrsarans themselves were a uniquely beautiful blend of people, human in their appearance. It was only subtle differences that set them apart. Some had eyes so dark they had no pupils. There was a glorious mix of all races, as on Beta. Some even had skin that was translucent, as if made of cellophane. Some had wildly bright hair, while others were covered in scales or fur.

The mash-up of kingdoms was unique, with warriors in three different shades of armor, all hefting sleekly designed swords or spears from their respective territories, the steel in natural shades of gold or black or deep cerulean. Karr peered deeper down the sweeping green valley, the lush grass full of tents that held merchants selling plump blue fruits and enormous spiked vegetables. Other groups, on the outskirts, drank black oil from intricately designed clay mugs. They danced and laughed and had the merry look of musicians and artists, dressed in colorful garb and playing instruments strung together with vines or carved from animal horns.

Karr grinned as he watched them, imagining the way he'd sketch their smiles, how he'd douse the background in blue, as if they were all emerging from the sea.

They were a group Karr would have imagined himself drawn towards, in another life. If he had another name. *Another family.*

The Garden of the Goddess and its visitors all wove together to make a wondrous nebula of cultures and styles.

It reminded him, in some ways, of Beta Earth.

But where Beta was shiny and new—a technological masterpiece that felt plucked from the pages of a fantastical storybook—Dohrsar felt strangely like home, despite the fact that it was a faraway land. He would have wanted to find a quiet corner here, sit down with his tablet and sketch for a while, if he were planning on staying.

If what Cade said was true, Geisinger believed this planet, this place, held the key to curing the Reaper's Disease. There were so many planets out there across the galaxy, he'd never be able to visit them all in a thousand lifetimes. And none of them had yet to offer the cure to what had ravaged the—

"You."

Karr turned and found himself face to face with a young woman.

She looked like she'd marched right out of the pages of an old western novel that he'd once borrowed from Jameson. She wore leather shorts, a torn and dirtied tunic, and a long leather duster coat that waved in the wind, stitches piecing together one of the sleeves. A shimmering blue-and-black sword hung at her hip, and her body was covered in wicked scars.

A soldier.

This was a soldier.

She wasn't alone. A tall man followed in her wake, a duster billowing behind him, a wide-brimmed leather hat concealing his features from view. By his posture alone, Karr could tell the Dohrsaran could split him in two if he wished it.

"You," she said again.

The girl's words filtered into his ears, clear as day thanks to his translator chip inside his S2 helmet.

"Me?" Karr asked, and he felt like an idiot the moment the word left his lips. But what was he to say? Her eyes burned with intensity, her voice harsh and demanding.

"Your ship. It's been here before." She placed her hand on the pommel of her sword, curling her scarred fingers around it. Karr had no doubt she could remove it in an instant, dismember him limb from limb.

He cleared his throat, unsure of what to say. "I haven't..." His words trailed off as his brows narrowed. Her stance tensed even further. "We haven't been here before."

He looked into the distance, where Cade was still speaking to the three royals, none the wiser that he'd slipped away. Perhaps it had been a bad idea.

Karr had executed, quite flawlessly, *plenty* of bad ideas before.

"Ten years ago," she said. Her voice was rushed, breathless. As if she'd been waiting on this moment for a long time, or was worried time itself would run out. "You came. And you took something that was not yours to take."

"I'm not the captain," Karr said. "I'm just one of the—"

She held up a hand.

It silenced him at once, that strong, demanding motion.

The young woman reached into her duster, revealing an ancient journal from the deep pockets. A Dohrsaran horse, fierce as it reared up on the front cover. The girl slammed it down on the grass, just before the toes of Karr's heavy S2 boots.

"This is your sigil, is it not?"

She knelt before him, opened the journal, and with practiced finges, flipped to the very first page.

The sketch was faded, drawn in black. But Karr found himself leaning forward as he recognized it. He knew it like he knew his own sketches in his quarters aboard the ship.

It was a phoenix, a mythical bird of ancient lore.

And it was the very same one painted on the bottom of the *Starfall*.

CHAPTER 14

Sonara

"Ten years ago," Sonara said, tapping her fingertip on the worn page as she knelt before the Wanderer. This one was much smaller than the others, a square jaw and plain face barely visible from inside the tinted helmet. She'd seen him step away from the group, then slip quietly away, unnoticed. On instinct, she'd gone after him. "A ship with this insignia came in the night. And yesterday, your ship arrived, bearing the same exact fowl."

Her heart was a war drum pounding against her ribs.

"I saw it with my own eyes. You have been to Dohrsar before, and you did *not* leave empty-handed."

The Wanderer, behind his mask, simply stared at her. As if he hadn't understood her words.

"You're wrong," he said suddenly. She couldn't sense his aura beyond the damned suit, couldn't decipher a truth from a lie, a threat from peace. But she did not miss when his gaze dropped to the sketch again, and narrowed just the slightest before he looked back up at her. "We've never been to Dohrsar. I'd remember if we had. But if you want to talk to my captain—"

His words trailed off as he glanced back towards the table where the queens and Jira sat, still speaking to their leader. None had made a move, *yet*, towards this plan Azariah and Thali spoke of.

But the suns were beginning to dip lower, the sky shifting colors as they did.

Dusk would arrive soon, and Sonara would lose her chance, when the Wanderers moved.

On instinct, she reached out and grabbed the Wanderer's wrist.

The strange armor he wore was cold. Lifeless. Almost skeletal, like a sand beetle.

She dropped it at once.

"You know the truth," she said. Her hand went back towards Lazaris. "You stole him."

Slow down, Sonara, her conscience whispered. But her blood was getting hot.

She scooped up the journal and held it out again, the pages rippling in the wind. "What did you do with Soahm of Soreia?"

"Touch me again, and you'll regret it," the Wanderer said.

Inside, Sonara's curse writhed, trying to escape its cage.

She hadn't meant for it to go this way. But he was smaller than the others, and *alone*, and since they hadn't arrived with their ship as she'd hoped, she'd taken the chance to seek her answers the easy way first.

"Sonara. That's enough." Behind her, Jaxon stood at the edge of the crowd, eyes pleading. "This is not the time."

Oh, but it was. She'd been waiting for it to be so for ten long years. "Back away, Jaxon."

He shook his head. "Please." His eyes flitted towards the Wanderer leader, the queens and the king. Her mother would take notice soon. *Jira* would take notice, and perhaps recognize the very girl who'd bathed his throne room in blood.

Sonara turned back to the lone Wanderer. She had only moments.

"Tell me the truth."

Sonara's grip tightened on Lazaris. She could swing. She could lift her brother's old sword and swing right now, stab that beautifully honed blade against his armor. Perhaps it would work.

But then she would leave without her answers, without Soahm.

So she swallowed the taste of bile in the back of her throat, telling herself that an outlaw was only as good as their self-control.

Revenge wasn't always best served cold.

Sometimes it needed to fester and fever like an old war wound.

"I only want the truth," Sonara said, snapping back the reins on her rage. She tapped the drawing of the flaming bird again. "Is this not the very same symbol on your ship?"

She thought she saw him sigh, as he took a step closer. "It's the exact same bird. Maybe… it's possible that my parents once came… but of course, there's no way that they would have taken some*one*. Some*thing*, always, but some*one*?" He spoke like he was trying to solve a riddle in his own mind.

The others suddenly joined him, five Wanderers in their crimson armor, faces hidden beyond heavily darkened visors.

"Karr!" A woman Wanderer, judging by the voice, but far, far taller, stopped just behind him. "Is there a problem here?" Her hand flinched, as if she wanted to reach out and place it on his shoulder. She lifted it instead, signaling the others to step closer.

The short Wanderer, *Karr*, glanced backwards. "It's fine, Jameson." He lifted his own hand into a fist.

The others stopped.

As if *he* commanded *them.* So strange, for his voice and his face were far younger, his size so much smaller than the group behind him. "We've never taken a soul from any place we visit. Talk to the Captain, if you don't believe me." He pressed a hand to the side of his red helmet. "Cade, there's someone who'd like to speak to you."

A pause.

His hand dropped, and Sonara assumed he was speaking to her again. "I'm sorry. I've nothing to offer you, and the Captain is otherwise engaged."

She was about to speak again, to choose her next question wisely, when a new aura suddenly grabbed her curse's attention.

An ancient and furious presence, gnashing its teeth, like the last warm trickle of sunlight before an endless, frozen winter.

It was the very same one from the journey here, the one that had sent Sonara tumbling to her knees. She wobbled, feeling the world tilt sideways and back again before she steadied herself.

"Sonara?"

Behind her, she felt Jaxon's presence as he stepped from the small crowd that had gathered, but she could not speak.

Her eyes watered from the pure power of the aura. She tried to swallow it away, but before she could, it surged again.

More insistent this time, like it was pushing her to pay attention. For a moment, she felt whisked away from her body, cast into her curse as it pounded its fists against the cage and roared. She could sense her own sword. Not the *blood and metal and bone* but the ancient steel within it. The hands that had once forged it, female and long forgotten and laid in a deep sandy grave.

It was impossible.

The aura flared outwards and away from the pommel, beckoning her towards the Wanderer boy. It landed where his heart pulsed in his chest beneath his red armor, his blood sharp as iron as her curse inhaled without her consent, breathing him in.

It laid out a path for her. A path she felt she was compelled to follow.

From sword to Wanderer heart.

Kill him, her curse whispered.

It sounded, suddenly, like the voice that had spoken to her ten years ago, when she'd been cast into an otherworld of half-darkness, half-light. *Choose*, the voice had said then.

Kill him, it said now.

Terror surged through her. For she tried… Sonara *tried* to push it back, to harness her curse and force it inside of its cage. But she was helpless to its spell.

The hair on her arms stood on end as she felt her own hand responding to the order. She looked down, horrified as she fought back to no avail. That aura and the voice that came with it, so strong her curse would not relent, commanded her very motions.

No, Sonara thought, overcome with panic. *You have no power over me.*

Her grip tightened on Lazaris anyway.

Sweat beaded on her brow, but she could not release the blade.

And then, as if in a dream, she felt her own arm moving, lightning quick. She saw the blur of black and blue sweep past her vision as she lifted Lazaris, and in one swift motion… it slid right through his sleek armor as Sonara stabbed the Wanderer boy in the heart.

CHAPTER 15

Sonara

The Wanderer bleeds red.

It was the only thought that came to Sonara's mind, as she removed her sword in one fluid motion, the blade slicing through a gaping wound in his chest. It had sunk right through his armor, blood and metal and bone.

Someone gasped in shock, before a scream erupted from the tall Wanderer at his side.

Well done, Sonara's curse hissed. She felt it settle back down into its cage, satisfied.

And then Sonara was stumbling backwards, a bloody Lazaris still in her grasp, as Jaxon yanked her away from the chaos and hauled her into the crowd, pulling them away just as another scream rang out from behind them.

"SEIZE THEM!" the Wanderer woman shouted.

Sonara's feet moved of their own accord as Jaxon ran, hauling her along, cursing under his breath as they shoved past fires and campsites and beasts awakening from their slumber as the screams intensified, following closely behind on their backs.

Jaxon stopped, yanking her into the shadows of an empty makeshift booth, wares packed away and locked up for the night. A crate of hand-woven carpets leaned against the booth's edge, and Jaxon pulled her down behind it, yanking Sonara to her knees as she shook, Lazaris still locked in her iron grip.

"What the hell?"

Jaxon shook her, his eyes wide and… afraid. Jaxon was *afraid.*

"What the *hell*, Sonara?"

She couldn't stop shaking. "I don't know, Jax. Goddesses damn me, I don't know what happened!"

She looked down, saw Lazaris in her hand, and dropped it, hands shaking as she tried to wipe away the trickle of the Wanderer boy's blood that had flowed down it.

"My curse… it… controlled me," Sonara tried to explain, but the words failed her, for what could she say, *how* could she make him understand what had just come over her, standing before that Wanderer boy? How could she tell him the strange voice that had made her choose a side in that otherworldly half-place before death, that had been whispering to her all these years since, had finally taken hold of her?

Too many times, her curse had gone awry.

"Stay here," Jaxon said, untying the red bandana from around his neck. He scrubbed at her hands, trying to get the blood away. She gripped the worn fabric like a lifeline. "We're getting out of here. Far away, and then you'll explain."

He stood, creeping around the edge of the booth as shouts rang out, and a group of Soreian and Wasteian warriors ran past, shouting questions at passersby. Some of Jira's Diamond Guard stomped past after, spears in their hands. The queens, the king and the Wanderer leader had to be aware by now.

They had to get out of here before someone discovered her.

"The job," Sonara said. "The Princess."

"Screw the job," Jaxon growled as he crawled back over. "Jira's daughter can do her own damned mission."

He removed his worn hat from his head, placing it over Sonara's hair. "We're going to find Markam. His curse can help us get you out of here unseen. Head down. Hand over mine. I'll lead you."

"But—"

She didn't get to finish her thought before there was a shout.

She peered out of the shadows as a group of Dohrsarans closed in around one of the Wanderer soldiers, shouting curses.

The Wanderer held up his hands, as one of the Dohrsarans shoved him… but then another Wanderer jumped in. Others followed from each side, and soon there was an all-out brawl.

The unease spread like a cloud, stretching its dark fingertips across the valley, snaking its way around Dohrsaran and Wanderer until there was a rift that had not been there before.

Sonara could *feel* the tension, a palpable monster birthed to life as shouts grew and weapons were hoisted, and the peace between the two was shattered.

And suddenly a shot rang out.

Sonara couldn't see if the body that fell was Soreian, Wasteian or a Deadlander… but all kingdoms, all allegiances seemed to have been swept aside as screams tore across the Garden of the Goddess, and the Wanderer leader gave the command to attack.

***

All around her, the Garden of the Goddess melted into chaos. Shots pierced through the screams, screams turned into gurgles of blood, blood stained skin as bullets hit home in Dohrsaran chests. The world became a blur as everyone ran in different directions, the need for escape controlling their actions.

The aura intensified with every retort of a Wanderer weapon, with every thump of footsteps as the people around her scrambled for escape.

There were no kingdoms now.

There was only survival.

"Run!" Jaxon yelled in Sonara's ear.

She laced her fingers through his as they sprinted through the crowd, stumbling over fallen bodies as bullets sprayed. Jaxon stumbled over a crumpled booth, flames licking up the sides of the fabric. Sonara tightened her grip, crying out as she hauled him back to his feet and they ran.

On all sides, tents crumpled or erupted into flames. People cried out, trampled under rushing feet. Sobs of others mixed in, holding their dead, the clang of swords and hiss of Wasteian soldiers loosing arrows against the Wanderers.

In seconds, the peace had been shattered and an all-out war took its place.

And Sonara had done it.

Sonara had been the catalyst.

Another wave of *bitter, cold revenge* swept her curse up.

Movement, everywhere. Dohrsarans running, soldiers from Soreia, the White Wastes and the Deadlands grouping together as the queens themselves dove into the battle. They lifted their blades and spears and faced their sudden enemy. Beasts stormed about, knocking tents over, stamping through fires that blazed and spread high. The vines on one of the goddess' fingertips caught flame, the glowing flowers melting as the fire licked upwards, ever higher. Wanderer soldiers closed in on all sides, shooting her people…

Goddesses, what had she *done*?

Sonara felt like a sword had been stabbed into her temples as she screamed and her curse unleashed itself full force. She gasped as it swarmed every sense, making it impossible to breathe.

"Markam!" Jaxon shouted his brother's name. "Help me with her!"

"Oh, Sunny, what did you do?" Sonara felt Markam's gloved hand grip her other arm.

"Get us out of here!" Jaxon commanded as they helped guide Sonara along.

Her legs felt numb. Her body felt like it was shutting down.

"The exit is blocked," Azariah said, emerging from the smoke with Thali at her side. "There are too many trying to leave at once. It was not supposed to go this way."

Something in the distance exploded, and heat scalded Sonara's face. The ground rumbled as if a bomb had gone off.

Duran's soul-ember flared white hot in Sonara's chest. He was panicking, wherever he was.

"Duran!" she shouted. "Where is he?"

She couldn't see him.

Steeds ran everywhere, the herds let loose from their pen, but he wasn't among them. She remembered his panic, ten years ago when he'd run from the Wanderer ship that stole Soahm… would he leave her now, lost to his own panic again?

Desert cats sprung and attacked, without their riders to control their terror. A flock of wyverns soared into the air, screeching as they left the chaos behind. One fell, its wing ablaze, and tumbled headlong into the mountains, carrying its riders with it.

Metal, Sonara's curse told her.

A great wave of it coming from the north, growing stronger with each second that passed.

"It's coming!" Sonara gasped out. "Jaxon, their ship is coming!"

They kept running.

The grass was ablaze now. Flames licked across the sea of green, leaving smoke and ash in their wake. Then the wind kicked up, fanning the flames higher. Sonara felt her heart slam against her chest, as the ship from her childhood appeared again, the flaming red bird aglow as the engines screamed.

The ship's belly opened wide over their heads. A great black orb shot from its depths, the size of a steed, with wire connecting it to the ship. It tumbled down to the sand, where it landed with a thud that Sonara felt in her bones.

She stared at it, shock slowing down the moment she took in its details.

The giant orb was made up of hundreds of strange metallic beetles, as if they'd all locked together to form a hive. It remained motionless, but she swore she could hear it, *feel* it humming as they ran past.

As if it were alive.

"This way," Thali directed, as an opening emerged through the smoke. "Hurry!"

There was Razor, appearing through the crowd. Three

Wanderers aimed their rifles at her belly, but Razor let loose a war cry, dipped her head left, and blasted them with emerald fire.

The Wanderers melted before her.

Her great tail lashed out like a whip, sweeping aside three other Wanderers closing in nearby. Their bodies soared across the Garden of the Goddess like falling stars.

Markam practically threw Azariah onto her back, Thali right after. "Go!" Jaxon shouted, just as Duran's hooves thundered past. He hoisted her onto Duran's back, then leapt on behind her, his strong arms wrapped around her middle as her fingertips locked into Duran's mane. Then they were galloping away, the beat of Duran's hooves beneath them, the shadow of Razor above. She could see the exit now, the lone road down the mountainside. They were going to make it. They were going to get out of here, *safe*.

The screams rang out, louder and louder.

They were nearly there.

Darkness, Sonara's curse hissed a warning. A shot rang out behind her, a breath later.

A terrible, beast-like cry came from Jaxon, and his fingers slipped from her waist.

It was too late when she realized, with horror, that he was falling.

"NO!" Sonara screamed. She reached for him, kicked her heels and tried to turn Duran around, but he was going too fast, overtaken with fear. He reared beneath her, a screech of terror.

"DAMN YOU!" Sonara screamed at him, demanding him to listen through their bond. "GO BACK FOR JAXON!"

But the chaos was a monster, raising its ugly head, baring its rows of teeth.

Duran only ran faster away from Jaxon. His body was fading, his hand reaching out for her as his edges blurred from the distance, and in her mind, Sonara saw Jaxon turn into Soahm, lying on the sand, screaming, *Wait, Sonara, wait!*

Duran reached the mountain pass just as the orb of beetles came to life.

It exploded outwards, a mighty swarm of darkness. Buzzing filled the air as they soared across the valley. Sonara saw, with horror, one of the bugs collide against a Soreian soldier, latching on to the back of his neck. Blood burst as the metal bug burrowed its legs into the place where spine met skull. All around the Garden of the Goddess, the metal bugs found hosts, and dug their sharp claws into Dohrsaran necks.

When they were done, a crackle sounded from the ship.

Sonara watched as that same blue light from ten years ago shot down from its belly and stretched across the valley like a blanket. It tucked itself close to the ground, nestled up against the sides of the mountains surrounding them, stretched high up towards the ship.

The Dohrsarans running towards it were suddenly thrown backwards, as if the light had become a glowing wall.

A prison, that trapped everyone inside.

TWO HOURS LATER
Geisinger Tower, Beta Earth

The message came at midnight.

The young assistant stopped at the heavy wooden door that led to his boss' private sitting room, pausing for a moment to steady his nerves before he knocked twice.

"A message… sir."

His voice shook in time with his knees. He waited, wondering if he'd already made a mistake. If perhaps, like the last assistant had warned before rushing from the office, the monster had finally come out to play.

No mistakes, boy.

You do what he says at a moment's notice.

You get in, you get out, and you certainly do not ask questions.

"Come in."

The answer was more of an ordered bark, so he opened the door, shuffling inside with the small chip held carefully on a silver tray.

Friedrich Geisinger sat in a wingback chair by the glass wall that overlooked the entire city. A cup of tea sat untouched on the table beside him, surely gone cold now.

Beside it, two small black pills.

His second batch of the day.

"What is it?" Geisinger asked. He sat with his back to the door, staring out the wall as rain pounded on the glass, warping the view of the city beyond.

The assistant walked closer, holding out the transmission chip. "It came in just moments ago, from one of the jobsites."

"I have plenty of them," Geisinger said, voice teetering on the edge of anger and annoyance. "Details, boy. They make every story you'll tell one worth being heard."

"Dohrsar," the assistant blurted out. "It came from one of your camera drones on Dohrsar."

Friedrich plucked the chip from the tray, then slid it effortlessly into a small dock on the arm of the chair. Two taps of his fingertips across the top, and a hologram appeared before them, flickering against the glass.

It was a king, a veritable giant, standing amid a cloud of smoke. Soldiers in crimson suits stood around him, flames flickering in the distance.

"It is done," the king said.

The transmission paused at a tap of Geisinger's fingertips.

"Leave me," he commanded. "I'm not to be disturbed until morning."

The assistant left as quickly as he'd entered. Hours later, he still couldn't erase the image of the alien king from his mind. Couldn't stop seeing the grotesque, hollow socket on his face, where one of his eyes should have been.

PART TWO

METAL

CHAPTER 16

Sonara

Darkness had never bothered Sonara.

In her earliest days in the Deadlands, she'd clung to it, for it was in the darkness that she'd honed her curse. Where she'd sat, for hours on end, pulling at the air around her, trying to decipher aura after aura; where each one came from, be it beast or man, and what they were feeling.

Jaxon and Markam had spent plenty of hours hiding out in the darkness with her, so she could train.

"Left," Sonara would say, *"twenty paces from me,"* and Jaxon's voice came from where he'd been hiding.

"Very good. Now tell me what I'm feeling."

"Proud," Sonara said. "But not of me. Proud of your own damned self, for thinking you're the one who taught me this trick."

His answering chuckle lit up the darkness.

Sonara sighed as she stoked the fire in front of her, suddenly hating her memories of Jaxon. Because, after all these years… he was starting to feel like Soahm. She'd lost them both to the Wanderers, to the *same exact ship*.

The fire crackled merrily across from her now, embers dancing upwards to fade into the shadows of the towering cave. A pair of bright red eyes flashed as a wyvern pup hissed and scurried around to the dark side of the jagged stalactite hanging over the fire.

Sonara sighed as the pup faded from sight. Was the goddess of fate tangled up in all of this? She'd always thought the goddesses to be just stories. Lights in the night sky that cared nothing for the people beneath them, or a series of clever little tales to explain the strange happenings on Dohrsar.

But perhaps she was wrong, for there were too many threads weaving together and tying their knots tight.

And then there was the curse in her veins, a curse that had caused all of this in the first place, combined with some new, unknown power… and the threat was far stronger than she'd ever thought before.

"Damn it," Sonara hissed as she tossed a stick into the fire. The embers danced skyward, causing more wyvern pups to scurry quietly after them, testing their new claws and wings. "Damn Jaxon for getting me out of there. Damn him for falling from Duran's back. And damn my useless curse."

She'd stabbed a Wanderer in the chest at the Gathering, succumbing to some new level of her curse as if she'd been a prisoner of her own. She should have been killed for what she'd done. And yet *she* was the one walking free.

But Jaxon… he was her blood brother, her counterpart, as essential to her as the suns were to the moons. Without him…

"You should not call your gift useless, Devil."

Sonara glanced to her right, where Thali sat leaning up against the cave wall, her Canis mask gaunt in the firelight.

"You're wrong," Sonara growled.

They'd resorted to hiding in the shadows, in a cold, forgotten cave just beside the Garden of the Goddess. It stank of wet earth and rotting bones.

And when she closed her eyes, Sonara could still imagine the sound of the screams from the prisoners in the Garden, and the small campfire Thali had made, crackling merrily, only served to remind her of the attack.

The deep eye sockets of Thali's Canis mask looked hollow as she stared at Sonara from across the flames. "It took over your senses. It had the power to control you. A power that strong, a magic that intense, Devil, is *not* useless. You should learn to wield it like a weapon."

"It couldn't save him," Sonara said softly. "It couldn't save any of us."

Footsteps sounded from the shadows as Azariah and Markam appeared, having returned from the network of tunnels carved out around the cave. There were miles and miles of them throughout the Bloodhorns, snaking all directions into the dark. They'd been carved out by miners that had passed through with shovel and axe in hope of uncovering priceless gold. But now these tunnels were abandoned, picked through as the search for gold had driven further north, towards Deadwood.

Sonara had sent Markam and Azariah out together with a torch and a sword, to seek food, blankets, or anything of real worth to help them survive while they came up with a plan.

And to talk through whatever cold tension hung between them, so palpable it made it impossible to be around the two.

But it seemed they had found only a single mountain rat, the carcass stinking and crawling with white maggots as Markam slammed it down beside the fire.

Azariah looked like she might be sick.

"Well," the princess said, as she glanced away from the carcass, her lips pursed tight. Dirt was smudged across her smooth cheek, and her cloak was stained with smoke and charred holes from the attack. It made her look, for all the world, like a runaway.

A far cry from the princess who'd hired them mere days ago.

"Well, *what*?" Sonara asked.

Azariah put her hands on her hips. "The… the plan? Have you come up with anything yet?"

A plan for *what,* exactly, Sonara wasn't sure. "There's no way in hell we can get through that sort of power."

Markam glanced over at her, eyes narrowed as he took out a small blade and appraised the rat's torso. "Who says we're going to try?"

She gritted her teeth and forced herself to speak, not snarl. "Your brother is trapped out there, Markam. And you'd sooner let him die than risk your own skin to save him."

"Self-preservation, my dear Sunny," Markam said. "You must take care to learn about it."

He drove the blade into the rat's belly.

"Markam has always been good at such things," Azariah said, as she settled beside Thali and tried very hard not to look at the rat blood pooling on the cave floor. "I don't know that he needs any help in saving himself."

Sonara turned. "You."

Azariah blinked back at her.

"*You* did this. You brought us to this damned place, and for what?"

"Leave her," Thali commanded. "The Lady doesn't answer to you."

Sonara chuckled. "The *Lady* can speak if she damn well pleases. She hired us to come here. *She* is going to explain what in the hell just happened at the Gathering, and what we're to do next to get them to *leave* this place. No one told us we'd be waiting for a bloody massacre. Did you know it would come to this?"

"That depends, Devil," Thali said. "Did the princess know that the very person she hired would murder one of the Wanderers, instigating *said* massacre?"

Sonara felt her blood thrumming in her ears. "It wasn't me."

Still, the guilt inside of her raged.

"Wasn't it, though?" Markam asked.

Sonara whirled around.

He held up his hands. "It's a simple observation, Sunny. It was your hand that drove the sword in."

"My *curse*," Sonara said, not for the first time. "It made me do it."

"It is because you are weak," Thali answered. "The Children of Shadow were never meant to be controlled by their great magic."

"There you go again, uttering nonsense." Sonara closed her eyes and forced herself to breathe deeply, to will her pressing need to *destroy* far, far away. She'd already done enough damage. And that blasted word—*magic*—wherever Thali had learned it, kept coming up. It sounded like some ridiculous term from the goddesses. From people who stared up at the stars each night and whispered their prayers to something long dead and dormant.

"It is not nonsense," Azariah answered softly. "Thali has taught me everything I know. My magic has become an asset. A friend."

"Yeah?" Sonara whirled on her. "And where was your *asset* when we needed it during the attack? You could have blasted them all away with your lightning. You could have helped *everyone* get free with the power that lives in your veins, and yet all you did was run."

Azariah did not move an inch. The flames of the fire were reflected in her dark eyes, as if she were a devil herself.

"Why?" Sonara asked. "Why did you do *nothing*?"

Azariah's face remained passive.

They glared at each other from across the fire as Markam sighed and said, "Because she knew the attack would happen."

The words swept across the cave like a secret.

"Markam." Azariah looked at him with eyes burning like embers. "You don't know what you're talking about."

He shook his head and barked out a cold laugh. "I'm a fool for agreeing to help you when you came running to me. I think you knew exactly what would happen here. I think you let it happen because you care more about getting your hands on the Antheon than you care about your own kingdom. Your own people."

"Oh, you're one to talk, *Trickster*," the princess spat. But there was pain in her voice, pain twisting her features. "Do we need to go over what happened in your short stay at Stonegrave? All you cared about was using me to get wealthier. It didn't matter that you stomped over my heart in the process!"

Sonara glanced between the two of them, their auras becoming too much for her to bear.

Not quite hatred.

But it burned close enough.

She turned to Azariah. "Did you or did you not know what it would come to when the Wanderers made a move?"

Azariah's shoulders seemed to sink in. "I… I didn't know the full details."

Sonara felt her hand slide onto Lazaris. "Jaxon is gone because you didn't warn us about what was to come."

Azariah scrambled to her feet, kicking dust on the fire. It flickered for a moment as she held out her hands, her fingers trembling as an aura of *fear* swam towards Sonara, sticky and sharp with the tang of iron, almost like blood. "I swear. I didn't know they would trap them in such a way, that they would do what they did! That… Dohrsarans would die. I only knew that they would come, that they would use force if they had to. But never this."

She looked at her hands as if they were foreign to her.

"They are my people," she whispered.

And suddenly her fear became *sorrow,* the aura's scent like a flower pressed in a book. Present, but no longer alive.

"I tried." She swallowed. "I *tried* to summon it, but I've never felt fear like that. I've never felt…"

"Like a coward," Sonara said.

But her voice lacked the harshness she'd originally spoken with. Because suddenly she was speaking of herself. In her mind, she saw the ghostly memory of Soahm again, and Jaxon beside him, two hands stretching towards her as she ran away. Was there more she could have done?

She already knew the answer. There was *always* more, always another way out, a solution to every problem. But she hadn't solved either one of them.

"A coward," Azariah said, and nodded. "I suppose… that is exactly what I am." She gently sat back down as she seemed to notice the threat in Sonara's voice had faded.

"It's a sob story, ladies, it truly is." Markam leaned back onto his elbows. "But there's nothing we can do to save them. We should be halfway across the Deadlands by now, holed up in a better cave, drinking the day away. We'll simply wait until this little feud with the Wanderers passes. Jira will get his Antheon when the Wanderers uncover it, and then they'll let the prisoners go. The end."

"Always so cold," Sonara said.

"I prefer realistic," Markam corrected her with a shrug.

"It won't pass," Azariah said. "That's… that's why we came in the first place. The Wanderers have only just begun. And once they uncover the Antheon, they'll come back, time and again, to replenish their supplies."

"And the king will allow this?" Sonara asked. "He's trapped in there with the rest of them."

"Not trapped," Azariah said. "They have a deal. He is on their side, waiting for them to find the source."

Somewhere beyond the mouth of their cave, out in the tunnels, a creature cried out in pain. It was distant, the threat far away, as if something bigger and stronger was devouring it, with no hope of being saved.

"They'll use the prisoners to dig up the Antheon," Azariah explained. "It's somewhere near the valley, from what my father's partner can tell. A great source of power, but it remains unseen."

"What partner?" Markam asked.

"His name is Geisinger," Azariah said. "A powerful Wanderer from another world. I've overheard them speaking. He sends messages by the Gazers that soar the skies. The plan is to make the prisoners work until their backs break. They'll take nearly all of it, and my father will receive a cut. And once he gets his hands on it… it will change him."

"How?" Sonara asked. She narrowed her eyes as the princess spoke, searching for any sign of a lie, or more truths to be uncovered. The aura usually came as a scent with another hiding beneath it. Like a cup of wine with a bitter poison mixed in.

"I saw him with it, only once," Azariah said. "I watched from my hiding place as his messenger arrived, with one of the Gazers. The orb has a hollow interior, I suppose, because I saw it open wide, a hidden compartment of sorts, to give my father a bit of the Antheon. I've no idea what trickery the man did to it, for it was originally just a bit of black stone… but he gave it to my father in the form of a small black pill. And when my father swallowed it…"

"What?" Markam said, leaning forward.

Azariah wrapped her arms around herself. "He *changed*. I could have sworn… I could have sworn his eyes turned to shadows, black as the night sky."

"The King will use the Antheon to gain power over all Dohrsar," Thali said. "He lusts for it, just like he lusts for the abilities of the Children of Shadow. It is why he arranged for the Wanderers to strike during the Gathering. So the queens of the north and south would be taken captive, an easy way to remove them from power in one fell swoop."

"No one is coming to save the prisoners, then," Sonara said. "No army to get word, no great leader to journey here to fight for them."

She felt like a hollow pit yawned wide inside of her, threatening to pull her in.

Jaxon will die in there.

You will be alone again, without him, without Soahm.

You are nothing, and no one, just as your mother once said.

Sonara glanced at the dark cave mouth.

She could run, *right now*. She could climb onto Duran's back, where he waited safe and sound outside the tunnels, and be away from here in an instant, a speck of dust carried away by the wind. For one moment, she imagined it. Allowed herself to close her eyes and *see* it. Perhaps that was true freedom, being alone, with no one to tie herself to.

But when she imagined it, all she saw was Jaxon's bloody hands reaching down to help her up, ten years ago, when he'd found her dying on the cracked ground. His smile, as he oversaw her plucking her first purse from a noble's pocket. His encouraging words, as he stood beside her and taught her how to release an arrow from a bow with enough accuracy to hit a fowl mid-flight. She saw herself teaching him how to wield a warrior's sword, using the same steps Soahm had once taught her. She saw him standing before a mirror as she taught him how to dress like a Lady's guard, how to speak like a noble, and how to get a steed to listen when the beast flattened its ears and pranced in disdain.

Sonara looked carefully at the group around her. A princess, a cleric wearing a wolf's skull, and a smooth criminal wearing a Trickster's grin. They weren't much. But they were something.

And she herself was the Devil of the Deadlands. Devils didn't run from fear. They created it. They shaped it into a weapon to use against whoever dared stand in their way.

And there *had* to be a way to break through that light barrier.

There had to be a way to save Jaxon from the monsters on that ship, to get them to leave this place for good. Sonara sighed.

"Then we will save them," she said.

"Oh, stars above... Sonara, I see the look in your eyes, and I don't like it," Markam ran his hands over his face in disdain. "We're a few people. We have no resources, no army, no *chance.*"

"There's always a chance," Sonara growled. "Jaxon is your family. He's... he's *my* family."

She shocked even herself by using the word.

"What good can we do against an army of Wanderers?" he asked. "What good can we do against their weapons?"

That pleading tone, the truth of his words. It made Sonara's insides curl.

"Just help me," Sonara said. "For once, help me, without a deal or a prize on the other side. That's all I'm asking of you. Just help me find a way to free them."

Silence, as Markam stared at her.

It was Thali who finally spoke. "The Great Mother has tied us all to this." Her voice was so strangely out of place, so youthful and bright in the darkness of the moment. "For whatever reason, we are all bound to this place. I will stand with you. I will help you."

"And I," Azariah said, lifting her chin. "I will fight to free my people and stop my father."

Perhaps it had been her plan all along, to get Sonara and Markam here, to see the horror of what lay before them, with the king and the Wanderer's plan. But Sonara didn't care.

"Then we start from the beginning, as we always do," she said.

She turned to look at Markam, who'd been watching the entire moment unfold with what looked like an ever-building sigh.

"Intel first. You're up, Trickster. And if you walk away from this, away from Jaxon…"

"I know, Sunny," he said, and got to his feet, swiping the dust from his pants. He adjusted the hat back on his head, settling it just so. "If I screw this up, you'll make me regret the day I was reborn."

"No," Sonara said, surprising him. She smiled sweetly. "I'll tie you up and hand you to Azariah instead, and I'll enjoy watching as she tears you apart, limb from limb."

***

"Spyglass," Markam said.

Sonara looked to her right, where he was sprawled on his stomach beside her on a rocky overhang of the Bloodhorn Mountains, his face shadowed beneath the wide leather brim of his hat. The suns hovered overhead; high noon.

Sweat dripped down Sonara's temples as she lay there, the heat sweltering beneath the duster spread over her back, the better to help her blend in with the rocks.

Jaxon's hat was on her own head, blocking the sun from her eyes.

She was grateful he'd given it to her at the Gathering, but she also didn't deserve the comfort of it, when he was down there, *trapped*. So close, but untouchable.

"We've been here for hours." Sonara passed Markam her salamander glass. He frowned and wiped her sweat from the copper. "They're just *standing* there, Markam. Why don't they fight? Why don't they do something?"

"This is why we never sent you on recon missions."

Sonara raised a blue brow at him.

"You're too damned tense to lie in waiting all day. Now relax your jaw, before you shatter your teeth."

He lifted the spyglass. The old eyeball, plucked from a beast that lived beneath the ice in the White Wastes, swiveled in its liquid glass casing as Markam shook it, setting the eyeball right before he peered into the glass. He whistled softly. "No breaks or folds." He slowly peered left and right, then up and down. "I don't see a way out of it."

The network of tunnels surrounding their cave had several entrances and exits, *none* of which—much to Sonara's dismay—led into the Wanderer camp as she'd been hoping. She and Markam had settled not far from their cave, where a dark, forgotten mining tunnel spat them out on a small rocky ledge on one of the mountain peaks neighboring the Garden of the Goddess.

The light-wall spread before them, visible even in broad daylight.

Power like this... she'd seen only a glimpse of it, ten years ago, when it had stolen Soahm.

Today, it was tenfold.

A rippling wall of pale blue light—not opaque, for they could see clearly through it—spanned down from the belly of the ship. It seemed held aloft by some invisible power, a constant hum that sent the fowl, that so often flocked to the valley, soaring far from it.

Not a single flock of them had flitted across the blue skies in the hours she and Markam had been here watching.

Not a single beast at all had shown itself. No herds of black mountain goats, not even a damned snake had slithered past them. It seemed all life had been scared away from the Garden; as if nature itself was repelled by it.

Sonara looked back at the ship, and the blue wall of light spanning from its belly. Every so often, fingers of lightning crackled and snaked their way across the wall, like it was swimming with it. *Made* of it. She could sense the power in the air, taste the crackling burn of an endless storm upon her tongue as her curse stretched its fingers through the bars of its cage.

The entire light-wall spanned from the continuously hovering ship to the valley floor, like it had been sealed shut, seamless in its design.

And inside…

Sonara forced herself to look through the shimmering pale sheet of light, her entire body tensing up like a spring. "They've trapped them down there, like steeds in a slaughter pen."

She had no idea what had transpired in the hours since they'd run, seeking shelter in the neighboring mountain caves. But while they'd been watching, the scene inside the Garden had shifted.

No longer were there bodies sprawled across the grass, or the burned remains of what had once been a bustling market day. The rubble of tents and market stalls had been moved aside, the once-emerald, sweeping grass of the valley charred in a wide circle that left the Garden barren at its base.

The river that spanned across its center, stretching down from the fingertips of the goddess, looked dim, filled with ash and muddied by what seemed to be a constant trail of feet stomping through it, or the fat tire marks of the Wanderers' black vehicles that were now parked beside the river.

The Wanderers themselves stood paces apart, in groups of two, holding their rifles as they made a wide circle around the prisoners.

A herd of them, as Sonara had said. All kingdoms were gone. They'd been shoved close together, warriors and artists and merchants, nobles that had come to be seen and peasant revelers that had come simply to witness the Gathering's glory. All of them, now made *one* people, sent to their knees. Jaxon was among them. Alive…

But kneeling, just like all the others.

"Why?" Sonara asked. "Why don't they make a *move*?"

They all had one thing in common, one thing that set their classes and kingdoms aside: the metallic black beetles that had swarmed at the end of the attack. They clung to the backs of the prisoners' necks, their sharp needle-like arms digging into the skin, like ticks sucking the freedom from them.

Little red lights, on the backs of each beetle, glowed like devils' eyes.

"There," Markam said suddenly. "Something's happening."

He passed the spyglass to Sonara.

She swung it around to where Markam was pointing, pressing it to her eye so that she could see him up close.

The Wanderer leader, adorned in his crimson armor, emerged from the back of the largest of their vehicles, a massive metal wagon on six fat tires. And beside him…

King Jira.

They walked side by side, as if they were *equals.* Jira, with his massive frame, his gold tunic tied at his waist by a belt of diamonds. His crown of bones was upon his head, but it could not distract from the gaping socket in his face where his eye should have been. Sonara's lips spread into a devious smile as she beheld it. And remembered, suddenly, that the king was without his sword.

She had no time to question Markam about the whereabouts of Gutrender, forgotten in the chaos, as the Wanderer leader steered Jira towards the group of prisoners. Wanderer soldiers in crimson armor bowed their heads as they passed, stepping aside so that the Wanderer and Jira could stand at the front of the group.

Would it have happened in this way—this brutality, so many dead—if she hadn't given in to the sudden call of her curse and stabbed the Wanderer boy?

Sonara could feel the tension building as they watched Jira traitorously stand beside Dohrsar's enemy. His own *people,* that had journeyed with him here, soldiers and flagbearers and his musical troupe, kneeling with the others.

"Look," Markam said. He nudged Sonara. "Movement, in the crowd."

She swung the spyglass left, where suddenly a group of prisoners sprung to action.

A single, fell swoop of attacks to *escape*, as one kingdom. Soreians and Wasteians and Deadlanders, all together, lunged at their captors.

But the Wanderer leader scarcely reacted. He simply tapped the side of his armor, a button on his wrist. There was a crackle.

A *pop* that sounded like a single bolt of lightning.

The beetles on the backs of the prisoners' necks constricted. Their lights turned green, a flash of uniform brightness across the entire crowd.

The screams that came after shook Sonara to her soul.

The strongest, fiercest warriors of Dohrsar, who'd been to war and swung blades and rode steeds into battle… they all fell to hands and knees, writhing on the valley floor as the bugs on the backs of their necks began to glow a cool blue.

There was Jaxon in the crowd, his hands clawing at the beetle as his eyes bulged and his entire body shook like he'd been struck with lightning.

Sonara's curse slammed against its cage, and she hadn't the strength to hold it back as it blasted through the opening and tried in vain to catch the aura of obliterating pain Sonara knew she would sense coming from Jaxon, if he wasn't so far away.

His eyes… oh, goddesses, his eyes were bloodshot and wide and that was *panic* in them, panic she'd never seen before in all her years of knowing him.

Sonara gasped, ripping the spyglass from her face as she backed away from the ledge, dust scattering around her in a cloud.

"Sonara, get *down*," Markam hissed. "They'll see you!"

But panic had overcome her, because if the Wanderers were doing this to Jaxon, what had they done to Soahm, all those years ago? Her breath hitched in her throat, and Jaxon's panic became her own as…

Markam's arms wrapped around Sonara, pulled her close to his chest. She tried to fight him, shocked and repulsed by the sudden embrace, but when she looked down at where his hands should have been, where she should have seen their bodies pressed close together…

She saw nothing at all.

Only the ledge where they should have been standing.

She felt the coolness of his curse, his power wrapping around them both as he whisked their image right away from the world. If the Wanderers looked up, following a sudden cloud of dust on the mountainside… they would see no one at all.

"Breathe," Markam whispered.

She felt his breath in her ear, but couldn't see his face. Felt his warm cheek, the scratchy stubble and even smelled the leather of his hat, but saw only the blue light-wall and the ship towering in the sky.

He rotated her around, pulling her with him, until they were in the shadows of the cave tunnel again.

"I'm going to release you," Markam said softly. But he held her a moment more, and she did not miss how his own heart hammered against his ribs, how his own voice was changed, as if what he'd seen had shaken him to his bones, too. As if he didn't want to let go, for fear of his own panic overtaking him. "When I do, you'll be visible again. And then we're going to head back to the tunnels, back to Thali and Azariah, and we're going to come up with a plan to destroy the Wanderers. To make them pay for what they've done. Okay, Sunny? Are you with me?"

She nodded against his chest. "I'm with you."

He released her slowly, and that strange coolness faded from her body. Markam materialized before her, looking every bit as disheveled as she imagined she did. They stood like that, just out of reach of each other, staring in silence.

"Well."

They both turned, as a flickering torch appeared, and Azariah and Thali emerged from the tunnel. Azariah lifted a brow and passed the torch to Thali. "We came to check on you, to make sure things were going alright with the intel but… it seems you've been busy doing something else."

Sonara backed away.

"It's not *at all* what it looks like."

Even Markam lifted his hands before him in surrender. "Goddesses, no."

He cleared his throat, and the strange moment of togetherness, of non-hatred between them, melted.

"They've trapped them," Sonara explained. "With a power I have never seen before. Torture that renders them useless should they try to fight back."

Thali stepped past them and peered out the mouth of the tunnel, down at the scene below. Sonara risked a glance. The prisoners were standing now, all in a line. The torture, it seemed, had ended. The Wanderers were passing them tools from their massive vehicle. Black axes and strange sharp-pointed drills.

"We'll go back to the cave," Markam said. "Come up with a way to strike. At nightfall, perhaps, because—"

"Strange," Thali said suddenly. She leaned a bit further out of the tunnel, as if she wasn't sure what she was seeing was true. But she was looking *up*, not down. At the starship hovering in the sky. "I thought you killed the Wanderer, Devil."

"What?" A strange coldness crept across Sonara's skin as she approached the cleric. "I did. I saw him fall to the ground, after I pushed the blade in deep."

"Not so," Thali said softly. "*Look.*"

Sonara took the spyglass from Markam's outstretched hand and pressed it to her eye as she swung it upwards, looking at the small landing dock that jutted from the side of the hovering ship.

A balcony of sorts, where the smaller transport ship was parked. And there beside it, leaning over the railing to peer down at the prisoners below…

The Wanderer she'd stabbed, killed beneath the power of her curse.

Now very much *alive.*

CHAPTER 17

Karr

One moment, Karr Kingston was in agony, lying on his back in a kingdom made of fire and ash.

The next, he stood alone in a throne room, in a palace carved entirely out of ice.

He shivered, his breath forming a dense cloud as he turned in a slow circle. His body was miraculously free of all pain.

The left side of the room was all white, untouched by color or shadow. It was ornately designed, a jagged sort of beauty that reminded him of the mountains. Ice curtains were pulled back from towering, sharply carved cathedral windows. Beyond them stood the ghostly outline of mountaintops far away, the telltale diamond-shape of a flock of wyverns riding the wind between their peaks.

Karr gazed past the curtains, to the walls of the throne room, which were carved with thousands of tiny snowflakes. Each one of them unique in shape and size, but all shimmered with a dusting of frost as his gaze slid past. Rows of towering ice columns lined the throne room, bearing depictions of crystalline beings that could have been goddesses. They had crowns upon their heads, but no faces. Swords in their hands, but no enemies, for Karr realized the base of each column was carved to look like bones; ones each goddess, on each pillar, had slain.

The artistry was impeccable, so meticulously carved that their heavy gowns looked to be flowing in a forgotten wind.

Far overhead, the ceiling came together to the sharp peak of a single twisting spire. All of it, the purest shade of white.

He swung his head to the right, and gasped.

It was still *ice*, he was certain, shimmering and frozen, and slick as glass… but the color had turned black.

A mirror image in shape and design, the same jagged, frozen beauty. But *everything* was made of black ice. If Karr looked close enough, he swore he could see movement beneath the dark ice, like living shadows that slithered past.

He glanced down, in the space where he stood.

Unease crept through his senses as he realized that the space in which he stood was not black or white, but solid grey.

A carpet of grey, a single strip of muted color down the center of the throne room, rolled out to split the space in two. The design on the frozen grey carpet was beautiful, with foreign constellations he did not know broken up by snowflakes. Each one of them woven different from the next.

The carpet rolled all the way to a distant throne, carved to look like an exploding star.

Half of the throne was slick black ice. The other, purest white.

Karr shivered again, his bare feet cold on the grey rug. It was the only space in the room where he could not be touched by darkness or light, unsure of which way to go.

He knew only that he'd fallen into a long and dreamless sleep, and if he wished to wake up…

"Choose."

Karr flinched as the whisper echoed through the throne room. He looked around, but there was no one to be found.

"Choose," the whisper came again. *"Choose a side."*

Karr felt it rumble into his bones, as if the word were sidling up beside his very soul.

Not a suggestion, but rather, a command.

He knelt and reached a fingertip to his right, to touch the dark black ice. It was surprisingly warm and welcoming. Frozen, yes… but like tendrils of sunlight reaching out to soothe a shattered soul.

He turned left, and touched the white ice next.

It was cold and chaotic, a spiraling wind let loose from a raging storm. So bitter cold, it felt like it burned his skin. He flinched away from it.

Back and forth, Karr tested the two sides, wondering about each of them. The dark was sweet, and safe. But the white light was intoxicating, a taste that kept begging him to come back for more. A little tug and pull that whispered like a devil on his shoulder, its bony finger waving for him to draw near.

Karr wanted to obey. He wanted to sink into that white abyss, that pool of sly whispers, and let it swallow him whole.

He took a step.

Then another, his feet sliding on the grey rug, as he stepped away from the light.

It was then and there, Karr standing with one foot halfway into the dark, that the child suddenly appeared on the throne.

Bone-white hair cascaded down her shoulders, shimmering as if the strands were alive. When Karr looked closer, he saw that her hair was made of stars. Hundreds of thousands of them, a galaxy hanging in strands down to her waist. And it wasn't just her hair, Karr realized. Light poured out from the girl's body, arcing and swirling, as if she had a force field surrounding her. Planets ebbed and flowed across her skin. Nebulas danced in her eyes.

A blink, and suddenly she faded from the throne before reappearing on the rug just before him, a smile on her lips.

For a moment, her presence pulled Karr away from the dark.

He took a step back into the grey and faced the girl.

"Who are you?" His voice was missing the shock that, in any normal world, it would have been drenched with. "Where am I?"

Her laugh sounded like a song. "I am the Beginning," she said, and though Karr knew in his heart that he'd never met this girl, he had the strangest sensation that *she* had met *him*, that she knew more about him, perhaps, than even he knew about himself. "And so are you."

Her eyes were ancient and all-seeing. In her gaze, he felt laid bare.

She stepped closer to him. Though her head only reached his chest, when he looked down into her knowing eyes, something inside made him feel as if he were really looking *up*.

"Karr," she said. "The lost soul."

The light around her pulsed and expanded, until his eyes ached just from looking at her. She placed her hand flat on his chest, and for one moment, he saw a vision of blue light; of raging wind; of hot blood sliding towards his bare toes.

"Choose," the girl whispered. "Darkness, or Light?"

She stepped aside and held out her arms.

Tendrils of swirling, cool white snaked towards Karr's hands, while warm, delicate darkness swept around his feet.

"Choose."

It was impossible.

The pale abyss to his right whispered his name, and promised power and pleasure, greatness and glory, while the shadows from his left sung sweetly a single word: *Peace.*

"I can't," Karr said. "I can't choose."

"No," the girl shook her head, her hair shimmering as it danced. "No, I did not think you would be able to decide."

She smiled sadly at him, one last time.

Then she exploded into stars.

They radiated from her eyes, her mouth, her fingertips, swarming around her, in and out and through, until Karr could no longer see her or anything else at all.

Pain, everywhere.

He was burning with her. They were made of fire and flame, and nothing could put them out. Before they turned to ashes, the ice melted, and an ocean yawned wide beneath his feet.

He sank into the sea as a gentle whisper calmed his soul.

Not yet, my heart.

Not yet.

CHAPTER 18

Sonara

Alive.

The Wanderer is alive.

Sonara stomped through the tunnels, following the flickering torchlight as Thali walked ahead to guide them back towards their hidden cave.

"I felt the blade go in," Sonara said, more to herself than anyone else. "I saw him die, right there in front of me."

If Jaxon were here, he would have agreed, for he'd seen the entire thing happen. He'd given her his scarf, so she could wipe the Wanderer's hot blood from her hands. And it had stained her blade. Lazaris hung at her side, cleaned of the evidence by now, but Sonara was no fool.

She knew what it felt like to end a man, to feel the blade sink deep enough to stab through the heart. The Wanderer died, right there in front of everyone at the Gathering, and it was her uncontrollable curse that had caused it.

"Well, he's obviously not dead," Markam said. His voice echoed off the damp, roughly carved tunnel walls. "But that hardly matters now. Our focus is not on him. It's on finding a weakness in their boundaries and exploiting it."

He was right, perhaps. But that didn't ease the tension Sonara felt building in her shoulders. Something was amiss; a feeling she couldn't shake, that had her wrapping her arms around herself as they walked, wishing for the warmth of Duran.

The sooner they solved this problem, the better. Then she'd ride free with Jaxon, away from here. Perhaps she'd try her luck pillaging in the west again, where the endless sands turned to dry, brittle ground and flat-topped mesas. She didn't particularly enjoy the massive, skeletal spiders that walked the Earth there, but it would be best to be *far* from the Garden of the Goddess for a while.

"The Great Mother is at work in all of this," Thali said from up ahead. "She meddles, Devil. And it is clear she has chosen *you* to meddle with the most, if the Wanderer that called to your magic has risen from the dead again." She looked back over her shoulder, the teeth of her Canis mask flashing in the torchlight. "Much like the Children of Shadow. The Great Mother must not be done with him, yet."

"Then you believe me," Sonara said.

Thali's Canis mask bobbed as she nodded. "I believe that you are the catalyst in what is to be a great quest, perhaps to uncover a message that will turn the tide of this world."

Markam chuckled from the shadows. "Ooh, a quest. Will there be a prince waiting for Sonara at the end of it all?"

"You should not mock her, Markam," Azariah said softly. "Thali knows more than most do about the strange happenings on Dohrsar. If Thali believes the Wanderer was dead and has risen again, then I believe it, too."

"Your time with him is not over, Devil," Thali said. "I believe soon, you will face each other again."

Sonara said nothing, for the cleric had spoken plenty of nonsense in their time together, and she feared that if she spoke her thoughts, she wouldn't be able to hold them in for the rest of the night. She wanted silence. Time to think, and plan, so they could move from talking to *action*, and set the prisoners free.

The tunnels stretched on and on for miles, a network pattern in all directions. Old wagon tracks were gouged in the first few miles of tunnels, sprouting left and right where powerful steeds had once been harnessed and used for hauling gold back and forth. Some of the tracks ended in caverns deep enough to house cities, while others ended in caves where night beasts waited to snatch up careless prey.

The Bloodhorns were not a sanctuary for the lost. They were a living and breathing grave, their purple-and-red color an omen for any who entered.

If Jaxon were here, how many bones would he be able to call upon? How many dead would whisper to his curse, begging to find life again?

Sonara's magic hissed, coming awake again. From within its cage, she could just barely sense the reek of death, an aura she felt quite often in her travels. "So what are we to do?" she asked, ignoring the painful pulse in her temples. "How are we to strike against them?"

"We'll watch them around the clock, in shifts," Markam said. "We'll learn their patterns, try to decipher their plans. Then we'll come up with a way to attack."

Sonara stepped over an unfinished track, the wooden cart

abandoned, the side railing of it splintered and broken through, as if a massive beast had taken a bite out of it.

Release me, Sonara's curse whispered. *Let me dance in the dark.*

She hated the feeling of it.

The pressure it put on her skull, the fire it brought to her senses.

But she refused to open that cage again, to let it take control over her the way it had so many times lately.

The torchlight flickered as Thali took a left at a fork in the tunnel, heading back towards their cave. Here, the rounded walls pressed in tighter, the ground unstable. Sonara ducked her head, avoiding a jagged bit of rock protruding from the wall.

Sonara's boot crunched on something hard.

A human skull, eye sockets dark as pits, stared up at her. Hollow and void of life. She hadn't seen that before, on the way out of the tunnels.

"Thali," she said. "I think you took a wrong turn."

"There are no wrong turns," the cleric responded, "only detours, and I believe this one is a shortcut."

Sonara stepped past a ribcage that was now a jungle for glow worms to inch their bodies through. They carried on, as more bones grew in piles. Evidence that perhaps soon, they would face a beast lurking in the darkness.

"Thali."

Sonara's curse hissed and gripped the bars of its cage. She found herself stopping, tilting her chin to sniff the air as if she could sense what was wrong on her own.

The smell had shifted. The air had *changed*, warmer somehow, as if there were a daytime breeze blowing at the back of her neck.

"The smell," Azariah said from the back of the group. "It's *awful.*"

That warm breeze tickled Sonara's skin like a sigh.

Release me, release me, her curse hissed.

It pounded against the cage, setting Sonara's teeth to clenching as her temples pulsed and she tried to keep it in.

"Oh, for the love of..." Sonara turned to see Markam's shadowy outline as he lifted a foot, a thick substance clinging to the bottom of his boot. "Damn the goddesses for all time. These are real leather."

Sonara glanced to the right as something in the darkness shifted.

"Thali, we need to turn around."

The cleric continued to murmur about something as she lifted her torch and held it to the rounded wall, where it looked like something dark had been smeared across it, staining the rock.

"Blood," Sonara whispered.

Her curse hissed again in its cage, and suddenly the pressure of holding it back was too much to bear. The cage *clanged* inside as her curse shook the bars with its shadow claws, trying to tell her something. But goddesses, she was *so tired,* and...

The cage door blasted open.

Her curse soared out like a fowl taking flight, sensing the ripe earth, the natural scents that she knew the rest of the group could smell, but beneath it all...

Hunger.

A sharp aura that had Sonara spinning around, searching for the source of it. Again, she felt that warm, sighing wind, a pattern that felt like a breath being released, after having been held for too long...

Something hot and steaming dripped onto her shoulder, just as Azariah screamed from the back of the group.

Sonara's curse pointed upwards, sensing *dust and rotting flesh. Poison, oozing from pincers that were reaching, reaching…*

Sonara glanced up just in time to see the massive, dripping jaws of a Hadru open wide.

***

Out of the darkness, it came, a carrier of death.

Lazaris sang as Sonara drew the blade. She stopped the Hadru's pincers a moment before they snapped off her head.

The Hadru was enormous, a hideous crimson beast that was covered in scraggly patches of hair, with eight disjointed legs extending from a bulbous abdomen that ended in a long, coiled tail. A poisonous barb was at the end of that tail, able to be lashed like a whip and render its victim motionless in a single strike. A second strike would stop their heart.

The beast hissed and scuttled down the rounded wall, turning on Azariah next.

The Princess did not even utter a scream as it approached her, tail uncoiling slowly. She shook from head to toe, her pupilless eyes wide in shock, as if fear had overcome her fully.

"Run!" Sonara yelled.

The tail struck.

Markam tackled the princess aside a breath before the barbed tail reached her. The rock exploded from the impact instead, left with an oozing drip of acid that reeked of rot, of sulfur and death.

Sonara swung. Lazaris bounded off of the Hadru's armored

side. The beast whirled back around, a blur of red and brown so perfectly camouflaged they would not have seen it without Sonara's warning curse. Its tail uncoiled again and struck out, narrowly missing Sonara as she ducked and dove to the side.

Lazaris scraped against the ground as Markam helped her stand. "The belly is its weakest spot. I'll go for the legs."

She nodded, and they parted. Markam clapped his hands loudly to draw the beast to him before he used his curse and disappeared. Sonara heard his footsteps running down the tunnel, towards where Thali stood motionless behind her torch, unnoticed by the beast. Perhaps it was the Canis mask, or the reek of bones she carried.

But the cleric did not know how to fight. "Stay back," Sonara commanded her.

The cleric nodded silently, backing further away with the torch.

Sonara turned, assessing the situation. The Hadru was focused on Markam, who appeared and disappeared, using his dagger to strike at the disjointed, sinewy bits of flesh that connected each leg to the abdomen.

Azariah was on its other side, back pressed against the rocks, hands pressed to her mouth as if she could hold her terror in.

"Strike it down!" Sonara ordered her. Then she lunged out with Lazaris, aiming between the beast's back legs to swing at its fleshy underbelly. She managed a single slice, earning a screech from the Hadru, but it was not deep enough. She'd have to get closer.

"*Use your power*, Azariah! Now!"

One strike from the girl's lightning would have the beast down.

So why didn't she move?

Sonara danced, avoiding the Hadru's pincers, catching glimpses of Azariah every so often. She had lifted her hands, holding them before her as her entire body shook.

A spark formed, between her palms.

A tendril of lightning formed, but it died out, as soon as Sonara saw it.

"DO SOMETHING!" Markam screamed.

The Princess stared at her hands, her eyes wide. "I… I can't!"

The Hadru turned again, tail rising back in a striking position. Poison dripped from the sharpened tip as it struck another near-death blow.

Sonara's body moved on instinct. Her muscles remembered the steps Soahm had once taught her, sweat in their eyes, hot air rushing from their lungs as they'd rehearsed move after move, step after step, so that she could defend herself. So that she would become a young woman that did not have to fear those who wished to prey on the weak at night.

Markam appeared suddenly again behind the beast, dagger in his hand as he finally dismembered one of its legs. Acidic blood sprayed, eating at Sonara's duster and burning her flesh beneath.

A rabid hunger, zooming towards the left side of a victim's neck.

Sonara's curse warned her just in time. She turned and swung Lazaris in a death arc. Blood sprayed, so dark in the shadows that for a moment it almost looked black as one of the beast's pincers sliced clean off. It hissed and roared, tail jabbing the air.

"AZARIAH!"

"I'm sorry!" the princess whimpered, her voice so soft it was almost lost beneath the roar of the Hadru. "*I can't do it.*"

Sonara's curse beat against its cage.

Release me, release me, let me have at it, let me win.

The pain in her head exploded with each slam of her curse's shadow fists. She couldn't fight two things at once. She slammed her eyes shut, willing the damned curse away. Not now, *not now.*

"Sonara!"

She opened her eyes just as Markam slammed into her, both of them going down. Lazaris flew from her hand as a chunk of the rock exploded. Markam let out a guttural cry as a large piece of the rubble knocked him in the temple.

Blood dripped from his head. His body was suddenly a dead weight upon hers. She fought beneath him, trying to wriggle her way towards Lazaris, but the blasted weapon was out of her reach. Too far, *too damned far* as she stretched.

A click sounded out over them both.

The hair on the back of Sonara's neck rose as she looked past Markam's motionless body. The Hadru loomed in the shadows, rising up on its remaining legs.

Over its head, its tail snaked skyward, aiming like an arrow on a bow.

Sonara shook Markam. But his head lolled to the side. She heaved, trying to shove his body from hers, but he was too damned heavy.

Release me release me release me.

The Hadru was two steps away.

Release me or die, Sonara's curse hissed.

Out of options, she opened the cage.

Out her curse soared, searching for the Hadru's aura. It found it at once, its pain, its fury reverberating from the barbed tail as it readied for a death strike. *Slick as oil, a desperate hunger that swelled and turned foul, a poison that dripped and oozed, a tail that needed to drive deep and kill.*

This was *not* how the Devil of the Deadlands would go out—stuck beneath Markam of Wildeweb, in a stinking, forgotten cave.

Sonara cried out, lifting her hands before her on instinct as the beast struck.

It felt like the world slowed; like everything paused in the space between a single breath.

Sonara *pushed*, as if she could physically shove her curse forward and direct its path. The Hadru's rage… so dark, so desperately starving for blood…

Devour its rage, Sonara's curse whispered. *Take it for yourself and shape it.*

She screamed as she pushed her curse towards the Hadru, where it wrapped around the hideous beast like a leash of its own, devouring its aura. Then she clenched her fists and yanked backwards, pulling her curse's tether and the Hadru's aura with it.

As if she not only sensed it—but removed it from the beast's very soul.

Sonara's entire body shook as she hauled the aura into herself. She was suddenly *desperate* to escape from Markam's weight so she could seek a meal to become hers. It wasn't just hunger, it was *rage*, deep and demanding. As if the Hadru's aura was overtaking her own emotions, overtaking her own need to survive.

Sonara screamed as she fought against that rage, imagining other things; Duran and Jaxon and Soahm, and the future they could all have if she survived. If she fought off the Hadru and the Wanderers and found freedom.

Peace.

Peace like the suns setting over the sea. Peace like the wind dancing through her fingertips as she held out her arms and rode Duran as fast as the wind.

The furious aura melted away on her tongue, fizzled out like a candle, and Sonara swore she saw the Hadru's tail lower… swore she saw it back down from the fight as she sent that peace back towards it. But she hadn't the chance to know for sure, because out of the black, Thali finally appeared.

The cleric set the torch aside as she scooped up Lazaris and, with a sudden finality, shoved the blade deep into the beast's belly.

It let out a rattling sigh.

Then darkness came, as exhaustion pulled Sonara abruptly into sleep.

CHAPTER 19

Karr

It started as a simple tingling in his fingertips, gaining strength as it spread through him. It warmed, like the first kiss of daylight.

Then, without warning, it turned hot. *Blazing hot.*

Karr Kingston screamed, his entire body seizing as if he'd touched a live wire.

He opened his eyes to bright sunlight.

He blinked once, twice. His vision flickered out, then back again, fuzzy at first until he was seeing clearly. Not sunlight, then, but a lightbulb hanging above him. Bright as the heavens—and annoying as hell.

His head pulsed, *beat, beat, beat,* and Karr had the strangest sensation that he'd drunk far too much again. The memories were gone, only a thick haze was in their place. *Definitely* alcohol, Comet Whiskey, if the past was any indication of the destruction he often caused under the stupor of the hellish drink.

Karr lifted a hand to his eyes and groaned. "Can someone shut that damned thing off?"

A crash sounded from his left. A chair, toppling over as Cade leapt from it, his footsteps far too loud as he rushed over to Karr's bedside.

"I thought… Oh, God, Karr, we all thought you were…" He fumbled to form words as Karr's muddy mind tried its best to keep up.

Tears ran down Cade's pale face, and Karr thought, for a moment, that perhaps his older brother had gone insane. Until he blinked a final time and took in the white room in which he lay. The medical bay of the *Starfall*.

"Cade, what's going on?" Karr's voice ached from disuse. He sat up slowly, feeling like his head might topple off of his shoulders. It wasn't just his head. His entire *body* felt like it had been hit by a runaway Rover. Karr reached up, placing a hand over his aching chest. "What the hell happened?"

Cade sniffed and straightened himself again. "It's my fault. I never should have brought you here. I should have left you on the ship with the others, kept you safe from it all." Tears and snot streamed down his face, stealing years from his appearance. He looked, not like the seasoned captain he was, but like a scared child.

That shocked Karr more than anything else, for he had never, not even when their parents were murdered, seen Cade lose his composure like this.

Cade lifted a wet hand and placed it on Karr's cheek. Then he pulled back. With haunted eyes, he said, "You died, Karr. You were… you were *dead*."

"Dead?"

The word hung there between them.

It took Karr a moment to conjure up the memories, twisting

and tugging at the lock on his mind. But finally it broke and the memories tumbled forth.

A blue-haired girl drove a sword into Karr's heart. It sank right through his S2, splitting the armor like a hand parting through cool waters.

There was pain, but not as he'd expected. A cold, creeping feeling washed over him.

Jameson screamed from beside him. Cade ran over, his face warping in horror beneath his visor.

"He's gone, Captain," Rohtt said. "Leave him."

"Do it!" Cade screamed. "Take them all down!"

Shots rang out, and an all-out war began.

"I'm not dead," Karr wanted to scream. But his voice was gone. His body was cold. He'd hovered above himself, fading away as he rose, like he was soaring towards the stars. He saw Rohtt hauling Cade away, shoving him into the safety of their bulletproof transport, Cade howling and stretching for Karr amid the chaos as the Dohrsaran warriors closed in.

His body was left there, lifeless on the valley floor.

But as Karr hovered there above himself, he swore he saw fingers of black that swept up from the ground. They wrapped themselves around his lifeless body like they were alive, swarming into the gaping hole in his chest until they filled it again.

Then he saw nothing at all.

Panic took over. Karr's heart slammed against his ribs, and then he was fumbling for the sheets, tearing them away from his torso. He swung his legs over the side of the bed, tugging at the white medical gown he wore.

Cade was still speaking, apologizing until his words all rushed into one—*I'm-sorry-I'm-so-sorry, my-God-you-were-dead*—but Karr wasn't paying attention.

He yanked the gown over his head, not caring that he sat naked in the stark white room.

He stared down at his chest, searching for the dried blood. The scar. The mark of death upon his skin.

No slash marks on him, no puckered skin where a sharp warrior's sword was driven through, to send his soul into that strange place of darkness and light, where he had the faintest memory of not being completely alone.

"Dead, Cade?" Karr heard himself say. "Then how do you explain this?"

He looked up at his brother, revealing the place where the scar should have been.

But there was only fresh skin.

CHAPTER 20

Sonara

"Fifty Wanderers, not counting Jira's soldiers," Sonara said. "And a hell of a lot more Dohrsarans. One hundred and twelve prisoners, to be exact."

The moment she'd come to after passing out in the tunnels, she'd left a still-unconscious Markam in Thali's care, took the bloody Lazaris from the cleric, and she and Azariah had set out to watch the Wanderers again.

Sonara swung the salamander glass to the left now, following the perimeter of the light-wall. Her head throbbed, and her body was exhausted.

She hadn't experienced that level of power from her curse before. Not in such a way. What had happened at the Gathering was different. This time… she'd almost felt like she'd controlled it.

She'd pulled the hatred right out of the Hadru, in a breath.

Then she'd pushed her own feelings, her own aura, right back towards it. Almost like she gave it *peace.* The energy toll it had taken was great, for Sonara felt like she may vomit up the meager rations she'd eaten on the walk back up here. And she still needed a night of true sleep, a luxury she hadn't received since the Gathering.

The sooner they ended this and got out of the Bloodhorns, the better.

The mountains had offered nothing but trouble, thus far.

"It's like a net," Azariah said softly now. "Keeping everyone inside."

She looked different, in the moonlight… like an outlaw, filthy and bruised and still willing to put up a fight, so different from the polished princess she'd been, when she rode into the desert to help save Sonara from the prison wagons.

This was the first bit of time they'd spent alone together since they'd joined forces.

Sonara had no female friends, and no desire to gain any.

Most men were relatively simple to understand, often wanting glory or gold or a lover. They said exactly what they felt, and Sonara understood them as much as she understood herself.

But women… She saw them all with a face that looked like her mother. All that ever did was push her away.

Sonara sighed as she looked at the light-wall, still finding no way inside. "We need to find a blade that can cut through it."

"Certainly not metal," Azariah said stiffly. "I'm afraid that would blow you backwards. Stop your heart."

"Then we'll send Markam," Sonara said.

The Princess lifted a brow.

Sonara shrugged. "He has no heart."

Azariah's eyes glittered with the hint of a smile. "May I?" She held out her hand, her gloves still intact to hide her scarred skin.

Sonara held the eyeglass out to her, and together, they watched in silence.

The Dohrsarans had begun to move, forming a solid line that stretched towards the rocky side of the Bloodhorns beneath them, the very mountain in which Sonara's hidden cave sat.

Down below, six workers manned the Wanderers' great drill. It rumbled and whined as they powered it up, red light surrounding the sharp point of the drill as they pressed it against the Bloodhorns.

The rock melted little by little as the drill spun, and the Dohrsarans shoved with all their might to keep it pressed close. It was backbreaking work. The kind that would have broken a weaker man or woman, but the Wanderers had chosen the strongest to man the machine in shifts, to swing hammers and axes, cutting through the mountain with brute strength. The warriors, the weaponsmaidens, the steed trainers.

The others followed behind, carting away the rock by hand. Soon, they'd cleared an entryway into the mountains, the entrance of a narrow tunnel that faded from view.

Still, those metallic beetles were attached to the backs of their necks. The lights on them glowed red, but every so often, if someone stepped out of line…

They turned green.

And not *one* prisoner was taken down, screaming and thrashing through the pain of whatever the hellish beetles were doing to them. But *all* of them suffered together, from a single act of defiance.

"There he is," Azariah said softly. "Your companion."

Sonara took the eyeglass from Azariah with a nod of thanks, and there he was again.

Jaxon of Wildeweb.

He looked different without his hat. His eyes, always so bright with life and laughter, were dulled, his long scar stark on his face. He stared straight ahead, just as the others did. Never looking left or right, only focusing on the job at hand. He was injured, his arm wrapped in a bit of dirty cloth. But he marched onwards, carrying load after load of rock.

The Garden of the Goddess had turned dim, too. At night, the flowers that snaked along the fingertips of the goddess usually glowed bright, like stars that had been plucked from the sky and placed in artful spirals around the towering monuments.

But now the moonpetals were gone, having burned to ashes in the attack.

The beasts that had survived the attack, noble steeds and great wyverns that hadn't flown away, were harnessed and used to haul the rubble.

It was something that would have taken months to plan, and a great deal of knowledge about the Dohrsarans, and how their Gatherings worked, to be able to pull it off. But this was an entire operation, set up in a matter of days.

"Your father will pay for this," Sonara said, glancing at Azariah to check for a reaction.

The Princess only nodded. "Good."

Down below, Jaxon took a breath as he dumped another heavy rock into the pile. Then he turned, following the others back towards the gaping mountainside. The silver beetle on the back of his neck reflected the moonlight. His skin was red and swollen where those awful legs dug in deep. Bruises bloomed around it, stretching into his hairline.

Look up, Sonara wished she could tell him. *Look up, and see that we're still here. We're going to set you free.*

The Wanderer soldiers stood around the perimeter, clad in their red armored suits, overseeing the work as it went on into the night.

It had never struck Sonara before, just how different the Wanderers were. What sort of world had they come from, where they could craft weapons that could blow apart a person in a single, earsplitting shot?

Where they could arrive to a kingdom by the sea, and whisk its prince away without anyone trying to stop them.

"It calls to my magic," Azariah said softly.

It was suddenly not so strange to see her lying on the rocks, her face dirty, her hair disheveled. She was a Shadowblood. She had power that made her, in many ways, greater than the father that had once killed her in hope that she'd come back again.

"What do you mean?" Sonara asked.

"I can feel a current in the air. It is always there, much like the wind; something I can feel but not see. I can sense when a storm is brewing on the horizon. How far away that storm is, whether lightning will rain from the skies. How strong each bolt will be. The blue wall feels like a storm. Like someone took the power that runs in my veins and changed it. Stretched it out, to form a sheet that sweeps across the Garden of the Goddess. There are no breaks, no folds. Its energy never seems to run out, either. As if whatever current runs through it is being powered by something endless. If we can find a way to shut that power down… we'll have our way inside."

"Assuming you're correct," Sonara said.

Azariah nodded. "All we can do at this point is assume."

"Your power," Sonara said.

Azariah smiled softly. "Magic," she corrected her. "It is called magic."

"You're afraid of it."

The Princess flinched, but did not disagree. She sighed, looking at her hands as they lay side by side on their stomachs, the rock beneath them cooling with the night. "Freedom is a tricky thing, Devil. I've spent a lifetime dreaming of it. Hoping that someday, it would be mine. And now that it's here… I'm not so sure how to handle it."

"You did just fine when you helped free me from the prison caravan," Sonara said.

Azariah frowned. "Perhaps it is because then, he was far away." She looked down at the valley, where her father's massive frame could be easily picked out of the crowd.

"You're not his anymore," Sonara said. "You never were."

"A statement I know to be true," Azariah answered, as the wind blew, and Sonara's curse winked open a single shadowy eye. *Sadness, like the withering roots of a plant forgotten and left to die beneath the boiling suns.* "And yet, in his presence, I still feel like the chain is around my throat."

"Then you have to kill him," Sonara said. Azariah *did* balk at that. "You have to kill him, as he once killed you," Sonara explained, as she swallowed the sadness away. "But this time, you must ensure that no being—no goddess or planet or great source of power—will be able to bring *him* back."

As she said it, her eyes were focused, not on Jira, but on another figure down in the crowd.

A queen with blue hair who stopped her work and looked south with weary eyes, as if she were searching for a glimpse of the faraway sea.

***

For the next two days, the group took turns watching, and waited for hours on end to learn all they could about the Wanderers and their patterns, and how to disrupt them.

And each night, the Wanderer Sonara had killed came to the loading dock and stood alone, looking down at the Dohrsarans below.

Sonara watched him, taking note. Each day, without fail, he came.

"He stands in the same place, staring out at the horizon, like he's just watching. Waiting," Sonara said.

Beside the small landing dock that jutted from its side, the rest of their skyship was fully enclosed. It was still held aloft by some invisible force, hovering beside the fingertips of the fallen goddess. Their blue light-wall did not falter. It remained intact at all hours of the night and day. The only access to the ship was the landing dock where the Wanderer stood, open to the air.

"My father once had an enemy he couldn't defeat," Azariah said, on the way back from their next stakeout together. She and Sonara were more relaxed, their words flowing a bit easier with each hour they'd had to spend together in the sweltering heat, watching the Wanderers. "He swapped brute force for cleverness. He captured his enemy's son. Tortured him, got the information out of him, and when he was done… he delivered his head in a box."

She said it so matter-of-factly, as no other princess Sonara had ever met would do.

"Then that is what we must do," Sonara said. "We will steal the weakest of them." She pointed behind her, where the Wanderer that was once dead, now alive again, turned back and disappeared into the ship. Like clockwork. "We'll take *him*."

Azariah, to her credit, did not object. "But… how do you propose we do that?"

Overheard, a flock of fowl suddenly flitted past, their presence surprising Sonara. They screeched and turned when they got too close to the light-wall, but they rose with the wind.

Higher.

Soaring *above* it, until they reached the other side.

Sonara smiled as she finally found their way in.

"We'll get to him the only way we can," Sonara said. "From above."

CHAPTER 21

Karr

He should not be alive.

But Karr's heartbeat was as steady as it had ever been, a constant thrum in his chest as he paced on the exterior landing dock of the *Starfall*, his head aching from the effort of trying to discover *how.*

How—after being stabbed through the chest with the warrior's blade—had he survived?

Karr had always thought that one would be able to decipher what happened in the afterlife. That some part of him, hidden beneath the stupor of disbelief in the impossible, would reveal to him what had occurred in the moments he'd stood in that strange otherworld.

But he came up empty every time.

He knew only one thing for certain. It was a place evenly split between darkness and light, and he *hadn't* chosen a side.

Just as he hadn't chosen a side with Cade's plan.

Karr stood on the landing dock of the *Starfall* and leaned against the silver railing, feeling sick as he stared out at the world.

All around him, the peaks of red and purple mountains

stretched into the sky above the valley, jagged and unforgiving. To his left, the strange monumental towers of rock protruded from the valley below.

It had been beautiful when they arrived at the Gathering, only days ago.

Had it been just *days*?

Karr gripped the railing tightly, his palms sweaty beneath his S2 gloves. So much had already changed.

He closed his eyes to right himself, but the call of the wind made him feel uprooted. His damned helmet felt like it was pressing in against him.

The audio transmitter picked up on a strange melodic cry of an alien bird. It echoed across the valley, bounding off the mountains like a mournful song.

Far off in the atmosphere, the planet's rings shone in the night sky; pastels that seemed to dance with life. He'd always loved ringed planets, as if some great artist had painted them across the sky or taken extra time to mold and shape them. Karr knew he should wish to capture the sight of the rings now, sketch their smooth arches and spread the images across the top of his bunk.

But the magic of the scene was broken by the truth.

For each time the wind blew, it carried the sound of a drill driving into the mountainside. It was a constant, ever-present reminder that signified Cade's horrific choice.

He'd started a war, and it was one that Karr wished, desperately, he had no part in.

The wind sighed. It was acrid and hot, and Karr breathed deep inside his S2, feeling the strange absence of pain in his chest where a sword wound should have been.

He felt sick. When he looked down below, inside the electromagnetic walls set up beneath the hovering *Starfall,* he saw the prisoners.

So many Dohrsarans who'd welcomed them to their planet. Who'd been willing to exist, side by side, with armored creatures from another world. And Cade had taken them all captive.

He'd joined with the Dohrsaran king, the monstrous warrior whose one eye glittered darkly as if he were always waiting for a chance to strike. How long had Geisinger been in talks with the king? And how long had Cade held the truth of what he would do when they arrived here?

"Hiding out again, little brother?"

Karr did not turn at the sound of Cade's voice. He simply sank deeper into his stance as he leaned over the railing.

Cade's crew-turned-army, so helpfully run by Rohtt, stood guard around the clock, their weapons ready to fire should the prisoners revolt again. But it didn't matter.

Karr now understood the true meaning of the blueprint he'd seen in Cade's room. He wished he'd dug a bit deeper, had had time to discover the hundreds of mites hiding in the cargo hold.

He'd never seen ones like this before in person; hadn't known the tech was fully completed, though there had been talks of weaponry such as this on the horizon.

Each mite was like a tiny droid soldier, whose mechanical "bite" reacted with the cerebral cortex of the imprisoned host body.

If a host revolted or acted out of turn, it sent a signal to the mites, which sent waves of pain throughout every host, firing against every nerve. He'd seen Cade signal those mites with a button on the wrist of his S2. But Karr knew it wasn't that simple.

There had to be something in control of them all. A power source somewhere on the ship that was continually running. Perhaps it was the ship itself. Karr knew his way around tech, but nothing such as this—nothing that could run both the mites *and* the electromagnetic wall he'd trapped everyone in, used to keep prisoners inside, and to keep enemies *out.*

It was all sickening.

The crew: Jameson and Doerty, Rivers and Stacya and Balu. They were his family, the ones that had stuck around the longest. They'd shared laughter and drinks and meals during what seemed like endless interstellar travels. They'd explored new places together, sang stupid songs and gotten so drunk they couldn't tell their right feet from their left.

But now they'd done what no human should ever do; what no human could ever come back from.

They'd stolen someone's *freedom.*

"Karr, look at me."

Karr flinched. He'd forgotten Cade was there.

Again, a wave of sickness washed over him. He swallowed the bile away, and said, "I thought I told you to go and stick your head further up Geisinger's ass. It's in there so deep, I'm surprised you can see the light of day."

Cade's outline was blurry in his peripherals as he joined his side. He was wearing his captain's S2, the black set him apart from the crimson suits of the crew. He crossed his arms over the railing and stared out across the horizon.

Out.

Never down—at what he'd done.

"Why, Cade?" Karr asked. "Why are you doing this?"

"I've told you a thousand times." Cade's voice was heavy. "The outcome is worth more than the risk. When the job is done, and it *will be done…*"

"What about them?" Karr cut him off.

"They'll be freed. It will all have been for *true* gain, and not simply ours. They're aiding the galaxy in something that will truly change things for the better. The eradication of the Reaper, Karr. Gone for *good.* Earth will be liveable again. A planet ten times this size."

"And the ones that died in the attack?" Karr asked.

Cade faced him fully. His eyes were dark, the shadows beneath them even darker. "How many times must I remind you that *you* were among those dead? They struck first."

"I'm not *dead*!" Karr screamed. His blood pulsed in his ears. His body shook with the need to *do something*, but what could he do? How could he do anything that would undo *this*? "So what if they struck? You defend your own, and then you get the hell away! You don't turn it into this. You don't start a…" His words trailed off as nausea tugged at his insides. "You don't start a bloody *war camp*, Cade."

He turned away and stared out at the Bloodhorns, trying to pick patterns out of the strange swirls of rock. But everything had blurred together.

It didn't make any sense. Cade had always been *good* at his core, despite his unlawful activities… but everything he'd ever done was for their survival. For the good of their family. Hell, when they were younger, he was Karr's hero.

Now he'd changed sides.

"You took a job for a man who doesn't care about anyone but himself," Karr said. "His own gain."

"Geisinger is *good*."

"Money doesn't make a man good. Oftentimes it has the opposite effect."

Cade threw his hands in the air. "Says the looter who's spent his whole life wishing for a mountain full of riches!"

Karr's hands curled into fists. "That's not the same. We work for our money so we can survive."

"And that's exactly why I took this damned job!" Cade growled. "Because I promised you, just as I promised *them*."

In his mind, Karr saw their parents' death plaques, stuck in the wall alongside millions of others. *I'll take care of him*, Cade had said, long ago, when they were mere boys visiting from their orphanage. Before Jeb had come to collect them. *I promise, I'll take care of Karr.*

He always had.

But not like this.

"They would be ashamed of you," Karr spat. He wanted Cade to feel his pain, to feel the truth of what he'd done. "They would be horrified to call you their son."

Cade's face changed at that statement.

"You didn't know them," Cade said through gritted teeth. "Not like I did. Don't pretend as if you ever did."

The space between them yawned wider. Karr knew if he kept going, he might not ever be able to reach Cade again.

"Look at yourself," Karr said softly. "Look at what you've become." His breathing grew heavy behind his visor. "Give me a reason to believe that you're still *you.* Please. Tell me the truth. What does he have on you? What does he have on… on us? Because I've gone over and over it in my mind, Cade, and the only conclusion I can come to is that he's threatened you, or…"

"You're wrong," Cade said. "You're not thinking clearly. You're acting like a child. You can't go through life without taking a risk, Karr, without seizing an opportunity when it comes. You'd know this if you'd ever had to think for yourself, to make decisions, but I've protected you from that burden. *I* make the hard choices, *I* keep us alive, and *you* follow. That is our way."

Karr felt like he'd been slapped across the face.

"How proud Jeb would be of you, Cade," Karr said. "You've turned out just like him."

"Just… listen," Cade pleaded with him.

"How many died in the attack?" Karr asked. "I want you to say it."

Acid filled his stomach as he waited for the answer.

He took a deep breath.

The ground felt like it was too far from his feet, as if he were standing a hundred stories tall. For a moment, it was all he could do not to topple over. He closed his eyes, forced himself to take another breath.

"How many?" Karr asked again.

Cade shifted. "At least… two hundred."

Karr nearly sank to his knees. Dohrsaran *and* human, for Karr couldn't stop seeing the faces of their own crew that had fallen. Higgins, with his tall, broad frame and constant frown. Sampson, with his untamable mane of hair. Lex, who had a family back on her home planet. *So many sisters it's hard to count*, she'd told Karr once.

Now there was no one to send money back home to those sisters.

Now there were three empty bunks and more holes in Karr's heart that he didn't think he'd ever be able to refill.

"Get away from me," Karr said.

Not a shout but a whisper, full of pain.

"Get away from me, and don't come back until you're ready to call off this war and set them *free*."

"I can't," Cade said. He closed his eyes, and behind his visor, Karr saw how shallow his cheeks had become. "I cannot, and will not fail, Karr. This is the only way."

The door to the loading dock slid open with a hiss, and Rohtt marched onto the platform, heavy footfalls mixing in time with the workers' hammers and drills down below.

"Geisinger on the line," Rohtt said with a sneer, looking past Karr as if he were only a part of the horizon.

Cade sighed. "I'll be there in a moment."

"Geisinger doesn't have a moment, Kingston." Rohtt crossed his scarred arms. For the first time, Karr realized that Rohtt had probably been on the wrong side of the Great War. Crossman or not… it was like he had no soul. Karr wondered where those scars had come from, and what victims likely lay in shallow graves on the other side of the story. "There will be time for your little family fits when the job is done."

"*Go*," Karr said. "Run to your new god and worship him."

Cade glared at him. He turned and was almost to the *Starfall* doors when Karr spoke up.

"Is it worth it?" he asked.

"Is it worth what?"

"Your soul," Karr said.

Cade didn't answer.

He only swiped his palm on the scanner beside the door. It slid open, and he disappeared inside the enclosed halls of the *Starfall*, leaving Karr alone. The longer he stood here, the longer he allowed himself to stare out at this planet, the memory of that place returned clearer. The half-darkness, the half-light.

The place where he'd been asked to make a choice before he came back to life.

The whine of the drill started up again.

Loud and shrill, like a painful scream.

Disgust swelled in Karr's chest. It squeezed at the place where his sword wound should have been. He placed a hand to his chest, falling to one knee.

What was there that Karr could do to turn things back around? Rise up against his brother and Rohtt and the crew? Steal a rifle, shoot the Crossman, and then what?

He'd get nowhere.

He'd never been a fighter.

And down below was an army and a monster king.

"Nothing," Karr muttered beneath his breath. "You can do *nothing*."

Because he was a coward. Because he always had been, when it came to truly living. He'd been beneath Jeb's fist, and then beneath Cade's, and when he'd tried to run and start a life for himself… well, that escape pod was never a true plan.

He'd come here and he'd died.

And he didn't know how in the *hell* he'd come back to life.

His heartbeat pounded like a war drum, in time with the workers below as they dug into the mountainside. Each hit, his chest tightened, like he couldn't breathe.

He bent over, leaning against the railing to try to calm himself.

You're fine. Deep breaths, Karr. It's all in your head.

But when he sucked in another breath… his lungs failed him. The oxygen readings on his S2 screen were in the green; he shouldn't be struggling for air. Karr gasped, but again, it felt like nothing entered his lungs. He felt like he was *drowning,* pressed beneath the heavy weight of water.

"Cade." He gasped his brother's name into the com.

Only static answered.

"Cade."

He barely got the word out as he stumbled towards the door, his vision filled with flecks of white. A few more paces, and he'd reach the door. Another thirty seconds, for the airlock to clear and open the door wide.

He wouldn't make it inside.

Karr's legs went out from under him just as he reached the door. He stretched, trying to reach the lock panel.

Breathe! his body commanded him. But he was suffocating, buried alive inside his helmet.

Some part of him still tried to hold on as his body reacted on instinct, reaching for the latches on the back of his helmet. He flipped the latches and yanked the helmet free, then took a gasping breath of Dohrsaran air.

He'd expected pain. He'd expected his lungs to fold inwards

and revolt against the poisonous alien atmosphere, but at least he'd be able to take a single breath, get himself inside the airlock and pay the consequences in the med bay.

Instead…

Karr took another breath. It was dry air, the kind you'd expect from a land made of sand and no sea.

But it was not painful.

If anything, it was *fresh,* a far cry from the air inside the helmet, and certainly the air inside the *Starfall*, which always held a hint of metal to its taste.

Karr turned and hauled himself to his feet as he stared out at the planet. He risked another breath. The wind sighed gently by, tickling his skin. He could feel his heart, a steady beat inside. It was almost calm. *Almost,* if it weren't for the sound of the hammers and the drill below.

Beat, hammer, beat…

Beat.

Beat.

Karr looked skyward. For suddenly the sound was growing louder. And coming closer.

Beat.

…Beat.

…Beat.

He was certain, *certain* there was something above him. He heard it, *felt* it, his hair moving as if caught in a strong breeze. But there was nothing above him save for the sky, the rings of Dohrsar still glittering bright, the monumental red rock towers off to the right.

"You're losing it," he told himself, over the sound of the

wingbeats. Perhaps the air *was* poisonous. Perhaps it had gotten to his brain.

Not a second later… Karr's helmet fell from his hand and landed with a dull thump against the loading dock.

For out of the sky, a monster appeared.

It burst into existence, a wyvern as black as night. Its wingbeats carried it closer, dark scales and sinews undulating as it stroked its mighty wings once, twice, then tucked them close to its body and spiraled down towards the ship.

There were two riders atop its back, outlined in the last dregs of sunlight as the day shifted into cold, unfeeling night.

The first was a man wearing a hat, a leather duster coat rippling behind him as it caught the wind. The second was the very same blue-haired woman who'd driven a sword through his heart.

He stumbled backwards, tripping over his own feet as he tried to get to the airlock. The wyvern landed before him. Its mighty claws screeched against the metal, black jaws oozing as if it couldn't wait to swallow him whole.

"P-please," Karr gasped, holding his hands before him as the young woman dismounted, swift as a river, and strode across the landing dock to stand above him. "*Please.*"

He wanted to scream, but his voice had been stripped from him in the face of fear.

"Oh, look at that," the woman said, raising a blue brow as she frowned down at him. "The beast begs."

Terror washed over Karr, freezing him to the spot as she took the very sword from his nightmares, spun it around…

And with a single hit across his skull, sent him spiraling into the dark.

The last thing he saw was his own blood, pooling across his vision as he fell.

Not crimson.

But dark as night. As if it were made of living shadows that danced away on a hot desert wind.

CHAPTER 22

Sonara

The Wanderer boy bled red like the rest of them.

Sonara had seen it with her own eyes, felt the warm wetness of it melt into the spaces between her fingers as it oozed down Lazaris.

Red—like the bird painted on the belly of his ship. A crimson that spoke of Soahm's mystery.

He *had* bled red. Sonara was certain of it.

But when Lazaris' pommel hit true on that landing dock, and the skin atop the Wanderer boy's scalp split open…

Her curse went wild.

For it wasn't crimson that seeped from his wounds, like the last time she'd drawn it from him. It was *shadows*. Shadows like her own, not pooling from beneath his skin, but soaring. Little ghosts formed out of the darkness, sprouting wings and taking flight.

And then she'd sensed it with her curse: that *something*, the strange zing that came from Shadowbloods alone. Along with something else. Something that had set Sonara's knees to quaking, something that was…

"Impossible," Azariah said now, the very same word Sonara and Markam uttered when they'd loaded the Wanderer's unconscious form onto Razor's back and soared away.

Azariah kept her distance from the Wanderer, her lips set in a frown as she stared down at him. "So he came back, then," she said. "In… in the same way we did. But how?" Her pupilless eyes found Sonara and Markam, who understood that moment of coming back from death to a second life. "He's not from here. He's not Dohrsaran." She frowned. "How is he breathing our air? He's not wearing his helmet."

Thali emerged from the edge of the cave, her Canis mask stark against her dark robes. "Who are we to say that only natural-born Dohrsarans should receive the Great Mother's gift? It is a miracle," Thali said. She knelt and pressed her gauntleted hands to the cave floor as if she were touching a holy relic. "Something I have *never* come across, in all my readings or travels. A Wanderer, come to Dohrsar, and *changed*." Her voice wavered with reverence. "The Great Mother's hands are upon him now. He is forever bound to this place."

"No," Markam shook his head. "Tell your *mother* we don't want him."

"I will do no such thing," Thali hissed. "To do so would be heresy."

"But he's a Wanderer. Whose people shot the hell out of ours."

"And now he is a Child of Shadow, too." Thali stepped closer. Her eyes glittered from deep within the sockets of her mask. "I wonder what magnificent gift swims within his blood, alongside his bones."

Azariah approached the Wanderer slowly, eyes narrowing as if she were waiting for him to spring to life and strike like a snake. With a deep breath, she removed one filthy glove and touched the young man's forehead. Her skin was no longer burned, though deep scars that looked like jagged lightning ran across her wrists, towards her elbows. "He is warm. Feverish."

"Rags and cool water," Thali said, then faded into the darkness at once.

"So he's our pet now?" Markam asked. "We're going to care for him, and feed him and—"

"He's collateral." Azariah looked up with narrowed eyes. "Language I would think you, of all people, would understand."

Markam stiffened. "It was *years ago*, Azariah. How long will you make me pay?"

She lifted her chin. "As long as it takes."

The two froze like that, glaring back and forth at each other; his hand on his dagger, her hand on the Wanderer's forehead.

"Nevertheless," Azariah said, backing down from the fight, "we have to keep him alive until we recover what is rightfully ours. Watch him. I'm going to help Thali gather supplies to care for him."

She stood and glided past him, her shoulder grazing his.

Markam muttered something under his breath, then marched across the cave to his pack, cursing as he shoved his bedroll aside. "Who the hell went through my things?"

Sonara swallowed her shock and focused on Markam. "We have a Wanderer turned Shadowblood, and you're worried about who touched your things?"

Markam shrugged. "Steal a man's wineskin, and you may as well ask to borrow his blade, too, so you can stab him in the heart."

Sonara sighed and knelt before her own things. She flipped open her saddlebag and began searching. Over her shoulder, she added, "Azariah, find something to bind him with."

"The boy is one of us." Thali returned from the shadows, an old pail full to the brim with water and strips of cloth in her gauntleted hands. She set them before the Wanderer, then turned her Canis gaze up at Sonara. "We will do no such thing."

"We *will* tie him up, unless we want to risk losing him when he wakes to find himself in a blasted cave, surrounded by a pack of outlaws, one of which wears a corpse for a face and another being the one who killed him in the first place," Sonara practically growled at the cleric. She didn't have time for Thali's games, her strange belief in magic and miracles. There was only good and bad, darkness and light. Everything else was happenstance. "We needed a prize to ransom. We got it. Bind him."

"A Child of Shadow is not a prize," Thali said. "The Great Mother—"

"Can kiss my outlawing ass for all I care," Sonara said. "Bind him."

She turned back around, not waiting for the others to answer, for she knew Markam would eventually take her order and see it done. At least he knew the way of jobs such as these. Feelings weren't allowed in the mix.

Though, perhaps he'd let that rule slide, judging by whatever had happened between him and the princess in the past.

Sonara continued to dig through her pack, rummaging for that ever-present form of Soahm's journal.

She had to find it, had to make sure that she didn't lose the scent she'd picked up on when…

"Sonara."

She turned, and there was Markam. Holding her journal in his outstretched hands, a look of compliance on his face. "Don't kick me in the balls, please. I do rather like their current form."

Leave it to Markam to make her laugh, despite herself. Sonara chuckled softly, then took the journal from his hands, pressing it to her chest.

When she caught Markam's gaze, that little spark of pride in his eyes, she relaxed her grip and placed the journal into her inner duster pocket. It was all she had left of Soahm.

"Look who's rummaging around others' belongings now," Sonara said, swallowing and turning away as she repacked her bag, shielding her face with her blue curls.

"You dropped it. In the attack. A simple thanks would suffice."

"I'm all out of thanks," Sonara said, glancing past Markam to the Wanderer's unconscious form. He was now tied against one of the spiraling rock pillars, his head slumped forward in sleep. That strange suit still covered the rest of his body, but without his helmet…

He looked like a Dohrsaran wearing a Wanderer's skin.

She hated the very sight of him.

Azariah and Thali cleaned him up, using the cloths to wipe the dried blood from his forehead. They'd wrapped and bound the cut tightly. Thali held her bone-covered hands before her, murmuring softly as if she were praying over him.

A Wanderer, right here in the flesh, turned Shadowblood.

"You haven't spoken much since we saw what he was," Markam said as he sat down beside her.

Sonara sighed, and placed Jaxon's hat back over her head, the scent of him now long gone. A sickening ache twisted in her stomach.

Goddesses, she was so *tired.* There was a weariness in her bones that just wouldn't quit. "I never speak until I have words worth doing so," Sonara said.

"What did you sense when we captured him?" Markam asked.

"I don't know what you're talking about."

He raised a dark brow, and she knew he saw right through her lies. He always had, for how could anyone trick a Trickster? This was Markam's game she was playing, not hers. "We were partners for years, Sonara. Lovers, too."

She wanted to retch at that thought.

He chuckled as if he understood. But then he narrowed his eyes. "I know that look when I see it. It means something dark. Something dangerous."

"It was nothing," she said.

He reached out, lifting the brim of Jaxon's hat with one finger, so he could better look into her eyes. "It wasn't nothing."

Sonara stood, tired of holding it back. She grabbed Markam's sleeve and pulled him closer as she lowered her voice.

"Soahm," she whispered. She pulled the journal from her pocket and flipped open the worn pages. Sketches of Wanderer loot flickered past as she went page after page, flashes of words sketched by hers and Soahm's hands. But it wasn't the drawings she'd needed. It was the *scent,* tangled up in the pages. "The Wanderer's blood," Sonara said, angling her chin at the unconscious boy. "The moment I drew it from his skin, it was like… like I could sense Soahm all over it. Like he was right there with me."

"But you never knew Soahm's aura," Markam said, and for

a moment they were their old selves again, no lies between them, and certainly no lust. Just two new Shadowbloods trying to make sense of their second chance in the world. "You didn't have your magic when you were together in Soreia."

"No, I didn't," Sonara said. "And stop using that word."

"Sorry," Markam glanced over his shoulder, where Thali still tended to the Wanderer like a mother beast. "The she-wolf won't shut up about it."

"She won't shut up about a lot of things." Sonara lifted the journal again, the aura of *charcoal and dust, memories and dreams* filtering into her senses. "But when he bled, I sensed *this*. That same aura, every time I open the pages. It's like..." She breathed deep now, but the scent hadn't lingered this time. It never did for long. "Like he's here with me, talking about doing so much more. Dreaming of being the leader our mother never was; someone kind and gentle and different from the warrior mold Soreia has always known. This journal was Soahm's before it was mine, and I like to think it carries a piece of him with it. Like his soul is inside."

Like the Antheon that can turn a regular man into a Shadowblood, Sonara reminded herself. *That would turn a king into a conqueror, should Jira get his hands on it.*

She was beginning to wonder where the line was, between fact and fancy. Lately, it had been blurring more and more. And now that a Wanderer had been chosen by the planet?

Blast, she couldn't be sure.

"So you're saying... what, exactly?" Markam asked.

His brow was scrunched, the very same way it always was when she asked him questions about math. Or modesty.

The two things Markam was not very well versed in.

"I don't know what I'm saying," Sonara said. Her head ached, heavy with exhaustion. And now she doubted she'd sleep tonight again, though she longed to lay down her head. For this wasn't a part of the plan, a dead Wanderer come back to life to be just like her… and to carry with him Soahm's scent? "Soahm must be in that ship, Markam. He's close. I can sense it all over him. And whatever that Wanderer knows… I'm going to find out."

"By what sort of means?"

She gave him a smile worthy of her outlawing name. "The usual. Maiming. Dismemberment. Whatever is necessary, but you'll need to keep Thali and Azariah busy. They've developed a fondness for their new friend."

Even now, Sonara could taste their *wonder* as they sat off to the side, watching the unconscious Wanderer. Or perhaps *not* a Wanderer any longer? Strange, that his helmet was missing. Stranger still, that he no longer seemed to need it, unless that was the reason for his still-unconscious form.

"I'll be pleased to do so," Markam said. He lifted his hand, and a set of playing cards appeared. "Azariah needs to be brought down a notch or two."

"Keep pushing her, Markam, and you'll lose her forever," Sonara said. "Don't mess it up, when you only just got her back."

She turned, but Markam caught her wrist and spun her gently around.

"Promise me one thing, Sunny," he whispered as their eyes met, and her curse latched onto his aura. For a moment, she allowed herself to breathe it in. To remember the good times they'd shared, when they were only comrades. When she'd learned that he harbored a darkness that she harbored, too. A darkness that Jaxon and his sunshine smile would never quite get.

"I don't make promises anymore," Sonara said.

Markam smiled. "All I ask is that you don't kill him in the process. We don't yet know his curse. He hasn't been a Shadowblood for long. You don't know what he might do in return, once you begin to question him."

"Is that *worry* I hear in your voice, Markam of Wildeweb?"

"Yes," he breathed. He dropped her hand. "But it's not you I'm worried about. It's him."

***

Sonara wasn't sure when she'd fallen asleep.

But she awoke in a sudden panic, sliding Lazaris into her palm with an effortless motion—only to find the fire melted down to mere embers, Markam's rumbling snores filling the cavern. She'd forgotten how soundly he slept.

Sonara sat up, unsurprised to find the Wanderer was still unconscious, his bindings in place, though she could see the rise and fall of his chest. She watched him for a moment, wondering if perhaps he was faking it, waiting for his chance to escape. But his breathing was long and even, as if he truly hadn't yet woken.

She'd already been waiting for what felt like hours, but it was no use, trying to interrogate someone in that state. She'd wait as long as it took.

She yawned, stretching her aching shoulders. As she breathed in, an aura flickered to life in her senses. Her curse was often hardest to harness upon waking.

Curiosity. That ripe zing that begged for her attention. And mixed with it…

The aura she'd sensed before, when the Wanderer ship soared across the skies over the Bloodhorns.

Fear.

Not coming from within Sonara, but *without.* Around her.

Sonara stood, swiping cavern grit from her palms.

Some auras were simple, easy to manage as they skated across her tongue. She could swallow them away like a bit of cool water, forget that they were ever there. Others were more insistent, like an embarassing memory that constantly tried to re-form in her mind. Sonara couldn't quite decide which category this aura fell into now. For on the journey to the Garden of the Goddess, at the Gathering, and facing the Hadru, it had overcome her like a monstrous thing. But tonight… it beckoned.

Like a song she longed to draw nearer to, if only to hear the melody a bit more.

This way, the aura sang. It pulled at the threads of her curse, dragging it deeper into the cave. *This way.*

Sonara wondered if she was making it up herself, or if perhaps the voice was somehow hers.

The aura was like a ripple in the current of the air, far past the rock formations that surrounded this open entry space. Deep, deep, into the shadowed edges of the cavern, and the stars only knew just how far it went.

Foolish, to walk into the darkness alone.

Sonara knew this as well as she knew that the red suns always rose and set.

But she still found her feet turning towards the darkness.

Taking one step, and then another, as the aura beckoned her forth. She scooped Lazaris up, along with a small, still-smoldering stick that she pulled from the fire, the light just enough to cast a tiny glow ahead of her. She was only a few steps into the dark when footsteps sounded just behind her.

"Where are you going?"

Sonara turned to find Azariah awake and rubbing sleep from her eyes.

"Nowhere," Sonara said.

It wasn't a lie, exactly.

"Then I'm going nowhere with you," Azariah said. She crossed her arms as if daring Sonara to defy her.

"Don't fall behind," Sonara said. She turned on her heel, not checking to see if the princess followed.

Onwards, she walked, past the spiraling rocks, further into the outskirts of the cavern. Water trickled past her boots, that tiny little stream, and she realized it was flowing downwards. Following a pattern it had driven into the red mountain rock, likely from years and years of running the same route. In the barest light of her fire, the water across the red rocks looked like fresh-flowing blood.

"My father would be shocked to find me here, crawling through a cave with the night beasties," Azariah said softly. "He didn't let me wander often."

Sonara held the torch a bit closer to her, Azariah's collar scar just visible in the dim light as she glanced back. "Did he keep you locked up?" Perhaps it was pushing, but they'd spent enough time together by now that the awkward walls were beginning to crumble.

Azariah tucked a lock of hair behind her ear, revealing the scar even more.

"I used to wander the castle grounds as a child," she said softly. "Always under watch, of course. But after Markam… my father worried I'd gotten too brave. He said it was foolish for a demon like me to ever hope for *love.*" She spat the word like it was laced with poison. "He chained me up after that. Said I'd never leave his side, for *he* was the one who'd given me life, and if I wished to keep it, I'd never dream of escaping again." She reached up and ran her fingertips across the collar scar. "Three years, he kept it around my throat. And every night, I went to bed dreaming of the day I'd wake up and finally find a way to break free. I didn't have the means to until I met Thali."

"Duck," Sonara said suddenly.

A flock of wyvern pups soared past their heads just after, little black bullets in the darkness that she'd sensed just before they arrived.

"She could teach you how to hone your magic," Azariah said with wonder, as she stood straight again. "It's how I broke free, after I discovered my father's plan with the Wanderers."

"How did you do it?" Sonara asked. "How did you escape him, after all those years?"

Her curse picked up on a gust of *hunger*, spiraling around another rock formation, from the winged creatures that perched upon it. Azariah followed her when she ducked, or sidestepped left or right, her curse showing her a map of sorts, pulling at whatever living or breathing beast it could find to help guide the way.

Right now, it felt normal to use the curse.

Almost gentle, like she was fully in control.

"We started little by little, learning how to light a candle with a single spark, learning how to simply warm my hands without burning anything at all. Eventually I was able to control it enough to melt the chains that bound me. Thali and I had a plan to meet a group of riders in the city that night. We'd nearly made it out of the castle grounds when my father realized I was missing. He sent fifty of his guards after me and… I lost control."

She paused, and Sonara turned to face her, sensing the princess' sudden aura of sadness. It was a muted scent, one that reminded her of the time just before the setting suns, or before a long-awaited goodbye. Azariah's bottom lip quivered as she spoke.

Sonara had always hated emotions, *hated* the way they overcame her. She hadn't cried, hadn't allowed herself to feel them, since the day Soahm was stolen. Since the night her mother forced her and Duran to make the Leaping.

But tonight, she wanted to listen.

She wanted to stand beside the princess in the darkness and hear a story that was just as sad as her own.

Somehow, it made her feel less alone.

"I killed them all," Azariah whispered suddenly, as if she were revealing a secret she'd kept buried for too long. She started walking again, as if she needed the motion to keep herself talking. "We made it to the courtyard. I could see the road into the city, just down the hill. I could see *freedom*, and then they swarmed us, all around. I've never been so afraid, so desperate. I knew he was going to chain me up again, perhaps lock me beneath the castle walls, where I'd never feel the sun on my face. My magic exploded from me. I couldn't hold it back. The courtyard… it became a pile of ashes."

Sonara could see it all in her mind, the same place where she'd been taken captive by Jira's guards not long ago.

Azariah looked down at her hands, gloved once more. "I've been afraid of myself ever since." She blinked, as if she'd surprised herself by speaking her truth.

The torch was slowly beginning to dim, but they'd reached the end of the cave.

The space they stood in was still large, though not quite as wide as the entrance where their companions slept. Here it looked untouched, not rounded walls like in most of the Bloodhorn tunnels, but just the natural, rocky ceiling of a wide cave.

No skulls of the dead.

No bones, waiting to be buried.

Nothing except for the large pile of rubble, the disturbed rock. It was far, far larger than she'd realized, stretching into the darkness left and right.

"Maybe the entrance to another old cave," Sonara said aloud. "The miners often close up the places where too many have died. I came here because..." She wasn't sure why she was telling the princess, but she felt like now there was an opening between them. A comfortable place in which to speak freely. "My curse was calling me here."

"What do you sense?" Azariah asked.

Sonara shook her head, frustrated that the aura had deserted her. "Nothing."

And that struck her, again, as strange.

"Thali says that the planet lives and breathes," Azariah said. She knelt to look at the rubble. The rocks were carved, from the looks of it, by ancient hands. Azariah held one to the light, illuminating symbols that Sonara didn't think she'd seen before, though she felt a little tug of memory. "Maybe it's calling you here to send you a message."

Sonara snorted. "You truly believe the planet lives?"

"Of course I do," Azariah said. She passed the rock to Sonara, who took it in her hands to get a closer look at the markings etched within. Swirling lines, with hash marks driving through them like blades. "I had the same disbelief as you when Thali first came to the castle. Clerics are either deeply relatable, or terribly misunderstood. It seems there is no in-between. But I'm not ashamed of what I believe in now, because Thali taught me the truth. Your magic holds power over you, enough to control you and command you, and you are bowing to it. I once did, too. And once I can forgive myself for killing those men..." She nodded to herself. "I will be able to unleash it once again."

"I cage it," Sonara said. "I set it free when I need it most. Otherwise, the pressure, the pain of it, is far too much to bear."

"I once felt the same way." Azariah gently set down the rock in her hand. "You love your steed, don't you?"

A drastic change of subject, but Sonara nodded. "We have a bond. We came back to life together."

"And now you ride him free. Unbridled, unsaddled. It's rare, for any rider and steed. But a beautiful thing to behold."

"Duran deserves his freedom," Sonara said. "He spent most of his life being caged, too."

The moment she said it, she knew she'd walked headfirst into the princess' clever little trap. Azariah smiled beautifully. "Your magic is the very same. It pains it to be held back. It's a living, breathing thing, just as the planet is. It deserves to fly free. It is your heart and your soul."

"I didn't ask for it," Sonara said.

Azariah lifted her hands and smiled softly. "Neither did I. But we have a gift, and we must keep reminding ourselves of that. To be different is *beautiful*." She smiled again. "Have you ever heard the tale of the first Shadowblood?"

Sonara thought back on the tale. It changed often, like all stories did. But some details remained the same. "It was a girl," Sonara said.

Azariah nodded. "Eona."

An old northern name, common enough in the White Wastes. But Azariah spoke it like a song.

"Eona was the very first Shadowblood. A princess, not much younger than you and I are now, whose father was a nomadic warrior king. Jira's ancestor, no less."

"She rode a northern steed," Sonara said. "One as black as the night."

In the tale, the king set out on a journey from the north, slaying all in his path. But he lost a great battle along the way, so he and his warriors found solace for a time, to rest and recover somewhere in the Deadlands. It was there that her father and his court discovered the heart of the planet, and Eona laid eyes upon it for the very first time.

"There are many written accounts of the First King," Azariah said, "though the original texts seem to have been lost with time as to what truly happened that night while they camped. But the scholars in Stonegrave believe that the First King came upon a great source of power. It pulsed with it… and seemed to beat with the answers to all things."

"Like a heart," Sonara said.

The Princess nodded. "The First King was like anyone who wishes to rule. I believe there is always a kernel of greed within them. A little portion of their souls that begs for *more*, and it is up to them to decide how they will feed that kernel. Will they shower it with good, or will they nourish it with evil, as my father does? The First King had discovered the planet's very heart. And in his nearness to it, he decided to give in to that darker side of himself, for his lust for power was strong, and that lust was heightened by the pulse of the planet's heart. He removed a piece of it himself. He cleaved it from the Great Mother... broke her, if you will."

Sonara sat and pulled her legs to her chest. "What did it look like? The heart."

"Shadow. A mass of shadow, pulsing, moving. *Alive*. The First King discovered he could do great things with that piece of the heart. The tale, of course, is that he used its power to raze every defiant army across Dohrsar, solidifying his title and beginning his long reign."

"And what happened to the piece he removed?"

"Another relic, lost to time," Azariah said with a shrug.

"If it's true that he removed a piece of the heart, how can you claim the planet is still living?" Sonara asked.

"The proof is all around us."

"But no one can live with half a heart."

Azariah lifted a brow. "And no one can come back from the dead, or walk the Earth with shadows for blood." She carried on, satisfied with having silenced Sonara. "After the First King learned of the power that small piece of the heart gave him, he wanted more. He returned with a full army to remove the rest of it. And it was that night, while everyone slept, that Eona first heard the planet's whisper."

Sonara hadn't heard that part of the story before.

"Eona crept closer, certain that the whisper came from the heart itself. *Save me,* it said. Eona could feel its terror, as if the planet were anticipating what was to come when morning arrived. She was clever. Too clever, as many princesses are." She winked at Sonara with a casual smile. "She managed to steal the king's mighty sword while he slept."

"Gutrender," Sonara said. "At least, the story says that the sword once belonged to him."

The sword that started this whole mess in the first place.

"The next morning, when the First King awoke, he found Eona standing over the heart of the planet, the golden sword in hand."

"To save the heart?" Sonara asked. "To fight off her father and protect the planet, like the good little heroine she was?"

She hated stories like these.

Why was the princess always so perfectly pliant? Why did the princess never answer the call of the shadows, never bathe herself in blood or sidle up next to the sweet simmer of sin?

You do, Sonara told herself, but it sounded like Soahm's voice. *You are the Devil of the Deadlands, the heroine from Soahm's story come to life.*

Sonara was surprised when Azariah frowned. "It's quite the opposite. Thali says that Eona's true greed appeared as she listened to the whisper of the planet. As she stood over the heart, staring into its inky depths, she tasted the power she could have. With it, she could surpass her father's strength, and become something far greater than he. She used his sword and slew his army in a great bloody battle. She nearly delivered the death blow to the First King… until someone stopped her."

"Who?" Sonara asked.

There was no *someone* in the other versions of the tale.

"Her brother," Thali said. "Her twin brother, Eder. She did not expect him to stand in her way, so perhaps it was the element of surprise that helped him to take Eona's life. Alas, that part of the story does not remain in the holy texts. But it was his goodness, his purity, that stopped her from stealing the planet's heart. He saved Dohrsar."

"But then Eona became a Shadowblood?" Sonara asked. "Why her and not Eder?"

"As she lay dying, the planet brought her back. You know how it goes. Tendrils of shadow, sprouting from the ground to fill your body and give you a second life. Have you never considered what those shadows are?"

Of course Sonara had.

She and Jaxon and Markam had talked about it over countless hours, musing about what they now were. But there was never a true answer.

"The shadows are pieces of the planet's soul," Azariah said. "The planet lends us some of her soul, and gives us magic with it. The power to command the aether. The power to call upon the bones of the dead. The power to sense the emotions of others." Her eyes lit up as she looked at Sonara. "You're an extension of the Great Mother, Dohrsar. A Child of Shadow."

"But why bring Eona back, and not her brother?" Sonara asked. "She tried to kill the planet. He's the one that saved it."

"We could not possibly begin to understand the Great Mother's choices, just like our Wanderer that lies in waiting for us, back at camp."

Sonara shook her head. "But why bring *any* of us back? What makes us chosen?"

Azariah shrugged. "Does anyone truly know? You must remember your time in that fold between life and death. The planet decides."

Sonara nodded. "Darkness. Light. A realm that held none other, save for… a voice."

"A whisper," the princess said. "Another detail that every Shadowblood remembers. Thali says it is the planet, speaking to us. You may not want to believe the truth, may not wish to worship the Great Mother… but you can at least acknowledge the fact that she lives. That she exists."

Sonara's breathing stilled.

Azariah's words, strangely, made sense. For if the planet really had given her some of its soul, then that would mean her curse *was* alive. That it could possibly find a way to slip out of her control, to remove the leash she'd kept it tethered to all these years. That it could possibly even grow strong enough to command *her.*

There was both comfort and unease in considering that. Perhaps that was the answer to why her curse had exploded at the Gathering. But if that was true, then why did the *planet* command her to kill a Wanderer… someone who wasn't even from here?

"What happened to Eona after she became a Shadowblood?" Sonara asked suddenly.

"There are many stories about her. Many accounts that she walked the planet, using her magic to seek others like her. Powerful

Shadowbloods… some of which she created herself, by slaying those who had unique giftings in their first lives. Who knows how many of them were blessed enough to be chosen and come back a second time?"

Sonara shivered at that. The torch was nearly gone now, the flames having eaten it whole. Soon it would burn to embers.

"What happens if we find the heart?" Sonara asked.

Azariah stood and picked up the dwindling torch. "I suspect that you came here because, perhaps, like Eona… you're hearing the planet's call. It sings to your magic, beckoning it to grow stronger, and answer." She pressed her hand to Sonara's arm, gently. "You must be careful, Sonara, which path you choose to take."

CHAPTER 23

Karr

Karr dared not move.

The intruder was still there on the bridge, kneeling over his parents' bodies while his knife dripped with their blood.

Plink.

A droplet upon the grated floor of the Starfall.

Plink.

A droplet on the silver pistol that his father had not been able to fire in time, now discarded beside his dead body.

"Hurry up," a voice hissed.

A new pair of boots entered the bridge. Pretty, polished things, a triangular symbol stamped into the leather on the side of the heel. "Find the keycard and let's move."

Karr sank further into the shadowed space beneath his father's pilot chair; further away from the pool of blood, and his mother's outstretched hand.

Her eyes were still. Unblinking, as she lay on the grated floor, her lips parted, her gaze distant. She had always watched Karr closely, with a look that only a mother could give. One that was full of equal parts lesson and love…

But now she looked past him. Through him. As if she no longer saw him at all.

"Not here," the voice said.

"Then check the husband."

The first pair of boots, unpolished and worn, turned. "I already did."

"Well, it's not here."

"It has to be."

"Then find the damned thing!"

Karr began to shake.

The men were growing angrier. He could sense it in their tones, the urgency of their harshly muttered words as they searched the bridge, throwing journals from their casings beside the dash, opening his father's lunch crate, tossing aside his mother's hand-knit blanket she kept slung over the back of her chair for long trips through hyperspace. A framed photo, normally magnetically held to the dash, was thrown to the floor. It shattered, the glass splitting across the faces of the Kingston family.

The boots stopped moving.

A pair of gloved hands scooped up the broken frame. "Oh, hell. Kids, man. There's kids."

"Not on board, I didn't see—"

Karr hadn't meant to cry. He hadn't meant to let out that awful, revealing little squeak. But Cade wasn't here. Cade was running errands in the small market just beyond the ship docks, and Karr…

Karr was utterly alone.

The two pairs of boots turned towards the dash, facing the space where he hid just below them, in the shadows.

He saw knees appear. Then the shadowed face of a man, as he knelt. "Hello, little one." His teeth were jagged and golden, sharp as a shark's as he smiled. "You can call me Jeb."

***

It was dark when Karr woke, gasping himself back into the land of the living.

He cataloged several things at once:

There were ropes around his chest, binding him, *a prisoner.*

The cave he sat in was dark, but not so fully that he couldn't make out its vastness, broken by the distant light of what must be a crackling fire, for he could smell the telltale scent of wood smoke. He tried to glance left and right, but his skull hissed in pain, and the throbbing worsened… which Karr promptly remembered came from the very same young woman who'd stabbed him in the chest, days before.

Think, Karr.

He looked around as far as his bindings would allow him. The rock itself was red. Not a muted brown or grey, like most planets. But a deep, bloody crimson shot through with veins of deepest purple, as if the rock had been prepared by an artist's hand: the same rock that made up the Bloodhorns that surrounded the valley.

If any luck was on his side at all, he might not be too far from where the *Starfall* was docked. Had the crew seen him get taken? Had anyone noticed he was gone? By now, they had to have seen his helmet, left behind.

He was still breathing. Still *alive,* without it.

But *how*?

Panic began to set in, for with each breath he took, more of the Dohrsaran air entered his human lungs.

How long did he have, until the poisonous atmosphere got to him? And if he ever got back to the safety of the *Starfall,* would there be long-term effects?

He took another shuddering breath. There was no telling how long he'd been out for. Surely by now, Cade was searching for him. Until then, Karr simply had to get himself to stay calm.

Nothing good was ever accomplished under the guise of panic.

All around him, twisting spirals of rock jutted into the black abyss above. Creatures huddled in the corners of the cave, some of them only visible by their dimly glowing green eyes, the slits of them flashing as they blinked, then reappeared again.

Somewhere behind him, he thought he heard hissing. Perhaps a snake, which gave Karr one more reason to panic.

Relax, he told himself. *Settle your mind.*

He'd been in plenty of sticky situations before, but never one quite like this. At least not without Cade or another member of the *Starfall*'s crew. Jameson was always his closest comrade. If she were here, she would have made a joke. Something to calm him first, before she got them both to thinking.

Footsteps sounded ahead.

Karr looked down at his bonds, wriggling side to side as he tested the strength of the thick rope. But he could scarcely *breathe,* let alone move to get free. His hands were numb from the mere tightness of it.

Think, he told himself again. *Just think!*

His brain had always been his greatest asset. But the voice in his head sounded like Cade's, and when he thought of Cade… he thought of what his brother had recently become.

The footsteps grew louder, and soon they were joined by the flickering orange glow of a torch coming around a thick, spiraling red stalactite. And the person holding it must be…

The woman from his nightmares.

There she stood with her blue-and-brown hair, and an old worn leather hat perched atop her head, the wide brim dipping her features in shadow. Her shorts were tattered and torn, but her ankle-length duster looked sturdy enough. Leather boots came halfway up to her knees. She walked with the confident swagger of someone who did not need protecting, and as she came close, jamming her torch into a small hole in the ground, the light kissed the weapon attached to her leather belt.

Black-and-blue steel that Karr knew well. Suddenly his chest ached again as he beheld the sword. As if his body remembered the feeling of the blade eating its way through his skin.

"You stabbed me," Karr said.

He paused.

His voice… he hadn't uttered the words in English, but rather in *her* language. He'd spoken Dohrsaran as clear as day, as if he were fluent, and had been all along. But that was impossible.

She tilted her chin, removing the shadows from beneath the wide brim of her hat. Her eyes were a muddy brown, matching the strange dark streaks in her blue hair. Those eyes fell upon Karr and did not waver as she said, "And yet here you are."

He understood that, too.

His face scrunched up as he tried to hide his shock.

She sat down, far enough away that his legs, sprawled before him on the rocky ground, could not reach her. But not so far away that she faded into the shadows without her torch.

"Where is Soahm of Soreia?"

More words, in her tongue, that he understood as easily as if she'd uttered them in English. She did not ask it like a question. It was more like a demand, and Karr remembered suddenly that she'd asked the same thing at the Gathering.

He hadn't known then, so why in the hell would she think he'd know now?

He swallowed. "I don't know what you're talking about." *Again, in Dohrsaran.*

She nodded once, her face impassive. But she gently slid her sword from her belt, twisting it round in her grip.

"Do you know, Wanderer, why a Soreian warrior gives a weapon a name?"

She ran her fingers across the steel, black with a stripe of blue running down its center. Was she going to kill him in one fell swoop? Or would she play with him first, the way a cat toyed with its food before sinking its teeth in deep?

If Cade were here, their situations swapped, what would he have done?

A mask, Cade always said. A mask to swap out for every situation.

Karr considered this, wishing he were as good an actor as Cade, but one could only work with what one had. And Karr had always had a decent smile. They'd used it to get into plenty of high-profile places on jobs. "I'm not very well versed in the ways of Dohrsar," he said, placing that smile on his face. A little sideways grin that pulled at the dimple in his cheek. "I'm sure there will be plenty of time for me to learn, while you and I discuss whatever matters you brought me here to…"

Her sword spun in her fingertips.

The blade stopped an inch from his eyes.

"We give a weapon a name," she said, "so that when it slays a man, he will remember it. Even in death."

Perhaps the smile was a bad idea.

"Lazaris," she said, flashing a grin that looked more like a snarl. "That is her name."

Perhaps he *was* to be her prey.

Karr's hands began to shake, the fear spreading all the way down to his toes.

"Why am I here?" he asked, willing his nerves to settle, his heart to steady. "You asked me if I knew about this Soahm." He tried to think back on the memory of that night. The chaos, the fire, the screams and Cade's fury before Karr sank into that world of darkness and light. "You asked me and I told you I did not."

"People lie. Especially Wanderers."

"I don't know a man named Soahm," Karr said. "I *swear.* I've never been to your planet, and I don't even captain the damned ship. You've got the wrong prisoner if your goal is to find answers."

This time it was *his* turn to glare at her.

Because God help him, suddenly Karr was no longer afraid. He was furious.

He'd died. He'd *died* because of this girl, but a miracle had brought him back.

"Why did you stab me?" he asked. It was the question that had plagued him more than the truth about the place he'd sunk towards in death. And if there was anything he knew about circumstances such as these, it was that you had to keep your captor talking. Or, at least… Karr thought you did.

"Where is Soahm?" the girl asked, instead of answering his question.

"I just told you. I don't *know*." How could he make her believe him? She seemed intent on exactly the opposite. "There's nobody on board my ship with that name, nobody but a bunch of grunts from across the galaxy and—"

"You lie," she said. "His scent is all over you."

She pointed the sword at him.

"I didn't lie!" he yelled. "I don't know Soahm! He's not on the damned ship!"

"*Lies*," she hissed, leveling that blade ever closer.

Karr yelped in sudden panic, his hands grappling for something, *anything*, but the ropes were too tight, and all he got was a sharp slice on his palm from a bit of rock protruding from the ground.

He stared at his hand in horror.

Because something was wrong with the image before him, as his palm throbbed from the cut. He felt like he was in someone else's body, wearing the skin of an imposter as he looked down.

The blood on his hand was all wrong.

Karr stared, open-mouthed, as he watched it soar from the wound.

Not drip, as it should have done, as it had *always* done. But *soar.* Like it was weightless, smoke trailing from a candle just blown out.

It was not blood.

It was shadow.

"What's happening to me?" His voice sounded distant.

"You bleed shadows," the woman hissed. "Shadows that have the very same aura as him."

"What did you do to me?" Karr gasped.

His hands were shaking beneath his bonds.

He wanted to get free, wanted to scream and run but he feared that his body was no longer his, that even if he tried, he would not be able to control it.

"Tell me where my brother is." She stood and drew closer, her sword swinging back towards him. "Tell me where you're keeping Soahm of Soreia."

"I don't know!" Karr said, shaking his head.

The atmosphere was poisonous. Had it turned his blood, addled his brain so that he thought he was speaking her language? He could hardly concentrate as he saw the deep, dark blood slip from the wound, as if it had been hiding inside of him like some sort of living poison. Shadows whisked away into the darkness, gone in a puff of black.

"Your ship stole Soahm. Ten years ago, in the night, I saw the red bird fly away with him. And now you've returned, and your scent carries his. Lie to me again, and you will never forget Lazaris' name."

"*Please*," Karr said, shaking his head. "I don't know! My helmet, oh God, where's my helmet?"

It was terror that wrapped him up now, and he was sinking, falling into an abyss he feared he would not come back from.

He was dying, surely, from the poisonous atmosphere. And if he didn't die from that, he'd die when this woman killed him for good.

The panic roiled.

Deep inside of him, he felt something shift; a rift, forming in his chest. As if a beast had been in slumber, and now his own terror was forcing it to awaken. His skin crawled, as if his blood was boiling inside, and if he did not let it out, he would burn to ashes.

"He had blue hair. Blue eyes." She towered over him like a monster. "He had a family and a future and a crown—and it was all stolen from him."

"Please," Karr begged. "*Please,* I don't know a thing, just let me go."

But a growl rumbled in the girl's throat, and then she was gripping his shirt with both fists, her weapon discarded, her face close to his, the breath shared between them. She was so close he could see subtle hints of blue swimming through her brown eyes. Blue like the sea, blue like the sky, a pale color so drastically different from the shadows now swimming from his skin.

He felt like he was back in the *Starfall* again, watching his parents bleed out. But this time there were no shadows to hide in, because they'd all disappeared.

Now he was bleeding those shadows.

Now… he had a monster hiding inside of his own skin.

What had this girl done to him when she'd killed him?

"You have a final chance to speak the truth," she whispered. "After that, you will know true pain."

She lifted the blade, angled it towards his chest.

"*Sonara!* Stop this madness."

Two figures emerged from the shadows: a beautiful girl with dark hair, and behind her, a woman that looked like she wore a skull for a head.

He was hallucinating now. Would they tear him apart, would the woman with the skull-head *devour* him?

He wanted to live. Oh, God, he wanted to *live.*

The sickness swelled, the heat inside of him rising. The entire cave seemed to tremble, as Karr's body shook.

And just before she pressed her weapon into his chest…

Karr screamed. He put all his terror into that scream, all of his desire to *live.* The rift widened, and something felt like it broke inside of him. A heavy, weighted darkness dropped from a fraying string. It tumbled down, down, into his soul where it settled beside something warm and waiting and entirely brand new.

Yes, it seemed to whisper. *Here I am.*

Release me.

Karr's body shook as that heat spread from him, pooling in his fingertips, his toes. He yelled and tried to shove the pain and the fire away.

A loud crack resounded, and the woman shouted and dove to the side as the ground actually fractured beneath Karr's sprawled legs.

The fault line spread until it reached the far side of the cave, where it drove upwards into the rounded wall. The wall shifted, that raw crack of power splitting it in two, wide enough to reveal a small hidden alcove of rock just beyond.

And at the end of it, standing in the shadows as if it had been there for ages, just waiting to be discovered… a door.

CHAPTER 24

Cade

The message was scrawled in something so dark it could only be dried blood. The translator in his S2 shifted the strange letters around, morphing them slowly until Cade Kingston could read the ransom note, clear as day:

Free the prisoners or he dies.
You have until the suns set.

A lifetime, Cade Kingston had spent protecting Karr, only for it to come to this.

He couldn't lose him a third time. And yet here he stood, holding Karr's discarded S2 helmet in his hands. To remove it would mean death, for the air on Dohrsar was poison.

His hands shook as he replayed the recording he'd pulled from the loading dock camera.

As he saw Karr just after he'd left him last night.

In the recording, Karr stumbled, scraping at his helmet as if there were something *inside* of it attacking him. He fell to his knees, then crawled for the loading dock door in desperation.

Cade zoomed in, close enough to see the whites of Karr's eyes as he removed his S2 helmet. He didn't know what he'd expected to see on the recording, but certainly not relief.

Certainly not his brother, lying on his back as he gulped in the poisonous air like he was chugging a flagon of fresh water.

Moments after, the wyvern had emerged from the sky.

The two Dohrsarans upon its back had dismounted, and Cade saw, with a sudden hatred that flared in his gut… the woman that had stabbed Karr at the Gathering, days ago.

Jameson confirmed it, along with three more of Cade's soldiers.

The Dohrsaran woman knocked Karr unconscious with her blade, then loaded him onto the beast's back. The video cut off, the wyvern having soared out of the camera's view before he could accurately see which direction it went.

Karr had been gone for twelve hours now. *Twelve hours*, enough time for the poisonous air to kill him. But there had to be hope. There *had* to be. For he hadn't come all this way, survived all that he'd already been through with Geisinger, for Karr to die. Not once, but twice.

Cade set the helmet down, unable to look at it any longer.

Was this his payment, his penance, for what he'd done to the Dohrsarans?

They hadn't stopped working. They'd made it half a mile into the Bloodhorn Mountains, the tunnel sloping deep into the earth. Already, they'd removed their first hint of Antheon. It was real. It would pay off.

But at what cost?

Cade winced as he stood, leaving the helmet at his feet. His back ached, his legs trembled, and his chest felt like it could split open. A small price to pay, compared to losing Karr.

Why had the woman taken him? She struck where it hurt him the most, as if she'd somehow known exactly which crew member would be best to take.

He composed himself as he heard the door to the loading dock slide open behind him.

"Kingston." Rohtt strode through the doorway, dressed in his Crossman black. He had a prisoner with him, the beautiful southern queen who walked at his side as if she were his confidant. Cade could just see the fringes of the silver mite's legs curling forward from the back of her neck.

A painful way to take a person's freedom.

He felt a twinge of guilt, a sickness that reminded him of just how deep he'd gone down the rabbit hole.

But the mites worked exactly as Geisinger had promised they would. Cade knew that truth all too well.

Rohtt gripped the queen by the back of the arm, pushing her forward onto the loading dock. She kept her chin high, her blue braids perfectly smooth atop her head, unshaken by the raging wind.

"We showed the footage to the prisoners, Captain," Rohtt said as he halted a few feet away. His dark eyes flitted towards the discarded S2 helmet. "The Queen says she has knowledge on his captor."

Kidnapper, he should have said. But Cade couldn't quite bring himself to correct Rohtt and utter the word. He'd lost Karr too many times. Was it possible that the fault had always been his?

"Speak," Rohtt commanded the woman.

She tilted her chin ever so slightly away from him, as if he carried a particularly unwelcome scent.

"Captain Kingston," the Queen of the Southern Kingdom said, and Cade fully looked at her for the first time. With two simple words, she took command of the conversation.

Despite the mite, she still held herself with a straight-backed pride of royalty. In the days since her capture, she had refused to bend, to lift a hand to work, accepting the pain of the mite to the point that it had nearly killed her. It was only when she realized her actions caused her people pain, too, that she relented.

"You have information for me?" Cade asked.

He cared not, about keeping his usual mask of indifference.

This was Karr.

The wind soared past, whistling as if it knew where Karr was being held, but did not wish to share the secret with Cade.

"Information in exchange for a deal," the queen said. "Your liaison was accommodating enough, and has already ironed out the terms with me. Myself and my court will walk free tonight."

"Why would I be inclined to take this deal?"

His eyes went to Rohtt. Damned fearlessly bold Rohtt, who worked on Geisinger's word alone. Cade was never in true control. The moment he'd signed on that dotted line in the room in Geisinger's hospital, he'd given his own freedom away.

It had only grown worse, when Rohtt arrived in the hospital that night, and began the painful work that led towards shaping Cade into their man for the job.

But it was worth it.

It had to be, once he recovered Karr.

"Because if you don't take it… you will never see your brother again," the woman said. "You are dealing with no ordinary enemy. You know *not* what monster you face."

Cade could still see the dried blood and the helmet on the ground, the spot where she'd slammed Karr over the head with her blade. He angled his body ever-so slightly away, trying not to think about Karr shivering in the darkness somewhere, suffocating slowly beneath the weight of the planet's poisonous atmosphere.

How long, exactly, would it take until it killed him?

No, this job had not gone cleanly.

And once Cade found Karr's captors, the mess would only get worse. He would kill them. And he would make sure he did it slowly.

The Queen glanced at the screen still held in Cade's hands. "A Shadowblood." She hissed the word like a curse. "An enemy of Dohrsar, and one with mighty powers that come from the depths of darkness. Some say they have found a way to break open Hell's very gates and breed with the demons that have sprung forth from there. If it's a Shadowblood you're facing, it is not likely that you will ever see your brother again."

Panic raced through Cade, but the queen was not done explaining.

"I caught a glimpse of her at the Gathering. And though I did not believe it at the time… what I have seen is indeed true. It is her, in the recording. I recognize the face, and I recognize the stolen blade she carries." Her eyes narrowed in what looked like fury, before she lifted her chin ever higher, the mite's legs stretching against the back of her neck. "I give you a final offering of peace between my kingdom and yours." Her voice was diplomatic.

But her eyes were as cold as steel. "The girl is someone I regret to know well. A demon that should not walk this Earth. There are a great many outlaws across Dohrsar, and for years, there has been a tale about a Devil ravaging the Deadlands. A Devil that stood against your very ally, the king. You can keep the prisoners from the White Wastes, but you must set *my* people free. You'll still have enough to complete the job."

She nodded to Rohtt, as if he were not the man holding her captive, but her servant, set to do her bidding.

Rohtt snapped his fingers, and out of the doors behind him came another set of guards, hauling in a shackled man.

This one was tall and lean and made of muscle. Though he was wounded, a filthy bandage over his arm, Cade had the faintest feeling that should he come too close to the prisoner, he might need to call upon the power of the mite. His dark eyes met Cade's without bitterness. Only a calculating glance that went first to the dried blood on the loading dock. A slight tilt of his head, before he glanced back to Cade and the Queen.

"Jaxon of Wildeweb, confirmed by the king as the man who walks with the Devil," the queen said with a smile, inclining her head towards the imprisoned man. "Threaten to kill him… and it is my belief that the girl will do anything you ask."

PART THREE

BONE

CHAPTER 25

Sonara

Sonara knelt in the darkness.

The ancient door before her was heavy, rounded at the top as if it belonged in an ornate castle, instead of buried deep inside the recesses of a cave in the Bloodhorns. It was made of deep red stone, with strange, ancient symbols carved into its surface.

The door had no handle, no hinges, no visible way of entrance.

Her curse, nestled inside its cage, blinked weary eyes at the door. Curious, but not quite ready to test its aura.

The one time I need you to do something, you remain passive, Sonara thought to her curse.

It only blinked wearily, then backed away from the bars of its cage.

"Markam?" Sonara glanced over her shoulder as he approached, blood on his stubbled chin, his duster filthy. "You try. You're good at breaking and entering."

Markam approached the door, though Sonara doubted he'd find any way past it.

The Wanderer's power was immense.

Sonara hadn't meant to make him do *this*, she thought pointedly, as she looked at the ancient red door.

She wasn't sure what she'd hoped for, exactly, when she questioned him only an hour ago. Answers about Soahm, perhaps, or some knowledge about what the Wanderers were doing, and how to shut them down.

Certainly *not* an ancient red door in the middle of the very cave they'd spend their time hiding in.

A door that had kept Thali seated in silence behind her bone mask, as the Wanderer slept beside her, his raw surge of power having stolen every ounce of energy from him.

"Terra magic," Thali said. A torch flickered in her bone-gauntleted fist. The light cast an eerie shadow across her Canis mask. "It is the greatest, rawest power of the Children of Shadow, for it is a connection to the Great Mother herself. A power I have not seen before in the flesh."

"And the door?" Azariah asked. She looked at the Wanderer; the blood on his head, dried black as the blood that ran through all their veins, except Thali's. "What do you think…"

Sonara could sense the princess' curiosity. But among it was also fear.

The aura was thick and oily on Sonara's tongue, coming off Azariah in waves as she looked from the Wanderer to the red door and back at Thali again. "Is it…"

Sonara knew what the princess was leaning towards.

Knew it, because just the night before, they'd spoken of such impossible truths, about the first Shadowblood, and the heart of the planet. But it was only a tale. A tale that had begged her to listen and had *felt* like a deep history of Dohrsar, nonetheless.

Now the door felt like another page of that story. Another chapter to the ancient tome that was the beginning of Dohrsar.

"Perhaps it belongs to one of the old kings. An old storage hideout, or bunker," Markam said, as he gave up on trying to open the door. He'd even foolishly kicked it with his boot, earning a yelp and a bruised toe.

"Possible," Sonara said. She looked at the princess. "Do you know if your father has secret hideouts across the Deadlands?"

Azariah nodded. "Of course he does. What royal wouldn't, when the history between all three kingdoms has always been war? But… I'm not sure he would have created one this hard to reach, and this far from the palace."

Markam lifted a dark brow. "What, you mean he didn't stash a door hidden behind a solid wall of rock, only accessible by a Wanderer-turned-Shadowblood's strange new Terra magic?"

Thali gave her torch to Sonara. She knelt before the door to examine the symbols. "All my life I have studied. All my life I have committed myself to worshipping Her. But I have never felt so close."

"What do you mean?" Sonara asked.

Thali breathed out slowly. "These are the Great Mother's symbols."

With trembling hands, she reached out, her bone gauntlets stark against the red door. She pressed her fingertips to the symbols, and her whole body seemed to shiver. "The planet has spoken to the Wanderer, calling to his magic." She glanced back to Sonara, the torchlight flickering behind the Canis' jawbone. "Just as she spoke to *you,* Devil, to bring your sword to strike the Wanderer's heart, and draw him back as a Child of Shadow made anew."

"What do the symbols mean?" Sonara asked.

Her heart had begun to hasten its pace. Her curse, curled up in its cage, winked open an eye again and began to sniff the air, as curious as ever.

"I cannot be certain," Thali said. "But I believe this door leads to a sacred place. One that may very well contain the heart of Dohrsar itself."

In any other time, Sonara would have laughed.

But now that conversation she had with Azariah, deep in the shadows, felt all too much like a history lesson instead of a fireside tale.

Across from them, the Wanderer groaned and began to wake.

"Start a fire," Sonara said to Azariah. "We're going to have a talk with our Wanderer, and see just what fate Thali's *Great Mother* is leading us to."

CHAPTER 26

Karr

He was in the half-place again.

But today the scenery had changed, a throne room swapped out for the shores of an ancient, endless sea. The waves were split down the center, rolling towards where Karr stood, barefoot upon a grey sand shore.

He stared out at the sea, wondering which side, given the chance, he would choose.

The left half of the sea was dark and furious, the wind raging, the white waves tossed about until they exploded upon the sand.

The right half was calm. A gentle ocean of dark waves. They barely kissed the shore as the wind danced like a delicate thing, in time with a song that was unheard.

Both sides collided against each other. One crashing furiously, the other gently lapping.

Together, the sounds made a word.

Choose.

But he'd already chosen.

The grey sand was warm beneath Karr's bare feet. He wiggled his toes, feeling as if he were home.

"It is far more interesting than the last place," a voice said. Delicate, like the tinkling of bells or a wedding song. "Memories are fascinating things. You never know what sort of picture they might paint."

Karr turned, and there she was.

The child made of starlight. He hadn't the chance to look at her closely, the last time he met her in the half-place. But now he saw her in full. Little glowing planets rotated across her skin as if she were their axis. They swam through the starlight that made up her long coils of glowing hair, then danced across her collarbone, into her arms and her fingertips and back again.

"I chose," Karr said.

The child rose a shimmering brow. "Did you?"

"No," he said, shaking his head. "I guess not." He glanced back at the half-sea. "What is this place?"

"The center of us all." She pointed her finger at Karr's hand. "May I?"

He lifted his palm and held it out to her.

A tendril of starlight shot from her fingertip, a tiny galaxy stretched like a rubber band. Heat seared his skin as the starlight sliced a cut along his palm, drawing that strange, ghostly black blood. It soared off into the sky, half splitting towards the white sea. The other, barreling towards the dark.

"The shadows," Karr said. "What are they?"

The child laughed. Her eyes were like nebulas, swirling with colors he could not even name. She motioned for him to follow, and together they walked along the grey shore. The half-sea followed them, always crashing in part darkness and part light, always keeping them in the center of the two. "Not shadows, my heart. They are tendrils of soul. They dance within us, always keeping the balance. Half-darkness. Half-light. It is what sets the Shadowbloods apart. What keeps them worthy."

"Shadowbloods?" Karr asked.

"Yes, my heart. It is your second chance." Her smile was tired. The starlight that made up her skin seemed to dim, some of the lights winking out, some of the planets growing still. They walked in silence for a time.

Karr knew he was asleep, lost inside of his dreams. But it felt real, the warmth on his bare toes, the stinging pain on his palm, the little scab of black beginning to form over his cut.

They stopped when shapes began to form in the distance.

A castle the color of sand, on the fringes of a city that unspooled towards the sea. Like a child's seaside creation; a fortress that felt vaguely familiar to him, as if he'd seen it in a storybook, flipping past the pages with his mother and father before their lives were cut short. He gazed at it for a time, wishing he could run to it. Lose himself inside of the castle halls, discover the secrets that waited within.

"What is this place?" Karr asked the child.

"Memories," she said. "Every Shadowblood has them."

"But they aren't mine," Karr said.

"My dear lost soul." The girl's nebula eyes met his, and there was sadness within her gaze. "You do not remember. But there is one who does. Soon you'll discover the truth. When you do, you must be ready."

"For what?" Karr asked.

The star child smiled. "The end, my heart. You must be ready for the end of the end, where there will be another choice. And this time, you must choose a side."

She reached out, placing her fingertip upon his chest.

It went through him, searing past his skin, past his blood and his bones, into his rib cage, where she removed his heart.

Not flesh, as he had suspected.

But solid black.

The Antheon that Cade was after, but today, it pulsed in the child's grip.

Like a still-beating heart.

***

When he woke, Karr Kingston's captors had prepared a feast for him.

Or so they'd said.

But by the looks of the hideous creature rotating on a makeshift spit over a fire, its jagged teeth poking out from a charred, fleshy head… he wasn't so sure.

Sonara, the blue-haired woman had called herself. She'd dragged him here by his ropes, setting him before a stack of unlit wood, where the rest of the group sat. Dirty and not heavily armed, there were only four of them in total.

The beautiful one, with black, depthless eyes, had held her hands before her, her dark brows knitting together as she concentrated.

"Find your peace with it, Azariah," the small-framed one, in the wolfen mask, leaned forward and seemed to sigh. "Settle your soul into the depths of the Great Mother and let your power *soar*."

A spark of blue shot from Azariah's palms, sparking the fire to life in an instant.

Karr hardly believed it—for that was magic, living and breathing, in front of his very eyes.

Magic the likes of which he himself had achieved yesterday. Impossibly, he knew it was *his magic* that had done it, *his* power that had split the cave floor.

He remembered that awful heat, that roiling darkness that had broken inside of him, tumbling into an abyss in his soul where something living had been waiting for him to open it.

That great surge of power had shoved the very cave walls aside, revealing a crimson door, as if it had been there in hiding.

The firelight spread further, revealing that very door now.

There it stood in the rock, sealed shut.

He had done that.

But *how* had he done that?

The question made him look at the group differently, for this wasn't any normal prisoner-of-war situation.

Something had changed drastically in himself, and it made him desperate to try to discover what other secrets this group, this planet, might be hiding. For was it possible the people who'd taken him captive were *all* like him? Was it possible that others, on Dohrsar, had this hidden magic?

He looked to Sonara, who sat cross-legged on the other side of the flames, her hand resting on her black-and-blue sword.

"Why did you kill me?" Karr asked cautiously. "And why did I come back changed?"

She picked at her teeth with a bone. "I ask the questions. If you answer mine, you'll earn the right to ask me one back. Is that clear?"

Azariah simply ran her hands through her tangled hair as if trying to remove the knots. The one in the wolf-skull mask was motionless, looking towards the red door in the rock, and the man beside her, whose eyes danced with mischief as he twirled a dagger between his fingertips, was watching Karr like he might bolt.

Like he *dared* him to bolt and see just how far he could run before he sank that menacing dagger between Karr's shoulders.

"Fine," Karr agreed. He'd play her little game.

Sonara tossed the bone behind her and sat back in a casual, relaxed lean. "What business do your people have on my planet?"

He chose his words very carefully. "I'm not in the business of taking people captive. I'm not in support of this mission at all."

She narrowed her eyes.

"My captain didn't offer me the truth about the mission. All I knew is that we were to come to your planet, dig for a black substance called Antheon. He never explained the details. Never said it would come to this, to taking your people captive and using them as workers. If I'd known, I would have tried to stop it."

He hoped she believed him. He hoped her magic sensed his honesty, his truths.

She nodded. "Alright. Markam?"

Markam sighed and stood to approach him, his hand on the dagger at his hip.

"I-it wasn't a lie!" Karr said, as he watched the dark-eyed man approach with a sickening swagger. "I told you the truth."

But instead of reaching for Karr with some horrible magic that would squeeze the air from his lungs or suck out his eyes… Markam only turned the spit, removing the hideous creature from over the flames. "Relax, Wanderer. You've earned yourself a meal with that first truth." He ripped off a roasted ear from the creature and held it out. "The first taste."

"Oh, goddesses, hold me," Azariah groaned. "You said you were done with torture."

Markam raised a brow. "I beg your pardon, Princess?" He tossed the ear into her lap. "Perhaps you'd like the first bite?"

She swept it from her lap as if it were on fire.

"Enough." That was Sonara again, drawing the situation back to her. She grabbed the ear and popped it into her mouth. Her gaze flicked to Karr, who realized suddenly that he was relaxed. That his heart rate had slowed, no longer on edge.

For in that small bit of chaos, the situation had shifted again. He'd seen more than captors in these strange, magic-bearing Dohrsarans.

He'd seen humanity.

And at that glimpse, he saw hope.

Perhaps they would see reason, decide to set him free, if he could convince them he'd had no part in it.

"My brother took the mission of his own accord," Karr said. "He was hired by a man named Geisinger, a king in his own right, from a planet called Earth. Cade brought us here, said he was going to have a crew waiting to dig beneath the planet's surface to find the Antheon. Said Geisinger had set it all up. I pressed him for answers, but he gave none. And then when we got to the Gathering, and you," he looked pointedly at Sonara, "*killed* me… I'm guessing it set things into motion. Now it's my turn. Why did you kill me?"

He felt so strange asking the question, speaking of his own death as if it were a casual topic. As if they were old comrades sharing a drink together by a warm hearth.

Sonara cracked her neck. "To understand the truth, you must know the origin of it all. I'm a Shadowblood, brought back from death to live a second life."

That word.

The Child of Starlight had spoken it, in his dreams.

Karr leaned forward, holding onto her words, desperate to understand them.

"My blood has been replaced by living shadows," Sonara said, "and those shadows have granted me a curse. Each Shadowblood's curse is different, perhaps pulling at some strength they may have had in their first life. With mine, I can sense the auras of others. Their truths and their lies, their emotions, their anticipation before a swing. Before they try to escape." She smiled wickedly at him. "I killed you because my curse deemed it so. It directed me to end your life, for some reason deeper than us both. And now here you sit before me… A Shadowblood, made anew."

A shiver of fear ran through Karr. But it was also followed by something that seemed to slip past the fear. Curiosity.

"*Why?*" he asked.

Karr's heart was pounding in his ears again, like a tub of water set churning down a drain.

"The Great Mother chose you," the woman in the skull mask said. "The planet itself. Dohrsar. She lives and breathes… and chooses. And *you* have been chosen, Wanderer. The planet commands all magic. Commands all things. I believe it spoke to Sonara. Urged her to make the choice, taking hold of her magic so that it could set things into motion. Just as it urged your magic to reveal that door to us." She looked over her shoulder at the crimson door nestled into the rock. "For whatever reason… the planet needs you here. Your fate is intertwined with Sonara's."

Karr swallowed. Was this girl, this Child of Starlight in his dreams, some incarnation of the planet's soul? It was impossible, but so was magic such as this…

He'd seen plenty of strange things in all his travels.

He'd met plenty of people that believed in things others would call ridiculous, religions that he'd never given much thought to, while others gave their entire lives to the cause.

Eventually, one of those religions had to be found to be *true.* He just never suspected he'd be the one to discover real proof.

"And all of you," Karr asked, "you have been chosen, too? You have this shadowed blood?"

"It's terribly complicated, I'm afraid," said Azariah. "When I was only a child, my father murdered me. He slit my throat in a golden temple of his own making, and I came back as one. Most of us meet a horrific end before we're brought back."

Karr felt like he might be sick. And not just from the smell of the smoldering cave rat.

Thali spoke again. "It appears you have Terra magic. The depths of your abilities, we cannot yet be sure. But they all have their own. Lightning runs in Azariah's veins. Markam can make illusions appear true."

Sonara glared at her. "*Details*, cleric. Hold your tongue."

But Thali did not seem fazed by the command. There was something unique about her, beyond her appearance. It was the ease with which she carried herself. The calm certainty. "He is one of us now. Even if he came from that ship."

"The ship that has taken our people captive," Sonara said back.

"And still holds Jaxon and Soahm with it. They took everything from us." Her gaze became icy, the same way it had when she'd nearly taken her blade to his skin. "*Everything.*"

"*He* did not," Markam corrected her. "You told me that yourself. He spoke true, about Soahm. He knows nothing."

"But his people do," she said. "I'm certain of it."

"Certainty and desperation are two very different things," Thali said softly. "You would be wise not to confuse the two, Devil."

Silence fell between them.

"Continue to speak truths, Wanderer," Sonara said to Karr again. "Or you will die."

"He will *not*," Thali's voice hardened beyond her bone mask. "No Child of Shadow will be harmed on my watch. Harming him would be to cause harm to yourself, because for whatever reason, Devil, *you* and this Wanderer are bound by fate. Do not test the planet, by hurting him now."

Sonara crossed her arms over her chest and stared across the flames at Karr.

Beneath her gaze, he felt like he was in someone else's skin. He stared back at her, unblinking, looking at the lines of her face.

This wasn't happening to him, truly. Was it? But he could feel that the strange sense of the power in him was real.

"Fine." Sonara sighed. "You will not die today, Wanderer."

"*Child of Shadow*," Thali corrected.

"My apologies," Sonara shot back. "You think you know so much about the planet. Why in the hell would it bring back a Wanderer? Seek and find *that* truth."

Thali's next words were a whisper. "I will not pretend to

understand. But it remains the same. We took him captive, but he is not what he once was. He's not an enemy any longer. He shouldn't be bound."

"He will remain so until we decide where his loyalties lie. For now, they're with his people." She looked back to Karr. "But you should know that it wasn't my choice to kill you. And if what Thali says is true—as much as I'm inclined to disagree—then the planet decided for me. It felt like something gripped my power and pushed it forth."

"Yesterday," Karr said, putting aside the fact that she still looked like she *wanted* to kill him, "I split the cave floor. I did it, but it felt like my… my magic… was doing it of its own accord."

Azariah nodded. "It lives, just as the planet lives. It's a part of you now, just as the shadows are."

"What are they?" Karr asked.

"The planet's soul," Thali breathed from behind her mask. "A gift granted to you because in the place of darkness and light… you did not choose."

How could she have known what happened to him when he died?

"We all went there, in death," Markam added, as if he were reading Karr's mind. He shrugged. "A terribly boring place. Lonely."

"The details change," Sonara said, "depending on your memories. But the half-ness of it is the same. Part darkness, part light."

Karr suddenly had a flashing image return to him. Like a snapshot taken by a camera, displayed on the ceiling of his bunk inside the *Starfall*. "I wouldn't say it was lonely. The child was there."

A pause, as the Dohrsarans all looked to each other. There was something shadowed in their glance, like they were holding onto a secret Karr hadn't any idea how to unlock.

"What child?" Sonara asked.

"A girl," Karr explained. "She told me the half-place was made up of my memories." He saw the girl in his mind, heard the ghostly recall of her voice. But the exact words she'd spoken had faded like ashes on the wind. "There was something ancient about her all the same."

Markam shook his head. "There's no child in the half-place, Wanderer."

Thali's pale eyes met Karr's from behind her mask. The firelight danced in them, a blazing inferno that had him locked in her gaze. "What did she look like?"

Karr shrugged. "Like starlight incarnate."

Her eyes seemed to dim for a moment.

"I heard a voice when I was there," Sonara said. "I have heard that voice every day since. It is the whisper of my curse, the voice that begs me to pay attention. But it never had a form. Never a body. Certainly not a child."

Silence swept across the cave like a heavy blanket.

"So… why am *I* here?" Karr asked softly. "What do you want with me?"

Markam plucked a limb from the rat and began to gnaw on it, the only sound in the cave besides the crackling fire. "You're a ransom, Wanderer. But for now, we need information. In exchange for offering it, we'll let you live for the time being, until your captain meets our demand."

"A fine reward," Karr said darkly.

Again, he thought of Cade. Of what would come when the Antheon was distributed across the stars, Geisinger's new creation.

"What do you know of this Antheon my brother seeks?"

It was Azariah who answered. "It… changes a man."

"In what way?"

She swallowed, looking about the group. They watched her closely, as if they too were waiting on her answer.

"I do not know. Not fully. But to see it land in the hands of this Geisinger, and of my…" she cleared her throat, "of the king… I fear it would give them a great deal of power. A great deal more than they deserve."

"You have a mighty power," Thali said. "The *both* of you, for whatever reason, are being called. Your fates are intertwined. I suspected as much with you, Sonara, but… but now, it seems the *two* of you are called. Joined."

"The heart of the planet," Sonara said. "The place Eona found."

"Who the hell is Eona?" Markam asked.

"The first Shadowblood," Sonara explained. "She tried to steal the planet's heart. To take it for her own and wield it. To become the most powerful person this planet has ever known."

A face flashed in Karr's head suddenly.

Cade, standing beside the Dohrsaran king as they looked at their prisoners cutting into the mountainside, a hunger for *more* always shining behind his eyes.

"The heart," Karr asked slowly. "Is it a *true* heart?"

"The source of all things," Thali said. "When a Child of Shadow is chosen, she lends to them a bit of her very soul. The heart… well, as the records show… it has no limit to its power. It can do all things."

"In the story," Azariah explained, "Eona was drawn to the heart. The pulse of its power was too deep for her to resist."

"Like your magic," Thali said. "When you reached a place of great fear, it struck out as raw as a babe's first cry in the world. The heart of the planet, I believe, is calling you and Sonara both. Beckoning you to pay attention. To listen close. The heart is a beautiful gift, the source of life. But to others, it is a dangerous weapon, the kind that only a monster would want to control. To take it would be to kill the planet. To take it would be the end of the end."

The end of the end.

Only a monster would want to wield the planet's heart.

A monster like Geisinger.

A monster like *Cade,* now that he'd taken the wrong side.

"We have to stop him," Karr said. "If the heart exists. If it's true…"

"Of course it's true," Thali said. "The Great Mother's beauty is upon the very door you revealed."

"The source of all things," Karr said. "The source of life, with great power."

He pieced it all together.

The energy source that was constantly appearing on Cade's scanners.

Like a pulse.

A beat.

A beating *heart.*

He felt sick, suddenly understanding it all, even though he'd never heard the full story. Even though this planet was not a place to call his own. It had changed him, that much was true, with this power that roiled beside his blood and bones.

"We have to stop Cade," Karr said. "I think he's after the heart. He doesn't realize it—he thinks he's just seeking out Antheon, this powerful substance, but if Thali is right… what happens if the heart is removed?"

The woman in the mask pressed her hands to her chest as if she wanted to calm the racing of her own heart. "The planet would cease to exist. For what living being can survive without a heart?"

He had to stop it.

For this place may have been where he'd died at Sonara's hand.

But it also gave him a second chance at life.

To see it fall at Cade's hands… his brother had no idea what he was about to uncover. What he was about to destroy. All these people, these creatures, the ringed planet that looked like a glittering jewel nestled among the stars. All of it would fall, if it was true. If Cade discovered the planet's heart.

How many other planets were out there, like this one?

How many others had a source of life, and Geisinger was sending missions out across the stars, conquering entire worlds, enslaving their people and devouring the very planet's source of life?

Karr knew it would take all of the group's magic combined to shut down Cade's mission. To destroy the *Starfall*'s energy source and set the prisoners free from his brother's command.

But Karr would do it, for something in Cade had changed the moment he'd taken the job from Geisinger. When he'd discovered Karr trying to fix up the escape pod in the belly of the ship, there was a new light in his eyes. Karr had mistaken it for excitement, for the promise of freedom.

Now he realized it was hunger.

A hunger for power.

For money.

For a life that offered *more.*

Some part of him wondered if they'd ever be able to get out from Geisinger's fist once he stopped this job. But Cade wasn't buying them freedom. He was just placing them in thicker shackles.

"Tell me the story of Eona," Karr said. For he feared that it would mirror Cade's greed. "All of it, please."

Thali nodded.

She motioned for the others to join her. Azariah helped Karr stand, and they all led him towards the door, where Thali sat close, examining the details on the rock as she spoke.

"The first Shadowblood was a young princess named Eona," Thali said, her voice mixing in with the sound of the crackling fire. "She discovered the heart of the planet, and died trying to steal it for herself, so that she could conquer the world…"

As she spoke, Karr gently pressed his hand to the door.

The story of Eona washed over him, and he could have sworn he felt a gentle pulse beneath his palm, coming from the other side.

CHAPTER 27

Cade

He'd never had to don a mask this wicked before, but he wore it gratefully, for it would bring back his brother safe and sound.

It was a carefully crafted one, the kind that Jeb would have worn were he in charge of a mission gone awry. A mask of indifference—of utter cold—that Cade slid upon his soul.

The Deadlands night wind howled like a vicious wolf on the prowl, and whisked away the warmth that had been here earlier today as his prisoners worked.

Geisinger had only given him a few more days to complete the mission.

There were eyes across the stars, ones that would come to call, should they learn about the work.

Remember your part, Cade told himself, and calmed the furious shaking in his knees as he stared out at the horizon. From up so high, here on the loading dock, he should have felt like a king in this world.

Instead he felt sick as the prisoners continuing to cut into the mountainside far below.

"They're late," Rohtt said with a grunt now. He stood to Cade's right, arms crossed over his chest, the picture of a military man who obeyed orders and didn't ask questions. That was Rohtt's way. It had never been Cade's, until this job. "I told you not to get your hopes up, Kingston."

He hated Rohtt.

He truly did.

But the man acted as Geisinger's eyes and ears, and tonight Cade was grateful for the distraction.

Cade leaned forward, trying to get the feeling to return to his toes. All day, he'd paced upon this loading dock in the sky, waiting for a glimpse of the Devil. She'd left no way to contact her; and Cade knew she was out there somewhere, watching.

Free the prisoners, had been the Devil's command.

Cade wouldn't do it. He *couldn't* do it, not if they wanted to complete the mission on Geisinger's time. His hands were tied. Geisinger would take Karr from him if he didn't.

There was no winning when his brother's life was being threatened on all sides.

Three soldiers stood to the right of the dock, three to the left, all of them armed.

Cade's *new* prize for the Devil was the man now bound and kneeling on the loading dock, a dark sackcloth over his head. Jaxon, a part of her troupe. A criminal with crimes similar to Cade's.

Queen Iridis had sworn that if Cade threatened him, the Devil would not destroy the rest of his plans. His work could go on, with fewer workers, fewer prisoners. But Geisinger would still get his Antheon. Cade would still get his payday. And Karr would still live out his future as rich and protected as a king.

It was the life he deserved, the one Cade had promised he'd give to him, long ago, when Karr was saved from the raiders and their knives.

"By nightfall," Cade said now. He glanced to Rohtt, who held the imprisoned Jaxon in his grasp. "She said by nightfall, or Karr would die. What if we've made a mistake? What if she hasn't seen our message?"

All day, they'd left Jaxon bound and fully visible on the loading dock, surrounded by guards. All day, Cade had paced, watching and waiting for a sign of the Devil.

He knew she was watching him, too, out there somewhere in the wilds.

Queen Iridis swore the Devil would come for Jaxon…

But perhaps she was wrong.

Rohtt grunted. His eyes glittered darkly behind his visor. "Trickery. Bastards always think they can do things on their own terms."

"This *is* on their terms, you Wanderer buffoon," the prisoner Jaxon said, his words muffled by the hood over his head. "You'd be wise to treat it as so. The Devil will kill you all, for what you've done."

Rohtt slammed him in the back with the butt of his rifle.

Jaxon crumpled, his body bruised and battered from the countless beatings Rohtt had given him upon interrogation. The mites had done their job, taking the Dohrsaran to the edge of consciousness, countless times when Cade pressed the command button.

But Jaxon had also been wounded in the Gathering attack, according to Rohtt, with a broken arm that had left him unable to defend himself when they'd discovered him holding a mighty golden sword, the hilt like a scorpion's tail poised to strike.

They'd taken the blade from him without a fight, Cade certain that its weight in gold would be worth something, somewhere across the stars.

But even in his pain, Jaxon had offered Rohtt no information. Only a cruel smile and four whispered words.

The Devil will come.

Cade looked back to the sky now, the planet's rings dancing in the distance. Colors so beautiful, he knew Karr would have longed to capture them in one of his drawings.

His hands clenched into fists. And then his heart clenched, too, as if it were a fist of its own. As if it wanted to squeeze every drop of terror from his blood until Cade had nothing left.

"There," a soldier said. "Movement."

Cade's head snapped up.

He followed the flow of the wind towards the Bloodhorns that held Geisinger's Antheon beneath. Tricky, to uncover the hotspot of its power, *the Queen of the Hive*, as Geisinger said. For it seemed the Antheon's energy moved. Appeared sometimes on the tracking radar, then faded the next, like it was a living thing.

"I don't see anything," Cade growled.

"There it is again," another soldier said. He lifted his rifle. "The black wyvern."

"Weapons *down*," Rohtt commanded.

Ghostly, those Bloodhorns, with twisted mountaintops that looked like jagged glass capable of carving a hole in the sky.

Cade shifted his gaze as a dark mass lifted from between two peaks, the moonlight cascading down to show the arched back of a dragon. A mighty head, sharp scales curving from the top of its neck down to a barbed tail that flicked and twisted as the beast soared across the sky.

First, there was no sound but the wind. But then the beast's roar arrived, and the great flapping of its wings carried across the pass as it grew closer. And *larger*, every second, large enough to take up half the loading dock with its sheer size.

"Hold your fire," Cade said into his helmet com, grateful that his mask of indifference held in place, for he'd seen plenty of alien beasts before.

But never dragons, not until Dohrsar. It was a beast that matched the night, spiraling downwards, snapping out its wings to catch the wind as it landed upon the dock. Its mighty talons screeched against the metal as its wings hovered overhead, casting them all in shadow.

Upon its back sat three figures.

A man wearing a wide-brimmed leather hat to match his duster coat, the shape of two blades visible as he slid down from the dragon's back with ease, keeping a hand upon its sinewy side.

Next, the young woman called the Devil, blue-haired and ferocious with a too-large leather hat on her head and a cerulean sword hanging at her hip, the same one that she'd driven into Karr's heart.

And then Karr himself.

He was there atop the dragon, his hands bound, a hood over his head, but it was *him.* Cade would know that lazy posture anywhere, from his gangly arms to the scar that was visible just above the cut of his shirt, protruding from his collarbone.

The Devil climbed down from the wyvern's back. It huffed out a mighty breath, two plumes of smoke trailing from its snout, and the smell whooshed across the platform, even through his mask's filtration system. It reeked with the stink of death. Its eyes, easily the size of Cade's head, focused on him. Dark and pupilless. A low growl rumbled in its throat.

"Easy, old friend," the prisoner Jaxon said from beneath his hood. As if he knew that growl well and feared it not. "We'll be reunited soon enough."

The wyvern whimpered. Then lowered its head to the platform, eyes watching him intently.

Cade swallowed, wondering if perhaps he'd made a mistake in bartering the life of a man who commanded a wyvern as a child would a family dog.

"Welcome, Devil," Cade said to the blue-haired woman. His voice remained strong, even with the howling wind. "I believe you have something of mine, just as I now have something of yours. We can do this trade quickly. No harm need come to anyone."

"Save your diplomacy for the next planet you invade," she said. She marched towards him on worn boots, that sword remaining on her hip as silence seemed to sweep across the landing dock. The soldiers leveled their guns at her.

"Hold your fire," Cade commanded, lifting a hand.

They froze just as she did.

She curled her hands into fists. Her eyes dropped to the hooded Jaxon, her jaw tightening as she seemed to take a deep, steadying breath. "Can you read, Wanderer? Because it seems you have not agreed to my simple demand. Free *all* the prisoners. Then you'll receive Karr."

It was Rohtt who spoke this time. "Free Karr, or your comrade here will receive death. We've already given him more mercy than he deserves."

He pointed his rifle at Jaxon's head. They'd removed the mite from his neck, knowing full well the Devil wouldn't take him with it still intact.

The wyvern growled.

"Kill him if you wish," the Devil said. She shrugged and removed her hat as if to shake off the dust. "He means nothing to me, despite whatever intel you must have received that speaks otherwise." She paused and smiled with two rows of teeth. "But… I should warn you. The moment you harm him, Razor will turn you into a delicious steak. And she likes her meat well done."

"Charred, actually," her male companion said. "To the point of smoking."

As if in response, emerald smoke plumed from the dragon's nostrils. Its mighty tail twitched, and… Cade thought he saw something move.

Not something… but rather some*one*.

CHAPTER 28

Sonara

It was a stupid plan, really.

Perhaps even verging on outright outlandish, that they'd ever thought it could work. And yet, as she stood there on the loading dock, the wind tugging at her hair, the ground so far beneath her…

Sonara lifted her chin high and thought for one moment that the plan might actually work.

"I will *not* free the prisoners," the Wanderer leader, Cade, said. There were ten guards in total, spread evenly across the dock; five on each side, with loaded rifles. Sonara watched them in her peripherals as she sighed and tapped her toe against the hard metal.

"A foolish decision," she said. "And *not* in accordance with my demands."

Casually, she reached up and adjusted her hat.

The signal, decided upon hours ago, for the rest of her comrades to move.

If she concentrated on it, she could just barely feel Markam's curse behind her, like a cool tide ebbing at her back; something she only knew because of how often he'd hidden their troupe in the past, on jobs that had gone awry.

Today, he'd fashioned a visual shield of sorts, to hide the truth from Cade and his soldiers. For it was not just Sonara, Markam, and the prisoner Karr that had arrived on Razor's back.

The others, if they obeyed her signal, were stalking just behind Sonara, hidden by the veil of Markam's curse. Sonara dared not even try to make out their forms for fear of drawing too much attention to the fact that something was not quite as it seemed.

She thanked the wind for how loudly it howled past, mixed with Razor's heavy breathing to help muffle any sounds. Sonara kept the conversation going, giving the others time to make their way past the soldiers unheard.

"Well?" she tapped her toe impatiently on the dock, showing not an ounce of fear.

Cade held out his hands. "I have a job that must be completed. When, *and only* when it is done, your people will go back to their lives, their kingdoms. They'll continue on as if this was only a blip in the history of Dohrsar."

"Except the dead," Sonara growled. "They will walk this planet no more."

"You murdered my brother," Cade said, the words tumbling out like they were laced with a bit of poison. His comrade, a man called Rohtt, glanced his way, eyes hardening. "You drew first blood, before I moved against your people."

"And yet he still lives," Sonara said.

For just a moment, her insides squeezed as she caught the

barest glimpse of Azariah's outline slinking between two guards; so thin, it could have been a mere trick of the light.

Come on, Markam, she thought, fighting back panic even as she kept her expression cool as the night wind. *Hold the veil.*

She was so close to the inside of the ship.

So damned close, to getting everything she wanted in one fell swoop: the truth about Soahm's disappearance, *and* freedom for Jaxon and the rest of their people.

But one wrong move from the others, one footstep placed too loudly on the metal, and their cover would be blown.

A guard to Sonara's right shifted, his eyes tracing the space where Azariah had just been.

He blinked, narrowing his gaze as if he'd caught the ghostly image of her, too.

But Sonara cracked her knuckles, shifting her position to draw the guard's gaze to her. When she looked back, the flickering image of Azariah was gone.

"I'm growing impatient," Sonara said loudy. "You have sixty seconds, or we'll soar away from here and you will never see your brother again. Free my people. *All* of them."

"Free Karr," Cade countered. "I will offer you this single prisoner in return. Nothing more."

She laughed. Every part of that laugh felt *wrong*, as if she were betraying Jaxon as he knelt before Cade, so close to the deathly barrel of his soldier's guns. As if she cared nothing at all for the blood brother from Wildeweb who held half of her heart.

"Very well, Wanderer," Sonara said. "I'll agree to your trade today. But know that this war is not over. It's unwise to go against an outlaw's demands; far worse, to go against a Devil's. I will return again."

She glanced over her shoulder at Markam, who leaned against Razor as if he were merely relaxing. But she knew he *needed* the support of the mighty wyvern, his strength slowly waning as his curse flowed from him like an endless river.

"Karr?" Cade called across the space, to where the hooded Karr sat on Razor's back, hands bound. "Are you well?"

Karr did not answer.

"Gagged," Sonara said. "A precaution. But I assure you, he's unharmed. Answer me this, while Markam unbinds him." By now, the others had to have reached the loading-dock door. She had mere moments left before Markam's strength would fade, and the illusion would break. "Ten years ago, your ship came to Dohrsar. It stole a Soreian prince and soared into the stars, never to return. Until now."

"I have captained this ship for eight years," he said. "If it's answers about the missing prince that you seek, I'm afraid you won't find them with me. And the ones who captained it before me are long gone."

But she sensed something.

A scent that slipped from him as the lie tumbled off his lips.

It was sickly sweet; a drop of poison placed into a drink.

He knew more than he let on.

Markam's hand touched Sonara's back as he moved past, hauling the hooded Karr with him.

He had little time left to hold the veil.

So Sonara looked at Cade. "We trade at the same time. Jaxon? Can you stand?"

"Well enough," Jaxon answered from the ground. Cade nodded to Rohtt, who roughly hauled the man to his feet. Cade pulled Jaxon forward, as Markam led the hooded Karr towards them.

They all met in the center.

"That's close enough," Sonara said. She fought the tremble in her hands as she reached out and pulled the hood from Karr's head, desperately hoping Markam's strength still held.

She relaxed, as Karr's face was revealed.

He'd been fashioned to look a little beaten, a little bruised, his hair falling over his eyes to help muddle the imperfect color. He kept his gaze down, his shoulders slumped…

"Free Jaxon," Sonara said. "*Now.*"

Cade shoved him forward.

Sonara had only a moment to grab him by the shoulders. To squeeze him tightly, hoping he could see it in her eyes, feel it in her touch. *I came for you. I did not leave you behind.* There was that summertime smile, a sign that he was unbroken, despite the green bruises wrapping around his throat, the scabs that showed he'd been a prisoner beneath the power of their metallic mite.

"Go," she whispered as she released him, giving him a helpful push towards Razor.

He climbed on her back, not questioning her even when Markam whistled, and Razor obeyed his command. In one massive beat of her wings, her body lifted from the dock, soaring away with Jaxon as if they were one with the wind.

Safe.

He was safe, and he was *free*.

"Come here, Karr," Cade said. He took his brother in his hands, then pulled him off to the side.

Sonara saw the moment he noticed the change. The way Karr's shoulders probably felt far thinner than they usually were. The way he smelled different, moved different…

"Now," Sonara said, "It is time you learned, Wanderer, what happens when you cross the Devil of the Deadlands."

She looked pointedly at Karr, and grinned.

"The punishment is grim," Karr said. But his voice was not *his* voice. It was too high, too airy and feminine. Karr's very body *rippled* like a coin dropped in water. And then he was changing. Morphing before their very eyes, until suddenly Cade was holding the shoulders of a young woman, dressed in Karr's suit.

But upon her face… a mask made out of a wolf's skull.

"Hello, Wanderer," Thali said.

Cade stumbled back in horror as the illusion fell, revealing that his brother was *not* his brother… that Markam's curse had painted Thali into Karr.

"Take the Devil alive," Cade gasped, his whole body trembling with rage and disgust and *fear,* heavy upon him as Sonara's own curse thrashed. *"Kill the others."*

His guards aimed.

But Markam had saved just enough of himself for one last push.

And just like that, Sonara felt his curse wrap over her body as his hand closed tight over hers.

And together, they disappeared.

Cade's soldiers fired, but Sonara and Markam had already moved, lunging to the right and sprinting towards the loading-dock door.

She could see the others now. The *real* Karr, and Azariah, their previously illusioned bodies now in full view at the loading-dock door as Karr placed his hand upon the scanner and furiously typed in a code. The door whooshed open.

Three steps away, and they'd be inside.

Cade's soldiers shouted, turning at the source of the noise.

"Karr!" Cade shouted.

The real Karr stepped aside from the doorway to let Sonara, Markam, and Azariah dive in.

A bullet lodged into the metal just beside him.

"No!" Cade shouted, but the door was already sliding shut.

The look on his face was one Sonara would remember forever.

Pained and broken, twisted in agony as he stood there, helplessly fooled by his own brother while a group of outlaws snuck aboard his ship and locked it from the inside.

CHAPTER 29

Sonara

It was eerily silent as the door slid shut behind them.

As if they'd stepped through another veil, or a portal into another world.

The only sound inside the *Starfall* was Markam groaning, as he dropped Sonara's hand and slumped to the floor, eyes closed and head leaning against the cool metal. Shadows poured from his nose, a look of pure agony on his face.

"He did it," Karr said. "I can't believe he *did* it."

"Believe it," Sonara said, even though she was just as shocked herself. "Markam is strong… insufferably so."

"It was too much to ask of him," Azariah said, as she knelt beside the Trickster. For the first time, she reached out and touched him, placing her gloved hands upon his cheeks so she could turn his gaze towards her.

Gone was the animosity between them, that palpable hatred Sonara's curse had always cast. There was still tentative mistrust, but… it seemed she cared enough that she didn't want to see his curse suck him dry.

"Magic that powerful, used for that amount of time, has a great cost," Azariah said. "Markam, can you walk?"

The Trickster groaned but nodded. "I just have to…" he grimaced as he fought off the unbearable headache Sonara knew he was likely experiencing. "I just have to catch my breath."

Sonara knew she should have been worried.

She'd brought nothing with her. No water, no food to give him energy to recover after he'd illusioned Thali into Karr. The cleric had decided upon it early that morning, so willing to give her life over to protect the planet's heart.

There was no telling what would happen to her now, stuck outside with Cade and the others.

But she'd insisted. So much so that she'd spent the entire morning praying to the planet before they'd left on their mission.

Sonara turned now to get a good look at the space. So long, she'd dreamt of finding this ship, of going inside and finding Soahm here waiting for her. Alive and well, after all these years.

This was another world entirely.

Silver, rounded walls and ceilings, as if the whole ship were made of hardened moonlight. Red lights glowed softly along the floor every few feet, giving her the strange feeling that they were in the belly of something living. The air felt stale, cold and crisp beyond the sleeves of her long duster.

Sonara sniffed the air, searching for a trace of Soahm.

But there was only *cold.*

Only the muted metallic tang of the ship's walls, like a handful of fresh coins pulled out of a pocket.

And there was a strange, muted sound of humming beneath

her feet. She took a step along the metal, feeling like the floor could fall out from under her.

If magic was what Thali and Azariah wanted to call a Shadowblood's curse…

Then this was *dark magic.*

Every part of Sonara screamed to turn back around, to rush into the open, endless air of Dohrsar. But the job was not finished.

"I can't believe I just betrayed my own brother," Karr said softly.

"It's not betrayal when you've finally chosen the right side," Sonara said. "Now what?"

She itched to move. To go deeper into the belly of the metallic beast and discover any traces of Soahm.

Karr worked at the wires in the small panel in the wall. "We find our way to the source. We shut down whatever's powering Cade's force field, and I'm guessing that'll take out all the mites with it."

"Guessing," Azariah said.

Karr shrugged. "Educated guess."

***

The ship felt like a living cage.

Sonara shivered as they jogged down the halls, sickened by the constant gentle thrum beneath her feet. Karr took the lead, turning this way and that, and Sonara kept her curse upon him, unafraid.

She would be ready, should he decide to turn on them.

Azariah and Markam took up the rear, Markam able to walk,

but clearly in pain as he followed numbly along, silent for once. Should the door to the loading dock be opened too quickly—the only way inside the ship from the small transport pod that went to and from the ground—they'd be the first line, the strongest defensive powers shared among them.

"The crew level is down one," Karr whispered.

He paused before an opening, a split in the hallway, as something red rolled past.

A tiny creature, seemingly made of painted steel; a Wanderer beastie, on three black wheels, that beeped and dragged a trash bin behind it.

"Sweeper droid," Karr whispered, as Azariah lifted her palms before her as if she wanted to attack. "*Not* a threat."

The droid beeped once more as it turned the corner, out of sight.

Duran would *not* be pleased, if he ever ran into one of them. It put a fleeting smile on Sonara's lips as they moved on. They passed by closed door after closed door, the lights flickering every so often. Still, that incessant humming beneath Sonara's feet.

Her curse lifted its head from inside its cage, sensing the hum… hungering for it. She could taste it, like electricity that mirrored the light-wall. But this was different, condensed and somehow stronger at the same time.

"It's below us," she whispered. "The source of the power."

Azariah nodded, as if she, too, could sense it. "Electricity, like I have never felt before."

They'd nearly reached the opposite end of the ship. It was too calm. *Too* easy.

They made their way through another arched door. Inside, a wide room with metal tables and chairs scattered about.

"Mess hall," Karr explained.

They jogged silently past portholes on all sides, windows that offered small glimpses of the outside world. From here, the Deadlands felt distant. Like she was back in Soreia, staring out at a view that would never be the same again, without Soahm.

Through the mess hall, they journeyed, until they reached what Karr called an *elevator.* A small metal boxlike room held aloft by magnetics, it would lower them towards the ship's engine room.

"It hasn't been fixed in ages," Karr said. "But it's quick enough. Four levels to go down, and we'll be at the storage bay. Easy as breathing."

He waved his hand before the panel on its side, and the doors opened with a cool hiss.

The metal room stared back at the group. A cage, more like. Sonara went first, pressing her back against the cool metal wall, her left hand on Lazaris' pommel. Markam stopped at her side, Karr and Azariah shuffling in next.

Karr pressed a button on a panel just inside the elevator. The doors slid shut.

Then the room *shook*, lowering them.

Sonara drew Lazaris in an instant.

"It's fine," Karr said. His lips tugged into a smile. "Trust me."

"Easier said than done," Sonara said back.

"Four levels down, the doors will open, and the storage bay door is just right down the hall," Karr said.

The elevator suddenly paused, only one level down.

"That's… not right," Karr said.

He pressed a button on the panel, his features twisting to a frown.

Anticipation, sweaty palms tightening over the handle of a metallic weapon.

The aura slammed against Sonara's curse, warning her only a second before the doors slid open and a cluster of armed guards stood waiting, just beyond.

CHAPTER 30

Sonara

Enemies, filling the hall.

Sonara counted ten in the breath of a moment before the first one lunged forward as if to grab her.

Sonara's blade was in her hand in an instant, the space so small she could only angle it forward, a single swipe of Lazaris that managed to cut a wicked slice through the man's abdomen.

He stumbled sideways as another came forward.

"Shut the door!" Sonara shouted.

Karr fumbled to shut it, but the doors were too damned *slow.*

"Fire!" the guard in the back yelled.

Bullets sprayed. Karr threw himself to the side, out of reach. Markam and Azariah hit the floor just as the bullets slammed into the back wall of the elevator, landing themselves in the metal. They were red-tipped, zapping with a spark of blue that left a smoke mark on the metal.

"Stunner bullets," Karr said, as the identical click of ten guns reloading sounded out.

"Az," Markam said. "We need you, *now.*"

"I can't," she said.

He ripped off her gloves. "*You must.*"

Her eyes met Sonara's as she spun.

The *pop* of the guns going off sounded out, but the bullets never landed. Because at the same time, with a scream of terror, Azariah threw her palms together, as if she held a blade, pointing it towards the guards.

There was a satisfying *crack* of electricity. The bullets melted as a bolt of her power spiraled from her palms, creating a sheet before her just as the doors slid shut.

Silence, once again, as if someone had simply put a pause on chaos.

"I… I did it," Azariah said in a breath. She held up her own hands, a triumphant grin on her face as if she'd found the key to her joy once more.

"What the hell?" Sonara whirled on Karr.

"They're using stunner bullets," Karr explained, plucking one of them from the back wall of the elevator. He dropped it to the floor with a tiny *ping*. "Cade gave the order to take you alive. Get hit by one of these, and you're *done*." He tapped the lowest button on the paneled wall three times, in rapid succession. "It's not responding. They're going to meet us on every level. They can use the stairs faster than we can ride on this. They'll be waiting."

"Stairs," Markam said. "We could have taken the damned *stairs*?"

"We'd have made too much noise, given ourselves away!"

"More than *this*?" Markam yelped. As he spoke, the elevator slowed again.

"How long?" Sonara asked. "How long before the doors close, once they're opened again?"

"Twenty seconds, give or take," Karr said.

The elevator jolted to a sudden stop.

Blast, Sonara hissed in her mind. Her curse slammed against its cage, knowing full well that enemies awaited them just behind those slow-opening doors.

"Don't move," Markam hissed as the doors slid wide.

The guards were already there, just as Karr said. Ten in number, their weapons raised and ready. But they paused, confusion twisting their features.

"It's empty, Jacques," the guard at point grunted.

Beside him, a lithe woman stepped forward, her large eyes narrowing. "It can't be. They were *just there.*"

Sonara saw it then… a shift in the air before her. Like a rippling wall of fabric where the elevator doors remained open, bathed in Markam's Trickster curse.

Twenty seconds before the doors would close again, and the elevator would be on the move. Sonara's heartbeat hammered in her throat.

Hold it, Markam, she prayed, even to the goddesses, for they were sitting beasts in this metal box, and what good could one sword do against ten soldiers with Wanderer guns?

Markam grunted behind her, so softly she almost didn't catch it.

Goddesses, it was near impossible how much power he'd used today. She'd always known him to be strong, but he'd never had a true mission, never put his mind to something like this.

The female guard tilted her head, as if she'd caught the sound of his grunt, but still saw nothing inside the elevator. She stepped forward, eyes narrowing, not two breaths from Sonara's face.

Hold the illusion, Sonara begged Markam. Her hand squeezed over Lazaris' pommel. She didn't dare breathe.

"I think..." The woman stepped forward, her rifle almost touching Sonara's chest. "There's something off about—"

Markam gasped, and the illusion broke as his strength gave all the way out.

"*FIRE!*" the woman yelled.

Sonara lashed out with Lazaris, the masterful blade shoving the rifle to the side just as the woman fired.

Behind her, Sonara heard Markam yelp as the bullet hit home.

Sonara lunged just out of the doorway and sliced the woman's hand clean off.

Blood sprayed as Lazaris split right through bone. The gun fell with it, and Sonara used the momentary lapse to wrap her arm around the woman's throat, yanking her backwards and using her body as a shield as her own soldiers fired in retaliation.

Three red bullets slammed against the woman's chest as the doors slid shut.

Her body was a dead weight in Sonara's arms.

"You..."

Sonara turned to find Karr wide-eyed, pressed against the elevator wall like a child in the face of a monster.

"You cut off her hand."

Sonara shrugged as she let the woman crumple at her feet, alive but unconscious. "Better a hand than a head."

He just blinked as the elevator dropped another floor.

A *ding* sounded out, and Sonara readied herself for a final wave of attacks—this time, without Markam's power.

He was slumped on the floor, unconscious, drool already

pooling onto his chest. But Azariah looked down at him as if she were looking at a beautifully chiseled statue, instead of roadkill left to rot beneath the desert suns.

"He… he saved me," she said. "He dove in front of me and took the bullet."

He'd never done that for *her*, Sonara realized. She nodded, surprised to find relief that the princess was still by her side, a comrade in arms. Perhaps even a *friend*. "Get your power ready, Princess. We're going to need it."

Azariah flexed her hands and turned to face the doors.

They slid open soundlessly.

But instead of nine guards waiting for them, there was only one.

The towering Wanderer woman who had stood beside Karr at the Gathering and screamed when Sonara drove her blade through his chest.

***

"Jameson," Karr blurted out, stepping away from the elevator wall.

Sonara eyed the scene quickly. The woman stood in a small hallway, a locked door about ten paces behind her; the entrance to the storage bay, where Sonara felt that *pull* towards the energy source.

Off to the right, another locked door. The paneling was removed and messed with, the very same way Karr had done when they'd snuck aboard the ship.

Sonara could hear pounding fists behind it, muffled shouts as guards tried to break through.

Jameson had gotten here first, it seemed. And jammed the door from the outside.

Her skin was tan, muscles rippling down her bare arms as she reached up to tap the visor on her helmet. It slid open, revealing her face beyond.

"Kingston," she said. "What the hell are you doing?"

Fear filtered from her aura, but as she looked at Karr, there was something else there. Desperation, a need to save him. Familial love, the kind Sonara held for Jaxon, for Soahm…

Her accent was similar to Karr's, lifting upwards at the end of her words. But there was *knowing* in her eyes, as if she were staring at an old friend. Her pistol wavered as she saw him, then steadied again as she looked at Sonara, Markam and Azariah.

"Don't. Please." Karr held out his hands. "Jameson, this isn't what it looks like."

"Then explain it to me. Because it looks to me like you're walking free, navigating a group of Dohrsarans through your own ship."

"I'm not a prisoner," Karr explained. "Step aside, Jameson. *Please*."

The woman's gaze landed on Sonara, eyes narrowing and hands sliding the safety of her pistol back. A series of beeps sounded, and then the gun was glowing blue, Jameson lifting it to fire.

"Dammit. Put your weapon down," Karr commanded. "That's an order."

But Jameson did not relent. "What did they do to you, Karr?"

"Nothing but help me see the truth. My entire life, we've been comrades. But I'd be more inclined to call us family, Jameson. You and me, we can out-drink all the rest of them."

The woman gave a nervous smile from inside her helmet.

And though Sonara sensed fear… Jameson's aura also revealed hesitation. A decision to trust Karr, already made. *A flower not quite ready to blossom, but swaying towards the kiss of sunlight, leaning closer to the call of the wind.*

Her hands shook. "Tell me why I shouldn't kill them, Karr. They kidnapped you. That one," she glared at Sonara, "tried to *kill* you just days ago."

Karr walked past Sonara, his hands outstretched. "It's true. But it was supposed to happen. I can't explain how I know. But it's the way things were always meant to go. I've seen other parts of this planet. I've spent time exploring it, and… it's changed me. Cade's mission is a death wish. Not only for this planet, but for so many more of them. What Geisinger plans to do with the Antheon could bring about the *end*."

"The end of what?" Jameson asked.

"Order," Karr said. "It's going to change people. It's going to cause chaos across the stars."

Her eyes narrowed. She lifted her gun again, swinging it towards Sonara. "You've never stood against Cade before. Not once. How am I to know they're not forcing you to do this against your will? That whatever they've done to you since taking you isn't what's driving this?"

"Drop your sword," Karr said. "Sonara. Do it."

"Like hell I will," Sonara hissed. It was a fool's request. But as she said the words, Jameson's aura changed, leaning towards the darker decision. The one that would end with Sonara and Markam and Azariah bleeding out with Wanderer bullets in their chests. With a deep sigh, Sonara lowered Lazaris.

Karr took a step towards his crew member. Who he claimed to be his friend. "She's not my enemy. She's not yours. You've always helped me see the lighter side of things. You've always been there with me, helping me understand that life is what you make of it."

The woman's hands were shaking now. The pistol was wavering in her grip, its blue glow beginning to fade as it powered down.

Karr took another step.

He was only an arm's length away.

"You've known since the beginning that what Cade is doing here is *wrong*. You did nothing to stop it."

"He made me swear," she whispered.

Then she was trembling full-out as Karr reached her and took the barrel of the pistol in his outstretched hands. But still, she did not let go.

"He made me swear that I wouldn't tell you. Because if I did… God, he knows you so well, Karr, it's like Cade *knew* you wouldn't stand for it. He made me swear I wouldn't let you screw with the job. That I'd do what it took to stop you if you tried."

"Bastard," Karr hissed. The hideous word made Sonara's insides churn. "And you chose to side with him? Like all the rest of them?"

Jameson nodded. "Of course I sided with him. He's my captain. He gave me a home onboard this ship. A place to lay my head."

"Then you'll have to shoot me. Right now. If you want to stop me, Jameson… go ahead. Do it."

The soldier released a shaking breath and dropped her gun, tears in her eyes. "I sided with him *then*, Karr. I sided with him because he promised it would make a better life for you. For all of us." Tears fell from her eyes. "But you know I'm not the kind to keep a bloody promise. I'm done. The second I saw you again, I knew I was done."

Karr whooshed out a breath, and then he was gripping her tight by the shoulder. She returned the gesture, and suddenly her aura was *pleasant, like freshly dyed silk drying on the wind.*

The locked door began to buckle, as if they were hitting it with an axe.

"They're going to break through, Jameson," Karr said. "And you'll have to explain why you didn't take their side. We're taking the escape pod, getting out of here after we shut this mission down. Come with us."

Jameson shook her head. "I can't. I already made mistakes, Karr. I knew it was wrong, but I stood down there beside your brother and let him do… the horrors that he and Rohtt and Geisinger planned. I won't live the rest of my life knowing I had a hand in it."

"So what, then?" Karr asked.

She stepped aside, motioning for them to move past her. "Go. I'll do my best to slow them."

"Jameson—"

"*Go*, kid. You've always been a thorn in my side. Defiant and self-glorifying, and so damn stubborn I don't know how anyone could stand against it." She pressed a gloved hand to his cheek. "Go. I'll see you when the stars go dim."

"Please," Karr said.

She nudged him away. "You can stop him. I know you can, kid."

Her words were final. Sonara sensed it on the woman's aura, as much as she saw it in Karr's slumping shoulders as he backed away.

Then he was running past her, stopping before the storage-bay door as he tried to bypass the locks. Karr cursed. But then another fumble of his fingers, and the door to the storage bay hissed open.

Darkness yawned from within. A massive room, unlit.

"Inside," Karr commanded. Sonara and Azariah dragged Markam's limp body along, heaving against his unconscious weight.

But Karr paused on the threshold, looking back at Jameson.

"Please," he said.

She just smiled again. "Good luck."

The door beside Jameson blasted open with a cloud of smoke.

Cade stepped through, Rohtt beside him, along with a flood of guards.

"Karr!" Cade shouted, as Karr stepped inside and slammed the button just inside the storage bay. The door began to slide shut, sealing them inside.

Just before it closed, Sonara saw Jameson root herself in the center of the hall, her rifle held in her arms as if it was the last time she'd ever hold it.

"I can't let you go, Captain." She pointed her gun at him, and held it steady.

Cade lifted his own rifle. They heard a gunshot, just as the door slid closed like the lid of a casket.

Karr dropped to his knees, not knowing in whose chest the bullet had landed.

Just as Sonara turned, staring out at the dark storage bay, her eyes wide.

Because he was here.

Soahm was inside.

***

She'd recognize the aura anywhere, like it had been a part of her all along.

Like sun-kissed skin and wind-blown waves, the salt that hung, ever present, in the Soreian air.

"Soahm," Sonara breathed.

The aura was overwhelming.

The others called out to her, but she was already rushing forward, sprinting past waiting rows of Wanderer machines chained down in their loading spaces. The room was *massive*, easily half of what made up the entire ship.

Her footsteps echoed like the retorts of bullets as she ran past crates and metal boxes packed into shelves against the walls, so many strange auras pinging at her from all around. Guns sat in their locked casings, the rifles that had brought down her people, shot them in cold blood. She slowed as the aura grew stronger.

Left, her curse sang.

Sonara turned, walking past shelving full of Gazers like the ones she'd often chased on Duran. Everything together, *all* of it, was like piecing together the answers to the attack. And everything leading up to it. The elements that had enslaved Jaxon, and all her people.

But Sonara cared not, in this moment.

For Soahm's aura, the memory of him, had never been so strong as it was here, *now.*

Twenty paces, her curse said.

Sonara slowed, searching for him. A tan and handsome face, pressed among the crates, or his body tied and broken from torture, or perhaps a jail cell, where he sat waiting…

The aura stopped at the entrance to a massive silver orb; the escape pod Karr had mentioned would be their way out.

The door was just barely ajar.

"Soahm," Sonara called softly.

She tasted salt on her tongue, not from her curse, but from the wetness of tears spilling down her cheeks, landing on her lips.

He was just inside. Her brother was only a few paces away.

"Sonara!" Azariah called out. "Wait!"

Sonara scarcely heard the princess' voice as she walked forward, closing the gap.

With trembling hands, she reached out to grasp the heavy side of the escape pod's door. With a mighty heave… it opened.

Soahm's aura rushed out in a wave.

Here.

"Soahm," she said again, his name like a promise on her lips, a promise she'd kept for ten long years, every hour of every day since he went missing. She swore she would find him. Bring him home.

But the escape pod was empty.

"It can't be," Sonara said. "*No.*"

She crawled inside, scrambling over the first row of seats. They were worn and emptied of their stuffing. Ancient. Smelling of decay and dust. Another row of seats, and then a pilot's chair, a dashboard with shoddy-looking tech. No spaces to hide, no spaces for Soahm to be waiting within.

"Where is he?" she growled.

She turned, abandoning the escape pod. She marched across the storage bay, striding past Markam's unconscious figure, past Azariah who sat on a crate beside him, until she reached Karr. She grasped the collar of his shirt. "Where is he?"

"*What?*" Karr asked. "Sonara, I—"

"I SAID, WHERE IS HE?"

She slammed him against the metal wall of the storage bay. His head hit with a sickening crack, but he did not cry out. He let her shove him against it, curling his shirt in her fists.

"He's here. I can sense his aura, all over this hellish place."

Karr's eyes were desperate as she growled and pulled him away from the wall, then turned and hauled him back towards the pod where Soahm's aura waited, whispering, *Here I am, Sonara. Find me.*

She shoved Karr to his knees, then whirled and pointed at the pod. "Where is my brother?"

"Sonara."

His palms were face-up. Pleading. She removed her sword—*Soahm's* sword that she'd stolen from Soreia on her way out—and pointed it at Karr. She no longer cared if he was a Shadowblood, no longer cared that he'd helped her into this very ship. He'd once carried Soahm's lingering scent as he'd bled. He had to *know something.*

"You'll tell me where he is," Sonara growled, and the words were bitter on her tongue. Full of her desperation, her rage. "Or I will drive this blade in deep, and this time, Karr Kingston, you *will not come back.*"

The space was silent.

She looked past his shoulder at the empty pod, certain that once she looked inside again, she'd see her brother waiting, that stupid sly prince's grin on his lips, his laughter bubbling over.

I've waited for you a long time, he would say. *I waited, and you finally found me.*

You win, She-Devil.

You win.

"Sonara. He's not here," Karr said. "I'm telling you the truth."

She crawled back inside the cramped pod. "*Please*," she begged her curse. She no longer feared it. She needed it, could not go on without it. "Please, show me the way."

A deep breath, from far within.

And then that ever-present voice whispered, *The dash, my dear little Shadowblood. Just there, to the right.*

Sonara reached out, realizing there was a small golden chain wrapped around the throttle of the ship.

Golden and… familiar.

Her hands shook as she grasped the chain. It was cool in her fingertips, clinking as she dropped the bauble into her outstretched palm.

She lifted it, gently, and breathed in.

There it was. The aura that had beckoned, that held Soahm within.

All from the stone. Not actually from him.

"It was his," Sonara said softly.

She turned.

Karr stood there, watching her with sadness in his eyes.

"But that can't be. It was my mother's," he said. "One of the few things she always held onto, was never willing to sell in all of their dealings and travels. She said it came from a friend. But I always suspected it meant something more. She was still wearing it when she was killed."

"Not from a friend," Sonara said, and she didn't know why

she felt so hopeless. "It belonged to Soahm. All his life, he wore it. He had it on the day he was taken."

"Perhaps he gave it to them," Karr offered. "If they were here, if they were still alive… we could ask them."

"They stole him from Dohrsar," Sonara said. "I saw it."

"They wouldn't have done it without reason," Karr said. "They were *good* people, Sonara."

"As good as Cade?" she asked.

His words died on his lips. He looked past her, at the dashboard. "I should get to work here… I should get ready to eject us once we stop the power source. Before Cade finds a way in."

She felt like time had frozen, like her skin had gone numb, the feeling spreading from the outside in.

Ten years of searching…

Ten years of hoping…

She had her answer. She had a piece of Soahm *here*, the most evidence she'd ever been able to find to prove that he'd been taken, that this ship was the one who'd hauled him aboard. She should be elated, as if she were close to finding the rest of him.

But something felt final.

Like this was all she would ever discover of her brother.

Sonara placed Soahm's necklace over her head, tucking the stone beneath her shirt to keep it safe. Soahm's scent faded as she settled down on the ground beside the pod, trying to breathe in the last of him. But little by little, the aura was fading, as if it had held on long enough for her to discover it.

One breath more… and she sensed it no longer.

"I think I found the power source," Azariah said.

Sonara glanced up, wiping her tears away.

The Princess stood over her, those dark eyes watching her closely.

"I am sorry, my friend," Azariah said carefully. "We have both lost someone we love today, in different ways." Sonara knew she spoke of Thali, her trainer and advisor and perhaps the only true family she'd ever had. "But we must finish the job we started. Only then, once the battle is won, can we take the time to sit and weep."

The words were brutally honest, but there was not a hint of coldness to her voice.

Only strength without judgement, so far from how the royals in Sonara's life had always behaved. And so different from Azariah's own father, Jira.

"Come, Devil," Azariah said. "Let's finish this together."

When she held out a hand, Sonara reached up and took it.

CHAPTER 31

Karr

Not long ago, he'd been in this very space alone, dreaming of another life.

Now Karr led the outlaws through the storage bay, past rows of tied-down crates that were now emptied. How long had Cade been planning this with Geisinger, while Karr drank his daylights out on Beta Earth, and ignored everything his older brother was loading onto the ship each night?

He hadn't known the crates were hiding assault rifles, a massive electric drill, and—

God forbid he even think it—the mites that kept the Dohrsarans prisoner.

But then again, if he had... what would he have done, back then? What level would he have pushed himself to, to stop Cade, before his eyes were opened by the people who walked with him now?

"It drops down lower," Karr said, stopping before the small rickety ladder that led to the ship's engine room. He'd spent plenty of time down here as a kid, hiding in the hard-to-navigate places.

Pipes slowly spat out steam, cooling the engine room as he climbed through the opening and down the rungs of the ladder, the others closely following.

"Cade can't be running the force field on the ship's power alone. That would have meant going into total shut-down mode, lowering the levels so that the only power was fueled towards the light-wall itself. And the mites... they'd have to have a constant source, too."

"There is power in this place," Azariah said, as she walked behind Karr, ducking around pipes and past the countless panels that blinked readings back at him. Too much for him to ever consider learning about beyond the basics he already knew.

This was always the mech's job, a position that swapped out as often as Karr swapped out bits of charcoal for his drawings.

They passed the *Starfall*'s main engine; a beastly, greased-up thing that rumbled softly, ever-present in its power. But not near enough to keep the ship aloft *and* keep Cade's tools of imprisonment running at the same time.

No, there had to be something else... something *more* that he wouldn't have taken any notice of. For how long had it been, since he'd come to this darkened space? Cade wouldn't have even *had* to hide it.

"It calls to me," Azariah said. "From just up ahead."

Sonara spat on the ground behind her. "It's putrid," she said. "The aura of it. Power like the volcano that lies in waiting out in the Black Waters. Like a sleeping giant."

There were only a few dim red emergency lights that glowed softly in the upper rafters of the cramped room, but it began to lighten as they came to the very center of the *Starfall*, where the ancient transporter base sat.

Not the actual transporter, for that tech had been outlawed ages ago, every last transporter removed and destroyed from all ships in the ITC. It was dangerous tech, the kind that allowed ships to soar into spaces previously thought uninhabitable or unwelcome, and simply remove what they chose—a tech that had the power to scientifically *lift* an object from the ground with a tube-like force field that slowly drew them into the waiting ship.

Battles were won with it.

Cities were ransacked and picked clean.

"It wouldn't be here," Karr said.

But even as he said it, he felt sick.

For there was a dim blue glow, and a warmth in this space. And there were dark curtains hanging in the engine room that had never been there before, splitting the space in two.

"Here," Azariah said. She held out her hands, her eyes narrowing as she nodded at the curtains before her, the blue light seeping under and around the gaps. "This is what calls to me. This is what we must destroy."

Karr's stomach churned, nausea suddenly washing over him.

He stepped forward and drew the dark curtains aside, knowing already what he'd find. Another unraveling thread in the truth behind Cade's plan.

Somehow, Geisinger had replaced the transporter inside the ship. Or redesigned it, perhaps, because what Karr saw now was tech he'd never seen on such a condensed scale, so perfectly balanced inside of a single starship.

An atlas orb; the kind of clean, endless energy that powered entire cities on Beta Earth, discovered by Geisinger's great-grandfather decades and decades ago on a planet at the edge of the galaxy.

The atlas orbs were *massive*, back on Beta, but this one was no larger than a globe.

It hovered there over an open hatch in the engine room floor, the distant ground visible far below.

The atlas orb crackled with power, slowling spinning like a tiny planet on its own axis. Beneath the orb, past the open hatch in the floor, Karr could see the walls of Cade's light-cage. They spanned from the center of the atlas orb, stretching far, far down to the ground like a cone, where it trapped everyone inside.

"What… is it?" Sonara asked.

Her face and hair were bathed entirely in cool blue; the exact shade Karr would have sketched her in, to paste upon the ceiling of his bunk.

"An atlas orb," Karr said. "I don't know how to stop it."

"Turn it off," Sonara said simply.

But as Karr looked at the orb, his eyes tracing the open hatch in which it hovered… he saw nothing that would give him any indication of *how* to stop it.

He'd never studied the atlas orbs, never knew how they were able to give such endless power, or if, once put in place, they could even be shut off. It was a job for scientists and specialists; a job for Geisinger, or perhaps Rohtt, who knew far more than he was letting on.

"I'm sorry," Karr said. "There's nothing I can do."

Sonara turned to him, hands on her hips. "We did not come this far…"

"I didn't know this would be here," he explained. "I didn't know *anything*, though I've told you that before, *countless times*, about your brother, but you refuse to believe—"

"Do not speak of Soahm!" Sonara spat. "We must stop this, Wanderer."

"I don't care about Soahm!" Karr practically growled the name.

Sonara retreated a step, her back pressing against a metal coolant pipe. "This very space," she said softly, "is where he was taken." She pointed at the open hatch in the floor, where the atlas orb spun. "That doorway opened wide, and a blue light carried him from the sand up into the ship. This is where he was taken."

It couldn't be the truth, for that would have been ten years ago, and if it was… that meant his parents were still alive, captaining this ship. It would have meant they'd been using a transporter, working with illegal tech and kidnapping an innocent Dohrsaran prince.

"It can't be true," Karr said.

But he knew it was, for why would a Dohrsaran know about transporters, and how they worked? It was a tech that should have been alien to Sonara… and yet she'd just explained it clear as day, like she'd never forgotten the moment her brother was stolen.

Karr sat down on the ground, his energy gone. "I don't know what else to do," he said. He looked over his shoulder, back into the winding metal maze of the engine room. Somewhere above, Markam was left unconscious, and the doorway to the storage bay would soon be blasted open. Cade and his soldiers would come through, and this little charade would be over.

Perhaps it was truly the end of Karr's last stand against this whole damned job.

"Thali once told me something I did not believe," Azariah said.

She stepped forward, slowly, to peer at the atlas orb.

Her eyes, pools of endless black, reflected the orb's pure ocean blue.

"She said that if one can only find a reason to give themselves over to the magic given to us—the bit of the planet's soul that courses through our Shadowblood veins—there is no limit to the power we can unlock."

She removed her gloves and dropped them on the floor, forgotten.

"Azariah," Sonara said. "Don't touch it."

"Those are my people down there," Azariah said. She reached out her hands, her bare palms facing the atlas orb as if she were holding them over a warm fire. "And it was *my* father who joined with the Wanderers to cage them. To make them prisoners, to cut apart the Bloodhorns until they discover its very heart."

She smiled to herself, closing her eyes as she seemed to bask in the moment.

"Thali did a great thing today, in handing herself over so that we could gain entry to this space."

"Azariah," Sonara said. "Don't—"

The Princess turned to smile at her. It was the kind of smile that belonged to a queen. A woman who deserved to rule, not with an iron first, but with love and light and respect for her people. "I am sorry, Sonara, for the second life you've lived on the run. But should I survive this… when I become queen, you will always have a place in my court."

Before anyone could stop her, she took another step forward.

And with a great *heave*, Azariah's magic erupted.

CHAPTER 32

Sonara

Fire exploded into Sonara's senses.

Beside her, Azariah stood with her hands outstretched, her skin glowing blue as her power struck the atlas orb.

Sonara's hair stood on end, her curse screaming as it was filled with *smoke, the scent of an ancient city burning to a pile of ashes on the ground.*

Azariah's lightning smashed against the orb, blue against blue, a Dohrsaran curse against Wanderer science.

Death, the voice inside of Sonara hissed, as she sensed Azariah's life, her very energy, like a candle burning low. The Princess screamed, her lightning crackling against the power-source in an endless death blow.

If she did not stop soon… she was going to burn out.

The atlas orb flickered. A tiny *blip* in the energy that Sonara's curse sensed as a momentary wave of smoke, like a candle guttering before growing strong again.

Incredible that Azariah was able to stand against it. And if she could keep going, there might still be a chance.

Like an extension of her body, a bit of her soul, her lightning forked from her outstretched palms and clashed against the atlas orb. The orb pulsed like a living thing, fighting back against her power.

Azariah dropped to her knees, her body trembling as she screamed against the power surging from her palms. Her arms had turned utterly black, with blue lines of lightning digging into her charred skin like etched burns. Slowly, the burns snaked upwards. Palms to wrists. Wrists to elbows. Elbows to shoulders.

She was giving everything, *everything*, towards shutting down the atlas orb.

So why wasn't it going out?

Release me.

Sonara suddenly heard the whisper inside of her; the call of her curse.

Release me and let me fight with her.

Take away her fear.

Take away her pain.

Years, Sonara had spent hiding from her curse, locking it inside its cage, for it was an uncontrollable beast. Years, she'd *feared* it, deep down, for the power it held over her.

But as Azariah screamed, as her lightning burned its way to her shoulders, the retort of each slam against the atlas orb like a whip cracking over and over again…

Sonara knew that each surge of power brought the princess closer to death.

Memories flickered through her like snapshots as she leaned closer to the power source, palms outstretched.

Sonara saw herself as a new Shadowblood, standing beside Duran as he drank from the Briyne. Tears poured down her face, and her head pounded with the effort not to breathe, not to sense all the auras spiraling past her, trying to claw their way into her senses.

The power source rippled as tears poured from Azariah's eyes now.

Sonara stepped closer to her.

Sonara, hands shaking as she tied a bandana tight around her own face, closed her eyes, and willed her senses to dull, to no avail.

Sonara, seated in a bar as she drank bottle after bottle of oil to try to dull the pain.

She could no longer hear Azariah's screams over the crackle of power, the fight against the atlas orb. But Sonara felt her own body turning hot, sweat pouring down her skin as she looked at the princess.

The burns stretched upwards, to her neck.

Sonara, years later, her heart slamming against her ribs as Markam pulled her into the shadows behind a saloon. She laughed as she kissed him, as his teeth tugged at her ear. He pressed a hurried kiss along her neck, and she no longer felt alone.

Not until the aura of lust, verging on love, was so strong, her curse trying to break from its cage that she shoved him roughly away.

"Why do you do it, Sonara?" he asked. "Why do you always push everyone away?"

She'd never kissed anyone again, after that night.

The memories sped forward.

Sonara, moving to the corner of a lively saloon, pulling her hood over her head to drown out the sounds of the music. Jaxon, laughing as he downed a mug of oil and asked her to dance, but she said no, always no, for the joy between them would do nothing but awaken her curse until it begged to devour the auras whole.

The only time she let it loose was when she swung Lazaris, when she cut through victim after victim, using her curse only in the moments it could help her win a fight; help her grab a payday; help her survive.

Laughter, joy, happiness… it was all too much to bear.

The strongest emotions, the purest ones, only begged her curse to break through its cage even harder.

It was fear she could squash most easily, anticipation or little white lies that she could force her caged curse to ignore. Still, the pain she got from releasing it would throw her down to her bedroll each night, for *ten years*, swearing to herself that someday she'd find a way to rip it out of her body.

"She's burning out," Karr yelled.

Sonara blinked as she came back to the present, and focused on Azariah.

Help her, be brave, the voice in Sonara's soul whispered. *Do it now, before her time runs out.*

The Princess' skin was beginning to flake away, like ashes on the wind.

Her dark hair was aglow, the ends rising all around her as she fought. She had become more than a comrade, more than a deal made in Sandbank. She'd become a *friend*, the only female Sonara had ever trusted.

She stepped forward, without thinking, and lifted her own hands.

Yes, her curse purred inside. *Release me now, Shadowblood.*

With a shout, Sonara blasted open the cage inside of her. Her curse soared outwards, stretching for Azariah, little shadow hands grabbing ahold of the princess' aura. It was pure terror, surging through her, hot and sticky and impossible to scrape from her skin.

But Sonara began to reel back the tether, remembering what had happened on the night she'd faced the Hadru. She harnessed the princess' fear, the terror Azariah felt now as she faced the atlas orb.

In one breath, Sonara pulled the aura of fear right from the princess.

She hauled it back towards herself, letting her curse attack it, devour it… and in a breath it was gone.

Azariah's body seemed to shift.

As if the fear that had been holding her back was the final weight that had to be lifted.

She drew herself to her feet, her entire body trembling with the effort as she kept her hands before her.

Sonara watched, amazed, as the princess shaped her lightning into a sword.

A mighty sword of pure Shadowblood power, far better than Gutrender could ever be. She lifted her hands above her head, the sword following with it, until it was poised above the atlas orb, ready to strike.

Take it down, Sonara thought to her.

The Princess slammed her hands down, and the lightning sword drove straight through the atlas orb.

A great explosion threw them all sideways as the ship shuddered.

The electricity fizzled out, collapsing in upon itself, fading from existence until it was no more.

Azariah collapsed, and somewhere beneath the ship, a great *hum* fell silent.

Sonara peered through the circular opening, the space where the atlas orb had just been… as the light-wall faded, its power gone.

The Dohrsarans were trapped by a cage no more.

***

The rush from the engine room was muddled and breathless, a moment of blurred time, full of uttered curses as Karr and Sonara hauled the princess up the stairs and back into the storage bay.

Her body was charred, smoke trailing from her hands, but she was alive… alive, and a savior.

Karr carried her towards the escape pod that sat waiting, the scent of Soahm no longer hiding inside. Sonara dragged an unconscious Markam in, too, strapping them both in haphazardly.

"You're sure this thing works?" Sonara asked, as Karr frantically started it up.

The lights guttered and came to life within.

The door sealed shut, just as Sonara heard a *boom.*

To their right, the door was blasted open, smoke pouring through the entryway as Cade and his soldiers sprinted in.

But Karr was not paying attention.

For the escape pod shook, a feeling that sent Sonara's stomach dropping to her toes, and then they were tipping forward, as the very side of the storage bay opened, practically spitting the pod out, shoving it *away* from the *Starfall* like a swatted fly.

Sonara screamed, clutching the straps in terror as they *fell.* As her stomach shot into her throat, and the small glass window in front of them revealed the ground drawing ever closer.

"Hold on!" Karr yelped.

At the last second, the pod jerked upwards as if it had sprouted wings. Sonara swallowed her scream as it carted them across the sky, through where the light-wall had once been.

Past the Dohrsarans below, they soared, over the valley and the hundreds that had been imprisoned, but were no longer held within the electric cage.

"Oh, hell," Karr groaned. He slammed a button on the dash, then pulled up on the small wheel before him, but the pod did not respond. The lights guttered out again, and then they were sputtering, bouncing like a wagon driving across uneven sand, as the pod died. Karr looked to Sonara with a strange sense of eerie calm as he said, "We're going to crash."

They'd defeated the atlas orb.

They'd shut down the light-wall and escaped.

So why, Sonara thought numbly, as the pod neared the ground… *why are the prisoners not running free?*

The answer never came.

Sonara's body lurched forward into darkness as the pod slammed into the sand.

CHAPTER 33

Karr

Karr woke in the half-place again, standing on the grey sand shore.

"You're nearing the end, lost soul. See how the sky falls?"

The Child of Starlight stood beside him, her nebula eyes turned to the night. The wind tugged at her hair, shaking the stars and planets that made up the strands. She pointed, a ringed planet shining on the tip of her finger.

Karr followed it with his gaze.

Above them, far above… a tiny star turned from its place in the sky. It shifted. Then it began lowering itself towards them, a tail of firelight sparkling in its wake.

"The sky isn't falling," Karr said with a small smile. For he'd seen that image countless times before. He'd been the boy inside of it, staring out a viewport as a new world beckoned below. "It's a starship breaking through the atmosphere."

The girl sighed and closed her eyes. "Can't you feel it?"

"Feel what?" Karr asked.

Across from them, the waves, in half-roiling white and half a calm, cool black, continued their constant dance. "Your magic calls to the planet itself. Reach out with it. Touch the breeze. See that it trembles as the darkness draws near."

She reached for Karr's hand.

Pain slammed into his chest, a piercing stab of blazing fire. But before he could gather the strength to scream, the scene shifted.

And suddenly they were standing in the shadows of a cave, peering out at the half-sea from within.

"Memories are hard to come by, when you have lived so many lives," the girl said sadly. She tucked a star-strand behind her small ear. "Come, little Shadowblood. Let us see what will be revealed to us this time."

She pointed, and to the right, two blurry figures arrived. They looked to be little more than ghosts, their color sapped, their voices muted as if they were behind a veil.

The first was tall and lithe. A young man, perhaps seventeen, with a jaw so handsomely square it could have been stone-carved. His cloak trailed behind him, snapping in the ocean wind as he walked. Slowly, with great pain, he seemed to move, as if he'd been injured in battle.

Beside him appeared a smaller figure, smiling as she flipped through a worn journal, not caring where she walked. She was a young woman, perhaps still considered a girl, her curls concealing her face as they tumbled about in thick, unruly waves. *"You're getting better."* Her voice felt like it was underwater as she pointed at a leather-bound journal in her hands. *"This one looks exactly like me."*

"Keep it," the young man said. *"Try your hand at a sketch, Little Sister. It's kept me busy during my recovery."*

"If I could spare you from the pain, lost soul," the Child of

Starlight whispered, her lips warm and glowing against Karr's ear, "I certainly would. But pain is what grows us and shows us who we truly are."

A cool wind crept through the cave, kissing Karr's ankles as he peered out at the scene. The hair on his arms began to stand on end. Beyond the mouth of the cave, the starship closed in on the beach.

"The darkness," the Child of Starlight sang beside him. "See how it blots out the stars in the sky?"

She'd just uttered the words when the ship slowed, finally noticed by the two figures, who'd taken a seat on the sand. They looked skyward, their eyes wide with terror.

Karr saw, unmistakably, the insignia stamped on the ship's belly in boldest red.

The phoenix. It was the *Starfall.*

"Run." The girl's voice trembled, the echo of her word fluttering like it had wings as she grabbed the young man's hand, abandoning the journal in the sand. "*Run!*"

She turned, leaping to her feet.

"Slow down!" The young man's outline blurred as he tried to stand, too.

Her hand slipped from his. For where she was fast and lithe, he stumbled, his gait unsteady as he winced and tried to keep up. *"Wait, Sonara! WAIT!"*

She was ten steps ahead. Then twenty, as she raced towards the mouth of the cave.

With a loud cry, the young man fell and crashed hard into the sand, his leg twisting beneath him.

The girl looked over her shoulder, her eyes wide as she realized, in her fear, she'd left him behind. She turned and had only made it a few paces out of the shadows, her hand reaching for him, when a beam of blue light erupted from the belly of the ship. Old tech, outlawed years ago; a transporter. The beam surrounded the young man, lifting him from the ground.

He screamed and thrashed, trying to escape, but he was powerless against the beam's hold. His arms stretched, a black amulet on a chain of gold dangling from his tunic, shining in the beam as the ship's belly yawned wide and pulled him inside before slamming back shut.

"See how the darkness steals," the Child of Starlight suddenly whispered. Karr had nearly forgotten she was there. "See how it leaves behind nothing but pain." Her warm glow flickered as she turned, pointing back towards the girl now hiding in the mouth of the cave.

Karr could not hear her scream above the roar of the *Starfall*'s engines as they powered up and readied to soar away. But he *saw* it, the agony in her eyes as her lips formed a name.

Soahm.

She reached out, her hand trembling as the ship rose to the sky and carried her brother away. A blast of hot wind soared into the cave. It pushed the curls from the girl's face, dried the tears as they fell from her eyes.

"Sonara," Karr breathed.

Her story was true. His parents' ship had come to Dohrsar. And if it was that long ago, then it explained why Karr thought he'd seen his father's face, peering down from the hatch in the ship's belly, where the transporter worked to swallow its Dohrsaran prize.

“They stole him,” Karr whispered.

The scene faded. The ship and the girl’s outline soared away like smoke on the wind, until the cave was empty again.

They had *stolen* Soahm, just as Sonara said. Abducted him in the dark of night.

“The darkness has returned again,” the Child of Starlight said. “I’ve given you all the memories I could hold. But now you must wake, lost soul. You must try to remember who you are. For this time… the darkness will destroy all.”

He knew what came next.

It didn’t make the pain any less as she drove her starlight finger into his chest, and sent him screaming away from the half-place, back into the blazing morning light of Dohrsar.

CHAPTER 34

Cade

"String her up inside the brig," Cade ordered, and wiped beads of sweat from his brow.

His soldier ran off to give Rohtt the command: to lock up the woman in the wolf-mask—who'd been acting as Karr—to torture her, if need be, and discover why the hell his little brother had taken *their* side.

Cade stood at the railing, looking down at the prisoners below, furious at himself for letting his brother get stolen in the first place.

He didn't have to guess what happened after that. Karr had probably been tortured by his captors. But then, as he always did, he'd wormed his way into their minds. Found a way to speak to them, figure out their plans, and then decided to take matters into his own hands.

Somewhere along the way, Karr had sided with the Dohrsarans.

Now he'd shut down the atlas orb and had soared away in his battered escape pod to do whatever it was he had planned for next.

Cade should have known. The moment Rohtt came aboard the

ship, Karr had seen through the man, seen the darkness in him, and probably decided right then and there that he would stop this.

Karr... troublesome, clever, good-to-the-soul Karr, Cade thought sadly. *You don't know what you're doing. You've joined the wrong side of a war you cannot win.*

***

Cade walked towards the brig, feeling weary. Burdened. His steps were heavy, his breaths uneven.

"She's asked for you." Rohtt's voice pulled Cade from his trance as he escorted him down the stairwell to the brig. "Only you."

"Then we'll give her what she wants," Cade said. He crossed his arms with a painful wince.

God, he should have told Karr everything from the beginning. Or better yet, he should have just left him behind, safe on Beta. If he had... it never would have come to this.

Cade peered inside the glass door that led to the brig. The wolfen girl was strung up by her wrists, which were covered by bone gauntlets. No one was inside with her, for she was laughing. Over and over again, *laughing*, like the electricity they'd used to question her had gone to her brain.

"There's something you should know about her, before you go in," Rohtt said.

Cade gave him a sideways glance.

"We've shocked her with so much, you think it would have killed her. Hell, it should have killed her three times over again. But she's still alive. Still just... laughing."

Cade swallowed and typed in the code, then slipped inside the brig.

The woman was waiting for him.

Her laughing fell silent when he entered. The smell of lightning was strong, like burned hair and singed skin. The girl's eyes, pale and pupilless beyond her wolf mask, fell on Cade.

"You *fool*," she hissed. "You have no idea what you're doing to this sacred space."

Cade took a stool from the corner of the brig. Its legs scraped against the metal floor as he placed it before her and sat down.

"Who are you? What were you doing with my brother? And why do you think you're vital to helping me complete my mission?"

Oh, the things she told him in that room.

She cracked like an egg and spilled all the contents: where Karr was, what he was doing, who he was with. The *magic* they all held. A woman with lightning in her veins, a devil who could taste emotions on her tongue and decipher truth from lies, and a trickster who could weave illusions like a spider would a web.

She admitted to him that she had no powers of her own.

But she had the answer… could tell him *exactly* where the Antheon was. And how to take it, once they got inside its hiding place, in the Bloodhorns. For the battle would not be simply in finding it. It would be in ripping it out of the Dohrsaran ground.

All she asked for in return was a sword.

A golden sword that had been taken from a Dohrsaran's hand

in the aftermath of the Gathering, as if it had been cast aside. Cade had kept it in his own private quarters, fascinated with the scorpion for a hilt. Masterful work, a blade he thought he could sell for hundreds of thousands when they got back to Beta Earth. Collectors there were fascinated by ancient alien artifacts.

"Why?" Cade asked. "Why make this deal with me?"

"Because," she said, "I've sought the planet's heart my entire life. But I have *never* been able to get inside of the sacred space that hides it."

Cade thought about it.

Thought and wrestled and told himself he didn't need the woman, but he knew inside that he did. For the damned energy trackers weren't keeping pace with the Antheon, a thing that constantly moved and flickered and was impossible for even the greatest programmers on his crew to pinpoint.

Without Thali, Cade didn't think he'd find the mother-source of the Antheon.

They could dig for weeks. For months, and only find small fragments here and there.

Geisinger needed it *all.*

And with Karr out there… Cade didn't have time.

So he walked out of the brig. "Cut her down," he said to the soldiers standing guard.

When she was free, she lifted her gauntleted hands to Cade like a queen. "The sword?"

"You can have it when we find the Antheon," he said. But he called for it and showed it to her like a prize dangled before a dog. Her eyes had glittered as she beheld its glory.

"Very well, Wanderer," she said. "We have a deal."

He offered her his hand, but she didn't need his assistance. She was strangely strong, despite the torture. Her pale eyes were alight as she looked to him from behind her wolf mask and said, "Then it is time we begin."

CHAPTER 35

Sonara

Sonara woke with the taste of blood on her lips.

And Duran licking sand from her hair.

"Leave it, beast," she groaned, but she let her hands fall against his soft muzzle, breathing in the taste of him. Her spirit brightened as the soul-ember between them blazed hot and true. He always found her through it, like a siren song that called him home. "Blast, it's good to see you, Duran."

In part because she loved the insufferable beast. But also, because seeing Duran meant she was alive, for there was no way she'd ever see him in Hell.

She smacked a kiss onto his nose. "You're just too pure."

She propped herself up on an elbow and took in the scene around her.

The sunlight was blinding, Dohrsar's double suns beating into her skin as the wreckage of the pod unfolded. It had cracked in half, like the discarded shell of an egg. Wires and computer paneling had gone dim, the entire flight down from the *Starfall* like some kind of sick dream now. The world had looked like it was melting as they fell, Karr cursing as he barely managed to control their descent.

Judging by the position of the suns, the long shadows sweeping across the Bloodhorns, it was late afternoon. Sonara shivered as she glanced past Duran, who busied himself with searching for some sort of snack in the wreckage of the pod.

During the descent, they should have seen the Dohrsarans running free, out of the dark tunnels and into the Deadlands day as the light-wall fell.

A sickening sense of dread spread like a poison through Sonara's guts, but she hadn't the time to consider it. She looked for the others, panic rising in her. But the headache… oh goddesses, it was pounding.

And now that she thought about it… her right arm was on fire with pain. It wasn't quite cooperating, as Sonara tried to push herself onto her hands and knees.

With a groan, she stood, walking on wobbly legs until she pressed her arm against Duran's broad backside. Goddesses, it was going to hurt.

"Still, beast," she commanded.

He simply huffed and swished his tail in her face.

Then she gritted her teeth, and, with a muffled shout, popped the arm back into place.

"Goddesses be damned, Sonara. You always do such… flattering things."

Sonara froze, the pain dulling at the sound of that voice.

She turned slowly, and there he sat astride Razor, the afternoon sunlight bathing him in burnished gold.

"Jax," she whispered.

Then she was running towards him as if her own heart had sprouted wings and had taken flight, desperately trying to carry her across the sand to him. He slid down from Razor's back, his boots squeaking on the fresh sand as they collided.

"You're home," she breathed.

He wrapped his strong arms around her, and Sonara couldn't help herself—didn't even want to stop herself—as the tears fell.

They pulled away from each other, hands on shoulders, eyes roaming one another's face as if that shared glance could tell all the tales that had happened in their time apart.

"You're okay? You're unharmed?" she asked, eyeing his wounded arm at the same time he practically shook her and blurted:

"You faced a bloody Wanderer army to save me! I always knew you were a wild soul, Sonara, but..."

She laughed, and then they were hugging again, and Sonara swore, *swore* to every single one of the goddesses that may have been watching, that if anything so horrific ever happened to Jaxon again, she'd tear them all down from the sky.

She'd rip them apart slowly, limb from immortal limb, if it meant she could keep him from harm.

"Ahem."

They broke apart, both wiping away tears.

"Such a sweet family reunion," Markam said. He knelt in the sand, shaking dust from his coat, a gash on his temple still oozing black blood. Somehow, his hat was still on his head. "I see you've returned my wyvern back to me safely, little brother. I'll only charge you ten gold coins, for the rental."

Jaxon chuckled, and helped Markam to his feet, gripping him

by the forearm. But then after a moment, he pulled his brother in for a hug.

Markam wrapped his arm awkwardly over Jaxon's shoulders, but accepted the embrace, before quickly backing away. He made sure to pull the brim of his hat low over his eyes, but Sonara caught the joy in them. "That's enough of that, Jax," Markam said, and cleared his throat.

"There's so much to tell you," Sonara said. "So much to—"

Several paces away, Duran snorted as he nudged a body in the sand.

"Azariah!" Markam yelped.

Markam stumbled, half-crawling across the sand until he fell at Azariah's side. Sonara soon joined him, a sickness spreading through as she thought, *Please, not now, not like this…*

A Deadlands warrior did not deserve to die falling from the sky in a Wanderer pod.

Strange, lightning-shaped burns ran across Azariah's body, stretching upwards towards her neck. Markam gently rolled her over and cradled her head in his lap, pressing his hands to either side of her face.

"Wake up." He shook her gently. "Wake *up*."

"She's alive," Jaxon said softly. He knelt and pressed his hand to Azariah's wrist. "My power… it tells me her bones are not yet ready to call upon. There is still plenty of life in her."

Something like hope grew in Sonara as she looked at the woman. Azariah's collar scar, once a hideous mark of King Jira's claim over her life… it was transformed.

Tendrils of lightning-shaped scars wound around her throat where that awful collar had once been, almost beautiful in its brutality. A work of art that was born of her own abilities. Her own *choice* to press herself to the brink of life in order to set countless others free.

"She shut down the light-wall," Sonara said to Jaxon, as she knelt by the princess and pressed her hand to Azariah's forehead. "She did it, for all of them. All of us. She's the one who deserves the credit."

"Ah, but you all had a part in the chaos," Jaxon said.

Now that he was kneeling on her level, Sonara could see the awful gouge marks where the mite had dug into his neck. Like whatever terrible Wanderer science it was had drilled four even holes into his skin and latched on tight, bruises and dried blood still plainly visible on his neck.

"It was a collar of its own," Jaxon said, glancing at the princess. "A pain that could make any man beg for death."

"Then it's good we destroyed them," Sonara said. "Good that we could set you all free."

Jaxon paused, his gaze darkening.

"Sonara..."

His words trailed off as Azariah groaned. Then she shifted and began to blink back the sunlight.

Sonara's body calmed with relief. She grinned, the kind of smile she hadn't felt graze her lips in a long time. It felt a little like waking. A little like stretching after a long, curled-up slumber in the lonely dark.

What Azariah had done in that ship, facing that atlas orb, and what *Sonara* had done, to rid the princess of her last ounces of doubt, of fear, would forever bind them.

The Princess had asked Sonara to take up a place in her court someday. It was not a decision to be made lightly. And not one Sonara was yet ready to make, but nevertheless, she felt she owed Azariah a life debt for destroying the Wanderer's power source.

"Karr is alive," Markam said suddenly, lifting his chin to Sonara as he found his waterskin and poured some onto Azariah's dried, cracked lips.

Karr sat twenty paces away, facing the Bloodhorns. They'd crash-landed on the opposite side, not far from the mouth of Miner's Hope: the entrance to the network of tunnels that eventually led back to their hideaway.

Sonara felt for Soahm's necklace, alarm rising in her for a moment as she remembered. But the weight of it was still there upon her chest, reassuring as she pressed a hand to Jaxon's wrist, then went alone to greet Karr.

For a moment, she sensed nothing in his aura. He stared ahead, glaring into the sunlight, unblinking. Not moving as he said, "I saw it."

"Saw what?" Sonara asked.

He turned, and there was an open gash on his forehead. The wind spiraled past at the same time, gentle. Timid. But it still carried with it a new aura on his black blood.

There was *Karr, like grease and wet ink,* and then there was a second aura.

One that was exactly like Soahm's. *Sand dunes and Soreian air and the glorious sea.*

Sonara wasn't entirely surprised any longer. For it had happened before, whenever Karr bled. And the more she began to piece the mystery together, the more she no longer wanted to solve it.

"I saw my parents take him," Karr said. "Your brother. You were there, too. I went to the half-place, and the Child of Starlight showed it to me, like a dream."

"You… saw it?" Sonara asked.

Karr turned to look at her, his expression grim. "Every detail."

"Then you saw that I left him behind," Sonara said.

She carried that truth with her like a dead weight upon her back. A moment in time, where fear had grasped her and she'd given into it fully.

If they'd run all the way into hiding together—if she'd waited and helped Soahm reach the cave—perhaps he would not have been taken. They knew the caves like they knew their own homes, Soahm's twisting halls in the Soreian palace, and Sonara's claimed space in the steed barns.

Karr nodded, but did not speak of what Sonara knew he'd seen.

I'm so sorry, she thought, as she reached up and closed her fist over Soahm's necklace. *I'm so sorry I left you behind.*

"It was like the Child of Starlight, whoever she is, needed me to see it," Karr said. His aura was full of fresh sorrow. "My parents were Travelers. Freelancers who went from planet to planet, usually the hardest ones to reach, and brought back goods for traders. Not the illegal kind, like me and Cade. They were good people. They never would have stood for *this.*"

Sonara felt empty inside, even as she breathed in that double aura of his and knew it was impossible, for he was not Soahm, and Soahm was not him. So why did the two share an aura that mingled like the moons and stars?

"But in that vision…" Karr swallowed. "Sonara, you were so young. So afraid. You did what anyone would have done."

"Don't," she shook her head.

"You watched as my parents abducted him. That beam of blue light, his scream, the wind blasting from the engines..." His eyes narrowed. "He had on that necklace. The day he was taken."

The chain felt sharp against her palm suddenly. But still, she held onto it, and for a moment, she was thrust back into that night. So many times she'd relived it over the years. She didn't want to again. But she *must*. For there were answers here. Secrets unburying themselves, shaking sand from their backs like beasts awakening.

"This child," Sonara said. "What purpose would she have in showing my memories to you?"

She could have been a goddess. She could have been some emissary from the planet itself, for now all of Thali's and Azariah's beliefs seemed to ring true.

"That's the thing, Sonara," Karr said. "It didn't feel like *your* memory at all." He swallowed. "It felt like..." He closed his eyes, pressing his hand to the gash on his head, like he was trying to think past the pain of it. "I keep trying to hold onto it, to understand the truth, but whenever it comes close I feel like it falls through my fingertips. And there's another thing. The Child of Starlight kept talking about the darkness, about the ship. She said that the darkness has returned. And this time, it will be the very *last time* to stop it."

"But we did," Sonara said. "We shut down the system. The prisoners should have been freed from it."

"They weren't," Jaxon said.

Sonara turned to find him standing there, his hands clasped in front of him as he lifted his stubbled chin and glanced at the Bloodhorns. The valley in their center, where he'd lost his freedom.

"What do you mean?" Sonara asked.

Jaxon sighed and ran a shaky hand across the back of his neck, wincing as he did so. "After you freed me, I landed Razor on the mountainside and waited, hoping you'd come back out of that ship again… hell, I even prayed. The light-wall fell, your pod crashed, and I came to you as quick as I could, once I discovered they weren't going to come find you in the wreckage. And… well, the prisoners aren't caged anymore, Sonara. But they're *not* running free."

"Why?" Sonara asked, but she could already sense the tension in Jaxon's aura.

The shift in him, as his hand grazed those awful marks on his neck.

"The mites are still controlling them," he said. "And now they're so far inside the mountain, I'm afraid if they keep going… it might already be too late."

Karr cursed, and spat in the sand. He pressed at his forehead, squeezing the spot between his eyes like he was trying to see through a heavy haze. "Somehow, Cade must have anticipated it. Planned for it to happen. Or maybe Geisinger did."

"A second plan," Markam said, coming up from behind them, his hat in his hands, duster waving behind him as he helped Azariah keep her balance. She smiled at Sonara, who nodded her chin in greeting. "Every good Trickster prepares for it."

"Room for error," Sonara said, thinking of all the times their missions had gone south, and they'd had backup routes ready in order to still complete them. "Perhaps he has a second power source somewhere?"

Karr shook his head. "No, he wouldn't have. There's no other place for it on the ship… power that deep would fry the engines, screw with the cooling systems… it had to have been the atlas orb."

"So what, then?" Sonara asked. "Where is it?"

Karr closed his eyes. "I don't know."

Sonara felt it, then.

A little tremble from her curse, like a warning message of a weapon readying itself to inflict a wound.

She spun around, searching for the source, but saw nothing at all.

"Sonara?" Jaxon asked.

And then her curse took flight, sprouting those little shadow wings and soaring away like a bird. Sonara yelped as it carried her vision with it, like a message was calling. Like her curse was going to be the thing that answered it.

Across the desert her curse soared, sucking in the scent of the bones and beasts buried beneath the sand, their *clever, clever* minds and *pinchers sharp as double-edged knives.* It spiraled through the beamed entrance to Miner's Hope, delving into the darkness of the Bloodhorns tunnels.

Hunger, Sonara sensed, coming from a beast chomping on the entrails of an unlucky victim. *Exhaustion*, from another as it hissed and curled up in a cold, empty skull for a long sleep.

Her curse moved, flipping and twisting, bounding off the walls where it chomped on history after history, all the people who'd bled and died and cut into the rock as they fought for the gold and glory the Bloodhorns held within. It soared until it reached their outlaw cave, where Sonara sensed the red door. She *saw* it, like she was seeing through her curse's eyes, the tether stretching further than it had ever stretched before.

Sonara's curse inched closer, slowing to peer at the symbols etched on the stone.

It sidled up against them.

Felt the pulse. Sensed the surge of power.

A beating drum, an ever-present rhythm from the other side of the red door. The salty aura of *fear, flighty and breathless*, came with each pulse. As if something alive were hiding within.

Save me, Sonara heard.

That same whisper, the one that had followed her all of her Shadowblood days, was speaking, and whether it was inside of her mind, or coming form the other side of the door…

Sonara did not know.

"We have to go to it," she whispered.

"Go to what?" Markam asked, as Sonara's curse snapped back towards her in an instant, until she was staring back at her crew, wide-eyed.

"The door," Karr answered.

As if in response to his words, the ground beneath them trembled.

CHAPTER 36

Sonara

They journeyed back into the mines, a breathless pursuit upon Duran and Razor.

With every beat of Duran's hooves, every grain of sand that shifted beneath his heavy weight, Sonara felt the pull of that red door inside the Bloodhorns; and with it, the gentle whisper that continued to utter its need for a savior.

She left Duran at the entrance to the mines, pressing a hurried kiss to his nose, swearing she'd be back to journey with him once more into the wind.

Then they'd gone, the five of them, into the dim.

No beasts appeared to stand in their way; they took no wrong turns, and their torches never once faltered as they finally found their way back to their outlaw cave.

All along, the ground trembled.

Little tremors; delicate shakes that had the dust kicking up, stray bits of rock tumbling down from the rounded walls.

The Wanderers, wherever they were on the other side of the

mountain, had to be close to the heart, their mad dash for their prize intensifying as time ran out.

"A door," Jaxon said, breathless as they stood before it. "Where does it lead?"

There it was, ancient as ever, standing in the rocky alcove Karr had created as if it had been there forever. It did not have a handle, or a keyhole, or any gaps that allowed them to peer inside.

"The heart of the planet," Azariah said. "An ancient temple, long covered up by time and power."

Jaxon, to his credit, did not raise a brow or utter a laugh at the pure absurdity of the statement. He simple shrugged, and said, "So how do we get inside?"

Sonara pressed her hands to the door.

When she closed her eyes, she swore she felt the pulse on the other side.

"I uncovered it," Karr said.

"With Sonara's help," Markam added.

"And her blade," Azariah said with a warning tone.

Jaxon looked to Sonara. "What exactly did I miss while I was gone?"

She shook her head, still trying to understand why the door called to *her.* Why she knew, without a hint of doubt, that the voice calling to her was no longer in her mind. And though she knew she was the only one who could hear it… it was coming from behind the door. From the other side.

"It was both of us," Karr said. "Both of us together, that made something react that first time. Could I…?"

He held out a hand.

Timidly, Sonara took it, and they pressed their palms to the door together.

Sonara winced, waiting for a great explosion, a shifting of the very ground beneath their feet. But nothing at all happened.

Instead…

The voice on the other side of the door *sighed.*

An impatient little sigh, like it was tired of waiting.

An aura followed. A burst of exasperation, *sharp like the tang of bitters dumped into a cocktail of aged oil,* and Sonara's curse took flight.

The tether pulled, soaring out of her until her curse slammed against the door.

Like a fist knocking.

Beside her, Karr gripped her hand tight, and Sonara began to feel the ground shake again. Not from the Wanderers drilling into the mountain somewhere nearby, but from Karr. He was gritting his teeth, trying to call upon the power that lived in his veins.

She could sense his curse, a *smooth bit of stone, the grit of sand* and *the damp smell of upturned earth,* as he pushed against the door with her, trying to shove it open.

Another *slam* of Sonara's power against the red door.

The whole cave trembled. The door itself shook beneath their joined palms, dust and loose rock pouring down upon them.

When the dust settled…

Sonara's curse recoiled and slithered back into its cage.

The door simply *clicked.*

And with a gentle creak, it opened wide.

***

The space beyond the door was inky black, as if inside it spanned a starless sea. A cold, spiraling wind slithered past Sonara's legs, kicking up the debris around her boots.

It faded, then returned again. Like a deep, ancient sigh, reeking with the aura of…

"Death," Sonara whispered.

The wind backed away, carrying the aura with it.

Behind her, a torch flickered to life merrily, as Markam held it out in hope that it would cut through the darkness.

Sonara dared to breathe it in again, letting her power stretch out and ease into the space before her.

She inhaled, pulling it back to her in a breath.

The rot of bones, ancient and trembling as that cold, sighing wind soared past them.

"Bones," Jaxon said suddenly.

Sonara nodded, for she knew he sensed it, too.

"*Hundreds* of them: skulls and femurs and knuckles and toes," he added. "Bodies left to decay upon old, ruined stone."

As if a great battle had taken place inside. As if the stories of Eona were all *true.*

"Well," Markam said with a sigh. "If you're all so interested in stepping inside the doorway of death and doom… I've suddenly remembered I have tickets to a show."

Sonara turned on him. "What *show*? There's no show."

"There is."

"Where?"

"North," Markam said. He pointed, then seemed to think better of it. "Or… south. Does it matter? I'm not going in there."

"I will go," Azariah said as she stepped past him. Her voice was raw, her eyes heavy, but she rolled back her shoulders and gave a reassuring nod. "I will join you beyond the door."

"I'll go," Jaxon said. "There's an arsenal inside, just waiting for me, with all those bones."

"It's too much, Jax," Sonara said. "The energy it would take from you—"

Jaxon only shrugged, as if he hadn't any limits or cares.

"I'm going, too," Karr said. "At this point, I can't turn back."

Sonara inclined her head to Markam again and raised a brow in challenge.

He chewed on his lip, then groaned and removed his hat so he could run his hand across his dark hair. "Fine," he spat. "I'll go. But I'm not happy about it. I'll take up the rear."

With that, Sonara turned back to the door.

The sighing wind carried its own scent, and it was then that Sonara noticed the wind had a rhythm. In, out, and back again. Not just a heartbeat, but breath. It was overpowered with the aura of shadowed blood. Something she'd carried with her for years, had sensed each time she met another like her.

"I feel it," Karr said suddenly. "The pulse." He had his eyes closed, his body leaning towards the open doorway.

That same *tug* came to Sonara, the one that had drawn her back towards the rubble when she and Azariah first journeyed into the dark together, and Sonara heard the tale of Eona. She followed it now, stepping forward into the dark with the torch held before her.

Its light reached only a few paces ahead. The space was full of stones like those that she and the princess discovered elsewhere in the tunnels. But these were larger, columns and pillars that were marked with the same ancient symbols, only their bases visible as they walked past.

Beneath their feet, Sonara sensed the rot of crushed bones.

A graveyard.

Sonara lifted the torch, trying to see deeper into the space.

"There," Markam said. "The torch, Sonara."

Just to their left, along the rocky wall, sat a carved ledge; a small carved-out line that spanned along the wall at eye level, into the darkness.

Sonara could sense the oil, already; the sticky substance left behind ages ago. But when she dipped the flames into it…

A trail of fire came to life, spreading steadily along the lip in the wall.

It went twenty paces ahead.

Fifty.

A hundred.

Then it trailed upwards, snaking along the stone pillars themselves, which lined the walls of what was a massive, ancient-looking temple.

Slowly, the darkness faded. Now they could see piles and piles of bones leaning against the pillars and stacked against the rounded cave walls, ten bodies high.

This was a place where the dead could not rest.

A place that had Sonara choking back the aura of death.

The sound of a heartbeat came louder.

It joined their footsteps as they made it past the rubble. They clustered together closely as they walked, as if to ward away the awful feeling of death.

In the very center of the temple the ground sloped downwards.

Wide stone steps were carved into the cave floor, each of the steps covered in those strange markings and painted a deep burnished gold.

They reflected the torchlight along the walls, and as Sonara and the others stopped atop it, she realized it was like a shining amphitheater.

More skeletons were strung along the steps, like they'd died trying to crawl towards the very center of the amphitheater.

Sonara trailed those steps downwards with her eyes, towards the middle.

Thump.

A heavy beat in the darkness.

Thump.

There it was: the heart of the planet.

It was not as Sonara had imagined it to be. Not a shimmering stone that was bathed in golden light, or a beautifully carved statue, or even a pulsing, writhing cluster of shadows.

It was simply a massive, jagged black rock that protruded from the smooth stone floor as if it had been planted there. It had the aura of pure shadows, like sorrow and sadness. Like *death.*

"The heart of the planet," Azariah said, as wind heaved from the stone. It pulsed once, the solid black shifting as Sonara realized shadows *did* swim around it. It pushed forth that wind again, cool and full of an aura that had her curse writhing from within. "It truly exists."

Her eyes glowed in the dark light from the heart. A black glow, if that were possible, that cast everything in a strange shadowed light.

Power.

Promise.

The purest aura Sonara had ever sensed. The heart called to her as if it were singing a song. A droning, sad refrain, one that she was certain had a voice. But she could not quite hear it.

"It's… real," Markam said suddenly. Out of the corner of her eye, the Trickster had stepped forward. The heart pulsed before him, sighing out again with its deathly wind.

"Markam?" Sonara said. "What are you doing?"

His eyes reflected the firelight as he leaned forward, almost as if pushed by a rogue wind. "Look at it, Sonara. Don't you see what it wants?"

He took a step down, into the amphitheater.

Sonara's body tensed, waiting for a trap; a threat, a great monster hiding in the shadows beyond the heart that they hadn't seen. But there was nothing.

"It wants to be taken," Markam said softly. "To be wielded by someone worthy."

A whisper of an aura pulsed from the heart. That song again, a melody that Sonara sensed inside, but wondered if anyone else heard. Beside her, she saw Karr tilting his head, as if *he* heard the song, too.

Markam swayed a little as he took another step downwards.

The song, pulsing in time with the heart… it had begun to form words.

Save me.

Sonara heard them at the same time her curse picked up on an ancient scent.

Fear.

Helplessness.

She was certain it came from the direction of the heart, as if the rock itself were speaking.

"Markam, stop," Sonara said.

He'd taken three steps down, and as he drew closer, the whisper from the heart grew louder.

Save me.

Markam removed his dagger from his belt, his hands trembling as he stepped over a skeleton and kept going. The bones crunched beneath his feet.

"Markam, I said *stop*," Sonara commanded him.

But he kept going, lower and lower towards the heart.

Save me, save me, save me.

It commanded Sonara to obey.

She lunged forward before she could stop herself, bounding down the golden steps and into Markam's path. His eyes were wild, as if he wanted to hunt the heart. Capture it and keep it for his own. His aura came to her, eager and desperate.

A monster on the prowl.

"Get out of my way, Sonara." He said her name like a hiss.

Her boots slid as he tried to move her aside, but she pressed against him, unrelenting. "What are you doing, Markam? Stop it!"

She slid Lazaris from its sheath, holding it before her.

"*I must have it,*" he hissed.

A warning aura flickered at the same time Markam lunged at her with his blade.

Sonara lifted Lazaris, blocking the hit with a clang that echoed up the amphitheater and around the massive temple cave.

But he recoiled and slashed again, eyes wild with the need for the heart. She slung Lazaris around, jamming the pommel into his nose. Shadow blood leaked out, but he didn't seem to feel the hit. He slashed again, aiming not for a wound, but for a *kill.* Something he'd never done, in all their years fighting together.

He aimed for her throat.

Jaxon shouted and ran down the steps towards them, while Azariah and Karr simply stood staring, in shock.

Sonara dropped to a knee as Markam's blade slashed the air. When she came back up, he'd lunged away, leaping sideways across the steps at the very same time his limbs began to fade from existence.

"Oh, no you don't," Sonara growled. "You're not going to disappear this time."

Behind Markam, Jaxon lifted his hands.

And one of the skeletons on the steps began to rise.

It was horrific, the sound of those rattling bones as Jaxon pieced the ancient dead back together. A clean skull bobbed atop shoulders that were bare of skin, and a rib cage that was broken at the chest—as if someone had stabbed it right through its long-gone heart—connected to long arms and splintered wrist bones. But the skeleton wrapped its unfeeling hands around Markam's arm, stopping him before his curse could render him invisible.

Sonara took the opportunity and dove. Her shoulders slammed against Markam's stomach as she knocked him to the ground, the skeleton cracking beneath them.

The blade flew from his hand, and his curse fizzled, his limbs solidifying again. *"I need it,"* Markam groaned. *"I need the heart for myself."*

He rolled, heavier and stronger than Sonara, until he was on top of her, her body pressed beneath his. He grabbed her hair, lifted her head and slammed it back down against the golden steps. Her vision sparked, flecked with white for a moment.

But she rocked and used her momentum to launch him upwards, driving her knee in between his legs. His eyes never wavered from the heart, hands stretching down the steps towards it, his aura reeking of *want.*

"A little help here!" Sonara called out.

At the same time, Markam's teeth found her throat.

He bit.

Hard.

Sonara screamed and dug her nails into the back of his neck. But then another pair of skeletal hands closed over Markam's throat, and began to squeeze.

Jaxon stood behind him, shaking as he held out his own hands and commanded the bones to obey.

The heart's aura kept pulsing, the dark death-wind sighing, and Sonara knew that each time Markam breathed it in, he fell deeper into its temptation. The power that it promised, the song that it continued to sing.

She heard *save me,* but some part of her knew that Markam heard a different set of words.

Take me for yourself.

Use me for your gain.

Somewhere beyond the cave, the mountain rumbled again. Cade and his soldiers, growing closer as they dug. Were they almost to the cave? Sonara's attention couldn't grasp on to which direction it was coming from, for Markam lifted himself on hands and knees, his face turning blue as Jaxon's skeleton squeezed the life from him.

Save me.

Sonara slammed her pommel against his head, but Markam did not falter.

"I must have it!" His voice was ragged, breathless and desperate.

Sonara went behind him and gripped his legs, pulling backwards. He flailed, kicking as she began to haul him away. Karr finally joined her side.

"I MUST HAVE IT!"

"Azariah!" Sonara commanded between gritted teeth. "Now would be a great time to step in!"

Lightning shot across the space, hitting Markam so hard he was blasted backwards until he slid to a stop, slung across the golden steps with the rest of the skeletons. His head lolled to the side.

Silence swept over the space.

"The heart," Azariah said with a gasp, as she slowly made her way down the steps to the rest of them. Blood trickled from her nose and soared away. "It calls to some stronger than others." She frowned down at Markam.

"Why am I not surprised it called to *him* in such a way?" Sonara said.

Its whisper still beckoned, drawing her near. She stalked towards it, as close as she dared.

"Don't get too close," Jaxon said. He wiped sweat from his brow as he sat on the steps to catch his breath. "It feels wrong, Sonara."

The heart was like a black seed sprouted from the earth, pulsing gently in its bed of stone.

Save me.

"I did," Sonara whispered back to it. But beyond the space, the cave rumbled once more. The walls began to shake, loose rocks tumbling from the ceiling to crash down around them.

Far more rubble than before.

"How close do you think Cade is?" Sonara asked. She sensed the answer was not one she wanted to hear.

Dust had begun to fill the cave, casting it in an eerie glow. "It won't be long," Karr said. He closed his eyes. "I can… I can feel pain." He rolled his shoulders and winced. "Like someone is cutting into my own body."

His eyes fell to the heart as it pulsed, the sigh of its breath pushing his hair back from his forehead as its wind soared up the amphitheater steps.

"It's calling to me. But not like it called to Markam." He closed his eyes again. "Like… like it wants me to come closer, and listen."

Save me, the heart whispered again.

Sonara glared at the heart, suddenly hating it. Suddenly wondering why in the hell she'd come here.

The heart pulsed, and an aura came with it.

An aura that had words, and the words said, *Come to me.*

She took a few more steps downwards, dropping to her knees as she got as close to the heart as she dared.

"Sonara, don't," Jaxon warned again, his eyes narrowing as Karr followed her. "Please."

"It's okay," she said over her shoulder. "Trust me."

She dropped to her knees, leaning forward at the same time Karr did. Their eyes met as they stretched out their hands. Together, they placed them upon the heart.

Sonara wasn't entirely surprised when the heart rippled.

When from deep in its inky depths, as she and Karr peered into the heart…

A child made of starlight stared up at them.

CHAPTER 37

Sonara

One moment she was leaning over the heart.

The next, she and Karr were tumbling into darkness, into an expanse that had no end.

They came to a stop on the bow of a boat, sailing across an endless black sea. There were no stars in the sky; only darkness that spanned left and right, as far as the eye could see.

"I have waited for an eternity."

Sonara looked to the right, and there stood the girl.

A Child of Starlight, Karr had said before.

And now here the child stood, her body woven out of planets and space and time and stars. Endless stars that sparkled as she turned, crossing her arms and raising a celestial brow at Sonara and Karr. "Perhaps… longer than an eternity," she said.

Sonara had the faintest feeling that she was being reprimanded.

"It's you again," Karr said.

The child nodded.

Then she snapped her fingertips, and the scene changed.

The boat sped forward, racing across the sea, and as it sailed, the girl changed, too.

It was like her life fast-forwarded before Sonara's eyes, the years adding to her age as she stretched taller so that the stars in her hair died, exploding and forming into new ones as her limbs stretched out. The planets upon the girl's collarbone and arms spun, lengthening and then multiplying so that more formed into existence. Upon her forehead, an image of a ringed planet appeared. *Dohrsar*. Her nebula eyes grew, flaring brighter as the girl's face shaped into something more mature.

She was a young woman now. A beautiful young woman made of the universe itself.

"It took you long enough," she said.

Sonara glanced over her shoulder, towards the others.

But they'd disappeared. Only the endless darkness remained, the black sky and the starless sea.

"Where are we?" Sonara asked.

Karr said, "My dreams. She only comes to me in my dreams."

The woman gave a gentle laugh. "You're not dreaming. You've come to my domain, lost soul. As I had hoped you would." Stars cascaded down her neck, falling with glittering trails of firelight behind them as she looked at Sonara next. "And you… don't you recognize the voice in your head, the whisper in your soul? I've spent years speaking to you, Sonara of Soreia, and you never truly *listen.* I'm surprised you made it here, and just before the end of my time. My spirit is growing weak."

"You," Sonara said, voice trembling. That voice, gentle, ancient and knowing all at once. A whisper that had asked her to choose, when she first became a Shadowblood. The voice of her curse.

"When I died, and fell into that place of darkness and light, ten years ago. It was *you* who asked me to choose, and…"

"You refused," the woman said.

Sonara had. For she couldn't find a stronger pull towards either side, both equally as appealing.

"As all the worthy souls have done before you," continued the woman, "and will do so after your time. Unless of course, the darkness wins, and Dohrsar ceases to exist."

"You… are the planet?" Sonara asked.

The woman tilted her head, stars tumbling from her hair to fade over the boat's edge, into the black sea. "No. I am her messenger. The spirit of the first Shadowblood she created." She bowed, holding out an arm before herself. A constellation created a bangle upon her wrist. "I am Eona."

Eona.

An enemy to the heart.

Sonara reached for Lazaris.

But her hands only scraped air. Her weapon was gone.

"You cannot kill me here, child," Eona said. "Not until I release you. And even if you did, the death would not be true, for I no longer exist. I am only Eona's spirit. The voice that speaks for Dohrsar."

"You were the one who forced me to kill him," Sonara said, looking towards Karr. "The one who has destroyed everything, time and again, taking my curse and acting like it's some sort of plaything in your hands."

"Oh, child," Eona spat the word. "Goddesses above. You use your magic but you still call it cursed. Dohrsar was right to choose you. The perfect balance. Deep down, you want to do good. But you don't fear the darkness, the acts you might have to do in order to protect the light." Eona sighed, shrugging her delicate shoulders. "It is just as I was, a long time ago. For part of me… half, at least, resides in *you*."

Sonara blinked.

The boat slid soundlessly across the sea.

"What is that supposed to mean?" Sonara asked.

Eona smiled. "Listen, for once, Sonara of Soreia, and the truth will be revealed to you." She looked to Karr with narrowed eyes. "And you. Dohrsar has been waiting for *your* fate to collide with hers, lost soul. For together, you are the answer to end an oncoming darkness. Dohrsar sensed it long ago, barreling across the stars. Such peace, Dohrsar once had from her place in the sky. But other planets have voices, too. They whispered to her, sent their warnings from star to star, until the message arrived. A call across space and time. *The darkness is coming*."

Eona's gaze deepened, the nebulas in her eyes churning like a raging sea.

"Those planets were unwise. They shriveled and died when the darkness arrived to them, for they did not create an army as Dohrsar did."

"Shadowbloods," Sonara said.

Eona nodded.

"I was the first. She gave me a choice, just as you both had… I looked at the darkness and light, and I could not choose."

"But the story says you tried to slay Dohrsar," Karr said. "You tried to take the heart for yourself."

Eona balked. The boat rocked, suddenly, as the black waves came to life. Perhaps Azariah had been wrong about the story after all, the details she'd spent her life believing warped as they slipped from lips to ears and onwards again.

"This is exactly why I will never understand your kind," Eona said. "I was once alive, like both of you. I have watched you, the living creatures that walk on Dohrsar's back, plucking plants and animals from her without ever thanking her for her gifts. You allow things to get twisted, stories to shift and change like the sands of time, until only the tiniest seed of the real truth remains. I was her first Chosen. Her first protector. It was my fool brother, Eder…" Eona's eyes narrowed, blazing bright. "Wicked, unworthy Eder, who managed to steal a part of Dohrsar's heart. Without it, she cannot be whole. She cannot unleash the power she holds inside to fight the darkness away."

"What darkness?" Sonara asked.

But Karr spoke next. "My ship. The *Starfall,* and Cade's plan."

Eona nodded, her nebula eyes grave. "A darkness much like the darkness that arrived when I was a living child, in my first life. My father found the heart, and in his greed, wanted it for himself. But I heard the planet's whisper. Heard the heart calling to me. *Save me.* Gentle and pressing but commanding all the same. My steed and I stood against him. Together, we fought with all that we had in our souls, for I did not want the planet to be stripped of what allowed it to exist. When I fell… Dohrsar brought me back. She gave me a piece of her own soul, the blood that roils with shadows. That part of her soul allowed me to have magic that was twofold. The ability to command the very land beneath my feet. And the ability to hear the planet's voice. To speak to her, not through words, but through tastes. She brought my steed back with me, for he'd been slain trying to protect the heart, too, loyal to the grave."

Sonara felt her very blood go cold, then.

Powers that were the same as hers. The same as Karr's.

And Duran.

Duran had come back to life, too.

She listened closer, wanting to understand why, of all people, the planet had chosen a girl who was unwanted. A bastard princess from Soreia, who had never been anything special at all.

"Oh, yes," Eona said. "You notice the connection. But the tale is not yet complete. You see, when I rose again—the planet's soul like living shadows in my blood—I sensed an aura of terror upon my tongue. The planet was afraid. I commanded the ground to quake. The cave entrance collapsed, killing my family with it. None but my younger brother Eder escaped." She looked past them, and in the sky came a flashing vision of the temple, the ruined arches and patterned stone strewn with skeletons. "This place became my home, for I chose to guard the heart with my second life. Because before Eder fled, he took with him the portion of the heart that my father had stolen. He declared that he would someday return and use that portion to take the heart for himself. I stayed for years, honing my powers, crafting a mighty underground temple to Dohrsar with my magic. Here, I worshipped her. In this sacred space, I listened to her whisper. She told me that the darkness she was warned of would someday arrive. So I began helping her craft an army. I crafted a door with my own magic, buried it in the earth and left the heart locked up behind it. I traveled across Dohrsar, where I helped to slay others, so that the planet herself could bring them back."

"You murdered innocent people across the planet," Karr said. "In hope that some of them would come back?"

Darkness, or light?

All Shadowbloods had to be held in the center of the two.

"Some sacrifices had to be made," Eona said. "We created an army. An army intent on protecting Dohrsar when that foretold darkness came." She seemed to still, and Sonara watched as her eyes shed tears made of stars. "Eventually, I met a Shadowblood from the south. Fell in love, as the living ones do. I had a child of my own, a beautiful girl who would someday become a Soreian queen."

More tears of starlight.

"Time and again, I would return to this space alone, to speak with Dohrsar. When she feared a threat was near, I came. And one day, my brother Eder *did* return. He brought with him that piece of the planet's heart. Tricky, he was, for he'd used it to fashion a weapon. One that I could not best with ease, for it held power from the planet's very heart. Eder and his army, hundreds upon hundreds of soldiers, nearly slayed me. And as I lay dying, I told the planet I was sorry. That I had failed her. Dohrsar mourned, the aura of sorrow on my tongue. I used the last bit of my strength to destroy this place. To bury it deep, destroying Eder, his army and myself along with it."

"But yet here you remain," Sonara said.

Eona nodded. "The planet loved me. Mourned for me, her first creation. But in that great explosion of my power, I gave so much of myself that I cast out my very soul. And with her own magic… the planet preserved it. She kept it here for a time, alongside my spirit. Keeping the pieces of me safe, until she could find someone else worthy to carry them. Someone to burn with the desires I had, to always protect Dohrsar, no matter the cost. She chose. Eventually."

"Your daughter?" Karr asked.

"No," Eona said. Her eyes turned until they fell upon Sonara, who felt stripped wholly bare beneath that ancient gaze. "She chose *you*, Sonara. The bastard princess of Soreia. My descendant, and a soul that was finally worthy."

Sonara froze as those words washed across her. "What did you just say?"

Eona simply smiled.

But it wasn't possible.

It wasn't possible at all, that Sonara would be chosen. For she was nothing. She was no one.

She was unwanted and unworthy, a sign she'd seen in her own reflection, all her life, when she looked into the sparkling sea and saw herself staring back: blue hair with streaks of brown, dark eyes that were not the cerulean of a true Soreian lineage.

"It can't be me," Sonara said. "I'm… no one."

"You carry blood of great strength," Eona said. "Have you never wondered, Sonara, why the Queen of Soreia hated you so?"

"Because I was a bastard," Sonara hissed, hating that word as it tumbled from her lips. "Because I was not created out of a fully pure bloodline. Because I was a stain on the crown, and a threat to the throne."

"There are plenty of bastards in each kingdom," Eona said knowingly. "They are swept under the rug, set aside… but the hatred goes deeper than that word, Sonara. You, my soul… you are perhaps the *most* worthy of any on Dohrsar. Because you are the daughter of a king *and* a queen."

"No," Sonara said, shaking her head. "My father was no one. A spoil of war… that's what my mother always said."

"How easily the living believe such petty lies about themselves." Eona smiled softly. "Your father, Sonara, reigns on a different throne. I believe you and your comrade recently removed one of his eyes."

Sonara didn't want to believe it.

But she saw the face in her mind, as Eona said, "Yes, my soul. King Jira sired you. *You*, a girl who has a claim to not one, but *two* Dohrsaran thrones."

"That's impossible."

"Is it? The King has sired hundreds of children, from hundreds of women across Dohrsar. How do you think your mother has kept the peace with Jira all these years?"

"Through strength. Through a steed army," Sonara growled. "Through a ruthless taste for bones and blood."

"Not so," Eona said, shaking her head so that more stars tumbled from her, landing upon her shoulders. "Your mother and Jira were lovers who met on the battlefield, and in secret, when they signed the Decree, they created *you*. A child that had the ability to bring both their kingdoms crashing down."

"No. I refuse to believe that monster is my father." Sonara's breath was growing ragged with horror. For that would mean… that would mean, all along, there was Jira's blood running in her veins. She was part monster, after all.

But then a different thought struck her, one that pressed back with a bit of light, as she realized…

Sonara's eyes widened.

Azariah was her *sister*. It all made sense now, the connection she felt to the princess. The strange sense of trust between them.

Sonara's hands began to shake. For the collar scar on Azariah's throat should have been on Sonara's throat, too. Would have been, if she'd grown up one kingdom over. "An entire life, I spent in the shadows," Sonara said, shaking her head. "When all this time… I could have been seated upon either throne."

"But would you have wanted them?" Eona asked. She clicked her teeth. "No, my soul, I do not think you would have. For your destiny is worth more than some pathetic mortal crown. You are the savior of Dohrsar. Well, half of you. The planet could not place all of her faith into one person again. Dohrsar made that mistake with me, for still, that missing piece of her heart is out there. I never got it back." She sighed. "So the other half of my soul went to an equally worthy person. A Soreian prince who was kind and pure to his heart, but willing to do what needed to be done to guide his kingdom to true light. He was named Soahm. Your brother."

Soahm. At the sound of his name on Eona's lips… Sonara felt like she was ready to shatter. Ready to break. "You're *lying*," she spat. She looked at Karr, begging him to agree with her. But he only stared at Eona, unblinking. "Azariah was correct, that Eona was the enemy to the planet, and she's twisting stories even now, trying to decipher a way for us to bring her back. To give her the power of the heart."

"Do you sense lies in my words, Sonara?" Eona asked. She shook her head. "No. Because inside you know I speak the truth. You've known from the very moment you became a Shadowblood that you were worth something. It is why you always fought for life. Why you fight for freedom, even now, for the ones who don't see value in you. Because you want them to believe you aren't a Devil. You want them to know that deep down, you are *good.*" She sighed and turned to face Karr. "This is where your destiny mingles with Sonara's and Soahm's, my sweet lost soul." She truly did sound sorrowful, as if she hated the words she would speak next.

"Me?" Karr asked.

Eona nodded. "The darkness *did* arrive. Not once, but twice. It is here now, to carry out the end of the end. But it came before, searching for a savior of its own. It found that savior in Soahm, and it stole him away, taking with it the other half of my soul before he could meet his death on Dohrsar, and become a Shadowblood. Before he could reach his destiny."

"But… that has nothing to do with me," Karr whispered.

Eona gently inclined her head. "It has everything to do with you, Karr Kingston. For inside, you carry the other half of my soul. Inside… you carry Soahm's heart."

CHAPTER 38

Karr

"No," Karr said. Beside him, Sonara had gone still and cold. So still he could no longer see her breathing, could no longer feel the warmth of her skin beside his. "I don't understand."

"You have the answers inside of you," Eona whispered. "I've given you the history, the memories… so many lives, my soul, mixing inside of you. It is no wonder your dreams are full of confusion, carrying you to so many places."

The frozen throne room, the floor of the *Starfall*, where his parents were murdered. The rocking sea, and the sand caves…

"You have lived not twice, as many Shadowbloods do," Eona said, "but *three* times, Karr Kingston."

"No," Sonara breathed out the word. "No. It can't be."

"The reality of it is painful, but that pain does not make it any less true."

"How?" Sonara asked. She was shaking now. Karr could feel her body trembling beside him. Her hands curled into fists as if she wanted to grab her sword and tear apart Eona, and the heart with it. "I need to know *how*."

Eona looked to Karr instead. "You know, Karr. Deep down, you already know… but time is fleeting. So I will show you."

She reached out again, pressing the tip of her star-finger to Karr's temple. He did not feel pain, as he normally did at her touch. Instead, it was like he'd been dipped into cool water as she pulled a strand of starlight from his temple.

She let it fall into the sea.

The water rippled, morphing from black to silver as the boat rocked with the waves.

"Come," Eona said as she knelt. She took Karr's hand, and Sonara's next, and pulled them down with her until they knelt, too. "It begins with me." She released their hands, then reached over the edge of the boat and ran her fingers through the silver water.

It rippled, and suddenly it was no longer a sea, but a memory.

They looked down at a land painted in white. A castle was carved right out of the ice, glimmering like it was made of fractals and glass. The scene zoomed forward, tearing right through the castle walls. Inside, he saw a young girl with pale, snow-white hair and a crown of stars upon her head, as she entered that very throne room Karr had seen in his dreams. The Child of Starlight, in the flesh.

"Eona," Karr whispered.

This memory came from *her* past, the part that her soul carried with it.

The image changed, colors morphing and swirling together until it cleared again.

In this memory, Karr saw that same sand castle in Soreia, but this time he was up close, staring down at the blue-haired young man he'd seen on the beach beside Sonara. *Soahm.* The prince was younger, standing on a balcony, a worn journal in his hands as he sketched the landscape, a sprawling kingdom by the sea. His rich blue cloak flapped behind him in the wind. He smiled as he focused his charcoal on a beautifully crafted stable that stood in the castle's shadow. Inside it, a blue-and-brown-haired girl with dark eyes, shoveling waste out of a steed's stall.

The image rippled, morphing again.

Until Karr saw himself. His own memory.

A child, so young at the time, but he recognized his own face. More specifically, the people standing over him as he lay in a hospital bed, sound asleep. His parents.

Karr's chest ached as he stared down at them, alive and well. He wished he could reach out; grab ahold of them, and beg them not to fly to Xurax, where they would meet an early end. Beside them, curled up in a chair, sat a much younger Cade. His cheeks were still plump with youth, his eyes limned in silver as he looked up at his parents.

"Karr is dying," their father said, placing his heavy hand on Cade's shoulder. The sound of his voice, so familiar, so long unheard…

"Dad," Karr breathed. He placed a hand over his mouth, holding his breath to ward away the tears. But they were already falling over the edge of the boat, rippling the memory like stones tossed into a pond.

"He's dying," his father said. *"And if we wish to save him, then we must do something unforgiveable."*

"We have to make a choice, Cade," their mother said. Her face, much younger then, looked heavy with grief. *"You must understand that the burden is ours to carry. But we must ask you to*

carry it after we are gone. To keep a secret from Karr, because if he ever learns the truth, Cade… we fear it would destroy him."

Karr didn't remember this. Perhaps his unconscious mind had held onto the truth, while he'd been sleeping in that bed. He'd been sick when he was younger, had a heart defect that had always kept him from playing with the other kids when they landed on planetary docks. But he'd grown up. He'd grown stronger, taken medicine all his life until he was older… and then he'd grown out of needing that, too.

"This is where it changes, my heart," Eona said. "This is where the truth is told."

Again, the image morphed until it became a memory that belonged to Soahm. The same thing Karr had seen in his dreams, watching the Soreian prince get taken just beyond the mouth of the cave. There was Sonara, younger and terrified as she ran, leaving Soahm behind.

The memory flickered back to the *Starfall* again.

It showed Karr on a table, unconscious as a man came aboard. A man that was tall, with dark eyes and a silver suit. Much younger than he looked now, but…

"Friedrich Geisinger," Karr said now.

At the same time his father, in the memory, stood to greet the man. *"Geisinger. You've agreed to help us."*

Geisinger nodded, looking down at Karr's tiny, unconscious body. Wires connected to his chest, and a tube inside of his throat, breathing for him. He didn't remember any of it. Unless… perhaps he did.

The flashes of pain, a bright room that came frequently in his dreams.

A man, standing over him with only his eyes showing, a mask over the rest of his face.

"It will not be easy, but the boy will live, assuming his body accepts the donor heart," the memory-Geisinger said. *"The Dohrsaran heart is genetically superior to the human's, having evolved to be able to sustain life for centuries in their poisonous atmosphere. It will be far better… capable of giving him new strength. A long and prosperous life. And the terms of our deal?"*

Karr's father wrapped his arm around Karr's mother. She sat, shaking at Karr's bedside as she held his tiny pale hand. She did not look away as she wiped her tears and whispered, *"Do it."*

Karr's father signed a contract. *"A lifetime of servitude,"* Geisinger said, *"in exchange for payment. It won't seem so bad, when your boy lives. Grows old. Has children of his own, and never knows the sacrifice you made in order to save him."*

"And the donor?" Karr's father asked.

"The abductee, from the dwarf planet?" Geisinger shrugged. *"He won't feel a thing."*

A new memory.

A shift.

Karr saw through Soahm's memories again, as he lay on a table, a shot injected into his arm. A poison, leaching into his system.

It did hurt, *dying.* It burned like a raging fire.

Soahm screamed from the inside, only the sound never made it out, for his heart stopped beating. His breath stilled on his lips.

His heart was removed, healthy and alien—and found to be much stronger than any Earthen donor's could dream of being. Geisinger placed the heart inside of Karr's open chest and sewed him back together, the scar an ugly reminder of what his parents had done… but one that would fade with time, with emerging science.

As Soahm's lifeless body was removed, Geisinger set aside an alien amulet: a black rock inside of a ring of gold, that had been around his neck.

Soahm's memory shifted into Karr's again, months later.

"This was given to us by a very dear friend," Karr's mom whispered, as she held him in her lap, and they stared out the viewport at a beautiful blue moon, a delicate orb that hung aloft in the black sky. This memory, Karr did remember. *"You should wear it. Keep it safe, always above your heart, and be grateful that you live."*

She placed a necklace over Karr's head, letting it fall just above where a scar sat on his skin. Soahm's necklace. The amulet that had been with him when he was abducted.

"Why are you crying, Mommy?" the memory-Karr asked.

"Nothing to burden yourself with, sweet boy." She wiped her tears away, and smiled down at him, beautiful as a star. *"I love you,"* she said. *"I would give anything for you. Even my goodness. Even my soul."*

The next memory was Karr's, one of the most recent, as he hid inside the *Starfall* and the raiders came aboard. He saw his parents' bodies, withering from existence. He'd been clouded by fear then, but he saw it all clearer now. He heard their words as they searched the ship.

"That's what happens when you try to run from Geisinger. When you don't honor his deals," the first raider said, staring down at Karr's father's body. *"No one can ever escape him."*

"Kids, man," the other raider said. *"Geisinger didn't say they had kids."*

That one was Jeb. He knelt down, his golden, shark-toothed smile widening as he found Karr hiding beneath the ship's dash. Karr had passed out, then. Fainted out of pure fear.

But some part of his brain must have held onto the memory. Or perhaps it was the new heart he hadn't known was beating inside of his chest… holding half of Eona's soul, the soul that had been entrusted to Soahm. And Karr had stolen it in the end.

The next scene showed Cade returning to the ship, back from his errands on the docks, to discover his parents, dead. His little brother, captured.

"You work for Geisinger, don't you?" Cade asked Jeb.

Jeb's nose was broken and bleeding, his eyes bloodshot as he held a gun to Cade's head. A second gun sat discarded, just out of Cade's reach. As if when Cade had arrived, he'd shot the other man, but fell to Jeb's strength in the end.

"You've been ordered to kill us, too?" Cade asked.

Jeb nodded, pressing the gun closer to Cade's temple. But it trembled.

And Cade looked up at him, a perfect mask of sadness spread across his young face. *"We will pay our parents' debt. We will do it. Say you killed us. But let us live. We'll do whatever you ask. We'll serve you forever… just let us live."*

The memories stilled.

The sea of darkness returned.

Eona turned away from the edge, facing Karr and Sonara with a sad smile.

"All this time," Sonara said. "All this time I spent searching for him… he was already gone." There were tears pouring down her face. Her body shook with rage.

Karr wanted to reach over. To grab her hand with his, but then he thought better of it. For what was he to her, but the boy his parents had killed her brother to save?

A monster.

A *child* of monsters.

That was what he was.

"Not gone," Eona said. "Not entirely. The portion of my soul that Soahm carried in his heart… it remains in Karr now. His memories are also held within."

"He doesn't deserve it," Sonara growled. "Soahm should have *lived*."

"My soul held on to his heart, because it chose him a worthy replacement," Eona explained.

Somehow the word *replacement* felt like a knife driven into Karr's chest.

"And now he lives again, through Karr. Your magic killed Karr so that he would come to our side. So that Soahm's portion of my soul would not be wasted. That it would be brought back home, where it belongs. And here he is, a chosen Shadowblood, who has half the power I once had. Together, you can stop the darkness."

"I will kill him," Sonara said suddenly. "I will kill Cade, and Geisinger, and whoever else had a hand in this."

She would not look at Karr.

And what would he do, if she did?

Karr swallowed his own tears away, the horrors that he'd seen. The reality that all of his life—his *lives*—had been some tangled, covered-up lie.

"Our time runs short," Eona said now. "For soon the darkness will break through the walls, into this sacred place. You must do what you can to protect the heart. To save Dohrsar from the soul that seeks it."

"Cade?" Karr asked.

"No." Eona shook her head. "Not entirely. Cade is only a pawn. There comes a deeper threat. Because there was another soul that survived, one that would not allow itself to be laid to rest. The greed, the desire to reach this place… it allowed my brother Eder's spirit to keep on living, so that someday he could make it back to the heart again."

She pointed upwards, into the sky. It had lightened, to show them an opening as the boat began to rise back towards the cave where the heart sat; where Azariah and Jaxon peered down, frozen like time itself had stopped. "My strength fades. My message is completed, my souls returned to this space. You will take over now. Protect the heart."

"How?" Karr asked.

"I'm afraid I have given you too much already. The afterlife will not be kind to me, the goddesses furious, for what I have already done. I have waited a long time to finally lay my spirit to rest. If I say much more, I fear that I will end up like my brother. That when Eder dies, too… we will spend eternity together, fighting a war that neither of us can win."

"Tell us how to defeat the darkness," Karr said. "*Please.*"

For when Cade arrived, there would be an army.

His power was not enough. A few Shadowbloods against an army… they would not win.

Eona was fading from view. The boat disappeared, and suddenly Karr and Sonara were back in the cave, kneeling over the heart as it turned solid again. But before Eona disappeared, he heard her whisper her final words. "Find the missing pieces of the planet's heart. You have all you need to awaken her. To put her back together again."

The heart solidified, and Karr felt thrown back into his body, as if perhaps all that had just transpired was only inside of his mind.

He pulled his hands away as time snapped back into motion again. Behind him, Jaxon's voice returned, his words picking up right where they'd left off. "Don't touch it!"

Markam's body was still unconscious beside Azariah.

It was as if nothing had transpired at all, while they were inside.

"His heart," Sonara whispered.

She pulled her hands away and turned to face Karr. She reached up slowly to grip the necklace around her throat that had once belonged to Soahm. "You carry his heart," she said. "It's why you carry his aura on your blood."

"Sonara," he said gently. "I'm—"

"Don't apologize," she said, turning her back to him. She seemed numb; as if all the rage and grief within her had been pushed deep down. "It won't bring Soahm back."

The space was still. Only the beating of the planet's heart, the sighing breath, the scent of death from the piles of bones, remaining from the battles Eona had waged against Eder.

The silence broke when the far wall of the cave temple shook once.

Twice.

Then it exploded, a rain of mountain rocks caving in, as a hole finally broke through. The silver tip of the massive drill stopped spinning as it was turned off from the outside, the screech of it dying out as it finally came to a stop.

Karr coughed dust from his lungs, waving his hand before his eyes as a small cluster of shadowed figures emerged first through the rubble.

Cade, and Rohtt shortly behind him. Following them, the Dohrsaran army stood waiting to widen the entrance, the mites still attached to their necks. Forced to do his bidding, or there would be pain; and then, death.

But there was a third figure who emerged and shook off the dust, then rose to standing at Cade's left, her hand on his wrist as he guided her over the rubble and into the clearing.

She dropped to her knees as she beheld the heart. Karr couldn't see her face, but he didn't need to, for the wolf skull gave her away.

It was Thali.

CHAPTER 39

Cade

Cade Kingston loved trouble, had lived it and breathed it since the day he'd come back from his errands on the starship docks, and found Jeb Montforth kneeling over his parents' corpses.

Jeb held an unconscious Karr in his arms, a bloody knife in his fist.

But Cade had his father's pistol, so he'd first shot the man with Jeb, and then he'd forced Jeb into a sparring match.

In the end, Jeb won the match, besting Cade because he was twice his age and twice his size. But looking back, Cade knew that he'd bound himself to trouble that day, that it would someday come to find him again.

And find him, it had.

"You work for Geisinger," Cade had said, when Jeb pressed him to his knees and held his father's gun to his head. *"You're here to finish us all off, because my parents tried to run from him. They didn't honor the deal they'd made. The payment."*

Jeb's hand was trembling on the gun.

Like he was bold enough to use a blade on a fully grown man, but too much of a coward to use a bullet on a kid.

"We'll pay their debt," Cade said. *"My brother and I. We'll work it off. We'll spend the rest of our lives doing his bidding. We'll go anywhere, steal anything. I've seen my parents work, I know how to run this ship."*

Jeb called Geisinger up, and gave him the counteroffer.

And just like that, the Kingston brothers sealed a lifetime of indenture to Friedrich Geisinger. But the man didn't want to deal with them. *Space trash*, he'd said, so Jeb himself became a bastard father of two. Geisinger would call upon them if he ever had need.

Karr couldn't know about the deal.

So Cade had spun a lie.

A lifetime of lies for a lifetime of trouble.

He wasn't entirely surprised, when, ten years later, Friedrich Geisinger himself forced him into the Dohrsaran deal.

Cade had done it. Not because he'd wanted to—the weight of the sins he'd have to carry, doing the man's bidding… what he'd have to do to the people there…

It was hideous work.

Unforgiveable.

But Cade had already committed a lifetime of unforgiveable sins.

So he'd taken the deal, in part because Geisinger swore it would be the final job to pay off his parents' debt. But also because Cade wondered, if perhaps, by giving Karr this gift—true freedom—he'd be able to save his little brother from burning in some locked cell in hell for his sins.

Sins by association.

Sins Karr didn't even know he'd had a part in committing.

"How can I trust that you won't run, like your parents once did?" Geisinger had asked. *"How can I trust that the sins of the father won't pass down to the son, and repeat themselves over again?"*

Cade had bet his life on this job. Because he'd needed it. God, he'd needed it, to set Karr free.

It was a stupid bet. Downright foolish, but not on Cade's part. It was foolish on Geisinger, because Cade never intended to leave this job *alive.* Fate was too fickle, a guiding force that he had decided, years ago, would not let him live to grow old.

He'd never forget the pain of that night, after he'd signed on the dotted line for this job.

When Rohtt came to his hospital room and wheeled him into surgery.

When the pretty nurse with a robotic eye had ripped Cade's chest open… and a queen mite was attached to his very heart. As long as the queen mite lived, the other mites lived, too. A complete failsafe, so that Cade would have no other option but to complete the job.

Do what Geisinger asked, return the Antheon, and the mite would be removed.

But if he failed…

All Geisigner had to do was hit *stop* on the queen mite that held Cade's life in balance.

Then he'd join his parents in whatever came after death.

The queen mite ached. He hadn't slept, hadn't eaten, and the more he wriggled and tried to scratch at the queen mite, at the flesh that had healed and cracked open again, despite the anti-rejection medication Rohtt pumped him with each night…

The queen mite was slowly sucking the life from him. Twice, he feared Karr had almost noticed, from the plans in his quarters, and the bleeding on his chest, when they'd landed on Dohrsar. But Karr had messed this mission up in other ways.

This was Cade's last stand.

His last chance.

And he would do whatever it took to finish the job.

***

The rubble cleared, and Cade climbed over it, past the point of the drill as he beheld the Antheon within. The pulsing black rock was *real*, nestled in the middle of a golden amphitheater, a ring of firelight casting a glow on the entire cave.

He'd done it.

Cade nearly wept as he walked forward, his eyes finding the Antheon. All the pain and the planning, all the lies and the sins he'd commited… it would all be worth it, when he commanded his prisoner army to rip it right from the Dohrsaran ground.

Cade reached the edge of the amphitheater, a grin blooming on his face.

But it fell, the moment he got a full view of the bottom.

"Karr."

Damn him and his resourcefulness.

For there his little brother stood, alive and well and still without his S2 helmet. Cade almost didn't believe it, didn't want to trust that his eyes weren't betraying him. But sure enough, Karr stood before the Antheon, his hair pushed back from his face as the rock itself seemed to sigh. To take a breath in and out, pull and release.

"You shouldn't be here, Cade," Karr said.

His voice echoed up the golden steps like a gunshot.

Cade swallowed, and held out his arms, considering how he'd perform this very last dance. How he'd get Karr to come back to his side, before all was lost. "Come here, little brother. It's not too late to return to your own people. Your family, Karr. It's all been a misunderstanding. We can keep you *safe*. That's all we want. Whatever effect this poisonous atmosphere has had on you… let's remedy it together. Come back to my side. We'll take the Antheon and soar away from here forever."

His voice carried out above the strange pulsing of the Antheon. The sighing of some sort of sickly smelling wind. Just as Thali had told him, it was *alive.* Like a creature in its own right.

"You can't have the heart," Karr said. "This job, and what you've done to these people to complete it… it's not worth it, Cade. Stop now, before I stop you myself."

Rohtt laughed out loud. "Fool boy. I should shoot you."

"You will *stand down*, Rohtt," Cade commanded. He glanced back over his shoulder, where his army was still clearing the rubble.

The drill itself had died out, smoking and smelling of turned oil. They'd have to dig by hand to widen the entrance, and if they dared stop… Cade would tap the control panel on his S2, commanding them to feel nothing but pain.

"This is the end," Karr said, drawing Cade's gaze back. "Stop it *now*."

The Devil stood at the bottom of the pit beside him, staring at Cade with a hunger—a hatred—that he had never seen reflected in the eyes of the living. There was the outlaw Jaxon, who Cade had traded and set free. And there was the beautiful young woman, Azariah, who had snuck inside the ship with the Devil. Finally, the illusionist Markam, who'd changed Thali's appearance—but he was unconscious, lying beside them.

Cade stepped closer, the dark space calling to him.

"Come to my side," Cade begged one last time. What had happened, in so little time, to change him? To make him choose *strangers* instead of his own flesh and blood? Cade had given everything, *everything*, to protect him. Was it the poisonous air? Perhaps it morphed the brain, changed the way someone thought. "Come back, and we'll talk about this. I'll tell you the truth, Karr. All of it."

"The truth doesn't matter anymore," Karr said now. "It won't change a thing."

The small group drew closer to Karr and the Devil, hands flexing as if they were preparing for a fight.

"Enough is enough, Karr!" Cade shouted. Fury sparked to life inside of him. "You're acting like a selfish child. I've brought you a gift. I've promised you a forever with it. Leave the heart. Come to my side, where you belong."

"I don't belong there," Karr said. He smiled sadly. "I belong right here. I always have."

Cade laughed harshly, the sound reverberating off the walls. It sounded a bit like the laugh Thali had given him inside the ship's brig. He silenced himself, checking his temper. He turned his gaze away from Karr, onto the Devil instead. "What did you do to him?"

"The question," she said softly as she drew herself to a standing position, her sword in her fist, "is not what *I* did to him. But what *you* did. What your parents did, the secret you kept. He's not your brother. Not fully."

Cade tilted his head.

Something squirmed inside of him. A feeling of sickness, of unease. How could she know the truth? It wasn't possible. Beside him, Thali seemed to perk up, listening closely for the first time since they'd entered the cave.

"What are you talking about?" Cade didn't have time for this. "Karr! To my side. *Now*."

The Devil drew her sword, a pathetic attempt at a threat from the bottom of the amphitheater, when Cade stood above with *real* weapons. But she snarled up at him, and said, "Do not speak to him as if he's your *beast*, forced to sit at your feet and lick the blood from your wounds. He's not yours to command. He never was. Not since the day your people replaced his heart with Soahm's. Not since the day you swore to keep that secret to yourself."

That squirming thing broke free inside of Cade.

It was terror. Terror, because how could this girl know the truth? For if she did… that meant…

"I know everything," Karr said next. He looked back at the Antheon, his fists clenching as he stepped away from it. When his gaze swung back to Cade, it was full of so many things. Sadness. Horror. Disgust.

"All these years, you knew, Cade," Karr said. "You knew that the *only* reason I am alive is because of a boy our parents abducted from this very planet. And now you dare to come back here, to the place I owe my life, and destroy it by ripping the very heart from it."

"You don't know what you're saying," Cade whispered.

"I know exactly what I'm saying," Karr said. "I saw all of it. I *see* all of it, and I keep seeing it, even when my eyes aren't open. It's the very worst when I look at you."

"I didn't choose," Cade started. "I didn't choose *any* of it, Karr! They did! *They* started this!"

Karr held up a hand. "Stop," he growled.

And as he did… the ground trembled.

Cade thought he imagined it. An aftershock, perhaps, from the drill breaking through the mountain.

"You are my brother, Cade," Karr said. "We share a lifetime of pain. A lifetime of things we did not deserve, but our parents brought it all onto us. And then you decided to continue it, when you made a deal with Jeb."

How did he know? How could he know?

Cade realized, suddenly, as his body felt dipped in ice… this was not Karr standing before him. This was a monster wearing Karr's skin. Perhaps his *real* brother died that day on the sand, when the Devil turned her sword on him and drove it into his chest.

The Antheon had brought Karr back. Geisinger said it had the power to do such things.

But what if it hadn't? What if it brought back a monster instead, some twisted version of Karr, that saw all and knew all, and…

"Enough of this," Thali said. "I've waited long enough."

She stepped away from Cade, walking forward into the unclaimed space between the two groups.

"Thali," the beautiful one called up. "It's okay. We're going to protect it from them."

"Silence, Princess," Thali hissed. "For so long, I have had to put up with your voice."

The woman below gasped, and took a step back, shock spreading across her face.

"All these years," Thali said. "All these years, I have sought to find a way to enter this sacred space. The heart lives. The heart breathes. It is so, so beautiful. I never thought… *never* thought I would finally find it."

"You shouldn't be on their side, cleric," the Devil said, her voice turning to a warning tone. "Care to explain what you're doing with them?"

"Hello, Eona," Thali said. Her wolf mask swung right, her eyes just barely visible in its shadows as she glared down into the pit to stare at the Devil. "How long have you been hiding in there?"

Cade watched, unsure what to do. Unsure when to command his people to move.

Karr's posture was rigid instead of lazy. His smile was wiped clean from his lips, and his eyes… they looked up at Cade with a burning intensity that they had never held within.

It was almost like hatred.

Cade couldn't look away from Karr, couldn't stop feeling like the brother he'd always known and loved and protected, that he'd given all of himself for… was *dead.*

CHAPTER 40

Sonara

Hello, Eona. How long have you been hiding inside of there for?

"You know?" Sonara asked Thali, as that greeting, more like a threat, entered her brain.

Her curse was going wild. It screamed at her, pounding at its cage from within. She let it out. She obliterated the cage door, let it fall to dust and rubble, for she no longer wanted to control it. Everything she'd ever hoped for, everything she thought she knew was true about herself, and Soahm… it was all a lie.

She didn't care.

She wanted to burn down the world.

She wanted to destroy everything in the wake of her rage, because Soahm was gone. Not just stolen, but *gone*, forever. It was some kind of sick, twisted punishment for her sins that Karr carried her brother's heart, her brother's aura, right back to Dohrsar.

Karr lived because Soahm was dead.

Karr carried half of Eona's soul because Soahm's heart was cut right out of his chest and given to him as a secret gift.

Thali suddenly knelt at the top of the amphitheater, drawing Sonara's gaze back to her. Giving her a place to focus her rage. And as she knelt, an aura filtered out from her.

That dusty, ancient scent, carried on the planet's breath.

Sonara breathed past it, trying to decipher Thali's next move. For the woman had apparently betrayed them, had secrets that went far deeper than anything Sonara expected. Secrets that tangled up in all the horrific truths Eona had shared with them.

"Thali?" Azariah called out to her once more.

Sonara swung her arm out, sword stopping the princess before she could move forward.

The Princess, somehow, was her half-sister. Another sickening twist of fate, that she'd had someone like her all along. A piece of her family, her blood, that she'd never been given the chance to get to know. She would *not* let harm come to Azariah today.

"Don't," Sonara growled. "She's not who she says she is."

Azariah paused, eyes wide, and for a moment, Sonara feared she would not listen. But the princess stopped. "Thali? Is this true?"

The cleric only laughed; a strange sound that had not come from her before. "You're a foolish thing, so desperate for love. All along, I thought… I suspected it was you. Three years I wasted, trying to train you. Trying to help you grow your power, so that you could lead me to the heart. And all along, it was the Devil I truly needed."

Azariah's aura deflated at those words. *Realization* and *betrayal* filtered out with each breath as she stood with Karr and Sonara and flexed her hands.

The hair on Sonara's neck began to stand on end.

"Not yet, Princess," Sonara whispered. "Hold it back. Save your strength."

For what would she have left, at this point? Azariah nodded, and the electricity in the space fizzled.

"I did not suspect Eona had *two* pieces of her soul that survived," Thali said. Her voice echoed through the cavern. "I know now that one of those pieces resides with *him*." She pointed her gauntleted finger at Karr. "A Wanderer from afar. Eona's spirit is always meddling, working with the planet, the two thinking they're some sort of preposterous team. Was it Eona's spirit that compelled you to kill Karr, so she could bring him back a Shadowblood? So she would make it harder for me to win in the end?"

"Who are you?" Sonara demanded, feeling like a beast whose hackles were standing on end. As if the piece of Eona's soul that she carried inside was growling. Warning her without words. "Who are you truly?"

"A lifetime of worship and sacrifice," Thali spat. She trembled as she removed her bone gauntlets, letting them fall to the floor with a hollow clatter. Sonara realized, as she watched, that she'd never seen the cleric's arms or hands without them. The scent of *decay* poured from her, that strange, dusty aura that Sonara had sensed on the woman the very first time she'd met her face to face, in the saloon. And now she realized why.

Thali's skin was decayed beneath those gauntlets. Portions of her skin had been eaten away to hollow, holes of green, dying flesh. As if her body had been devoured, little by little, by some sort of poison.

"A lifetime of seeking for a way to uncover the heart," Thali said, as she ran her fingertips across her ruined hands and wrists. Sonara fought back a gag from the aura as pieces of Thali's skin flaked away. "I knew it was here, close by, in these mountains... buried deep. But I could never get to its exact hiding place." She laughed again, but there was no joy in the sound. "But then Karr arrived, and he uncovered the damned door right to it. Of course, the door wouldn't let me inside. Wouldn't let me enter, because it *knew.* It knew that I carried its enemy beneath this shield of Canis bones."

Her ruined hands moved upwards, towards her Canis mask. She unclasped it from the back, three *pops* that sounded in time with the beating of the planet's heart.

Danger, Sonara's magic hissed. *Danger and darkness and the end of the end.*

"At long last," Thali said, sliding her ruined hands to the front of the bone mask. "I can bring Eder home."

She removed the mask. And Sonara nearly screamed at the sight of the girl's face beneath. Azariah gasped, stepping close to Sonara as she pressed a hand to her mouth.

Thali's skin was held together only in patches upon her skull, as if moths had eaten away at her face. Her ears were mere shreds, her nose down to the bone, her eyeballs hanging loose in the sockets, her eyelids eaten away.

An aura of *decay* rushed from her again, and Sonara now understood why.

She'd always thought the aura came from the poor remains of the Canis that had died, giving their bones to make Thali's mask and gauntlets. But it came from the destroyed skin beneath. Or perhaps from whatever lurked inside of Thali.

A darkness Sonara had yet to meet.

"I am weary," Thali whispered. She closed her eyes and cracked her neck on both sides, stretching in the freedom of no longer wearing a mask. "Hundreds of years, my ancestors have carried Eder's soul, searching for the heart so they could deliver him back to it again. They failed, but Eder's soul carried on, the same way Eona's did. Searching, always searching. Eventually he came to reside in me. I was determined to be the one to bring him home. He kept me alive, using his dwindling power so that I could remain a host. A host who loved him. Desired him. *Worshiped* him and gave *everything* so I could set him free."

She turned, lifting her hand to Cade.

"The sword, as part of our deal."

Cade stumbled backwards, as if he were horrified and disgusted at Thali.

But she moved, so fast it should have been impossible, and in a blink, Gutrender was in her hands.

Cade froze in shock, even Rohtt pausing beside him as they watched Thali admire her newly won prize.

She sighed longingly, then removed it from its sheath. Its golden color sparkled in the dark heart's glowing light, in the flaming torches littered all around.

"What are you doing?" Sonara called up the steps. "Thali, drop the blade."

"Eder's time was running low. Too much longer, and he would have vanished, gone forever. He held on as long as he could. So when I was in Stonegrave—when the poor little princess was sleeping, unaware that she was my pawn—I spoke privately to Jira. *I* told him about the heart's power. *I* convinced him to take the deal with Geisinger. To bring the Wanderers here, to dig it right out of Dohrsar. Because I knew that the planet would respond to the threat. That it would send forth a wave of terror and fear and draw the soul of Eona out of hiding. Make her soul act out and reveal itself, in desperation to save Dohrsar when the greatest threat it had ever known came calling."

She smiled with rotting black teeth.

"It worked. Eona's soul did reveal itself, but not as I suspected. I thought… I thought it was Karr alone. That Karr was the one holding her soul. I thought perhaps Eona's soul called to you, Sonara, and made you kill him, so that she could set things in motion. I wasn't certain *how* her soul had ended up in a Wanderer, but… Eder felt the whisper of Eona within him. And when Karr revealed that door with his power… we knew." Her hollow eyes fell to Sonara again. "It was you, Devil, that ruined things." She cackled, then hacked on a cough that had her spitting blood. "The Devil of the Deadlands, so unbelieving and undeserving of the planet's power. I should have known, but I never sensed it in you. Perhaps because you were too stubborn. Too afraid of your magic."

"How long have you known?" Sonara asked.

"Not long enough," Thali said. "You ruined my plans. I was going to join the Wanderers from the beginning, but then *you* initiated the attack, and I knew that Eona had made a move. I decided to stay with you, to see if you would do something else, led by Eona. But when it was taking too long… I offered myself up. You took me right to the Wanderers, thinking I was giving myself over as a worthy sacrifice to the cause. There, I was able to get Cade to see reason, to let me lead him here, the pulse of the planet's heart so powerful in its fear. So bright." Her eyes looked past Sonara, at the heart. She gripped Gutrender tighter, her fingertips oozing as the skin melted away. "This is far more poetic. Powerful. The way Eder would have wanted, for he once brought his own army back here, and fought Eona before the heart. Now he'll get to do it again. And this time… he will win." She turned to look at Sonara, her eyes protruding from her skeletal face. "Eder, my love. My soul. The time is now, for you to be set free."

Before anyone could cry out, before they could move to action, Thali lifted Gutrender.

And drove it deep into her own chest.

CHAPTER 41

Sonara

Thali did not fall.

Her body twitched, and she leaned forward on the golden blade, soaking it with her blood.

Then she moved. She lifted her head, cracking her neck side to side before looking down at the blade protruding from her chest.

"A hideous thing, this sword," she said. "I always wondered what my father saw in it."

But it was not *her* voice any longer.

It was a male's voice. Deep and horrific and rumbling like an undead spirit, risen again.

Her hands fell upon the hilt, where the miniature Hadru looked to be devouring the blade itself. "But so powerful. Not for its craft… for alone, it is just an ordinary king's sword. The First King's sword, ancient and hiding a secret."

Thali's fingers gripped the hilt.

"It is the stone inside of it that gives this sword its true power." She smiled, then pulled the sword from her chest. With a sickening *crunch*, the bloody metal slid out past cracked bones and rotting skin. "The small piece of the planet's heart that my father first removed, long ago, when he discovered the heart. I used it to destroy Eona, before. And I'll use it now to destroy her again."

Not Thali, then.

But…

"Eder," Sonara whispered.

Eder smiled from inside of Thali's body. His eyes had turned from Thali's cold, pupilless white to a solid shadow black, as he looked from Karr to Sonara and back again. "Hello again, Eona. Or should I say, the two halves of Eona, come together once more."

Behind Eder, the cave wall crumbled, the hole large enough now to let two people through at once. The first set of Cade's Wanderer soldiers appeared, hefting their rifles.

"Many thanks, Wanderer, for leading me here," Eder said to Cade.

"A traitor," Rohtt hissed. "A worm that should be squished beneath—"

Eder moved like a wraith as he spun in Thali's body, slicing the sword clean across Rohtt's neck.

Rohtt's head tumbled from his shoulders, a clean cut. Blood slung in raindrops against the tip of the drill as his torso teetered. Then it fell forward against the cave floor with a wet *smack,* to fall at the prisoner's feet.

"But you…" Cade sputtered. "You swore to be on my side."

"Wanderer fool," Eder growled. "Now it is *your* turn to die."

"Stop him!" Cade shouted.

The prisoners swarmed Eder like a wave, hefting their axes and shovels, their faces blank as they responded to Cade's command.

Eder slashed out with Gutrender, so quickly Sonara almost didn't see the blade swing.

Prisoners fell in his wake. The floor was littered with fresh bodies to mix with the dried bones.

All the while, Cade stood to the side, horrified.

Sonara had heard about Jira's conquests with Gutrender, why they called him the Scorpion King. She'd wielded the blade herself in Stonegrave, but she'd never seen it in action with her own eyes… never truly understood it until now, as she saw Gutrender at work.

Little by little, Eder began to descend the gold steps.

The power he held, and not just from the blade…

It was dark magic.

A power Sonara had never beheld before.

"Stop Eder!" she shouted to Karr and Azariah, as Wanderer bullets fired in the background and resounded throughout the cave. Sonara felt them rumble in her chest, and sing in her blood. "Stop him and get the sword before the gets to the heart!"

The cave turned into a bloodbath, a blur of bodies dropping and bullets firing, the rest of the Dohrsaran prisoners clustered together in the back, waiting blankly for Cade to pull them into the fray.

Eder slashed with Gutrender, stopping the bullets, *flattening them* before they hit the ground with a plink.

"Wanderer weapons against the might of the planet." Eder's voice boomed over the chaos. "Against a mere *portion* of the heart. Imagine what the entire heart could do if it were mine."

Gutrender swung left and right, arcing and twisting as Eder sliced through bullets, stopping them before they could hit Thali's body. Somewhere in the fray, Cade was now standing with his soldiers, shouting commands for them to stop him.

One by one, they lost to Eder. The sword was too mighty, too full of the planet's power from that one small stolen piece…

Eder's boots were on the second step of the amphitheater now.

Prisoners continued to fall as he walked, spinning and felling them in his wake.

Save me, Sonara's curse whispered as it picked up on the planet's terror. It was ripe upon her tongue. *Save me, my soul, save me.*

Eder was halfway down the steps.

Sonara backed up, her heels scraping the heart. She could feel its pulse inside of her, resounding as her own heart hammered in her chest. She could not fight an unfightable blade. Not with a regular warrior's sword, even if it had once been Soahm's.

There were so few prisoners now. So few soldiers. Only fifty left, perhaps, but still, they came.

The golden sword swung as Eder turned and leapt the last few steps, aiming for the heart, almost in slow motion.

Sonara lifted Lazaris, ready to take the hit. Certain that she would die trying to defend the heart.

But before Eder could cut her clean in half…

A jolt of electricity struck the sword. Gutrender smashed into it with a resounding *ring*, pushing the blade off balance.

Sonara looked to her right. There Azariah stood with her palms outstretched, a smile on her beautiful, lethal face, as she walked to join Sonara.

"I shared everything with this monster," Azariah said, her eyes sparkling. "It's time for it to die."

Eder swung, but Azariah's lightning struck the blade again.

"Shadowbloods," Eder growled, whirling to take out two more of Cade's prisoners before he faced Azariah again, and readied for another strike.

But next a set of bones rose to life, as Jaxon lifted his hands and *screamed* into his power. All around, the skeletons began to rise from the steps. They slunk across the amphitheater like an army, holding back Cade's prisoners, creating a wall so that none could pass.

Cade howled as he stood at the top, shouting for his people to *fight*, to find a way through the dead.

But Jaxon's army of bones was too strong, his power surging from him as he held his hands in the air like a conductor. The bones wove together like a wall that stood, ever-strong, around the bottom few steps of the amphitheater.

There was only Eder now.

"Worry about Eder," Jaxon said, as he looked over his shoulder at Sonara. "I'll handle the rest."

More bolts of lightning lanced from Azariah's palms, forming shields of blue that appeared in midair to meet the blade as Eder growled and came for them again.

The cave was filled with the crackle—the *boom*—of Azariah's power as she pulled at something deep inside herself.

Eder swung and sliced through the bolts with Gutrender. But when the electricity faltered, when Azariah didn't get a shield up in time, breathless and bleeding shadows from her nose… a boulder shot into the path, knocking into Eder. Karr shouted in victory.

Eder rolled sideways, Gutrender still in hand.

The fight continued.

Sonara's blade clashed against Eder's, and when she faltered, she felt the jolt of Azariah's electricity pushing Eder back. Azariah, *her sister*, and Karr, who carried part of Soahm inside of him.

Sonara fought alongside them, but Lazaris would not be enough. Soon it would break beneath Gutrender's power, and then what would she have left to defend the heart?

Magic, Sonara's curse whispered.

She closed her eyes.

There is no more cage, she told herself. *There is no more holding back.*

With a roar, she let her power soar from her to follow Eder's every move. She pulled at his emotions, his ancient and rotting aura revealing every step before he made them.

"Karr!" Sonara shouted, as she sensed Eder angling the sword towards where he stood.

Karr dove as lightning shielded his body, cracking like the Wanderer wall once had. And then Eder was recoiling again.

"Jaxon, to the right!" Sonara said. A skeleton stumbled into Jaxon's path, protecting his back as Eder lunged at him and cut the skeleton clean in half instead, the bones spilling only to quickly piece themselves back together again.

Rocks came up from the cave floor, as Karr called to the rubble. But Eder was too quick, spinning to cut right through the rocks, before turning again to cut through Azariah's lightning.

It was slash after slash, rock meeting sword and bone and lightning slowing its path, a deadly dance of darkness and light and earth.

But when the Shadowbloods began to slow, Eder did not.

Help us, Sonara thought. She pushed her prayer towards the planet's heart, not even sure it would listen. *Help us or we're all going to die.*

As Eder swung again, a shot rang out.

Thali's body jerked as the bullet went clean through Eder's chest.

He turned, snarling, to stare at the one who'd shot him.

Cade Kingston, his rifle outstretched, smoke trailing from the barrel like a bullet's goodbye kiss.

***

"Get away from my brother," Cade snarled.

Eder turned, sword steaming from the heat of the electricity.

Cade shot again.

The bullet went through Thali's eye socket.

"You cannot kill a spirit, just as you cannot kill a soul," Eder said. He swung the blade. Bits of blood fell from it like a sparkling red rain. Then he ran. Sprinting not towards the heart, but back up the steps towards Cade, blade poised to swing.

And Eder did swing.

But the blade never made it to Cade's chest.

Because the ground split open as Karr screamed beside Sonara, his body trembling as rage poured from him to create a deep crack in the ground. Eder stumbled, a foot caught in the crack.

Karr slammed his hands together, and the crack tightened around Eder's ankle, trapping him in place. He fell, face-first on the steps, helpless. Gutrender fell from his grasp.

It was almost silent as Karr took the bait and sprinted up the steps to finish the job. Sonara shouted after him. It couldn't be this easy.

She sensed the *anticipation* and *decision* on her tongue, knew that Eder was *not* ready to die… as Eder suddenly turned, aiming a small knife that had been hidden inside of Thali's cloak.

Sonara saw everything fading before her, like Soahm being stolen in the night.

Gone. Soahm was *gone.* He would never sit upon their mother's throne, take back his crown, give Soreia the king it deserved. Her whole life, she'd chased after the ghost of him, hoping she would find him, bring him home.

But perhaps he'd come back on his own.

Not fully. Not the way he should have been.

But as she watched Eder swing that blade at all that was left of Soahm… something inside of Sonara broke. All her sorrow, all her hatred for the Wanderers boiled within her, mixing and tangling until her own magic shifted.

She'd caged it her entire second life. Feared it, deep down, because she believed it controlled her. Like everything always had. When all this time, she could have been controlling it.

She pointed her magic—not a curse any longer—at Eder.

At the rotting, stinking thing that roiled within Thali's old veins.

Pain, she thought. The aura of pain…

And as she thought it, as she pushed it outwards with a scream, thinking of Soahm, thinking of the death he'd endured, the life he'd given so Karr could stand again…

Eder screamed.

Screamed, and that same *pain* Sonara had imagined poured from him. The aura she'd come up with, had manipulated into existence.

Sorrow, she thought, pouring her own emotions into her magic, wanting to use it to turn it into something more.

Eder began to weep, his aura pouring with sorrow as he felt what Sonara wove with her magic, tangled up in the crushing sadness from the loss of Soahm.

"Azariah," Sonara said, as she closed her eyes and imagined terror, the very same that the planet felt with Eder so near. "Get the blade."

Sonara shoved that terror outwards, sent it soaring on shadow wings. As it went, she threw herself along with it, until she was seeing through her magic, the very same way she had when she'd once taken a sword and shoved it deep into Karr's chest.

Into Eder's open mouth her magic soared, down into his rotting core.

Sonara told her magic to *sing*, to scream terror into Eder's very soul, and sing it did.

Terror, like Soahm's scream in the night. Terror, like Duran leaping from the edge of a Soreian cliff. Like a whip lashing upon a girl's open back, a kingdom full of people watching with hatred in their eyes.

Sonara laughed, as her magic sent Eder into the fetal position.

He curled himself up like a bug and trembled beneath the weight of the emotions she wove into him. Slowly, Karr called to the ground, widening the crack around Eder's ankle.

Pulling Eder deeper and deeper into the earth, as if Eder was now a part of the golden amphitheater steps.

"You cannot stop this," Eder growled, now only his face visible in the steps as they closed around him.

But Sonara told her magic to give him the aura of *terror, like a Soreian prince being stolen from a dark, once-silent shore.*

Eder screamed beneath the manipulation.

Azariah joined Sonara's side.

"Melt the sword," Sonara said.

Because Eona's words were coming back to her. The planet... it would wake. If given a chance, it would wake, if made whole again.

Azariah placed the sword on the cave floor. She pressed palms to it, and they began to glow. A soft blue at the start, then so hot they turned white. The sword, so powerful, so famed, should have melted beneath her magic.

And yet it remained.

Sonara dropped to her knees, her magic fizzling. Eder howled, thrashing against Karr's entrapment. The ground began to crack around him. He got an arm free, a rotting arm that reached towards the heart as Eder screamed.

"I can't hold him," Karr ground out. "I can't hold him, Sonara."

"Melt it, Azariah!" Sonara yelled.

"I'm trying," Azariah said.

She was sobbing as she pressed her hands to the sword, her power finally sapped.

Sonara sent another aura towards Eder, this time turning it into that blissful, beautiful glee she'd once felt, when Markam pressed his lips against hers. When all she wanted to do was sink into him, lay back, and do nothing but savor the moment.

Eder relaxed, giving Karr's own magic a chance to breathe.

Azariah sank, hands smoking.

Still the blade remained. "I can't break it," she whispered. "I have nothing left."

The blade was white-hot. "Take it," Sonara said. "Pick it up, Az."

The Princess nodded and scooped up the sword.

Sonara turned, practically blind from the intensity of using her magic, as she tried to force another wave of emotion Eder's way. But the creature only laughed.

"You cannot save the heart," he growled. "It will be here forever, beckoning the darkness to draw near. Someday, someone will arrive and claim it."

"Close it," Sonara said. "Close the earth."

Sonara could almost hear the world sigh as the ground trembled and closed fully over Eder.

The only sound left was the heart.

Thumping, slowly, as its aura whispered, *Save me,* that constant background noise that had not stopped since they'd entered this place. Silently, Sonara walked past the bodies on the floor. Past Karr, who lay there, watching, his brother beside him, the Dohrsaran prisoners gone.

"It's time to end this," Sonara said. "To put the heart back together again for good."

Silently, she took the sword from Azariah's hand. Her palm burned against the heat of it, but she sensed that pain inside of her hand, and breathed it in. So easy, to remove that feeling, the aura of pain that came with it. With a breath, she forced it away.

Her skin smoked as she held the blade and marched across the cave.

With a final bit of strength, Sonara drove the famed blade, with the original piece of Antheon, right into the heart of the planet.

Just as a gunshot went off.

As something pinched against her back, and shadow blood leaked from her chest, soaring past her vision so quickly she thought she'd imagined it.

"NO!" Karr screamed.

Sonara fell, catching a glimpse of Cade.

He stood with his rifle aimed at her as the pain from the bullet wound finally hit her.

She'd been shot.

CHAPTER 42

Karr

Karr screamed as Sonara fell, the sword sticking from the heart of the planet… and yet it had not worked.

"No!" Karr screamed again. "*No.*"

He scrambled to his knees, but then Cade was turning. Leveling the gun on him next.

Karr held up his hands. "Cade. *Please.*"

"I want to believe you, Karr, but…" Cade sniffed. There were tears pouring down his eyes as he stalked past Karr. "But all I see is a monster wearing my brother's skin."

Azariah and Jaxon moved towards Sonara, but Cade fired another shot. It struck the ground beside Sonara's body. "Nobody touches the Devil!" he shouted.

They held up their hands.

"Take the blade. Remove it from the heart," Cade commanded. "Or she'll die."

"Cade, please," Karr said.

Cade glanced at him, and his eyes were not *his* eyes. They were overtaken by pain and sorrow, by hatred and a burning rage. "You are not my brother. Not fully. Not anymore."

"I am," Karr said. "Cade, *I am*."

"This place, this hideous place… it's changed you, Karr. It's turned you into something I no longer know. And now I'm going to destroy it."

He marched onwards, his rifle still aimed at Sonara, who lay on the floor beside the heart, holding her side as shadow blood leaked out.

"You," Cade said, pointing his rifle at Azariah. "Remove the blade and toss it to me."

"Don't," Sonara ground out. "Azariah, I swear to the stars, if you remove that blade, I will come back and haunt you forever once I'm dead."

"Remove it!" Cade hissed.

Azariah reached out.

"Cade," Karr said. "You raised me as your own."

"Stop talking," Cade growled. He looked to Azariah. "The *blade*."

But Karr wouldn't stop. "You used to tell me stories each night before we went to bed. We shared a blanket at Jeb's place and I always got mad at you because you stole it, tossing and turning in your sleep."

"You have his memories, but you aren't him," Cade said.

"You told me once that we would be kings if we came to Dohrsar. But I never wanted to be a king, Cade. I just wanted to be free."

Cade was crying now. Karr could see his shoulders shaking, but he kept the rifle aimed upon Sonara. Still, he refused to believe.

"You can still stop this," Karr urged him. "We can find a way to escape Geisinger's path, start a new life somewhere, be together like you always wanted."

"There is no us," Cade said suddenly. He looked back at Karr. "There is no *us,* not after this."

He turned, pointing the rifle at Azariah again. "Take the blade. Use it to cut out the heart, piece by piece."

Behind him, Jaxon's skeletal army began to crumble.

Bone by bone, they tumbled, and Jaxon sank to his knees, unable to hold them any longer. "I'm sorry," he gasped.

"DO IT NOW!" Cade shouted.

With a sob, Azariah moved forward to pull the blade out.

But as Azariah moved… Sonara moved, too.

She reached out, with a wet, shadow-blood covered hand.

And slammed something into the heart.

Karr had only a moment to see what she'd done, as his gaze focused on the amulet. The amulet he'd spent his whole life wearing, that had once belonged to Soahm. It fit perfectly into a small hole on the side of the heart, like it had always belonged there.

The heart thumped once.

Twice.

Then the ground began to shake. The entire cave rumbled, like it was going to collapse and fall inwards on itself. Karr could sense it, feel it in the earth all around him as his magic picked up on the motion. Rocks tumbled from the ceiling, crashing down around the place.

"Get Sonara!" Karr shouted.

Azariah dragged her out of the way as the heart began to recede, sinking back into the ground. It swallowed everything in its path.

"No!" Cade screamed.

He threw his rifle and dove, reaching for the hilt of Gutrender as it sank with the heart.

His fingers grasped it, pulling him forward into the oncoming black as the ground shook, and Karr's magic told him that soon, it would all close in.

Karr dove and grabbed Cade's wrist.

"Let go!" Karr screamed.

Cade looked back at him, over his shoulder. His body trembled as he held onto the blade, still sinking slowly with the heart. "I must have it. I must have *something* to take from this place."

"You don't need it!" Karr said, tears in his own eyes, his body shaking as he tried to hold onto Cade. His magic lashed out, trying to hold back the heart. But it was sinking, too quickly, too strong, the space no longer responding to his magic. Against the heart, he would always be too weak. "Just let go, Cade. Let go of it all."

"I can't," Cade said.

His eyes found Karr's and for a moment, he looked like his old self again. Before the job, before their parents were gone. Before Geisinger and Jeb… before *everything*.

"I can't let go," he whispered. "But you can."

Any further, and they would both be sucked beneath the ground with the heart.

Together, they would cease to exist.

"Please, Cade," Karr begged him. "Please don't leave me."

"It's too late." Cade's hand gripped Gutrender so tight his fingertips turned fully white. Karr's fingers were slipping from Cade's other wrist, no longer able to hold him, to fight back as the heart sank and sank and sank. "If you're him… if you're truly him," Cade said. "Then let go, Karr. *Live*."

With a final cry, Karr's grip faltered.

"NO!" he screamed.

Cade fell, tumbling over the edge into darkness with the heart and the sword, as it swallowed them whole. The ground closed, swirling in on itself until it was solid again, the heart gone. Not even a mark to show that it had once been there inside the cave.

Gone.

Cade, and the heart of the planet… gone.

CHAPTER 43

LATER

Sonara

There was a Devil in the Deadlands, seated on the back of a once-dead steed as she rode towards the gates of Stonegrave, an army of freed prisoners at her back and a prince's sword hanging at her hip.

The past many weeks had been like a bad dream.

But Sonara had never feared the realm of nightmares.

It was the world of the living she shied away from, for the people and things in it were tangible. And dreams were not.

Dreams, like the idea that she could bring home a Soreian prince who'd been stolen by a Wanderer ship.

The very same ship that had once come to her planet, bringing with it a boy who bore that prince's heart. And inside of it, a piece of the very first Shadowblood's soul.

Sonara looked to the side, where that Wanderer rode now. Not on a steed like her own, but on a two-wheeled machine. A ripper, he'd called it. A bike that he trusted more than any worthy steed. He'd taken it from the ship that now sat in the desert sand, a relic. The engine, melted by lightning.

With the doors of the ship open, soon the desert beasts might move in. Or perhaps raiders would come and strip it down, sell the metal that made up its every part. The other Wanderers in Cade's army had been taken care of, sent to Deadwood to die.

The ship with the flaming bird on its belly was a threat no more.

Sonara had found her answers, not inside of it, as she'd thought she would. But in the heart of the planet itself.

Soahm was gone.

Sonara knew that now.

But pieces of him still remained. They resided in Karr, with his heart that beat as strong as the heat from the desert suns overhead. And in the leather journal Sonara kept in her duster pocket, heavy as it thumped against her hip with each beat of Duran's hooves against the sand.

Soahm lived on in her name, the one he'd come up with. And in the spirit of Duran, who Soahm had given her the gift of claiming, long ago, on a storming Soreian day.

And then there was Soahm's amulet. That was gone, too, though Sonara didn't truly feel as if she'd lost it. For when she'd lain wounded beside the planet's heart… she'd noticed a hole in the side. Another piece of it, cut out ages ago. It matched the shape of the amulet that sat upon her chest, hanging from a golden chain around her neck.

Soahm's amulet.

She'd pressed it in, the answer too simple, that act itself feeling like a dream.

But it had worked. The heart sank, receding into the earth, carrying the two pieces of itself with it. The sword and the amulet, both with their own stones. A bit of darkness had kissed Sonara's skin, healing her bullet wound… and giving her an extension on her second life.

A gift, perhaps, for returning Soahm's amulet to the heart.

Sonara had never known the full story of the amulet, only that it had been passed down from generation to generation, and started with the original Soreian queen. A young woman that had been kind and generous and strangely gifted in healing.

Sonara suspected now that *she* was Eona's daughter. That perhaps Eona had taken a piece of the planet's heart herself, and given it to her daughter to protect her, long ago.

The original Shadowblood. The chosen one, who'd balanced precariously between the realms of darkness and light. Not fully good, just like all Shadowbloods were. Perhaps Eona was just bad enough to steal a sliver of the heart she'd given all of herself to protect, and passed it on to her daughter.

Somehow, it had ended up right where it started again. It had saved Dohrsar, when the heart became whole. Some part of Sonara could still feel the heart's presence, deep beneath the planet's surface. It would always be there, alongside the mighty golden sword. Keeping Dohrsar safe.

"How long will you be mad at me for trying to steal the heart?" a voice asked beside Sonara. "You know I can't resist a prize."

Sonara glanced to her other side, where Azariah rode upon the back of a pale mare, glorious in the morning sun. Behind her, his arms around her middle, sat Markam.

"Not much longer," Azariah said.

Markam frowned. He wore his hat on his head, his duster soaring behind him.

"And I swear, Markam," Azariah said. "If you don't stop asking, I'm going to melt the eyebrows right off your face."

Their new respect for each other—perhaps even a mended relationship—was strange, and not what Sonara would have picked for a partnership. But somehow it worked, for the princess had a storm in her very veins. It would serve her well, if she were to spend her life once again loving the Trickster. Perhaps she'd never stopped loving him at all.

"We're nearly there," Azariah said. "Look."

She pointed.

And in the distance, beyond the looming statues of the great desert felines, the walls of Stonegrave awaited.

Her voice drowned out as a great screech sounded overhead. Sonara looked up, sensing the presence of Razor before she saw the mighty wyvern soar past, wings flapping in the hot wind.

Razor banked, landing before them, and Sonara smiled at the rider perched on the beast's back. It had taken a great deal of selflessness for Markam to allow Jaxon to borrow the wyvern.

That… and perhaps a small bit of coin.

"What is it, Jax?" Sonara asked.

He smiled as he stopped and removed his hat. A hat Sonara had kept safe for him, while he was prisoner to the Wanderer ship.

"Nothing," he said. "I only came to make sure the Devil is going to play nice when we get inside."

"Nice?" Sonara raised a brow. "I don't know the word."

Jaxon laughed, and his aura carried across to her, sweet as the suns setting over the evening sea. She breathed it in. Felt her heart flutter, as something inside of her shifted, and perhaps changed. "Jira doesn't know the word either."

"It doesn't matter," Sonara said. She swallowed those feelings away, saved them for a time when she could try to understand them more. "Because before the day is done, he'll sign the Decree."

Markam removed a sword from his side. "Well? How does it look?"

The sword balanced perfectly in his gloved palms. Golden, catching the rays of the sun as they winked down upon it. The Hadru on the hilt looked dangerously menacing, ready to kill.

"Passable," Sonara said. She looked to Azariah, who nodded.

"Oh, he'll consider it real," Azariah said. "Real enough to name me as his true heir in return…"

"And once he signs?" Jaxon asked. "What will it be, Devil? How exactly will we choose to kill him?"

Sonara shrugged. "Not my choice, actually. It's hers. She's the one who will take his throne."

Her half-sister, Azariah.

The Princess looked at Sonara, eyes widening.

"I…" she swallowed, pushing a dark curl behind her ear. Markam squeezed her waist gently and whispered something into her ear.

Sonara sensed an aura of *revenge,* carried upon the wind.

An aura she knew and loved, for once they were done with Jira, she'd turn Duran south. Towards Soreia, and the queen who'd shared secrets in order to set herself and her Soreians free.

"The Hadru will be hungry," Azariah said. "I think we should feed her a very kingly snack."

Sonara smiled with all of her teeth.

It was a plan.

And though plans did not often go as she wished… that was

the point of being an outlaw. A Devil. That was the point of living truly free.

"Let's ride," Sonara said. She smiled, catching Jaxon's eye.

He winked at her, and something inside of her clicked back into place.

He took to the skies, Razor screeching, the others racing after. But Sonara held back, Duran stamping his hooves eagerly.

"Hold on, Beast," she whispered, patting his neck. Breathing in his aura, *like fresh wheat stalks and sand grains and sweat.* She would never be able to thank Eona enough, for calling upon her own steed's spirit to bring Duran back from death with her.

Sonara waited as Karr returned, his bike rumbling as he pulled it to a stop in the sand.

He lifted his helmet, revealing his eyes.

She'd never realized until recently that they were a true blue. Blue like Soahm's. Blue like the sea that he'd once called home.

"Something wrong?" Karr asked.

Sonara nodded, casting her gaze out across the horizon, where she could have sworn she'd seen a metal Gazer. An eye in the sky, watching, as it always had been.

"Will he be back?"

"Geisinger?" Karr asked. He stared into the distance as if he could see all the way back to his home planet. "Maybe someday."

"And when he does?" Sonara asked.

Karr chuckled softly. "I suppose by then Eona's soul will have forced us to keep gathering together our army of Shadowbloods, and we'll be ready."

Eona's soul was insistent.

Obnoxious.

A little voice that spoke to each of them in her own ways, for even though the heart had sunk, she'd never quite gone silent.

"Unless you want me to go," Karr said. "There are plenty of places across the stars that I could explore…"

"No," Sonara said. "Dohrsar is your home now. Or… it is your home again."

A look passed between them, because they both knew.

For a time, there would be something broken inside of her, when she looked at him. And broken in him, when he looked back at the Bloodhorns' hulking shadow in the distance, the place his brother had sunk deep beneath the surface, chasing the endless dream for a future that he desperately wanted to call his.

It would take time for Karr to discover who he was. Who he used to be.

The dreams had plagued him. Sonara could taste the confusion on him, each night, when he woke screaming, the ground quaking beneath him, until she came to his side and reminded him to breathe.

Until together, they spoke of Soahm. And he fell asleep again, temporarily at peace.

Sonara smiled sadly down at Karr now. "I was just thinking… he would have liked the bike."

"Do you want to try it sometime?" Karr asked. Awkward, stiff conversation, but in time she hoped it would flow with ease.

Sonara laughed. "No." She patted Duran, as she pointed her gaze towards Stonegrave. "No, I think Duran would not be pleased with that."

With a smile, and a wink at Karr, she clicked her teeth.

Duran sprung into motion, the sand spraying behind him, blocking Karr's path as they galloped into the distance.

Onwards, towards the palace that sat waiting.

Towards a king that would sign the Decree to set Shadowbloods in the Deadlands *free.* And when they were done with him, they would turn south. They would fight, with outlaws and outcasts and prisoners set free, until the Decree was signed there, too. Then the north.

But for now, Sonara looked skyward, chasing the shadow of the wyvern as she rode.

Just like the kiss of the wind, just like the taste soaring from her steed, just like the cry she let loose as she threw her arms sky-high… the Devil of the Deadlands rode free.

ACKNOWLEDGEMENTS

FINALLY! I get to write the acknowledgements on a book I've been working on for years and years! First and always, I want to thank God for saving me and getting me through all things. You are first, I am second.

There's a massive list of people, as usual, that have had a hand in helping me complete this book, whether they realize it or not. To begin:

My agent, Pete Knapp, and the entire team at Park Literary, for helping this book find a home. Pete, you've championed me and this book from the start, and I'm convinced there's no better agent out there!

To my editor, Sarah Goodey, for seeing what I see in this book, and helping me find the true heart of the story.

To Cara Chimirri, thank you for the early eyes and insight on the manuscript!

To the entire team at HQ, thank you for the hard work and dedication behind all that you do. I'm so blessed to have BMB in your hands!

To KK, thanks for watching my son while I write and write some more!

To my amazing husband, thank you for being the inspiration behind Jaxon, whose summertime smile first originated with you.

To my family, I love y'all! Thanks for always buying copies!

To my family at Lifeway Celina, thanks for loving me just as I am.

To Craig Walker, thank you for coaching me into finding the best version of myself.

And to my readers… thanks for following me from genre to genre, character to character and world to world. I'm grateful for you all. <3

PRONUNCIATION GUIDE

CHARACTERS

Azariah: Az-uh-rye-uh
Duran: Durr-ann
Eona: Ee-oh-nuh
Eder: Ee-durr
Friedrich Geisinger: Free-drick Guy-zing-err
Queen Iridis: Queen Ear-ih-diss
Jameson: Jame-ih-son
Jaxon: Jack-sin
King Jira: King Jeer-uh
Cade: Caid
Karr: Car
Queen Marisk: Queen Muh-risk
Markam: Mark-um
Jeb: Jebb
Razor: Ray-zerr
Rohtt: Rot
Sonara: Suh-nah-ruh
Soahm: Soh-awm
Thali: Tah-lee

PLACES

The Briyne: Brine
Dohrsar: Door-sahrr
Soreia: Sore-ray-uh

OTHER

Antheon: An-thee-on
Canis: Can-iss
The Hadru: Hah-drew
Lazaris: Lah-zuh-riss

A QUICK CHAT WITH LINDSAY CUMMINGS!

What was your inspiration behind the world of *Blood Metal Bone*?

This book has been quite a journey. The concept first came to me in 2013, when an author friend encouraged me to write a book about horses—something I believe is hard to come by these days! I've had horses my whole life, but I truly fell in love with them as a young girl, when my mother was battling breast cancer. My horse became my escape during those times, and I particularly remember wishing I could just ride off into the sunset and leave my problems behind. Fast-forward to 2013, when *Blood Metal Bone* was born. I was sitting at a baseball game, of all places, boiling in the Texas summer heat, and the characters of Sonara and her loyal steed Duran just kind of came to me all at once. I wanted to place them somewhere different; a classic old western setting, with devastating heat, an endless desert, and girls who grew up wearing cowboy boots like me! A lot of Dohrsar, particularly the Kingdom of the Deadlands, was inspired by the classic cowboy western shows I used to see my dad watching as a kid, but I wanted to mesh the world with fantasy. I wanted to make the world itself more of a character than a setting, so Dohrsar became a sentient being: almost a true "mother earth" type of concept. Add in alien horses, and suddenly I was hooked!

Who is your favourite character in *Blood Metal Bone*?

I'd have to go with Sonara. I wanted to create a strong, fearless outlaw girl—I've always included strong female leads in my novels—but for Sonara particularly, I loved the idea that I could make her a person people fear on the outside... but they have no idea she's quite literally afraid of her own power, of what lurks beneath her own skin. I love that she learns to trust herself and come into her own capacity as a heroine, even though she's made mistakes and isn't perfect. I love her painful backstory, her desire to have a true family, and her "no quit" spirit. Her bond with Duran is perhaps the most autobiographical thing I've ever placed into one of my novels (without the soul-connection, but alas, we cannot have it all in real life. Sigh).

Where would you like to live on Dohrsar?

It's the one place in the novel not fully explored by the reader, but the White Wastes would be fascinating to me. I'm a mountain girl. I love the cold! I'd love to see ice castles and sprawling winter landscapes all the time!

Do you think there is a risk humans will behave like this when we start travelling across the stars?

I think there's always a risk. As humans, we're programmed to want more (to a fault) and if history has proven anything, we don't typically learn from our mistakes. I'm hopeful we'd do better, but I wrote Karr and Cade's side of the story because I wanted to show the unfortunate truth about people who crave power over goodness.

Would you like to jet across the stars yourself?
Honestly—no way!! I get carsick pretty easily, so all I can imagine is being space sick for months, and really regretting my decision to leave earth. LOL.

Do you have a writing routine?
I used to, before having a kid! Toddler life has taught me that you've got to just work on the fly, so I truly enter a sort of survival mode during my writing time. If I've got thirty minutes of time to write, I'll make it work! It's rare for me to have a long, drawn-out period of time to just focus on writing, like I used to—but honestly, I love it this way! It allows me to stay excited and use my time wisely when I'm given it. And coffee. I use my coffee very, very wisely.

Do you have any advice for anyone who wants to be an author?
Write more, care less. When I first began writing, I was so determined to see my books hit shelves someday that I lost the joy of writing along the way. I cared SO MUCH about the goal that I forgot to just enjoy the journey. If you want to write… write! Enjoy creating worlds and using your amazing talent! It's truly a gift.

Who is your favourite author?
I've got quite a few. I love Sarah J. Maas' brilliance in characters and plotting, C.S. Lewis' ability to weave deep concepts into

stories that kids can read and enjoy, Maureen Johnson's witty mysteries, Erin Morgenstern's absolutely buttery prose… too many to choose!

What is the book you wish you'd written?
Probably the entire Throne of Glass series, or *The Night Circus*. Those are very different books, but they've helped shape my writing style in their own ways.

What is your favourite way to relax when not writing?
I love going out to the barn and spending time alone, in the quiet, with my horse. Strangely enough, I also love working out, or reading a book by the pool, or going for a hike in the mountains, or journaling out my prayers. Anything that will help silence my mind for a while!